Their Dangerous Game

UNTOUCHED BOOK 1

C.S. BERRY

Author Note & Content List

Dear reader,

Okay this one is going to be a long one because this is the story that started them all.

First off, for the love of peaceful family gatherings, if you are related to me by any means, do not read this. If you do, don't ever tell me and if I catch you giving me that look like you know I know you know... just don't.

Well, fuck, I can't believe we're finally here. This book is only part of the multiple year journey that has been Untouched. I wrote this story because it was stuck in my mind and I needed it out and it just grew and grew. It was never meant to be published (not originally). It was just something I wanted to play with.

But then Private Listing did well and I thought why not put Untouched out there on Kindle Vella. I never expected anyone to love it as much as I did, but it found readers and it continues to find readers.

Now here's your fair warning: this is six books long. The six books are what's been published so far in serial. They are all written and going through edits. They all end on a cliffhanger. The six books end with a happy for now. It's a spot to get off the ride if you're happy. But there will be more books following it.

This book does have some darker themes please see content warning on next page if you're concerned. Your mental health is important and while some like to be surprised, if you need to know, it's there for you. Or on my website.

This is a steamy series not meant for readers under 18.

I'm so happy to finally have this in books! Untouched was a serial first only available on Kindle Vella – if you got it somewhere else, that wasn't me (pirates). It has been edited. Some of the scenes in the other books are intentionally shorter than the original serial, and there are some new scenes and edits.

If you're new to the Untouched books or only read part on Vella, strap in. It's going to be quite the ride.

XOXOXO,
C.S. Berry

Content Warning for the series:
Bullying
Stalking
Dubious consent
Spanking/bondage
Public humiliation
Group scenes (No swords crossing)
All characters are of age

Later books:
Attempted sexual assault (not by heroes)
Sexual assault (told by character as part of their story)
Stalking/threats
Being drugged
Kidnapping
Panic/sounds like guns, but no firearms are discharged in school
Trafficking is discussed
Death (not main characters)

CHAPTER 1

The Last

My high school motto: Stay under *their* radar.

The guys who will one day rule the world. Gods who choose to walk amongst us. Giant walking assholes who exploit everyone's weaknesses.

Eli Jacobs, Jack Hill, Caden Ross, and the worst of them all, Luke Foster.

Of course, they're all completely gorgeous with a long line of willing female victims to service their every need. They have it all. Money, looks, sex, and smarts. They rule our school. If someone doesn't cave to their will, they have the power to make that person's life hell.

Their nickname on and off the football field is the four horsemen.

Yup, like the apocalypse. Is it odd? Yes. But everyone accepts it. And the guys own it.

They destroy anyone in their path. Their drive and determination took the Sherman High School Mustangs to their first State Championship in twenty years. And their second. And their third. No one doubts this year will mark their fourth.

We're seniors now. One more year to avoid them and then off to college where the horsemen are just a footnote in my history.

It's not normal for an almost eighteen-year-old girl to play a game of hide and seek with four guys who don't know they're playing. But this town and this school make them powerful in a way that isn't normal.

I've always been a little bit of a loner. I have a single mom. Don't really remember my dad. Had one friend who moved away when we were in sixth grade. I got lucky when MacKenzie Campbell moved here and decided I'd be her friend back in middle school. It was around that time the popular boys were gaining more followers and power.

Until freshman year, I was your typical wallflower. Happy to sit back and watch other people live their lives. I thought in high school things would be different. We'd all be small fish in a much bigger pond.

Kenz and I even went to the cafeteria back then to eat. Until two weeks into freshman year. No one knows the whole story, but it's been gossiped about over the years. Apparently this junior cheerleader, who was queen bee, used her supposed virginity to pit Luke, Jack, Caden, and Eli against each other.

That's the theory at least. I mean, I was there and still don't know what she was thinking.

The guys were all at their own table. Even as freshmen, they were the center of attention. The table of cheerleaders were to their left and to their right the other football players. They made waves bringing in wins when even the varsity players had already lost their first two games.

In walked Kylie Elias in a short skirt and a top that showed off her breasts. Her blond hair was perfectly styled in soft waves and her blue eyes were narrowed on the horsemen's table. Her heels clicked on the linoleum floor as she made her way to the table.

When she sat in the seat between Eli and Jack, she leaned in to talk to Eli privately. Luke's cold blue eyes locked on her. He cleared his throat loudly, and Jack let out a laugh that captured everyone's attention. The hum of conversation died down to a murmur.

"What do you want, Kylie?" Luke asked, and you could hear a pin drop.

I held my breath, waiting.

"Fuck off, Luke. I'm talking to Eli." She turned her head away from him, and even I knew that was a mistake. But I watched the horsemen in middle school and knew to keep a low profile. Back then they weren't quite who they are now.

Luke laughed, and so did the other horsemen. It sends chills down my back even remembering it.

"What did she ask?" Luke turned to Eli, who smirked.

"She wants her panties back."

Laughter lit the air in small bursts from around the cafeteria. Kylie's face turned red and she slid her hands over the hem of her skirt. She stood up and put her hands on her hips.

"Well?" She held out her hand to Eli with an expectant look, choosing to brazen it out.

The guys all stood and reached into their pockets. Each of them pulled out a pair of lacy thong panties. They walked around the table and placed them in her hand. When Eli added his, he smirked in her face.

"Looks like you've lost more than your fair share of panties to us."

"That's not all she lost." Luke winked at her and leaned back in his chair like a king.

Her cheeks were red and her eyes narrowed. "You're nothing more than a freshman. Powerless."

The room grew quiet again. My heart pounded. Caden's laugh filled the silence.

Her gaze jerked to Caden.

"You didn't say that when you were riding my cock." He pressed something on his phone and sounds of moaning echoed in the room.

"Yes. Oh, fuck me, Caden, yes!" Kylie's voice was breathless but still recognizable.

"Guess our night wasn't that special after all." Jack sat on the table with his feet in the chair. "Was I even your first?"

Kylie opened her mouth to say something, but Caden said, "I was her first."

"Wasn't I your first?" Luke smirked.

She closed her mouth.

Eli leaned in but said loud enough for the whole cafeteria to hear, "Next time you want to lie to a guy about your virginity, maybe try not to fuck his friends first."

Kylie gripped the panties tight as she turned and hurried out of the cafeteria. My stomach twisted. There's no way I wanted to be party to any of their games. I couldn't risk being humiliated that way. I wouldn't recover.

It was the last time I went to the cafeteria, but they didn't stop with Kylie.

If someone crossed them, that person was either humiliated or beaten up. As freshmen, they were more powerful than the seniors. And now, they own this school.

And I avoid them.

It's the first day of my senior year. I get to my first class early so I don't chance a run-in in the hallway with *them*. I pick a seat near the front, away from the door. If one of the horsemen happens to be in the same class, they sit in the back row, but they almost always note who sits in the first row. So the second or third row is my spot, and by the windows so they don't have to pass me on the way to their seats.

So here I sit, wearing my favorite black skater skirt, knee-high socks, a Nirvana graphic tee—because vintage—and a pair of black and white saddle shoes. I even tied my long brown hair up in a high pony. It's cute, but not in a distracting way. At least it shouldn't capture *their* attention.

This is my last year in high school and I'm going to crush it.

Quietly. Without attracting *their* attention.

It would be easier if they were as ugly on the outside as they are on the inside.

Frankly they're beautiful, and I don't mind looking at the beautiful boys. What girl doesn't? But I'm not about to become one of their notches. They've made their way through almost every girl in school and rarely go back for seconds. But they don't fuck with freshmen. At least not after our own freshman year.

I've made it to the beginning of senior year and I feel confident I've managed to slip under their radar. It's a skill, not going to lie. I'm not one of their so-called unfuckables, or girls that aren't pretty enough to warrant their attention, but I'm also not the hottest.

I am, thankfully, unnoticeable.

They don't have any reason to mess with me. It's almost like a game that I'm so close to winning.

I check my phone as students file in, talking to their friends like they didn't spend all summer hanging out. There's obviously new gossip the first day back. One more year and I'm out of here. College will be where I can shine.

Kenz drops into the seat beside me. "Oh my god, I have to tell you about last night."

I slip my phone into my pocket and smile at my bestie. The only gossip I could think of is... "Let me guess, you finally went all the way with Brandon."

She grins and nods, leaning in to keep it quiet. "I'm pretty sure that makes you the last virgin in our class."

My brow scrunches up. That can't be right. "Margaret Carter."

"This summer. Band camp." Kenz holds up her hand. With each name, she puts down a finger. "Rachel Hayes, Eli Jacobs at a pool party. Parker Ford, Jack and Caden at her house."

"Wait, both of them?" Damn. That's one dedicated virgin to get a double hitter. Can't say I'm not impressed. To get not just one horseman but two on your first time is unheard of. Or was. From all accounts, these guys have the equipment to back up their reputation as huge dicks.

Kenz nods. "Melody Griffin, some other camp guy. Me, Brandon."

She wiggles her pinkie finger.

"Oh, fuck." That leaves me. Might as well paint a fucking target on my back for the four horsemen. Suddenly, I'm regretting wearing a skirt.

The horsemen make it their mission to defile virgins. Granted, it took them three full years to get through our grade level. Surely, there are plenty of junior and sophomore virgins to get through. It's not like they defile all the virgins, but they do seem to be on a mission.

Our class is a point of pride for them to leave no virgin unfucked.

Not dating or going to parties has assured I stay off their radars, but it also means I remain untouched. I'm not a prude, but I also don't want to be part of the game these guys play with girls. If there was a guy at this school I thought I might be able to date, I would have made an attempt. But honestly, the good ones are taken. And while the bad ones are gorgeous, I don't want to add to their numbers.

"They can't know, right?" I whisper to Kenz. I don't stand out. They probably don't even know my name. That's my hope.

"If they're keeping track..." She shrugs. "Probably not though. I mean, it's not like they know who's had sex and who hasn't unless it was with one of them. Girls talk but not to them. That would be stupid."

The hairs on the back of my neck stand on end and I can't help but look at the door.

Luke Foster. Quarterback extraordinaire. The dick who rules the horsemen and the whole damn school. If he weren't one of the hounds of hell, he could be an angel. Blond hair, cold blue eyes, and the body of Adonis. From the whispers in the girls' locker room, he isn't shy about his body and knows how to use it.

Normally I don't look when *they* walk in, keeping my eyes on my desk, but today, the reason the hairs rose on the back of my neck is because those blue eyes are locked on me with a determination that sets my poor heart pounding.

Shit. Shit. Shit.

I can't seem to look away as his gorgeous full lips tip into a cocky half smile and he changes direction from the back of class to cut through the desks.

Fuck my life.

My knee bounces uncontrollably. I got this far. So close to the finish line. I should have gone to band camp and fucked someone like Margaret Carter did. I should have been in band. Now I'm completely fucked.

Luke slips into the seat behind me, and heat engulfs my back. Kenz presses her lips together and faces the front.

That isn't where he's supposed to sit. He sits in the back. His desk presses against the back of my chair. His long, denim-clad leg sprawls into the aisle next to me, blocking my escape route. A sharp tug on my ponytail makes me feel like we're in middle school.

"Harper Davidson." His voice is like a soft caress against the back of my neck. It's deep and rich and melts panties like the fires of hell he probably holds in his hands.

I have no choice. Ignoring a horseman would set me up worse than being a virgin. I twist in my chair to meet Luke's cold eyes. His smirk is almost evil as he leans back in the chair like he doesn't have a care in the world.

"I heard a rumor you're the last virgin in the senior class." His voice is not quiet. The entire room is practically leaning forward with bated breath to listen to our conversation. He glances over at Kenz meaningfully.

She blushes and faces front. Her boyfriend is on the football team. Apparently boys do talk as much as girls do.

"I'm sure that's not true." I have to play this right or I'll become a target, if I'm not already. Maybe if they focus on someone else, I'll find a way to blend back in. Off their radar, out of their sights.

He sits up in his chair and leans forward on his desk, bringing him so close I can smell the mint on his breath and the fresh scent of his cologne. "Are you saying you aren't a virgin?"

His finger trails up my bare arm to tug on the sleeve of my t-shirt. Shivers trickle down my spine. I am so fucked. If I say I'm not, the target might not go away. Once they get someone in their sights, it's almost impossible to ward them off. He might want me to prove it.

"I'm saying I can't possibly be the last." I try to sound confident. Maybe I can take this year virtually. Surely Mom would understand the need to preserve my state of mind. I just have to get through today and then I can have a frank discussion with my parental figure over the virtues of staying at home for my senior year.

He lifts his eyebrows and scans my face. "How did you slip by us?"

"What?" My eyes widen.

"You're definitely fuckable. I'm sure those didn't just develop over the summer." He drops his gaze to my breasts. "I've seen bigger, but they definitely aren't small."

"Jesus," I breathe out. I feel the need to cover my breasts but don't. Again, antagonizing him would be a mistake.

"I know you've been here since grade school." He captures my ponytail and twists it around his hand. "But you escaped us until now."

I barely manage to keep from tugging my hair out of his hand. I can't afford to make him mad. I also can't give him what he wants from me. It's not that I'm afraid of sex, but sex with a horseman...yeah, not for me. I don't want to be party to their games.

"I'm not sure what you want me to say." Honesty might work best.

He leans in and pulls my hair to keep me from retreating. Tight enough to cause pain. He stares at my lips, so close to his.

My heart pounds a frantic rhythm. The truth is I spent so much time avoiding them, I didn't do what normal girls at regular high schools do. I haven't even had my first kiss. But normal girls don't have to deal with the four horsemen. At the time, it was worth it to lie low, but right now, that seems like the worst thing I could have done.

"I don't like to do anything half-assed," he whispers, and the words are soft against my lips. "Consider yourself marked by the horsemen. No one else will touch you until we're through with you."

My heart sinks and I shut my eyes at his words. My lucky streak has run its course. My only recourse is homeschooling. I would miss a lot in my senior year, but it would be better than being stalked by four guys determined to get under my skirt.

The door opens to the classroom and the sound of the teacher arriving filters through my brain. I open my eyes to Luke's icy blue ones.

"If you run, it'll just make it more exciting for us, unicorn."

"Unicorn?" I can't help asking.

"You're the last of your kind, Harper Davidson." His grin makes me flinch.

"Mr. Foster, could you please take your hands off Ms. Davidson so we can get started?"

Luke gives me a wicked smile before drawing his hand out of my hair and lounging back in his chair. "Of course, Mr. Wick. Do your thing."

"Thank you for your permission." Mr. Wick shakes his head and gives me a look to ask if I'm okay.

Fuck no, I'm not okay. The year just started and the horsemen have decided I'm their newest toy. I'm screwed unless I want to screw one of them and I most definitely do not. It may not be a huge deal, but I'd like to be with someone who actually *likes* me for my first time. Not being chosen just because I have an intact hymen. I should be able to choose who and when, not be forced to make a decision because they have a reputation to maintain.

I give Mr. Wick a small smile and face front. Turning my back on a horseman makes butterflies spin drunkenly in my stomach. I know I'm not worth their time, but how can I make them see it that way?

While Mr. Wick outlines our English course for this year, I notice

Kenz texting on her phone and feel the responding buzz of my own. I peek at my screen.

KENZ:

Holy shit, H! What are you going to do?

ME:

shrugging emoji

I lean to slip my phone back into my backpack, but a hand snags it from me. Luke.

Heat gathers in my cheeks as I start to ask for it back when Mr. Wick turns from the board. His eyes on the classroom.

My phone is unlocked. I didn't have a chance to hit the off button. So Luke could do anything he wants on it. Look over my dismal text messages. Check out my minuscule contact list. Verify my lack of a life with my level on Candy Crush. Scroll through photos of my cat.

What can I possibly do to a horseman? They run the school and if they want me, they can get me. No one will stand in their way. A shiver courses down my spine again.

The end of class draws closer and Luke still has my phone. I'm going to have to ask him for it back. What will he ask me to give up in return?

The bell rings. Fuck, I really don't want to do this. But I need my phone. Those butterflies start divebombing.

When I grab my bag and stand, Luke blocks my path. My breath catches.

"You're a small thing." He smirks down at me. My eyes land at the center of his chest. I'm not technically small. More average, but the horsemen are tall and built.

"May I have my phone back?" I clench my teeth even as my stomach twists into a knot. I add, "Please?"

"Mmm. I like it when you beg, unicorn." He presses something on the screen and his back pocket buzzes. "We have your number now. If you ignore us, you'll be punished."

I lift my gaze to meet his. My heart beats like a drum and my palms grow clammy. "Punished?"

His hand snakes out and his fingers feather down my arm to my hand. A trail of sparks follows in his wake. That's alarming. He lifts my hand and places my phone in my palm. "You're ours now until we decide you aren't."

He squeezes my hand around my phone. Hard enough to make me wince a little.

"Who knows? Maybe you'll give it up fast and we'll be bored in a week." He catches my ponytail and yanks me into him.

I gasp as his hard body presses into my softness. Sparks ignite everywhere.

He dips his head beside my ear and his lips move against my skin as he says, "I hope you aren't boring, unicorn. I think I'd like to play with you for a long time."

He releases me, and I almost fall back into my seat. He strides away, and all I can do is stare at my phone like it betrayed me.

I'm fucked.

CHAPTER 2
The Question

HARPER

Yeah, this isn't going to be my year. I barely have time to collect myself and move to my second class. I choose my normal spot and hope none of the horsemen have AP Statistics.

I glance at my phone and see Luke sent a group text with the back-to-school selfie I sent to Mom this morning and entered the horsemen's numbers with the names Death, War, Pestilence, and Famine.

These boys take this whole apocalypse thing way too far.

Death is Luke, of course. The pale horse. From his cold blue eyes to his shiny blond hair. Firm jawline. Cheekbones edged like glass. And lips that look pillow soft. If he was actually death, women would be falling over themselves to die for him.

War is Caden. The red horse. He spreads violence wherever he goes. Dark hair, green eyes. Deceptively pretty face. Not perfect though. His nose has a slight tweak in it from a fight. It suits him though.

Famine is Jack. The black horse. His blue eyes are stunning and have snared many girls. Jack has that darkness to him, not the violence of Caden, but something almost brooding and thrilling—at least for some girls. Except he rarely fucks the same girl twice.

Pestilence is Eli. The white horse. If Luke looks like an angel, Eli resembles a fallen one. Just as beautiful. Soft brown hair and eyes the color of melted chocolate. He rarely smiles and everyone knows he's rough with girls. Even I had the bruises to attest to it.

My sophomore year, Eli had come barreling down the hall after third period and I was in his path. I didn't notice because I was talking to Kenz. He grabbed my hips, lifted me out of his way, and went on. Granted, I barely registered to his six foot five self as I'm a full foot shorter, but I had bruises on my hips for a week. Luckily, he wasn't even aware of who I was, so crisis averted.

The back of my neck prickles again and I swear if Luke is in this class, I'll make myself vomit to get sent home. Vomiting is the absolute worst, but it may be worth it.

When I lift my gaze, it's not Luke in the doorway. But my relief is short-lived. Jack and Caden. And they spot me. FML.

If there ever was an unholy pairing, it's the two dark demons of the pack. Both built to tackle with speed and agility and brute force.

The only other time I got in a horseman's way was with them.

Junior year on the south lawn during lunch, I was sitting below my favorite tree reading with my legs outstretched. Caden was going long while Jack threw a football. Caden ran under the tree, not noticing me, and would have tripped over my legs if I hadn't pulled them back just before he reached me. That could have been disastrous.

It wouldn't have mattered that it wasn't my fault. If he'd gotten hurt or even embarrassed, they would have taken it out on me. I would have been in their crosshairs. Public humiliation would have been imminent.

Caden had jumped to catch the ball and landed on his side beside me. His green eyes roamed over my body for a hot minute as he grinned, but then Jack ran up and grabbed his hand to pull him to stand again. While they were distracted, I managed to run off before either could say anything to me.

Now I'm not as lucky as Jack takes the seat behind me and Caden drops into the chair next to me. Both give me almost feral grins. This would be a lot easier if any of these guys looked like meatheads or at least had a case of acne, maybe some scarring, but no, they're perfect. Tall, gorgeous, and dangerous. A teenage girl's wet dream.

I'd like to say not mine, but let's be honest. Who hasn't had a wet dream about a guy they can't stand, but is absolutely gorgeous? Yeah, that's what I thought.

I stare at the book in my hands and refuse to look at either of them. But then someone sits in front of me. Oh, no, not just anyone. Eli.

He sits sideways in his chair, and his dark eyes take me in. My heart pounds so furiously I'm sure they can all hear it. My fear probably excites them. Assholes.

Eli snatches my book from me. My empty hands slap the desk, but I don't try to get it back. I hope he likes historical romance. I should tell him to check out page 121, but I definitely don't want to give him ideas.

Jack pokes me in the back with the capped end of his pen. "Hey, Harper."

I draw in a deep breath and turn to him. Giving in today, at least during class, seems like the best idea. Maybe they'll get sick of me not rising to their bait. "Yes?"

"So what kind of virgin are you?" He gives me a sly half grin.

"What do you mean?" Engaging is a bad idea. I know it, but what else am I supposed to do? If I ignore them, Luke will punish me, and god only knows what that means. They've publicly humiliated students for years. I'm sure they've got their technique down pat. Of course, I tried to stay away from those public displays as well. Sometimes innocent bystanders end up on display too.

"Are you a technical virgin?" Caden supplies. "You know. Done everything but the deed. Just haven't had a thick cock filling your pussy?"

Okay, I can feel the heat and redness in my face. "I don't think that's any of your business."

Eli drops my book on my desk, making me turn back around. He grabs my chin and holds me still. "Now, kitten, is that any way to talk to your owners?"

That makes me bristle, but I swallow down the anger. It's early in the day. We still have to get through lunch, which is a fucking free-for-all. Now that they've caught my scent, I'm not sure I can hide from these beasts. I clench my teeth and meet Eli's dark eyes as he tsks me.

He traces his thumb over my lower lip, sending sparks through me.

"Some girls take a cock into their mouths and are still technically virgins if you count penetrative sex as losing your virginity."

Something settles low and warm in my gut as his thumb traces back and forth. Even his words cause a brief flutter in my stomach. Maybe I'm more attention starved than I knew.

"But I'm guessing you're the real deal, kitten." He releases my chin.

I refuse to touch my tingling lip. "Real deal?"

Caden perks up. "Never been touched before."

"Is that true, sweetheart?" Jack slides his finger up my spine to the nape of my neck. An involuntary shiver sweeps through me. "Have you been saving yourself for us?"

Eli drops his hand from the back of his chair to drag the backs of his fingers across my bare knees, along the edge of my skirt.

My lips part on a gasp. "Stop."

His eyes light up. "Why, kitten? Afraid you'll like it?"

What do I say to that? They won't rape me, right? I mean, girls talk and no one has ever mentioned the R-word. It's always been consensual. So what? They'll just work at breaking down my defenses?

I don't like these guys, so it shouldn't be hard to put them off. Sure, they're aggressive, but they wouldn't do anything that would get them put in jail. They're all eighteen. They wouldn't risk it. Right?

Besides, it's just this sudden focus on me that's spinning me out. Things will settle and I'll get used to them hanging around me.

"What about it, Harper?" Caden leans his elbows on his knees and looks up at me with those green eyes. "Are you untouched?"

I suck in my breath. It's too much. I won't last the day if they're in all of my classes. I mean, I'm not going to give them my virginity, but they'll continue to harass me.

"All right, class!" Ms. Ingrim gets everyone's attention.

Caden gives me a sly smile before turning toward the front. The three of them have me surrounded against the window. They can't enjoy being this close to the front. The teacher can keep track of whether or not they're paying attention. Surely tomorrow they'll return to the back of the class.

"These will be your seats for the semester," Ms. Ingrim announces.

Jack leans forward. "Guess you're stuck with us, sweetheart."

AFTER CLASS, I GET AROUND THEM AND LEAVE FOR MY THIRD-period class. My phone buzzes in my bag, and as soon as I get to art, I pull it out. At least none of them should be in here.

> **WAR (CADEN):**
> Answer the question

> **DEATH (LUKE):**
> What question?

> **PESTILENCE (ELI):**
> Is Harper untouched or a technical virgin?

> **DEATH (LUKE):**
> Answer

> **ME:**
> None of your business

> **DEATH (LUKE):**
> Wrong answer

Fuck.

Kenz comes into the art room and takes the chair next to me.

"Are you okay?" She puts her hand on my arm and squeezes it, giving me that worried mom look. Like I've contracted a fatal disease —assholitis.

"No." I hold out my phone so she can see the current conversation.

"Holy shit." Kenz puts her hand over her heart. Then she bites her lip and looks around before saying, "Do you remember Rebecca Forester?"

"Didn't she transfer after sophomore year?" I vaguely remember her. Rebecca was a nice and popular cheerleader. Not someone I talked to or hung out with.

"She was their pet project that year." Kenz leans in as more people filter into the room. "She swore she was a good Christian girl and was saving herself for marriage. They tormented her that whole year until she finally gave in."

"Why didn't she just transfer schools earlier?" Homeschool is sounding better and better.

"They wouldn't have let up. Once they have a pet project, they're all in." Kenz glances at my phone screen. "Just tell them, Harper. Maybe they'll go easier on you if you play along."

"Or it'll make them ten times worse." My phone buzzes in my hand. I sigh.

WAR (CADEN):

Since it's my question, do I get to hand out the punishment?

FAMINE (JACK):

I'm sure our girl will come through for us

DEATH (LUKE):

You have five minutes

Four

ME:

Untouched

Shit. Shit. Shit. My heart is pounding. The bell rings and I glance around the room. Third period seems to at least be dick free.

"I'm sure it will be fine." Kenz pats my back. "They're assholes but not actual criminals."

DEATH (LUKE):

Good girl

Seriously? What am I? A dog?

ME:

Do I get to know your sexual experience?

PESTILENCE (ELI):

Experienced

I purse my lips at that answer. I guess I need to be more specific if I want to know, but why would I want to know? It's not like I'm actually considering having sex with any of these assholes. They can make my last year of school hell, but like Kenz said, they aren't actual criminals.

I drop my phone in my bag and pay attention to my favorite teacher, Ms. Sullivan. I've spent the last three years in one art class or another, which is why I know a horseman wouldn't be in an advanced art class. So for at least one hour a day, I should have peace.

Of course, the next period could be the worst yet. Lunch.

CHAPTER 3

The Punishment

HARPER

A few years ago, the school decided it would be better to have everyone take lunch at the same time. That way clubs could meet. Students could talk to teachers when they needed to get extra help. And everyone got a break.

Great for everyone, right? Except that means all four horsemen will have lunch at the same time as me.

If they can find me. Ever since freshman year, I bring lunch from home because being in the cafeteria is hell for someone who wants to go unnoticed.

"Do you think this is a smart idea?" Kenz asks for the fifth time.

"Staying in the art room on the opposite side of the building from the cafeteria?" Duh. "Hell, yes. If they want me, I'm not going to make it easy for them to torment me. I'm not some lamb to the slaughter."

I rode under their radar for three years of high school and they never noticed me in middle school. Just because they finally decided I'm interesting because I'm a virgin doesn't mean I don't know how to evade those fuckers.

"Are you sure they aren't going to track you down?" Kenz picks at the sandwich she packed. "They have resources. They can find people when they want to."

"I didn't agree to their terms of ownership." I hold my head up high while I hide from them. "They can't force me to do anything."

I hope. I mean seriously, someone would have reported it by now if they did something like that, right? They aren't actually gods. They are high school boys. Fallible.

My phone buzzes a few more times, but I've been ignoring it since it started going off when the lunch bell rang.

"Don't you think you should check that?" Kenz makes a gesture toward the phone. "You might piss them off."

"So? If I piss them off, what will they do?" I shrug. Punish me? If they can find me. They have nothing on me. They barely even know me. They just found out I'm the last virgin and thought hmm, that would be fun to tackle. Fuck them.

"Did you check your phone after Luke gave it back?" Kenz cringes. Maybe she's worried she'll be punished by association. That's actually not an unreasonable assumption, but her boyfriend will protect her. "What if he put a tracker app on it?"

"He couldn't have. You have to have the passcode to add an app." I pick up my phone and glance over the messages.

DEATH (LUKE):

Where r u

PESTILENCE (ELI):

Come out, come out, wherever u are

DEATH (LUKE):

If you make us hunt you

You will be caught

PESTILENCE (ELI):

And punished

WAR (CADEN):

By all of us

FAMINE (JACK):

Last chance, sweetheart

DEATH (LUKE):

Answer

They don't seem to know where I am, but that doesn't stop the prickle of fear creeping up my back. It's not like I'm impossible to find. They've just never looked before.

The door to the classroom doesn't have a glass window in it like some do. They could be out in the hall right now. How hard would it really be for them to find out my schedule? These aren't regular students. They have access most don't. My throat tightens and my palms grow clammy.

It's fine. I'm fine. So what if they find me? What's the worst they can do? Scold me? We're at school and teachers are everywhere. I'm safe here.

My PB&J isn't settling right, so I put the other half back in my bag as I glance at the door. Okay, I need to think ahead. Is there anywhere to hide in here?

Shit, hiding sucks, but I got damn good at it over the past years.

The kiln room in the back doesn't lock, but would add another door between me and them. Besides, they won't tear through the entire building for me. I'm not that important. They have to eat too. They'll just realize I'm not worth it and give up.

PESTILENCE (ELI):

Ticktock, kitten

Eli can suck it.

"I could report them." I stand and look at Kenz.

Her eyes widen and she shakes her head. "Are you insane? Do you know what they do to people who take things to the principal? You think they're bad in school? They'd be all over you outside of school."

It wasn't even a good idea. I know better than that.

"I don't know what to do." I press my fingers against my temples. I can feel *them* like an ache behind my eyes. "This is so wrong. What the hell am I supposed to do?"

Kenz shakes her head. "I'd say screw the first guy you see, but I think that'd get you in more trouble. Unless that guy is a horseman."

"There has to be a way out of this." I look at the door. How long do I have until they find me? What do they mean by punishment?

I know what they do to guys. There's a reason Caden walks around with busted knuckles. But it's not all violence. No. Luke is cool and conniving. He can break someone with just a few words. They've ruined lives with a few choice rumors. Still, it's not all beatdowns or gossip.

Humiliation. As public as possible. I've heard whispers but, besides freshman year, never saw them in action. That might be the worst part. I don't know how far they'll go. My stomach churns.

"I should go home." I shove everything into my backpack and grab my phone to text my mom. She'll understand.

They haven't texted in a few minutes. What does that mean? Maybe they've given up. This could be my chance to escape. My gaze goes to the doorknob and I hold my breath, waiting to see if it turns.

"Harper, you can't avoid them forever." Kenz puts her hands flat on the table. "Just play along at school. They won't do anything right away, right? We'll have time to figure something out."

"I'm already fucking hiding from them and it's not even halfway through the first day. I don't know what punishment means either, and I don't think I want to find out." Pulling on my backpack, I head to the door. "I'll see you tomorrow."

I yank open the door and freeze. The four of them stand in the doorway, looking down on me. Jeezus, they're a lot. Tall, attractive—

My heart skips. Yeah, that might be the worst part. They're attractive. All of them. And a part of me doesn't really want to fight that hard against them. It's a small part, and I'll beat that horny bitch into the ground over time.

"Found you." Jack smirks.

I take a step back, but Luke grabs my arm. His hand is warm and firm on my bare skin. My eyes find Kenz, who looks pale. Earlier, Ms. Sullivan left the room for parts unknown. No one can help me.

"Not so fast, unicorn." Luke draws me forward into the circle of them.

Their heat engulfs my body, and the haunting combination of their colognes wreaks havoc on my system. Individually, they all smell great, but together it blends into something tantalizing and alluring, making me want to dive into their warmth.

Shit. No. Calm down, horny bitch.

"What did I say?" Luke brings his face down so we're eye to eye.

"Not so fast?" Fuck, I know it's the wrong thing to say, but what can I do? Admit I hid from them. That I'm afraid of them. That their attention is too much.

Caden and Jack chuckle, but the sound is far from reassuring. More like hyenas before they pounce on their prey.

Luke's eyes have an evil glint as he straightens. He doesn't release my arm but tugs me along with him as the group of them falls in step surrounding me. Like I'm their prisoner being led to my execution. Don't I get a last request?

"Is this really necessary?" I manage to get out around the lump in my throat.

"Yes," Eli says from behind me.

Glad that clears everything up. I try to glance back toward the art room and swear I see Kenz following us. I don't want her to get dragged into this.

Luke still holds my arm, but surprisingly, it isn't tight enough to bruise. I don't bother trying to drag my heels. With four men built for football, it wouldn't take much to be thrown over one of their shoulders, and I definitely don't want to show them or anyone else my panties today.

They're quiet as we move through the hallways toward the loud cafeteria. The noise escalates as we draw near, but as the horsemen step into the room, a hush falls over the crowd in a wave.

Eli, Caden, and Jack fall back, and I see them take up position by the doors. Luke makes a hand gesture to one of the other football players, who goes up to the teacher on duty. Within a minute, the two leave the cafeteria, and the doors all close.

The kitchen is closed since lunch is almost over. Holy fuck, it's only students in here and not a friendly face among them. Not that I know many of them personally. The instinct to run flows through me. Even though it would be pointless. It would add to my humiliation, so I tamp it down.

Luke drags me up onto a table in the center of the room. Eli jumps up to stand next to him, but Jack and Caden stand in the back near the doors.

I'm amazed the table holds our weight, but it wouldn't dare give out while the horsemen are on it.

My knees literally shake and I can't catch my breath. These guys can do anything to me. In front of all these students. Not one of them will help me.

Sure, I can report it after the fact, but right now, in this moment, the horsemen have complete control and that's terrifying.

"You all know Harper, right?" Luke's voice deepens and resonates throughout the entire room.

Some people mumble. I'm sure I've had classes with at least some of these students, but hiding from the horsemen means not making a lot of friends. The fewer people who knew me, the easier it was to slip under their radar.

"From now on, she's ours." Eli's voice carries in the large room. "That means you don't do anything with her. No talking. No touching. Pretend this is a huge game of cooties and you don't want to get them from her."

I can't help my glare at him. I do not have cooties, and who are they to say what I can and can't do?

"See, our little pet hasn't quite figured out her place yet." Luke pulls me close to him as Eli jumps down. I suck in my breath at the sensation of Luke pressed against my back. It's a foreign feeling. No one has ever touched me like this. Surprisingly, I don't actually hate it.

Eli walks across the cafeteria and grabs a chair. Luke's cologne is one of those soft, seductive scents, warm and inviting. It's so different from his coldness.

"She needs to know her actions have consequences," Luke says.

I look back at him, and he grins down at me. His pale blue eyes are just as cold as ever, but with a light of amusement in them that frankly doesn't reassure me.

"If you squirm or fight back, I'll make it worse." His words are soft and for my ears only.

My cheeks flush, but I refuse to acknowledge these psychopaths. My best bet is to ignore them as best I can. Of course, I can't exactly ignore them right now. The chair lands behind Luke on their makeshift stage. Eli's evil grin sparks fear in my heart. The reminder that, in here, they can do anything to me pulls at my fear.

My heart sputters as I search for one friendly face or teacher among the throngs of students eager to watch whatever the horsemen have in mind.

My mantra for today goes through my head: *I'm fucked.*

Luke sits in the chair and spreads his legs. Some guys make catcalls in the crowd. Eli takes ahold of my shoulders from the back and steers me toward the side of Luke's legs. The weight of Eli's hands on me sends a shiver down my spine.

"Lie down, Harper." Luke's voice is authoritative and his eyes dare me to resist.

Oh, fuck no. I draw back into Eli, the heat of his chest a far lesser evil than whatever Luke has planned. Eli smells like the outdoors on a warm day. Deceptive but alluring. Eli dips his head down next to mine.

"Play along and this will be over before you know it, kitten."

His breath against my ear sends a tingling sensation through me. That's not reassuring at all though.

I don't want to play along. When I look around, everyone looks eager to see what the horsemen have in mind. Not a friendly face among them. Of course they're eager when it's not them on the stage.

"Now!" Luke barks out, causing the guys to make an exaggerated *oh* sound like I'm in for it. They have no idea. Fuck, *I* have no idea. But this isn't going away. I can't escape this, but I can endure it. Yes, this is humiliating, but none of these students really know me. I just need to focus on the assholes doing this.

"How?" I lock eyes with Luke. His face shows no mercy.

"Stomach across my legs. Ass up." He pats his thigh, and his smile is so cold a shiver ripples through me.

"What are you going to do to me?" I ask quietly.

"Come here and find out." Luke pats again. "Don't keep me waiting."

I check that Eli is still behind me. Somehow, him getting a view of my panties is better than the entire student body ogling my backside.

My heart is beating faster than the wings of a hummingbird, but I lower myself awkwardly onto Luke's lap.

He adjusts me until I'm exactly where he wants me. My whole body feels hot and flushed as I hang over his lap. He flips my skirt up.

What the fuck! I try to come up. His hand presses into my back to hold me there.

"If you don't stop squirming, I'll pull your panties down and spank your bare ass in front of everyone. Is that what you want, Harper?" His voice is low and just for me.

"You're going to spank me?" I can't wrap my head around any of this. It's the first day of school and I'm being publicly spanked by the four horsemen because I didn't answer their text.

Fan-fucking-tastic. Great start to the new year. Way to go me. FML.

"We need everyone to count along." Jack's voice comes from the back of the cafeteria. Of course they do.

"Our pet is getting ten," Caden chimes in helpfully. Fabulous.

At least I didn't wear a thong today. I bite my lip to keep from telling them what assholes they are, but then Luke's hand comes down on my ass cheek. A cry bursts out of me.

"One." The crowd doesn't need to sound so excited about it.

I wrap my arm around Luke's leg and brace for the next one, but his hand doesn't come down hard again. Instead, he rubs where he hit, smoothing over the satin, pressing against the sting, and something shifts under the pain. What the fuck is happening?

He lifts his hand and stings my other cheek.

"Two."

I don't know if I'm going to be able to handle all ten of these. A flash catches my attention.

You know, if any of these fuckers are recording this, I'm going to personally track down every one of them and kick them in the nuts. And have Kenz record it. I lift my head as Luke rubs my ass again. I see the flash of someone's camera and turn in time to see Jack snatching the guy's phone and deleting the pic.

Luke brings his hand down on the first cheek again. I bite my lip to stop from crying out.

"Three."

No break and he claps the second one.

"Four."

I mean, they could have done a lot worse than spanking in the cafeteria, right? It stings, but it doesn't feel all bad, which is a little alarming. Especially when he rubs his large hand over the satin of my underwear. Edging closer to my center.

My breath catches. Oh, shit, liquid heat pools low in my belly.

I duck my head as a fresh wave of embarrassment slides through me. That small, little horny bitch rears her head. Fuck, I think I like the feel of his hand on me. Maybe I just like any touch after being deprived my whole life.

"Five. Six."

I bite my lip to keep in the moan that tries to edge out as he rubs the pain away. I feel like a fucking hypocrite.

"Seven. Eight."

I'm panting from all of this. I'm not sure if it's the lack of air as my breasts are pressed against Luke's thigh or the warmth between my legs. I can blame the blood rushing to my head for the redness in my face, since I'm practically hanging upside down. And not from being turned on from being spanked in front of most of my classmates. Add that to my mortification.

I grip his firm leg so tight and I can't help but wiggle a little to relieve some of the ache. My lip will bleed if I keep biting back the charged moans trying to escape.

"Ready for the last two?" Luke slips his finger along the edge of my panties. A gasp escapes me at the heat that flows through me from his touch. This isn't fair. It shouldn't feel that good. "Are you going to obey, Harper?"

I try to nod.

"I can't hear you." The slight laugh in his voice makes my stomach drop.

"Yes," I push out between my lips.

"Nine. Ten." The crowd shouts loud enough to cover the moan that leaks out of me.

My skirt covers my sore backside, and then Eli is behind me, lifting me to standing. He wraps an arm around my middle, and suddenly I'm grateful for the touch of a horseman. I'm not sure my legs will hold me upright. I try not to curl into his warmth and the shelter he offers. Somewhere to hide from all the eyes. Even though he's one of the reasons I'm humiliated.

I keep my eyes down, not willing to meet anyone's gaze. The bell rings and everyone filters out.

Luke stands and steps in front of me. He puts a finger under my chin to tilt my face up to his and studies my red cheeks before leaning down next to my ear. My back presses to Eli, but I can't get away from Luke.

"I could smell your arousal, unicorn. Tangy and sweet." His lips touch my ear as he speaks. "I wanted to taste it. Dip my tongue in and devour you. Then sink my cock into your quivering cunt until you come all over me while screaming my name. But it will have to wait."

My breath catches in my throat and the heat between my thighs is almost too much, but I try to maintain a straight face. I can't give them a reaction. That's what they want. They want me to break down and cry. Or throw myself at their feet for mercy. Or beg them to take me and make me theirs. All of theirs.

I inhale and hold his gaze. Daring him to do his worst.

Because guess what, bitches? It's going to take more than a few swats to make me fold.

CHAPTER 4

The Answer

Harper's sweet vanilla scent clings to me as I steer her down the hallway to our next class.

Harper fucking Davidson. The last virgin in our class. And all ours.

Such a sweet fucking surprise.

I'm hard as a fucking rock after spanking her. The sweet tang of her arousal along with the press of her body against mine was perfection. And the glint in her eyes afterwards.

Fuck me. She *is* a fucking unicorn. Untouched. Almost eighteen. Mine. Ours.

"See you next class." Eli slaps me on the back.

We need to meet after practice tonight to discuss this development and what we need to do about it. We need to thank Brandon for updating our list.

Harper surges forward a little as if she can get away from me. I let her because I like a little chase. A little defiance.

Most of these girls are easy. They flirt and wink as I pass. If I wanted to, I could drag any of them into a closet and have them on their knees servicing me. But not little Miss Untouched. She didn't even want to admit to her sexual status.

Her arousal probably mortifies her.

She's almost to the door when I grab her, stopping her, and push her against the wall. Not gently. I crowd in on her and catch her little gasp. Yeah, that's my hard dick pressing against your stomach. Get used to the feel of it.

She tilts her head back to look up at me. Her face is flushed red, and I wonder if she's still wet from the spanking. I could slide my hand under her skirt and feel it for myself. Rubbing her warm ass after spanking her wasn't enough. How much of a fuss would she raise if I slid my hand between her thighs?

Not yet. We just found this creature. We need to take our time. We need to agree on everything, so no one takes advantage before we all can.

"What?" she asks, almost belligerently.

I tsk her. "Want more spankings?"

"No." Her eyes are dark and spark with anger when she meets mine. Not submissive at all. I like that.

I drop my mouth next to her ear. "Maybe next time, I'll do it in private, where I can check how wet you get after every strike."

Her body tenses against mine. I chuckle as I pull back a little to look down at her. Her cheeks are almost as red as her ass should be. Her lips press into a fine line, but suddenly, she relaxes back against the wall and looks over my shoulder. Like she's giving in.

That's a new game. I'll let her play it this time. She needs time to adjust to us.

All of us.

I get it. We're a lot. Usually we come at girls one or two at a time, but not this one. Not the last. We want to savor her. Together.

I grab her elbow and steer her into our classroom. I guide her to the back and put her in the corner desk before taking the desk next to hers. She hisses slightly when she sits.

That makes me smile. Knowing that every time she feels that, she'll think of me.

Dropping her backpack on the floor, she gets her notebook out. She's not short, but not tall. She's got a good rack, a slim waist, and her ass...my fingers still buzz from smacking it. Nice bounce. It'll do nicely.

That long brown hair in a ponytail is fantastic to tug on. Her large eyes are dark brown. Her features are pleasant, even pretty. Small nose, dimpled chin, and high cheekbones. But her mouth...holy shit, why hadn't I noticed that mouth before this year? Her lips are full and shaped to perfection. A dark rose color that might be fucking natural. They'll look incredible stretched around my cock.

I lean back in my chair and stare at the students in the classroom. I notice the girl she talked to in first period. She approaches, but when she catches me watching her, she drops into the nearest seat.

I take out my phone.

ME:
Tonight. Talk about Harper

CADEN:
Pizza. My house?

JACK:
I'm game

ELI:
We need a plan

ME:
Exactly

I glance over at our girl. She's ignoring me still. After the spanking, I kind of expect the cold shoulder. Better than a weepy girl afraid of her own shadow. Much better. More to break.

JACK:
Did she cry?

ME:
Nah

CADEN:
Nice

ME:
She's angry

ELI:

I like an angry kitten

I refuse to smile, but I know Eli. He'd prefer a girl who spits fire than a weeping daisy. So far Harper hasn't disappointed. Most girls would be a crumbling mess after being spanked in front of most of their classmates.

Not Harper. Girl couldn't give a fuck.

That just means more boundaries to be pushed.

I reach over, grab her ponytail close to her head, and turn her to face me. I can see the pain in her eyes as I tug her hair, but she doesn't make a noise as she meets my eyes.

"We need to know how untouched you are."

"Why?" She presses those lips together again, considering what to say next.

I give her a moment. She should answer if she knows what's good for her.

She huffs out a breath. "Why can't you just leave me alone? It's only one more year. You haven't bothered me in the many years we've gone to school together. Just let me go my way and you can go yours. I won't be your sex doll."

If she thought that would put me off, she's in for a shock.

"It doesn't matter who you are. It only matters what you are." I lean in close enough to see the anger still flaring in her eyes. "You are an affront to our leadership. A hot little thing like you slipping through our fingers for years? Tell me, have you ever given or received head?"

She presses her lips together.

I want the answer to come from those lips. I want to see the truth in her eyes. She says untouched, but girls lie.

I tighten my grip on her hair until she flinches with pain. "There are other ways we can find out, unicorn. There's a janitor's closet three doors down. I can take you in there and find out exactly how inexperienced you are."

Her eyes flare with heat. "I don't have any experience. Okay?"

"None?" I narrow my eyes at her. How is that possible? I wonder if she's one of those religious types. Maybe daddy is a preacher.

"Some of us would rather not spread ourselves around," she bites out.

"Do you want to call me a whore or a slut, Harper?" I tip her head back, extending her throat. I can't wait to mark it up. Her pulse flutters.

She swallows. "If the shoe fits."

I smile and relax my hold on her hair. "Me and my boys have gotten around, but don't let that put you off. We always wrap it. We have plans for you, my unicorn."

I release her, and she shuffles back into her seat to face the front again. Her hand lifts like she's going to touch her hair, but she stops. Her eyes flick to me and her hand falls to her desk.

"Curiouser and curiouser," I mutter.

The teacher enters and begins the lesson.

I scoot my desk closer to hers and trap her in. "How about your breasts?"

"Excuse me?" she whispers, offended.

"Anyone get to second base? Seen 'em? Felt 'em? Sucked 'em?" I raise an eyebrow at her.

Her face flushes a light pink. "No."

"No?" My eyebrows draw together. What the fuck is with this girl? "Have you ever touched a cock?"

She shakes her head, once again trying to pay attention to the teacher.

"Fuck, Harper. Have you ever kissed a guy?"

Her cheeks deepen in shade, and she shakes her head again.

"Did you grow up in a convent?" The religious angle has to be it.

She turns her face toward me and gives me the most wicked, disparaging look that makes my cock twitch to attention.

"No, I didn't grow up in a convent. I grew up in this school where if I didn't want to be cornered by one of you assholes, I had to keep my head down and do absolutely nothing noteworthy. Only to find out the very reason you all want me now is the very thing that should have kept you away from me."

I grin. How can I not? The girl's got spunk. She's not going to bend to our will easily. Most girls cave easily. It just means she's got a slightly harder shell to get through. A challenge, but we're up for it.

She purses her lips and faces the front again.

I lean in to whisper. "I promise we'll correct that error as soon as possible."

She raises her hand. "May I go to the bathroom?"

Mr. Flack looks startled by her question before nodding. "Take the pass."

She stands and runs her hand over the back of her skirt before walking away from me.

Does her ass hurt from the spanking? I wait until she's escaped before raising my hand.

"Mr. Flack, may I go to the bathroom?"

He nods absently toward the other pass on his desk. I'm going to like this class.

I go out into the hall and stride across to the women's restroom. I push the door open and stroll in like I own the place. Only one stall is occupied. Otherwise, her black and white shoes would have given her away. I would have shooed out anyone else anyway.

I whistle a little tune from *American Horror Story* season one.

"You've got to be kidding me. This is the girls' bathroom." Her voice is sharp.

I lean against the sink across from her stall.

"We were having a discussion, and you left." I shrug. It's the middle of class. The likelihood of another student coming in is low, and once they see me, they'll turn and walk the other way.

"I was done with the discussion. Now please leave," she says.

"That's not how this works, Harper."

"You want to tell me how this works then, Luke?"

A realization hit me. "Do you have your panties down in there?"

"None of your business," she bites out.

I push off the sink and move toward the stall. The door barely reaches my chin. I look down at the top of Harper's head. Those pink panties are between her knees. My dick twitches.

"Need any help in there?"

Her head pops up and her gaze locks on me. "Oh, for fuck's sake."

"I mean, I assume you're in here to piss and I'm not hearing any pissing happening." I scratch my chin and give her a wink.

"Go away," she says sternly. Her eyes flash with anger.

"Answer my question then." I lift an eyebrow.

"You haven't asked one," she says through gritted teeth.

"We've established you are truly untouched. No one else has put a hand on that kickass body but me."

Her cheeks go red, but she holds my gaze. Those fantastic lips press tight.

"The logical question to ask is whether you've touched yourself. And before you qualify that, I'll ask explicitly. Have you stuck your fingers or anything else besides a tampon in your cunt?"

Her perfect lips part, and she looks completely dumbfounded by my question. "Are you fucking kidding me? Get out of the bathroom or I'll scream."

I narrow my eyes on her and smile bitterly. "You scream, you get punished. Remember, I let you keep the panties on this last time."

"I can't pee with you here. Go away." She drops her head, taking her eyes from mine.

"Fair. Answer my question." I'm not leaving until she gives me an answer. We need to know exactly what we're dealing with so we can put rules in place. I hate to tell Harper, but this won't be like the others. She's giving us much more than we've ever had before.

Even that wannabe Christian chick had taken a guy in her mouth before.

"No." The word is soft.

"I'm sorry I didn't hear you."

Her dark eyes flash back up to mine. "No. Happy? Now leave."

"You don't give the orders, unicorn."

She glares at me.

"But I'll give you a choice." I rub my finger over my lip, wondering how far I can push her. "Give me your panties."

"What?" She grabs onto them. "No."

"Or show me your ass. I want to see how red I made it."

"This has to fall under sexual harassment."

She won't tell on us. They never do. She'll beg for it by the end.

"You know us. Bringing in the administration will only make us ten times worse. Make a choice, unicorn. Ticktock."

Her mouth scrunches mutinously. "Fine. You can look."

She stands, pulling her panties up under her skirt, but I raise a hand to stop her.

"Unlock the door."

Her wide eyes shoot up to mine. Fear lingers in them.

"I promise not to touch." Much. I give her a smile meant to calm her.

She sighs and opens the door. I step into the stall with her, and she eyes me warily.

"Turn around," I say softly, anticipating every moment. I'd rub my hands together if I didn't think she'd start screaming. This will go much easier if I don't have to deal with the principal.

Pressing her lips together like she's stopping herself from saying something, she turns. When I slowly drag her skirt up, she gasps. But she doesn't stop me. One hand remains on her panties that she mostly pulled up. The other is clenched in a fist at her side.

I gather her skirt in my hand as I slowly reveal her pale thighs.

"Wait." She tries to turn, so I put a hand on her shoulder to keep her facing the toilet.

"Shh."

The skirt lifts to show her inflamed skin. Her muscles clench. I take my hand from her shoulder and trace the outline of my handprint on her cheek, feeling the heat radiating from the skin.

She gasps and tries to lurch forward, but I have her skirt captured in my other hand. "You said you wouldn't touch."

I lift my hand to her waist and yank her back against me. My denim covered erection presses against her bare bottom. "You don't get to call the shots anymore."

She sputters as she tries to come up with something. Anything to say to me.

Satisfied, I step back and drop her skirt in place. Her fist presses against the wall of the stall as she bites out, "Happy?"

I grin. "More than. See you back in class. Don't keep me waiting."

She grits her teeth, holding back probably every name in the book.

She'll have plenty of time to scream all the names she likes soon enough.

CHAPTER 5

The Plan

Eli

After practice, we head down to the rec room in Caden's basement with a bunch of pizzas. The room has a sixty-inch TV and a leather sectional. The walls are dark. It's the perfect hangout space. His parents work late most days if they aren't traveling, and tonight we have the house to ourselves. Perfect time to discuss our new pet.

These three have been my crew since second grade. We work hard together on the football field and we play hard off of it. We're top dogs at school for one more year before moving on to college. And frankly we're a little bored.

This summer was filled with parties and pussy. We had everything. No one defied us. We made good headway on the senior list of virgins until only one remains.

Harper Davidson is a challenge. Something that shouldn't have gone on as long as it has. We don't mess with girls who are already snatched up like that MacKenzie chick. But a single girl who looks like Harper shouldn't have slipped through our fingers.

"She's not going to go down easy." Luke shakes his head as he settles on the couch.

"They never do." Jack grins at his wordplay.

Luke ignores him as Jack holds an imaginary head down in front of his pelvis and thrusts at it. Caden throws a pillow at him. When it hits Jack in the chest, he falls onto the couch laughing.

"She's stubborn and headstrong. She made it to her senior year without us catching onto her." Luke is still mulling that over. She must have worked extra hard to stay out of Luke's sights. He usually keeps tabs on everything and everyone. Knowing everyone's triggers and weaknesses is how he stays on top.

He told us about the bathroom incident with Harper. Wish we all could have seen her ass red with his handprints.

"I've seen her around," I mention. She's noticeable when you look. Over the years, I've had classes with her. "She blends. One minute you see her and the next she's gone."

It's frustrating because now that I've locked onto her, I can't see anyone else. I don't know about the other horsemen, but I want to have her splayed out in front of me while I do nasty things to that firm, tight body with those wide eyes glaring at me the whole time, daring me to keep doing them.

I want to defile her over and over again. Not just one time to conquer the final virgin. I need to possess her.

I know Luke is all in, but I'm not sure if it's the girl or the control he wants.

"Yeah, I've seen her on campus too, but she's nothing special." Caden shrugs like he didn't light up like a Christmas tree when we found out she was untouched. "I mean, she's got nice tits and a firm ass, but she's not as hot as some girls in our class."

"Who have all been used so much they might as well be a toilet," Jack adds.

We've all been with them. The popular girls. Some are pretty good at giving head and some are a decent lay. We've even shared a few who were a little more adventurous between two of us. We've all taken virginities. It's almost a rite of passage at our school to have a horseman take your virginity. Most of the girls were technically virgins, but they'd done everything else. It wasn't much to push them a little further. Make them want and beg for a little more.

Most of them only had one or two of us. This girl should feel honored to have all our attentions.

"What are we planning to do with her?" I ask. I know what I want, but Luke leads us. He has his own ideas. "Share her?"

Luke sinks back on the leather sofa and lifts his bottle of beer to his lips. Fucking dick. Like he hasn't already thought this through and doesn't know exactly what he wants. He's always been like this. Whether he's leading us on the field or off. He takes his time and makes the right calls.

"We need rules between us and for her," Luke starts.

Jack leans forward and rubs his hands together. "She's clean. I say we do her raw."

My dick twitches at the thought of feeling her hot, wet heat surrounding it. I've always used condoms. We all have.

"What the fuck, man? You want a little Jack brat to haunt your college years?" Caden shakes his head.

"She's going to take time." Luke sets his beer on the coffee table. "We get her on birth control if she isn't already."

"That shit isn't guaranteed." Caden glances at us like we're stupid to risk it.

"It is if it's taken at the same time every day," Jack chimes in. His mom is an OB-GYN. She sat us down when we were twelve and explained all about birth control. She also makes sure we have access to condoms, which we always use. "Besides, it's actually more effective against pregnancy than a condom. And there are other options besides the pill."

"Does she get a say in this?" I have to ask. We've pressured girls before, but in the end, it's always their decision. Forcing a girl onto birth control? Maybe this one might go too far.

The other three look up at me.

"What? It's a valid question. Someone that uptight might not want to give it up. No matter the pressure. I'm not going to jail for some chick who cries because she thought she wanted it but changed her mind. We've got our futures to look out for."

"She'll want it." Luke seems utterly confident. "We need to control her first. Get her used to us and used to us touching her. Start getting over some of those firsts."

I flip on the Xbox and pass out controllers. If we're going to discuss this, we might as well kill something while we do.

I'm all for having a pet for a while and if I get to fuck Harper, then that's even better.

I get the game set up and then jerk my head toward Luke. "All right. Lay out your plan."

HARPER

KENZ:

Sitting pretty?

ME:

Ha Ha

It still hurts

KENZ:

Internet says ice

ME:

I'm thinking homeschool

KENZ:

sad face emoji

But it's our senior year

ME:

Better than dealing with those assholes all year

KENZ:

You could just give it up

ME:

Not going to happen

CHAPTER 6

The Launch

HARPER

I receive a text as I'm getting out of the shower on Tuesday morning. Yes, I still have to go to school. Mom refuses to listen to reason and swears it's better for me. I didn't tell her about the horsemen. That could be a whole thing.

And if she gets the administration into it, I might as well lay down and spread-eagle for them. They wouldn't let that shit fly.

> **WAR (CADEN):**
>
> Pick you up at 8

> **FAMINE (JACK):**
>
> Wear another skirt *winky face emoji*

I'm doomed. I dry my hair and grab a sweatshirt and ripped jeans. Sure, it's still warm out, but the air conditioning in the school can be frigid even this time of year. After having my panties showcased for the entire school, I need a little more coverage for the day.

My scalp still stings a little from Luke grabbing my ponytail, so I leave my hair down and let it dry naturally.

Fuck them if they think their little fuck toy should dress pretty for them. I didn't sign up for this job. And I can get to school in my own car.

I head to the kitchen and look at the schedule on the fridge. Mom's a nurse and her schedule changes all the time. Right now, she's working mornings, so she left before I even woke up.

I grab an orange and pack my lunch. By the time I'm ready to leave, I notice it's five to eight. Okay, as long as Tweedledee and Tweedledum are late, I should still be fine. Of course, I'll have an excuse ready for why I didn't wait so I don't get punished again.

When I reach the side door, I pull it open, and Jack and Caden stand there with shit-eating grins. Caden's face drops as he takes in my clothes.

"Change," he says as he pushes past me into my house.

"What? No. I'm fine. If we don't leave now, we'll be late." I don't mention I'm driving myself. One battle at a time.

"Then you should change quickly." Jack grabs my hand and leads me into the house. "Your mom working?"

I'm not answering that and tug my hand to get it back. They don't need to know I'm alone.

"She works at the hospital with my mom, so I know she's gone. This will go so much easier if you just work with us, Harper." Jack shakes his head and drags me toward the stairs.

"What are you doing?" I try to dig my feet into the rug, but Caden lifts me off them. "Stop."

Caden wraps his arms around me and holds me to his front. He's warm and smells like freshly baked cinnamon rolls. Not exactly what I thought the enforcer of the horsemen would smell like. A little too comforting.

Jack continues up the stairs and looks into my mom's room, then the guest bedroom, before finding mine. Caden drops me on the bed. I almost bounce right off it. I scramble to sit up immediately and glare at him. His lip twitches at the corner.

"Strip." He moves with Jack to my closet and looks through the hanging clothes. Brutes. Wait a minute. Strip?

I gape at their backs for a minute before crossing my arms. "I'm not stripping for you two."

"Take your clothes off, sweetheart. We aren't here to touch you, but we definitely don't want to show up with you looking like that." Jack turns to me with a grin and a wink. "We have a reputation to uphold."

"These are my clothes. There's nothing wrong with them." I stand and tap my foot. This is ridiculous. "I don't care about your reputations."

"Grab her clothes. I'll take care of her." Caden smirks as he stalks toward me. Hunger lurks in his eyes as he takes me in.

I feel a responding pulse between my legs. Seriously? My horny bitch is such a betrayer.

It's not like I don't get it. The cream of the crop wants to fuck me. Evolutionary-wise, my internal horny bitch is already lying down and spreading for them to produce the best offspring.

I swallow. Yeah, no offspring. That would be a disaster.

I back away with my hands out in front of me. I'm in my bedroom with two horsemen and they're trying to undress me. This isn't good. I should run out the door and drive as far away as possible. But worse will await me if I disobey.

Plus, this is my senior year. One year left. Mom can't afford for me to transfer anywhere else and homeschooling isn't an option.

"Come on, untouched. You said it yourself, we need to get to school. Stop delaying." Caden closes in on me until my back is to the wall. His warmth flows over me as his green eyes dance with mischief.

"Take off the sweatshirt, but we'll make do with the jeans." Jack shakes his head and pulls out a black top. "We need to take you shopping. Your closet is seriously lacking."

Caden reaches out and grabs the hem of my sweatshirt. I don't know what to do. Screaming won't do anything. They'll do what they want in the end. I'm not strong enough to stop them. But if they try anything more than taking off my shirt, I'll fight for all I'm worth.

"Lift your arms." Caden narrows his eyes.

I blow out a breath and put my arms up as he peels my sweatshirt off. A flash fills the room with light and I turn to see Jack lowering his phone.

"Did you take a picture of me in my bra?"

"Yup." Jack smirks and presses a few things on his phone.

"Delete it." I go to step forward, but Caden is still in front of me. He bodychecks me. I take a breath. My bra has good coverage, more than most bikinis, but Caden's darkened gaze rests on my cleavage and my bare midriff. Why did I decide it was a good day for a push-up bra? He licks his lips, and my panties dampen in response.

"Not going to happen." Jack leans against the wall opposite me.

I lift my gaze to Caden's. He's still blocking me in. "Excuse me."

He lifts his eyes to mine and quirks an eyebrow, then drops his gaze back to my breasts.

"I can see the appeal." His voice is low and almost reverent.

I press into the wall behind me as he lifts a hand toward my breast. My breath catches in my throat. I brace myself for his touch. They're just breasts. It's no different from Luke touching my ass yesterday. My pulse kicks up a notch at the memory.

"Caden," Jack says with a hint of reprimand.

Caden's jaw clenches. He gestures to my breasts and gives Jack a *but* look.

"Rules." Jack hands Caden the shirt he picked out.

"Fuck the rules, man." Caden turns the shirt over in his hands, but I reach out and snatch it from him.

Jack disappears into my bathroom. I quickly pull on the low-cut top. Kenz swore I *needed* it when we went shopping this summer. I put it on maybe once when I wasn't going anywhere. It shows a lot of cleavage.

At least it adds another layer between me and the beast in front of me before he gets too grabby.

"Much better." Caden gives a nod of approval and reaches out to straighten the collar next to my breast. The backs of his fingers brush over the swell, and I inhale sharply at the sensation of sparks lighting under my skin.

His green eyes darken as they capture mine. I can't breathe. He trails his fingers along the collar and begins to wrap his hand around the back of my neck. My insides churn, but not in an unpleasant way. I'm pretty sure he's about to kiss me.

Unbidden, my tongue slips out to wet my lips. His attention drops to them.

"Score." Jack's voice comes from the bathroom.

Caden takes a step back while letting his hand drop. His intense focus leaves me, and my breath rushes to fill my lungs. I collapse against the wall. Holy crap, would I have stopped him from kissing me? I'm not sure I would have.

Jack comes out of the bathroom holding up my pack of birth control pills. I charge forward to take them, but he holds them up out of my reach.

"Give those back."

He wraps an arm around my waist and tugs me flush against him. His blue eyes smile down at me. "Hoping to have sex or really bad PMS?"

"Irregular cycles if you must know, and knowing you all, you must know." I try to pull away, but he lowers his hand to offer me the pills. He smells like apples, crisp and sweet, and for a second, I pause as his warmth filters into me. The hard press of his body against mine.

He shakes the pill packet as a reminder, and I look into his laughing eyes. I snatch them away from him, knowing if he didn't want to let me go, he could have held me there.

Jack smiles and lifts his phone as I pass him to put them back in the bathroom. No doubt he's letting the others know of his findings. I'm sure they'll need to know my cycle next. God knows why.

"Time to go, sweetheart," Jack calls to me and holds his hand out for mine.

I bypass him and his hand and pass Caden, who's laughing at Jack. I might be able to get to my car before they come out. The house will lock behind them. I swipe my backpack off the floor where it dropped when Caden picked me up.

Before I reach the door, hands grab my hips, halting my progress. I glare up at Caden, who gives me a knowing smile. Jack walks by, tossing his keys in the air and snatching them quickly.

"You ride with us now." Jack holds open the door, but I don't move.

"You have practice after school," I remind him.

"Yeah, and maybe if you're a good girl, you'll get to watch," Caden says in my ear. Shivers ripple over me. Ugh, these guys.

"This is insane. I'll drive myself." I cross my arms over my chest.

Jack comes back until he has me sandwiched between him and Caden. The heat of them together seeps under my skin, making me jittery. "There are so many ways to punish you, sweetheart. You don't want to use them all up in your first week, do you?"

My cheeks flame, remembering Luke spanking me in the cafeteria. I waited all afternoon for someone to say something or snicker at me, but no one did. Still, I don't want to do that again.

I draw in a breath and almost go weak in the knees. Apples and cinnamon go together really well. I tip my head back against Caden's shoulder to look up at Jack. I should be mortified to be caught between these two. I should be, but it kind of feels good.

"Come on. We're going to be late." Caden wraps his arm around my waist and lifts me again.

Jack gives me his maniacal smile and turns to open the door.

"I can walk." It's feeble, but the attempt needs to be made.

"I enjoy toting you around, untouched." Caden leans his chin on my shoulder, his body solid against my back. "Maybe I'll carry you around like this all day."

I shut my mouth. He'd do it too. At least the cafeteria only had maybe half the student population, since the whole campus is open during lunch. Word will have spread. By now people are probably saying all the horsemen fucked me in the cafeteria in front of everyone. Because rumors suck and are rarely accurate.

I don't need to throw gasoline on the fire with Caden carrying me like a delivery everywhere. I seriously need a plan to deal with these guys. Ignoring them won't be an option.

WHEN I SETTLE INTO MY ART DESK FOR THIRD PERIOD, I breathe a sigh of relief. One whole hour without the guys. Yesterday afternoon had been a hellscape of different combinations of horsemen in each of my classes.

This morning, all the guys dropped their gazes to my cleavage every time they saw me like they'd never seen boobs before. The sweatshirt definitely would have been the better option, but it isn't like I have a choice anymore. Before I left AP Statistics this morning, Eli bent down to inform me where to meet them for lunch. I managed to forgo giving him a double bird salute when I left the room.

Kenz drops into the seat next to me. "How are you holding up?"

"Seriously considering whether giving them my virginity would be worth it if it means they'll move on from me." I put my head down on the desk. It's an option. Not a great one. But can I take an entire year of being dressed, stalked in the bathroom, picked up, or surrounded by four hot guys versus one terrible night of losing my hymen?

Kenz puts her hand on my shoulder. "I don't think it will be that easy, H."

"Why?" I lift my head. Her pinched face makes me straighten, suddenly alert. "Did you hear something?"

Her lips flatten and she nods.

Oh shit, this isn't good. "Just tell me."

"They plan on keeping you to themselves all year. The guys have spread it around that no one is to mess with you or it would be like messing with them."

My heart jerks in my chest. All year? I have to do this dance all year!

Kenz glances behind us to make sure no one is listening. "They don't just want to take your virginity. They want to own you."

"So I'm basically fucked either way." Hysterical laughter bubbles out of my lips. "Like literally."

"Maybe it won't be so bad, Harper." She flinches. Yeah, she knows it's bad.

This isn't just one guy with a goal in mind, but four of them with one singular focus: me. I hadn't given it much thought, but there are four of them. Do they expect me to fuck all of them? They're all attractive, but only one of them can take my virginity. Right?

Then again, they did double-team Parker Ford. Unbidden, I remember being caught between Jack and Caden this morning. Was that how it was for her? My insides buzz.

"I'm still in control of my own body." I say it out loud because I need to hear it. They can humiliate me daily, but they can't take my body unless I give them permission. "I just won't give them permission."

Kenz nods and smiles sadly. "Maybe." She grabs my hand and squeezes. "I wish I could help you."

I shake my head. No one can help me without a target being placed on them. This is my battle. Maybe that's why I avoided them for as long as I could. Maybe I've always known it would come down to me against them.

It feels like I'm in a battle for my soul.

"It might not be all bad." Kenz takes out her sketch pad and glances toward the door, but Ms. Sullivan hasn't come in yet. "The rumors all say they make it worthwhile. And there are plenty of needy bitches who go back for more, so that has to mean something."

"It means girls are as stupid as guys when it comes to sex," I say flatly. I may be a virgin, but I know about sex. What teenager doesn't? I read steamy romance novels and have seen porn. The porn didn't do much for me, but it was interesting.

Lack of opportunity and a healthy dose of sex-is-a-scary-fucking-risk-with-STIs made me not really want to travel that road as early as some of my classmates. The lack of opportunity probably had the most to do with it. So sue me for not having sex.

Now I have four guys thinking they deserve my virginity. Well, fuck them, it's not up for sale. They can keep their dicks to themselves.

CHAPTER 7

The Deal

HARPER

The cafeteria. I've spent three years avoiding this room. Yesterday I was tossed over Luke Foster's knees and spanked while everyone watched and counted along like some alternative demented Sesame Street timeline.

Now I have to present myself to the assholes so I won't be punished again. Coming into this cafeteria is punishment enough to be honest.

An arm slides around my shoulders from behind, and I tense.

"Easy, girl." Jack chuckles and tugs me into his firm side. "No one but us will touch you. Or Caden will break them into pieces."

"How touching." I roll my eyes as Jack directs me to a table off to the side. The other three are all there already. The tables surrounding it are vacant. It's time to put all the knowledge of these guys I gathered over the years to good use and help me out of this situation.

Caden is the largest of the group and the meanest. He's a fucking beast. He sits at the end of the table with his green eyes tracking me. He makes me feel like prey. Jack is right. Caden would decimate anyone who got in his way, just like on the football field. While the other guys are definitely not poor, Caden's family is wealthy and both his parents are too busy to ever show up for a game.

Even I show up for games. Game time always seemed like a safe space for me to be an actual high schooler, as all the horsemen are occupied on the field. So I've seen them all in action. I've even gotten caught up in the game and cheered for them a time or two.

Jack is a flirt. He guides me to the table and pulls out the chair next to Eli for me. I know it isn't optional, so I sit. Just being in this room makes me fearful of what punishment they might decide on next or if they'll just stick to spankings.

The girls at the next table call out to Jack, and he swaggers over to them. As he talks to them, he brings himself down on their level, leaning in and touching them occasionally. By the time he swaggers back to our table—fuck, *their* table—the girls are all giggling and gossiping behind their hands.

I get out my lunch bag and remove my sandwich. Caden reaches over and snags it out of my hand. I open my mouth, but what the hell can I do about it? Fight him? I need to choose my battles carefully or I'll give too much of myself away.

"Thanks, untouched." He winks and devours my sandwich in three bites.

It's not like I have much of an appetite with my stomach churning with worry anyway.

Eli pulls out an apple and offers it to me. Fuck if I don't feel like Snow White as I slowly reach for it. Poison wouldn't be a stretch for Pestilence, right?

"Thank you," I say softly.

"You're welcome, kitten." He spreads his legs and his thigh rests against mine under the table.

My stomach flutters. I don't pull away even though I really want to.

Pick my battles. I play those words on repeat in my head. They're used to getting what they want.

They could be a powder keg ready to blow, and my resistance could be the match. They aren't exactly known for their even temperaments.

Eli is a little bit of an enigma. He doesn't talk much, letting Luke run the show, but he's fucking brilliant. He's got a full ride waiting for him already at pretty much any university he wants to go to.

Luke clears his throat, and my eyes lift to him. Seriously, he's too pretty to be real. If he wasn't such a dick to everyone, he would still be just as popular and get just as much pussy. He's a little cold and calculating. His mother died when he was young, and his father raised him on his own. Maybe the lack of a woman's touch left out something fundamental in Luke's personality.

Like humanity.

"We need to discuss your schedule." Luke pins me with his cool blue eyes and steeples his fingers against his lips like the evil genius he is.

"My schedule?" I bristle.

This guy spanked me in front of everyone and then made me show him my bare, red ass in the bathroom. I have no doubt I will hate everything he tries to make me do.

Liar, that little voice that doesn't mind any of this whispers.

"We can't be with you every minute of the day."

Thank heaven for that. I bite my lip to hold in that response.

Luke tips his head as he notices my lip. I release it and lift the apple to take a bite. Please be poisoned. At least my death will be quick.

Instead, the apple is sweet and light, unlike my current lunch companions.

"You'll ride to school with one of us. Stay in the library and study while we have football practice. Be driven home or to wherever we require you to be after that."

"Wherever you require me to be?" The words taste bitter on my tongue.

Luke's smile is just a hint cruel as he leans on his elbows across the table toward me. "We own you, unicorn. You go where we want, when we want. You wear what we say and you do what we tell you to."

My heart is pounding. I can almost feel the rest of the horsemen leaning in to hear my response. They take up all the air around me, sucking it from my lungs. I feel like a gazelle surrounded by wolves and I can't see a way out of this.

"No." The word bursts out of me. I can't hold it in anymore. I set the apple down on the table and go to push myself back, but Eli's hand goes to the back of my chair, holding me in place.

I swivel to glare at him, but he just calmly moves my apple in front of him.

Luke's smile grows broader. Like he likes it when I'm defiant, like it gets him off. Noted. "What do you mean, no?"

Jack moves to the chair on my other side, sitting facing me and blocking me in at the same time. He might as well say checkmate.

"You can't just *own* me." There's more to it, but I'm trapped and I really don't want to put on a repeat performance for the students watching us. I'm pretty sure jeans wouldn't cut it for Luke's sadistic spankings. If he spanks me again, people will expect a spanking show every day. I'm not willing to provide our school with that much entertainment.

I want to run. I want to get as far away from these guys as I can before they take anything more from me. So far, they haven't taken much. Nothing I can't handle, but if they control where I can go...

My mind stutters to a halt.

Fuck, they could take me anywhere, and I'm supposed to shut up and go with four guys who have told me they want to fuck me. Yeah, I'm not that stupid. They'll claim I didn't try to get away. I chose to go with them. I'll be trapped. They'll keep taking from me until there's nothing left.

"What are you scared of, kitten?" Eli's almost gentle voice pulls me from the stare down with Luke.

I turn to face him. His brown eyes seem soft, but I'm not fooled by any of these guys. Their only loyalty is to each other. "I'm one girl against four guys. I'm guessing you can imagine what I'm afraid of."

It's not like they're subtle about what they want from me. I just don't know what all they want from me. How far are they willing to take this?

Eli captures a lock of my hair, and I wince, expecting a pull, but his fingers just drift softly down to the end. "Do you think we'll force you?"

His brown eyes focus on mine. He's not saying they won't. He's asking if I think they will. I glance around the table at these four guys. Again, no one has ever come out and called them rapists before. No gossip has ever been spread saying they forced someone. But that doesn't mean they aren't capable of it or they haven't made the victim terrified of coming forward. Their fathers have deep pockets when it comes to keeping their sons out of trouble.

I return my gaze to Eli. Currently, he seems like the lesser evil of the group. "You guys aren't exactly known for being nice guys."

Jack trails his fingers up my arm, leaving sparks under my skin in his wake.

I jerk my gaze to him. His blue eyes capture me as he trails his fingers back down to my hand. This is a major problem. Their touch doesn't repulse me. Not at all.

"Nothing will happen without your say-so." Jack speaks the words with such conviction, but can I trust what he says? Can I trust what any of them say? Do I dare to?

Just yesterday, Luke swore not to touch me and then caressed my ass with his hand. So yeah, I'm not exactly going to trust what these boys are trying to sell me. They seem to want me submissive and willing.

"I don't understand what you want from me." That's what frightens me the most. I don't know the rules of the game they're playing. How can I beat the game if I don't know what to do to win? Do I win if I keep my virginity?

"We want to own you." Luke's strong voice pulls my attention back to him. "In return, we'll protect you."

"Protect me from what?" I raise an eyebrow. I'll come back around to the owning part, but seriously? "The only people I've ever needed protecting from are you four."

Caden sits next to Luke, drawing my eyes. He's a beast of a man. No one in their right mind would call him a boy. His expression is blank, like we could be talking about the weather.

"As long as you do what we say, all of us will keep you safe and take care of you," Caden says.

"Do as you say?" My brain can't help turning to some pretty fucked up things they could make me do. "I'm still not seeing how this arrangement is beneficial to me. You want to take my virginity."

"We want you to *give* your virginity to us," Luke clarifies. His eyebrows lower. "We won't take anything you don't want to give us."

"You think I want to give you control over me?" I laugh, but it's a tight, high laugh, almost hysterical. Fuck these guys. "You know I only have one virginity to give, right?"

They all give hungry smiles at my words. Fuck if that horny little bitch inside me volunteers as fucking tribute. I'm going to need to bind and gag her, but I'm afraid she'd like that.

Luke leans in. "So many firsts to share with us. Sure, only one of us can push our cock into your cunt for the first time, but that doesn't mean we can't all be there when it happens."

I suck in a breath and recoil in my chair. All be there? As in all participate? I haven't been with one guy, and suddenly they want me to be with all four of them like this is normal?

I can't win this game. I feel it down in my bones. These beautiful, evil boys will take everything I have until I'm empty.

"Why would I agree to that?" I have to ask because they must know what they're saying is insane and no girl would willingly subject herself to it. Especially a girl who hasn't given up anything to one man, let alone four. "It's not like you're all agreeing to date me. You just want to use me to keep your perfect fucking record. Once you've had me, you'll toss me to the side like all the others."

Luke rubs his chin. I can almost see the calculations in his eyes. "What would it take?"

For me to agree to this insanity? I almost laugh out loud. I'll never agree, but they'll keep coming at me. Forcing me into situations where I have no choice but to do what they want or be further humiliated. They don't give a shit about what I want.

Fine, they want to play *let's negotiate for my virginity*, let's negotiate.

"A fucking choice to begin with. You could just forget about me." I lean forward, ready to bluff the fuck out of this. "I'll find a boyfriend and get on losing my virginity as soon as possible so you don't leave any virgin behind."

A growl on my left makes me glance at Eli. A shiver races down my spine. Oh, he doesn't like that option. Well, fuck him.

"What? You guys make exceptions for girls with boyfriends all the time. I'm pretty sure I can find someone who will only want to dick with me this year." I actually start turning like I'm going to look around the cafeteria for said dick.

Caden is the next to growl. Okay, so that sound does something to the primal part of me that doesn't mind being possessed by the hottest, strongest males around.

"Harper." Luke says my name sharply, drawing my eyes back to him. He folds his hands together in front of him. "We made those exceptions before. That's correct. But you aren't just any virgin we can pass off to the first male that piques your fancy. You've had three years to divest yourself of your virginity. Obviously, it's not a priority to you."

"But it is to you?" I mimic his posture.

Luke smirks. "Fine. If you can find one guy in this cafeteria willing to be your boyfriend and do the deed, we'll let you go."

I smile. Easy enough. What guy doesn't want a willing female? And I can hold off one guy all fucking year if I have to. Better one asshole than four.

"But"—Luke reaches out and grabs my chin, holding me so I can only look at him—"if you don't, you agree to submit to our rules."

"For how long?"

"As long as it takes." Luke gives me a filthy smile.

I consider the four guys who have their undivided attention on me. For now.

"Do you honestly think I want to get everyone's sloppy seconds?" I point at the table of still giggling girls Jack flirted with. Girls I've had in classes throughout school. Girls who talk about the horsemen in the locker room in bragging tones. "You all seem fucking excited that I'm untouched. But you guys have gotten around, and I'm guessing you don't have any plans on keeping it in your pants while waiting for me to come to terms with what you want."

"Are you asking us to be monogamous?" Caden leans forward. His green eyes flash with anger and something dark. "When you haven't even agreed to put out?"

"Yup." I cross my arms and sit back in my chair. "If I'm expected to give it up to you all, then shouldn't you have to give something up too?"

"The whole year." Luke draws my attention away from Caden's sputtering.

"What?" I'm not following Luke's train of thought as I try to race ahead.

Luke narrows his eyes on me. "We own you the whole year and we won't touch or fuck any other girl. But that means you play by our rules."

Something warm settles deep in my gut. I'm not sure if I'm happy because I got them to agree to something they obviously don't want, or if the idea of having these men to myself for a full year makes that bitch in heat utterly ecstatic. Kenz said they were going to keep me for the year. This is his move to make that happen.

I lean forward again and give him a forced smile. This would be too easy. What teenage boy would say no to guaranteed sex? Of course, I'll have to convince this mythical guy I'm not a sure thing after the fact, but that should be easy enough to do. One guy. A single guy to say *hell yeah, I'll date this chick*. Easy.

"So if I find a guy to date me in this cafeteria, you'll stop harassing me. But if I don't, I give you ownership of me for a year while all of you have to keep your dicks in your pants unless I want it? Did I get that right?"

"Not quite. You agree to play by our rules for a year, and we won't touch or fuck another girl during that time."

I narrow my eyes. Semantics, but when dealing with the devil, it's important to listen to the details. He left off the *unless I want it*. In the end, it's still my body. They can't force me to want any of them. At least not enough to fuck them. Sure, part of me is on board with this whole thing, but that part isn't in control.

Besides, I could probably find at least one guy willing to pull one over on the horsemen. So their deal is a moot point anyway. If not, I'll find another way out of it. Somehow.

It's worth the risk.

I hold out my hand. "Deal."

Luke takes my hand and says, "You have five minutes."

"What?" Oh, shit. Always confirm all the finer details in a deal with Death. I jerk my hand from his and can finally pull my chair back and stand.

At least three hundred students are in here, if not more. I can't possibly go one by one and check to see if the guy isn't just wanting me under his thumb in under five minutes.

One asshole versus four. This is my chance to escape them. Fuck it.

I step on the chair and then onto the table and yell, "Excuse me."

The noise in the nearest area quiets down. When the students see it's a girl on the horsemen's table, the room goes quiet. All eyes are on me, and I remember yesterday. I feel almost as exposed as when Luke had his hand on my underwear for them all to witness.

"Ticktock, kitten," Eli says.

"I need a boyfriend," I shout.

"You sure you don't need another spanking," a voice calls out from the back. Laughter drifts around the room.

Way to sound desperate, Harper. This is a lot more humiliating than I thought it would be.

"I need a guy to date this year, so I can live my life normally."

Jack shifts to sit on the table by my feet, and then Eli does so on my other side. Their shoulders touch my legs. It shouldn't ease some of the tension in me, but it does. A little. Even though they're probably glaring at the people looking at me.

I swallow my pride. "I've done everything in my power to stay out of the horsemen's sights, but now I just need a guy. Surely, one of you is willing to take on a girlfriend."

"If you want someone to fuck you, all you have to do is ask, baby," that same voice calls out. Asshole.

Someone else yells out, "Show us your tits."

More uncomfortable laughter scatters around the cafeteria.

"Don't you dare, unicorn." His voice low, Luke steps up behind me on the table. "You have two minutes."

Fuck my life. I have a horseman breathing down my neck and two more probably mean mugging the rest of the student body. Who knows what Caden is currently doing?

"Look, you all go to school here. You know who I'm dealing with. They've allowed me one chance to find a boyfriend to satisfy their requirements. All I need is one guy." Instead of four hulking ones who won't give a flying fuck about my feelings.

I scan the crowd. The girls look at me like I'm a thankless bitch, but I don't care about them. Or at least, I don't right now. If the other agreement goes into effect, I'll be cutting off their supply of premium dick— if everyone is to be believed—for the entire year.

The guys in the crowd don't make eye contact, especially with Luke breathing over my shoulder. I can feel the seconds slipping away along with my freedom.

CHAPTER 8

The Consequence

HARPER

Someone moves through the crowd toward the back, and a brief twinge of hope floats through me. But it's Caden, his dark hair and height unmistakable. That hope fizzles and dies. He makes his way toward the back, grabs a guy by his neck, and pulls him forward to stand before our table.

The guy is gangly compared to Caden and keeps dragging his feet. He's average-looking, and honestly, I could do worse.

The horsemen are all incredibly good-looking, but again, there are four of them. I'm pretty sure if I'm it for the year, they'll find a way to make me want it. And often.

My insides tighten, and I resist the urge to lean into Luke to absorb his heat. A part of me really likes the idea of having the horsemen as mine for a year. I should be appalled that the thought of four guys passing me around like a blunt doesn't bother me as much as it probably should. That the thought of each of these guys with their hands on me doesn't make me recoil at all.

Fuck, that's some scary shit to realize and all the more reason I hope this guy is serious.

Because I could totally hold off on giving up anything to him, and the horsemen would never know the difference.

"Grant Perkins." Luke grips my hips and pulls me back against him, then rests his chin on the top of my head. It's a possessive gesture that makes me want to settle back into him.

I think I'm losing my mind, but being held feels good. Maybe hiding all those years deprived me to the point that any attention, even unwanted attention, feels wonderful.

Fuck, I need to focus. I'm sure I've had a class with Grant before. I don't know him, but what do I care? Is he volunteering? Because I just need one guy.

"I was only having fun." The voice is the same as the heckler. I almost hiss in recognition as I recoil into Luke. Caden releases him but stands behind him.

"Do you want our girl, Grant?" Luke curls his fingers possessively around my waist.

Not exactly the guy I want to hang out with for an entire year. A coward who makes lewd comments. That would make my mom proud, for sure. But if it's him or the horsemen...

Then again, cowards are always cowards.

"Nah, dude, I was joking." Grant shifts his gaze uneasily between the horsemen. His eyes skip over me. No surprises there. He looks like he's a minute from bolting or peeing his pants.

"No one here wants this virgin sacrifice?" Luke's voice rings out, and I flinch.

Just bury me now. No one is laughing, but no one is stepping forward either. I rolled the dice and bet it all on a lost cause. No one will stand up to the horsemen. No one will go against them.

I just gave away my freedom on a stupid game of chance, where the odds were never in my favor. Yeah, I'm not exactly feeling like one of the smartest girls in the room at the moment. Of course, it doesn't really change anything. They were still going to keep coming at me if I didn't agree. At least I got them to give up something they didn't want to.

"Take off your underwear."

I swallow at Luke's words. My heartbeat ratchets up to a new level. I tilt my head to look at him, but he's not looking at me. Relief flows through me.

"What?" Grant stammers. "Nah, dude."

Luke gives him a predatory grin. His fingers tighten against me. "Caden, beat the living shit out of this guy if he doesn't give us his underwear in ten, nine, eight—"

Caden closes in on Grant, looking way too happy about fighting someone half his size.

"Wait." Grant shoves his jeans down and kicks off his shoes. "Wait."

Luke covers my eyes and whispers in my ear, "Can't destroy your innocence so soon."

"I've seen a dick before." I take a breath and my body brushes against Luke's.

His heat bleeds into me from behind. I can feel his hard cock against the base of my spine. He slips the fingers at my waist under my shirt and massages the skin of my stomach. Sparks scatter through my system as he chuckles low and dark in my ear.

"You haven't seen anything yet." His lips caress my ear, sending a delicious shiver down my spine. My insides melt.

Screwed. I'm screwed.

"Here," Grant says. I assume he's holding out his underwear for Luke.

"Put your jeans back on." Luke doesn't remove his hand from my eyes. There's rustling as Grant works to do as he's told and giggles of girls in the background.

I try to remain perfectly still because his body tempts me to relax into him. Like he didn't negotiate to own me.

Maybe I like the idea of being owned?

Yeah, fuck that.

Luke removes his hand from my eyes and lowers it to join the one currently still on my stomach, making even more sparks flood my system. I want to curl into him. These urges will hopefully go away.

Grant stands there with a pair of tighty-whities in his hand.

"Put them in your mouth," Luke says as easily as if he just ordered someone to pick up a piece of trash and throw it away.

Ew.

"Dude," Grant whines. It might as well be a *why* or *do I have to?*

Eli stalks forward and stops a foot in front of Grant. "Do what you're told."

Caden closes in on Grant's back. "You disrespected our girl."

Something soft twitters through me at them standing up for me. It's stupid and girly, but I can't deny it feels good. Almost as good as Luke's fingers tracing the edge of my low-cut jeans.

Grant levels his eyes on me, and I almost flinch at the hate in them, but I didn't force him to say what he said. I lift my chin. He should know by now what the horsemen are like. Fuck him.

Luke steps into me until his front is flush with my back. "Now."

Grant shoves the underwear into his mouth.

Jack walks over with a roll of duct tape. I wasn't even aware he left. He tears off a strip and puts it over Grant's mouth.

"Leave it on for the rest of the day." Luke lifts his hand from me and waves everyone else away. "Show's over. Go back to your lunch."

Caden slaps Grant on the back hard enough for him to jerk forward and let out a muffled *oomph*. When Eli walks over to me, he holds his hands up for mine. Pressing on my hips, Luke guides me forward a little.

I take Eli's hands as he helps me step down from the table. The fact I lost hasn't quite sunk in. I feel almost numb about it. Like I didn't give my senior year to the horsemen. Like this whole thing is a huge joke, and I'll wake up in my bed yesterday before school and laugh at the stupid dream I had.

When I sit and everyone else returns to their places at the table, Eli hands me my apple again. Fuck it. A girl's gotta eat.

"We'll find a suitable punishment for that stunt." Luke leans back in his chair and smiles. "Maybe a more private one."

I remember what he said yesterday about spanking me in private. I nearly choke on the bite of apple in my mouth. What the hell did I do now? It's not like these guys even like me. They only want to use me. And I gave them permission to use me for the entire year.

I don't say anything, and the guys finish their lunch chatting with each other about football. No matter how I twist this, I can't seem to think of a way out.

Fortunately lunchtime is almost over. Unfortunately my next class is with Luke.

"We'll discuss this more tonight at Caden's." Luke makes his way around the table to stand next to me. "From now on, you'll do as we say."

I press my lips together and stand, but I'm not going to agree to that. Luckily he doesn't appear to want a response.

As we walk down the hall, the others fall in line around us as if they've done this a hundred times. Each of them splits off until it's just me and Luke. Before we make it to the classroom, he backs me against the wall again.

I wince as he presses himself against me. Of course, he's hard again. I'm wondering if he's ever not hard. I try not to think of what that will mean for me, because that part of me I'm ignoring practically swoons.

"Don't be a sore loser, Harper." He lifts my chin with his fingertip. His gloating smile is almost too much. "We have so much to teach you and all the time in the world to practice."

I press my lips together, knowing anything I say right now will only get me more punishment. I want to yell and scream and tell him where he can shove his dick.

His gaze falls to my mouth, and he brushes his thumb gently over my lower lip. His soft touch stills all my internal fight. That should not feel as good as it does.

"Maybe I'll even give you a choice again." His gaze lifts to mine. "Tonight, you can choose your first lesson."

I want to say *gee thanks* as sarcastically as possible, but all I can think about is Luke's hand on my bare ass and exactly how he's going to figure out how wet I am. And what it would feel like to have his hand between my thighs.

Fuck me. My body doesn't know what's good for it apparently. I can't trust it to not fall into line with whatever they want from me.

"Maybe we'll start with your mouth." He pulls down my lower lip and dips the tip of his thumb in between my lips, tracing my bottom teeth. "After all, you haven't even kissed a guy before."

That reminder pisses me off again. I glare up at him. That falls on their shoulders too. If I'd dressed to find a boyfriend, *they* would have noticed me. Maybe I could have snagged a boyfriend before they developed an interest. Or sure, I could have been like some others and gone to camp where no one knows the horsemen. Of course, that would have meant being able to afford camp. But part of me doesn't want to give up that piece of me to just any guy.

Forgive me for being picky. Now I have the cream of the crop wanting me, but it's not by choice. And it's not like they want *me*. They don't even know who I am. They just want my virginity.

They want a body with no personality. Maybe they should find a blow-up doll.

"After school, wait in the library. I'll come get you myself." He lowers his head until his warm breath caresses my ear. "I can't wait to play with you tonight, unicorn."

CHAPTER 9

The Loophole

HARPER

I text my mom to say I have something after school today and then sit obediently in the library while the guys have football practice. My mind churns, trying to find a way out of this situation. I pull out my sketchbook and press the edge of my pencil against it. I like art, but I'm not really an artist. It helps me clear my mind. I'm not even planning on doing fine arts in college. But the way a drawing comes together, piece by piece—from nothing to a likeness of life—that shit makes me feel like I've accomplished something.

I sketch an oval and mark a cross where the eyes and nose should line up.

Today I need to focus. I can't do anything about tonight. Luke is driving me to Caden's. I'll be all alone. With the four of them. The problem is those fucking semantics I was too ready to ignore earlier because I was so sure that someone, anyone, would want to claim me when no one has tried in the past three years. Yeah, that really wasn't smart of me.

But these guys push my buttons and make me reckless, which fucking frightens me. Because I don't know how reckless they'll make me.

While the guys skirted consent, Luke flat out refused to include it in our agreement. And because of my awesome addition of monogamy, which seemed brilliant at the time, I'm going to have four horny horsemen circling me.

If they were getting some, they might go slower with me. Ease me into sex. Okay, even to me, that sounds laughable. When those guys want something, they go after it with unwavering determination. That shouldn't make warmth flood my chest.

If I were a little more sexually aware, I could use that as an advantage. But if anything, our new arrangement will make them press harder and faster and more often at my boundaries. I have no doubts these guys have sex a lot.

And I just agreed to be their one and only source. I might as well just say goodbye to my virginity.

Fuck my life.

The librarian stands and walks out the doors, probably to use the bathroom. I know Jack charmed her into watching over me. Not even teachers can control them.

Who's more powerful than a horseman? Obviously not any other student. The other guys wouldn't even stand up to them for free sex with a virgin. Fuckers.

Adults? Teachers, maybe some of them. Definitely not the librarian. She wouldn't be an ally, but some teachers like Mr. Wick seem to care.

Parents, possibly. I don't know about their parents. It seems like the horsemen do whatever they want to do. My mom would drag them around by the ear. She wouldn't put up with their shit. I'd love to watch her put them in time-out.

That image makes me smile.

Wait.

My mom.

Holy shit, she's like an ace in the hole. I can't let her know what's going on without getting the horsemen angry at me, but her words still have power. I pull out my phone and scroll to the horsemen's group chat. She's my trump card.

ME:

My mom just texted wondering where I am

She says I have to come home or I'll be grounded

I told her I don't have a car here

I actually smile at that. None of them will answer me because they're in practice. So once they're done, I'll already be safe at home. I spend the next ten minutes doing homework and then I pack my bag.

I text my mom to ask for a ride home. When she says she'll be here in five, I switch to the horsemen group chat.

ME:

My mom is coming to get me. I'm grounded for the next two weeks.

Sorry, not sorry.

Two weeks. Not too long but long enough. I don't think they'd buy I got grounded for the year because I didn't come home directly after school one day. But two weeks should give me plenty of time to actually figure out how to handle them and get used to the sparks that wind me up when they're near. Especially since I'll only see them in school.

Personally, I've never done anything to get grounded. I'm not sure my mom even knows the word, but those guys don't know that. My mom is about to become a really strict parent. My face stretches into a grin.

Check, fuckers.

I pick up my backpack and almost feel like there's a skip in my step. For now, I've won the battle. I just need to figure out how to win the war.

JACK

I don't know about the other guys, but I'm exhausted after practice. If they have plans for our new toy though, I'll rally. I'm not missing out on a hot piece of Harper.

Sure, I'm one of the dumbasses who didn't notice her before. But if what she originally wore this morning is any indication of what she normally wears, it's no wonder I missed her.

"Fuck." Luke glares at his phone like it personally did him wrong. He doesn't throw it, but I know he wants to. He can't afford to break another one right now.

I check my phone and see Harper's texts. I would have laughed, but I'm not stupid. Luke is pissed and would probably deck me. Grounded? Not that it will stop us. But that girl isn't stupid either. I doubt she even fought against the grounding. Her mom must be strict, which would account for Harper's current status.

Luke has plans. He wants a taste of our new pet project, and she just cut him off cold. From the redness of his neck, the guy is beyond pissed. He really doesn't like it when things don't go his way.

I almost feel sorry for Harper come tomorrow. Pretty sure she's in for another treat of public humiliation. Wonder if Luke will up the ante on public spankings or do something new?

Dude's creative with his punishments.

The underwear thing today was cold, but that dick thought he could get away with taunting our girl and talking back to us. He deserved to walk about with his streaky tighty-whities in his mouth. That ought to teach him when to keep it closed.

"We'll see her tomorrow." Caden shrugs as he packs things into his bag. As always, the big guy is hard to read. I'm not sure if he likes our girl or wishes we would drop her. He definitely isn't happy about only fucking one girl, especially one that isn't a sure thing. But I've also seen how he looks at her like she's a Heisman Trophy.

"Jack." Luke draws my attention. "Were you able to get on her computer this morning?"

I grin. "Of course."

While Caden had our girl pressed up against the wall staring at her tits, I got on her laptop and installed what I needed to get in. Camfecting isn't hard. I probably could have hacked her webcam remotely because her laptop is not at all secure.

Good for us, bad for her. Though I created an access point so I could make it more secure later tonight. Don't need some other dick getting off watching our girl. That tight body is all ours.

"Good." Some of the redness leaves Luke's neck. "Finish getting ready."

Eli comes back with a towel draped around his neck and another around his waist. He pauses and takes in Luke's tight lips. "What'd she do now?"

I grin. For a girl who spent years hiding from us, she sure knows how to make an impression. Two days. We've been on her for two days. I almost hope she keeps this shit up. Sure keeps it from getting boring.

"Grounded." Luke puffs out a breath. "Fuck parents."

"You believe her?" Eli opens his locker and pulls out his clothes.

That makes me pause. She hasn't been openly defiant much, but she definitely doesn't want to go anywhere with us alone. We don't know her mom. She might be super strict. After all, the girl is still untouched.

But then again, what parent is strict with someone who doesn't do anything for fun? Harper has never even been to a party, and I highly doubt she's broken curfew or snuck out.

I can't help the smile that tugs at my lips. Smart girl.

Luke's color starts to amp up again as he ponders it, obviously reaching the same conclusion. Of course, he looks less impressed and more pissed off.

"Who gets grounded for two weeks for being home late from high school senior year?" I can't help but voice what we're all thinking. "Especially a goody two-shoes like Harper?"

Luke's grin makes my skin crawl, but I'm excited to see what he's thinking. Dude has evil down to a science.

"Let her think she's won this round." Luke pulls his shirt on over his wet hair. "We can toy with her for a bit."

"Webcam party?" I arch my eyebrow as I gear up for what I'll have to do to make it happen. Computers excite me. Not like sex excites me, but there's something about sliding into someone's property without them realizing it. Not to do anything nefarious per se, but just to poke around. Look at the shit they don't want anyone else to see.

Even Caden grins when Luke confirms, "Webcam party."

Harper

ME:

Did I miss anything in history?

KENZ:

You mean when you were in the bathroom

At the same time as Luke?

ME:

No boundaries

KENZ:

I don't think they know that word

ME:

He also talked over the teacher

KENZ:

The nerve

ME:

It's not funny

KENZ:

I know, but it is a little

Not the whole ownership thing

ME:

Yeah, not exactly thrilled with how that went

KENZ:

I'll bring M&Ms to school tomorrow

And I'll take extra good notes in our shared
classes

ME:

You're the best

CHAPTER 10

The Sentence

HARPER

"Why didn't you just take your car?" my mom asks as we enter the house.

"A friend drove me and then ended up getting stuck after school." The loosest definition of friend ever, but I can't tell her two football players pushed into our house, forced me to change in front of them, drove me to school, and want to fuck me all year.

Yeah, pretty sure that wouldn't go over well. Though it might get me grounded for real, more likely Mom would also take it to the principal. And while the principal might try to make adjustments, the horsemen could make my last year unbearable.

That and the principal would have to fuck up my schedule to make sure I'm not with the guys. Any other year might have been okay, but I need these classes and most of them are only offered once during the day.

It's not like the principal will move the guys to different classes. To the principal, these guys are his golden ticket. Football stars, top of their class, rich parents.

Besides, Mom already has a lot of things to deal with. Her job is high stress enough. I can manage this. If it gets to be too much, I'll pull her in as my plan B.

"I don't want you to get stuck anywhere without a way out." Mom opens the freezer and takes out a frozen pizza. "Things are a little... complicated right now at the hospital."

I sit at the island and see the flinch on my mom's face when she says that. "What's happening?"

Mom snaps out of it and waves her hand. "Nothing to worry about. Just the normal, people are getting sick."

I nod. "That usually happens at hospitals."

She slides the pizza into the preheated oven she must have set before picking me up. Shaking whatever bothered her off, she leans on the counter and meets my eyes. Her brown eyes are curious but serious. She arches her eyebrows and gives me a conspiratorial smile.

"All right. Day two of school. Tell me how everything is going. How are your classes? Any problems? Any interesting boys?"

I almost scoff out loud at that last one. Interesting, yes.

"No problems." At least none she can help me with. "Classes seem good and doable, as always. Keeping my head down and my hands to myself."

I give her a self-deprecating smile. Well, trying to keep to myself, but I'm pretty sure this year is going to be pretty hands-on.

She rolls her eyes. "It wouldn't be the end of the world if you found a guy to date, Harper. You're seventeen. Your birthday is next week. You should be out partying on the weekends and doing things I don't want to know about. Even MacKenzie goes out."

"She's dating a football player."

"See." Mom holds her hand out to me. "You could do that. Football players make good boyfriends. As long as you use a condom."

"Mom," I say appalled. "Seriously, I'd rather not have sex with a sweaty football player." Let alone four of them.

"I'm just saying." Mom straightens. "Live your life, Harper. Hiding in the shadows might keep you protected, but it doesn't let you live."

"I suppose I could just sleep with the entire football team." I give her a wicked smile. "You know, make the most of my senior year."

Mom narrows her eyes on me and she points. "You know everyone needs a goal, but maybe just start with one guy and build up to the football team."

I laugh, but her words about hiding in the shadows get to me. I'm not in the shadows anymore. I've spent years trying to go unnoticed. To escape *their* notice. Hiding at school. Wearing things that wouldn't attract attention. It wasn't a fashion choice so much as a survival technique. Sweatshirts and jeans blend in really well.

But fuck that, I can do whatever I want now.

They've noticed me. Every other student knows I belong to them. I can dress however I want. Do whatever I want. I can stand out if I want. Because they put me on the map.

Sure, they want to control what I wear too, but fuck them. I've let them control everything about my life for years now.

In a fucked-up way, the horsemen granted me freedom by deciding to own me.

"Hey, Mom, after dinner, do you mind if I go back-to-school shopping? I could use some new clothes." I give my mom a grin. "You know, to get all the football players to notice me."

"*One* football player. Baby steps, Harper. And of course. Just use the credit card." Mom sorts through the stack of mail that's come in.

"How about half the team?" Yeah, I don't have the option to go baby steps.

She raises her eyebrow and gives me a look.

Laughing, I get out my phone and text Kenz.

ME:

Shopping emergency ASAP

KENZ:

I thought the dicks had you tonight?

ME:

Told them Mom grounded me.

KENZ:

LOL Sure.

What time?

ME:

Half hour?

KENZ:

I'll pick you up

ME:

thumbs-up emoji

AFTER OUR HOUR-LONG SHOPPING EXPEDITION, KENZ AND I pull into my driveway. We got to talk about classes and what I should be wearing. I think she realized I didn't want to talk about the guys.

I'm surprised they haven't texted me. They have to be done with practice and stewing over not getting to play with their new toy. Of course, the more time they have to stew, the more plotting they can do.

I take a deep breath, pretty sure this stunt is going to bite me in the ass. Tomorrow will be hell, but at least I now have the proper uniform to go into battle.

"They won't know what hit them." Kenz walks around to the trunk to help me unload my bags.

"That's the plan. I may not have the sexual experience to properly fuck with them, but I know how to dress to draw attention." It'll be nice to dress how I want for a change.

We take all the bags up to my room and put away my new clothes. Wonder if Jack will like my new clothes? After all, he said I needed new ones.

Where the hell did that thought come from? I'm dressing for me finally, not those Neanderthals.

My phone vibrates. My insides tense.

DEATH (LUKE):

Grounded?

ME:

Yes

DEATH (LUKE):

Pick you up tomorrow

ME:

Mom wants me to take my car. I'm not
allowed to hang out after school.

DEATH (LUKE):

...

It isn't a lie. She prefers me to have my car. I'm just not grounded. The three dots disappear. I walk over to Kenz and show her the conversation.

"You should let him drive you. You know it would be easier." Kenz drops to the edge of my bed.

A fire starts in my belly. "Sure, easier. Giving in to their every demand would certainly be *easier*, but I don't want to have sex with four bulked-up-on-'roids football players." I throw my hands up in the air. "It's not even a choice. I won't lie down and take it because they tell me to. Nine months. I have nine months left to get through this school year and get as far away from these guys as possible."

"H, it's nine months. Do you know how much shit they can throw at you in nine months?"

I don't really want to think about that. I'm just trying to survive this week. Next week I'll survive that one.

"Mom wants me to find a boyfriend." I roll my head toward Kenz. "Not that they qualify, but what do you think she'll say about having four?"

"You could do worse. Parker Ford said Jack and Caden were amazing." Kenz purses her lips. "A few girls say Eli's a little rough, but in a good way. And Luke...well, he has the equipment and the talent to use it apparently. You could definitely do worse for your first sexual experience."

DEATH (LUKE):

Tell your mother we'll get you to school and
home on time

I bite down on my lip.

ME:

You shouldn't miss practice

DEATH (LUKE):

That's for us to worry about, not you

I haven't forgotten about your punishment

"Ugh, this guy and his punishments." I turn to Kenz. "Because I asked for a choice, I'm being punished."

"You said the first punishment wasn't all bad." Kenz smiles suggestively.

I flush with heat, remembering that feeling under the pain. The moans he forced from me with every hit and subsequent rub. But it wasn't private, and I didn't dare meet anyone else's eyes, knowing they saw him do that to me.

"It was humiliating being spanked like a naughty child in front of a room filled with high schoolers. Oh, and it isn't like asking for a boyfriend in the same room the next day wasn't already embarrassing enough." I flop down on my bed and cover my eyes. "I thought maybe someone would have the balls to want to at least pretend to fuck me this year."

"I'm sure any of the guys, and probably a handful of the girls, would have taken you up on that offer, but not if it meant going against the horsemen." Kenz lies down next to me. "I mean, if you just want to be devirginized, you could use a dildo or vibrator."

"It would be an option." Not sure if I could actually go through with it though. I scrunch up my nose as I look at her. "Seems a little impersonal."

Kenz rolls to her stomach, pats my head, and gives me a wink. "Not if you do it right."

"If I'm being punished for trying to get a sanctioned dude to do it, what do you think they'd do to me if I took away their little prize?" I shake my head and stretch my arms over my head. "Besides, they want me to *give* them my virginity."

"Trust me, everyone has heard about the cafeteria today." She sits up. "If you keep going in there, they'll have to add it to the daily announcements. Yesterday in the cafeteria, Harper Davidson and the horsemen—"

Grabbing my pillow, I hit her with it. I hate being talked about. I hate being the center of attention. I don't want any of this.

"I can't wait to see you at school tomorrow." Kenz stands and heads to the door. "Those boys are going to flip out, and the guys who didn't step forward are going to shit a brick wishing they'd stepped up."

I smile, thinking of those reactions. "See you then."

"Peace." Kenz leaves my room and her footfalls on the stairs fill the quiet. Downstairs, my mom tells her goodbye as Kenz leaves.

I sigh and roll to my side. I haven't replied to Luke yet. Maybe Kenz is right. Maybe I should just take care of the problem. I shove the empty bags onto the floor and lift my phone over my face.

What would they do if I took away the prize? That old joke of *if I can't have your virginity, can I have the box it came in* comes to mind. I don't think it's really my hymen they're after. If so, they wouldn't want me for a whole year. My virginity is just part of the package deal.

I drop my phone on the bed and close my bedroom door before heading into my bathroom. After I shower, I stare at my reflection in the mist-covered mirror. This is something I can handle. It's not great, but I just have to get through each week. I'm almost halfway through this week.

Wrapping my towel tighter around me, I head into my bedroom and cover my mouth to stop my scream. Luke Foster lies reclined on my bed, with his ankles crossed and his hands behind his head like he has every right to be there.

"Don't mind me. I just wanted to enjoy the live version of the show."

His gaze trails to my laptop. On it are webcams focused on the other horsemen. Each in their bedroom. Caden sits on an enormous bed. Jack is in his desk chair. Eli must have his laptop on his lap in bed.

"You can't be in here," I whisper indignantly. I edge back toward the bathroom to put a door between me and Luke. I'm way more naked than in the bathroom stall yesterday, and I know Luke doesn't believe in boundaries. "My mom is downstairs."

I glance at my phone on the bed. I can't make a dive for it without him grabbing me. Maybe if I lock myself in the bathroom, he'll go away. Maybe not, but at least I have dirty clothes in there I could put on.

"Yes, your mom is downstairs, sleeping with a very loud show on, littered with death and mayhem. I'm sure one more scream won't make any difference." Right, screaming would probably turn Luke on anyway.

I slide my foot back an inch. "You're going to get me in even more trouble. I won't be able to leave the house for at least a month."

Luke rubs his jaw and creeps forward slightly on the bed. My heartbeat ratchets up like he's toying with me while he hunts me.

"Yes, you're grounded, which is why we've come to you."

I glance at the laptop screen again. I'm not sure if they can see me from this angle. My hair dangles in wet strands around my bare shoulders. Droplets roll down my skin to the towel, and the only thing between me and this asshole is the wet towel clinging to my body.

"I thought about punishing you in front of everyone again." Luke moves off the bed like he has all night. I don't know if I'll make it to the bathroom before he pounces.

I edge back again. The cold tile touches my heel. Almost there.

"But then I thought why share when what we really want is to see you crawl just for us." Luke moves so quickly I don't even realize his intention until he grabs my arm and drags me in front of my laptop. I clutch at my towel.

He tightens his arm around my waist and holds my back flush against him. The thin towel does nothing to hide the feel of him, the overwhelming heat of him against me. I'm just glad the towel didn't slip off in the humiliatingly brief struggle. I suck in a breath at his hard body pressing into my softness. My whole body buzzes with the realization that I'm practically naked and he's here alone with me.

He's too strong for me to fight off. He could do anything he wants to me. Fear collides with a trickle of curiosity. The curiosity shocks me so much I don't struggle in Luke's arms.

"Now, now, be a good little pet and look at your owners." He wraps his hand around my throat and tips my chin up, keeping his hand curled around my neck but not squeezing. "What do you guys think?"

His fingers burn into my skin, flowing heat down to the heart of me.

My skin burns like I've been lit on fire, but I can't separate the embarrassment from the desire.

"Lose the towel," Caden's voice rings out.

"What?" My voice is high-pitched. Panic shuts down the building desire. Them in my private space is enough of an invasion. I'm nearly naked as it is. This is all getting completely out of hand.

"No." I grab for my towel where it's knotted. My breath comes out faster, but I can't focus enough to think. I don't know how to get out of this situation any more than the others I've found myself in with these guys.

The guys all calmly watch me. Luke is a solid wall of force behind me.

If I scream, would my mom even hear me? If she does, what would happen? What would happen if she doesn't hear me?

Luke tsks in my ear. "You heard your owner."

The back of his other hand trails down my arm, sending off sparks in the flames already engulfing me.

"Please don't," I whisper, feeling as if my insides are caving into each other. It's one thing to have him spank my panty-covered ass. It's another to be naked in front of all of them. To bare myself in front of Luke. How do I trust he won't do anything I don't want him to do? How can I stand up against these guys? Maybe I can appeal to the kernel of goodness they must have inside.

He puts his arm tightly around my waist.

"Please, Luke." I meet his eyes in the video that shows me held by him. Cold, that's all I get from Luke. How can you negotiate with a psychopath? Shivers pass through me. This won't be like this morning or the spanking. I'm naked under this towel. No panties to hide behind. No bra to cover me. They will see every flawed inch of me.

"Kitten." Eli's voice is soft and soothing. I know it's a lie, but I can't help but turn to him for comfort and possibly help. My gaze swings to his video. "Luke isn't going to touch you. This is your punishment. You don't own your body anymore. It's ours."

I want to rail at them that it is my body. That they don't own me. That I choose what happens to me. No one else. Not the horsemen and not Luke Foster. But I can't provoke them more.

At least we aren't at school in front of everyone.

I take a deep breath and feel Luke's t-shirt dampened beneath my hair. It's only day two and they've already taken more than I want to give. I have to keep fighting. But again, choose my battles so I don't get punished more.

These battles are only the initial shots across my bow. I can take a few hits as long as I can escape the things that will cause the most damage.

Right now, they want to see my body. They won't touch it. They aren't even in the same room, except for Luke. I can't trust Luke, but maybe with the others watching, they can hold him in check.

I clear my throat and erase the emotion from my face.

"What am I being punished for?" I ask in a semi-steady voice.

Jack leans forward on his desk. "You tried to give away what's ours."

"You agreed—"

"It doesn't mean we liked it, sweetheart." Jack leans back in his chair. "You can fight us and get punished, or we can move this along. Get past the uncomfortable stuff."

"Easy for you to say. You're fully clothed." I sneer at the guys.

Jack stands. "Do you want me to get naked too? Would that make it easier for you?"

Caden scoffs. "I don't need to see your dick tonight," he complains.

I don't say anything, but Jack takes his shirt off and moves the desk chair out of the way. He's built lean, with muscles for days. A six-pack and an Adonis belt flowing into his low-slung jeans. A teenage girl's wet dream brought to life.

No wonder girls are stupid about him.

Luke's fingers tighten slightly on my neck as he drops his voice. "See, Jack is willing to play along. He's right, you know." He trails a finger along my jaw, sending pleasant sparks in the wake of my uneasiness. "This would be easier if you take your punishment. Follow what we want you to do."

I squeeze my eyes shut. I can't just do what they want. I'm already vulnerable to them. Is this something I can't stand to lose? Or is it like taking a shower in gym class with all the girls around? Sure, the girls probably won't be looking at me like free porn, but it's not much different. The girls notice things and the guys will definitely notice things.

Luke tightens his fingers a little more. I gasp and open my eyes.

"Look." His soft voice lures me.

Jack undoes his jeans and takes both his boxers and jeans down in one swoop. His dick is large and erect. I gulp.

"Like what you see?" Luke continues to whisper softly. "Can you see how much he wants you?"

I raise my eyes to Jack's. His blue eyes have darkened as they look at me. They grab at my insides and spin them like the tumbling of a dryer. It would be so much easier to resist if I wasn't attracted to them.

"Your turn, sweetheart." Jack winks.

The games these boys play are way beyond me, but I'll catch up. I have to. Maybe this will even give me a little power.

Luke releases my waist but keeps my head up with his hand on my neck. I know I'm supposed to look at the guys, but I can't. Looking at the wall over the camera, I untuck the towel and let it drop.

I hear a sharp intake of breath, but I don't dare look to see who did it. They might not like what they see. They might regret entering into a deal with me for the entire year. I have a decent body, but I'm not built like some girls I know they use repeatedly. I can feel the heat rushing up my chest to my neck.

"Look at us." Luke's voice in my ear makes my gaze flick down to all the horsemen. "You are wanted, unicorn."

Caden's blasé look is gone as he takes in my form, wanting. Eli steeples his fingers to his lips, captivated. Jack strokes his cock while his heated eyes stare at me with desire.

When I find Luke's eyes reflected in the camera, I instinctively back away, directly into him. His eyes aren't as cold as usual. His erection against my ass leaves little doubt of what he feels for me. Whether it's the control over me or my body or both, he wants me.

I should be terrified in this moment. I'm naked and vulnerable to this man in my bedroom, but I feel power surge through me as I meet each of their hungry gazes. The horsemen want *me*.

Scrap that. They don't know *me* to want *me*. They want my body.

I can feel their fervent gazes like caresses over my flesh. Even the cool air from the room on my still-damp skin can't diminish the heat that flows through me. My breath catches in my throat. Luke's hand wraps around my hip. His fingers burn into my naked flesh, and I want to sink into his warmth.

"Good girl," he breathes against my ear, and I feel a pulse between my legs in response. "You smell beautiful when you're aroused, Harper."

Heat claims my cheeks, but right now, I don't care. They want me and they'll have me if they keep this up. Because as much as I hate them, I want them too.

The Participation

CADEN

Jack has the right idea. He's jerking off. At least he's easing the pressure.

I look at our girl and really take her in.

Her brown hair is damp against Luke's chest. As she looks at all of us, her brown eyes widen. Her lips part slightly. Her face is scrubbed clean of any makeup and her cheeks are flushed from the heat of her shower and probably her embarrassment. Those lips of hers, dark rose lips, match her nipples.

Her body though...fuck me. I adjust my hard-on.

Her breasts are even better outside of the bra. Not small but not too big. Perky with hard nipples pointing straight at me. Begging me to taste them. I can't properly see her pussy, but there's no hair visible. Just slick, smooth skin. Her slender waist flares out in hips that will give me a good grip while I pound into her.

And I want to. Shit, I should just whip it out and give this girl a proper salute.

For years, while drinking and playing video games, we've talked about sharing a girl. Fucking her together. But I never put much stock in it. We aren't exactly picky, but each of us seems to like different types of girls.

The couple of times Jack and I tag-teamed a girl were great, but even then we overwhelmed the poor girl. Most don't ask for it again. The thought of all four of us probably terrifies our little untouched virgin.

I'm envious of Luke's fingers digging into her hip and clutching her neck.

"Turn her around." I lean forward to watch as Luke whispers in her ear.

I want to smell her arousal. I want to touch her soft skin. Watch those lips parted around my cock while I fist that long hair and fuck her mouth. Fuck, I'm going to cream my shorts if I don't stop thinking about the things I want to do to her.

She turns around to face Luke. Her eyes dart up to his, but who cares about that? Her ass is perfect. Luke said it has a nice bounce.

I want to look at every part of her. I want her to bend over so I can look at that untouched pussy, but I'm not sure Luke will allow it. Fucker likes to take control any way he can get it. So until I can get our girl alone, I gotta play by his rules.

Meanwhile, it looks like Jack is getting close.

"Untouched," I call out, "look at Jack."

She glances over her shoulder. Her eyes darken as she watches Jack stroke his cock. She wets her lips and turns around, almost mesmerized by what she's seeing. It's different from porn to watch someone get off when you know you're the reason.

I see that power in her eyes and I know if Luke touched her pussy, it would be soaking. Girl might be a virgin, but she wants it. We're just the guys to show her how to take it.

Consider it a public service.

By the end of the year, this chick will be so wired for sex nobody will compare to us for her. But when we set her free into the world, men will fall at our feet and thank us for helping our little nympho evolve.

Jack throws his head back as he comes. She can't seem to take her eyes off him. That's some fucking power right there. If she doesn't feel it, she's not worth our time.

"Sweetie." A muffled woman's voice comes over the webcam. "I just wanted to say good night."

"Don't come in. Just finished a shower. Getting dressed." Harper looks over her shoulder at Luke. "Good night."

"I've got work in the morning. You'll take your car, right? Stay safe." Her mom's voice sounds concerned with an edge to it. Maybe she is the type to ground her daughter.

"Of course." Harper dips down and grabs her towel. She watches Luke warily as she tucks it around her. "I love you, Mom."

"I love you too, sweetie."

No one talks for a couple of minutes. Harper could have ratted us out. It wouldn't have worked out well for her, but she could have gotten rid of us for the night. But she didn't.

Jack tugs back on his pair of boxers.

"She's in her room now." Harper tucks her hair behind her ear and doesn't lift her gaze to any of us. Over time, she'll lose that shyness.

Luke steps into her and tilts her chin up. "Leave the webcam on overnight. I'll be by to pick you up in the morning."

Harper searches Luke's eyes, and I'm not sure what she's hoping to find in that cold bastard's gaze. Anything good in him, his father destroyed. Much like my own did.

"Are you going to turn on your webcam too?" she asks.

He smiles, and I feel like I'm seeing something I shouldn't. Something intimate just between them. It's a weird sensation since I don't usually have any boundaries.

"You want to watch us sleep too?" His thumb traces her lower lip.

"Yes."

HARPER

I put on panties, a sleep tank, and shorts, aware of the camera the whole time. It's not like they can see more. They've already seen it all. I sit cross-legged on my bed as the guys move around their rooms, getting ready for bed. I want to study them and understand them better.

Eli moves his laptop onto the nightstand and picks up a book. I can't tell what it is though. He's stripped down to his boxers to sleep.

Jack gives me a wink and a smirk as he climbs into his bed. I feel warmth in my cheeks, remembering him getting off to me. The pulse and wetness between my legs was strong as he finished. I don't know what would have happened if Mom hadn't stopped at my door.

Caden watches me. Something feral and possessive in his eyes tugs at me. My insides burst with warmth. His growl from lunch moves through me again and my breath catches.

Luke kept his word and didn't touch me while I was naked. Well, not really in a sexual way. His presence alone made me uncomfortable, but I liked feeling his warmth. It would have felt more clinical if he hadn't been in my room with me. If I'd been alone with four guys watching me remotely.

A new feed logs in, and I see Luke. I can still feel his hand at my throat. He hadn't applied much pressure, just enough to hint at what he could do. It lit a small burst of fear beneath my skin, but also intrigue. I resist the urge to reach up and feel where his fingers were.

He walks around his room. Strips off his clothes and drops them in a hamper. His blond hair falls over his eyes as he looks down and puts his hands on his boxer waistband.

Curious, I lean forward. Will he show me his now that I've shown him mine? His eyes flash up to mine with amusement in them before he strides over to his bed. Boxer briefs firmly in place. Not that they hide much.

I lie down facing the screen. It's weird to watch these guys in their private moments, knowing they can turn and see me whenever they want to. I turn the sound down so if Mom comes by she won't hear guys in my room.

Being naked in front of them turned me on more than I thought possible. I've had fleeting moments of reading where something turned me on, but nothing grabbed at me quite like this. Nothing like the need to be touched while watching Jack get off. Or the whisper of Luke's clothes brushing my naked flesh. Or Caden's commanding voice. Or Eli's unwavering gaze.

Maybe I want all four guys. Not separately, but together. What does that make me?

I close my eyes just as my phone vibrates. It's the group chat. I pull the phone into the bed with me.

WAR (CADEN):

Way to nut for the camera Jack

FAMINE (JACK):

Jealous because you couldn't get off too?
You should have just stripped

PESTILENCE (ELI):

I'm sure Jack was enough for our kitten to
watch for one night

ME:

I didn't mind

I press send and hide down in the covers, peeking out to see if that got a reaction from the guys. Jack grins at the camera. Eli shakes his head, but there is a smile tugging at his lips. Caden shakes his head like I don't know what I'm saying.

WAR (CADEN):

Just so you know, little nympho, Jack is the
small one

eggplant emoji *winky face emoji*

DEATH (LUKE):

It's time to sleep

FAMINE (JACK):

Buzzkill

WAR (CADEN):

I'd sleep better with Harper in my bed

FAMINE (JACK):

If that's an option, I want in

PESTILENCE (ELI):

You two wouldn't be able to keep it in your
pants

But I would *winky face emoji*

DEATH (LUKE):

Harper can decide when that happens

Go to sleep

I glance over at Luke and his eyes lock on mine. He's giving me a choice. What will that cost me? My previous choice meant I stripped naked for them. Is this still part of the punishment?

Ugh.

ME:

Can someone give me a list of what will get me punished?

DEATH (LUKE):

Want more?

ME:

Can't avoid what I don't know

DEATH (LUKE):

You have a single command: We own you

That doesn't clear anything up. But I guess if I don't do anything to piss them off, I'll breeze through this. I set my phone back on its charger and turn off my lamp.

I watch as their screens all darken, except Eli's. He's still reading. If I knew my enemy better, I could figure out how to get out of this. Unfortunately, the information I do have is so I can hide from them. I doubt watching them sleep will give me much information, but maybe with time, they'll forget about the cameras being on and let something slip.

Movement catches my eye, and I look at Caden's screen. He's covered by his sheet, but the rhythmic movement beneath the sheet is hard to miss. I can make out his profile. His lips are slightly parted as he strokes himself, slow and steady. That pulsing starts between my legs again.

I slip my hand down between my thighs and press against the throbbing. My phone vibrates. A direct message comes in.

PESTILENCE (ELI):

Don't touch what's ours, kitten

My gaze flicks to Eli, who still has his lamp on. His dark eyes are on me.

PESTILENCE (ELI):

If you need relief, you have four willing men available and willing to service your needs

If you touch what's ours, you will be punished

ME:

So I'm not supposed to touch myself?

PESTILENCE (ELI):

No, kitten. Not your pert breasts. Not your wet pussy. Those are ours now

You've lost that right

Keep yourself clean and your pussy bare

Take care of what's ours or you'll be punished

I lift my eyes back to Eli and set my phone down. I show him both my hands belligerently. Take care of what's theirs? Puh-leeze. His dark eyes narrow, but he turns his light out.

I find Caden again. His pace is quicker. His gaze flashes to mine. I want to listen. I want to hear what he sounds like when he comes, but it's too much of a risk. Mom doesn't sleep well. Sometimes, she stops by my room when she goes to the kitchen.

If she heard a guy grunting in my room, she'd investigate. I could claim I'm watching porn, but I'd rather not have that discussion. Not tonight. Probably not ever.

Instead, I study Caden's face. The tip of his chin. His hand works beneath the sheet faster. He tenses. His fist stops. His shoulders ease down and he turns to give me a wicked smile.

I know he can see me. Even with the lights out, the soft glow of the computer screen reveals me. He gives me a kissy face before he rolls out of his bed, flashing me with his bare, toned ass, and walks across the room out of sight.

After a few minutes, he climbs back in bed and rolls onto his side, facing away from me. I blow out a breath. All the guys are trying to sleep except Luke.

His lights are off, but he's watching me. I should fear this man who can sneak into my house without anyone being the wiser. Of all of them, I know he holds the most sway and decides what they will do with me and when.

He owns me.

But as I return his stare, his eyes soften. He mouths *go to sleep*. I can feel the heavy tug on my eyelids. Like even they feel the need to obey him. As they slip down, I open them to see him still there. Still watching.

Instead of being creeped out, I feel safe and protected. I know he'll watch over me and nothing will happen to me while I belong to him. It's a small comfort, but enough to make me fall asleep.

CHAPTER 12

The Tactical Gear

HARPER

Our school doesn't have quite as rigid of a dress code policy as some schools. My new outfits would be a no-go at most places. I slip on a black hanky halter that leaves my midriff bare. My jeans come up to below my belly button and flare out at the legs. I slip on my red Converse high tops and pull my hair into two top knots on either side of my head, leaving two tendrils to curl on either side of my face. Long, dangly earrings flash in my ears.

It would have been dangerous to wear anything like this last year, but I already have the beasts' attention. I might as well live it up. I swipe on some bright red matte lip stain and add some eyeliner to my eyes with a touch of mascara.

I glance at my closed laptop. I don't want to give them a sneak peek. It was odd to wake up and roll over to see the guys sleeping. For a minute, I watched them. They didn't seem quite as fierce asleep, but I knew it was just an illusion as I closed the laptop.

Taking a quick selfie, I send it to Kenz, who sends me back the fire emoji.

The horsemen have all seen me naked. My cheeks flame at the memory. I'm definitely not showing as much as I showed them last night. My new clothes shouldn't matter to them. Yesterday, they changed me from concealing into something more revealing. So they should be thrilled with my new style.

I'm done hiding. I'm not changing. That's for damn sure.

I grab my backpack and head downstairs. This time I pack two sandwiches just in case Caden gets grabby again. After all, I do like to eat. I hear a light rap at the back door and sigh.

For a second, I hoped he would let me drive myself. I stare at the door like it could hold him back and straighten my shoulders. Time to face the day.

Slinging my backpack on, I walk to the door. When I open it, Luke stands there absolutely perfect in a black t-shirt that hugs his body, showing off his ripped arms, and jeans that should be illegal with how they form themselves to his body. Fuck, he's hot.

After a thorough appraisal, I lift my gaze to meet the ice king's melted blue eyes. His lips press together, and I wonder if he wants to tell me to change. He takes me in from my toes all the way up to my lips and stops there.

I press my thighs together against the feeling shimmering inside of me.

"Ready?" I ask, my voice a little breathless, and lift my eyebrow at him.

His eyes narrow on my hair. I don't think he likes it. Nothing to grab onto. But tough, it's cute and he can't pull me around by it. That's a win-win in my book.

He backs away and gestures for me to precede him.

Inhaling, I stiffen my resolve and walk past him toward his car. He's letting me wear what I want. I can ride to school in his car and let him figure out how to get me home. Mom wants me to drive, but she also said to be more social. What's more social than riding to school with the most popular guys in school?

I settle into the front seat and put my backpack at my feet.

As soon as he sits next to me and closes the door, he wraps a hand around the back of my neck and holds me still. Instinctively, I try to get away for a moment, but then I relax in his hold, inhale, and hold my breath.

I'm not sure what I've already done to offend him, but he hasn't hurt me so far. He raises his other hand and rubs a thumb against my lower lip, something he seems obsessed with doing. I exhale a shaky breath against it.

He lifts his gaze to mine. When he removes his thumb, he glances at it. "Good."

He releases me, and I fall back against the seat. What the fuck was that about?

"Don't wear lipstick that smears." It's an order.

"I don't plan to." The sharp words slip out before I can stop them. So much for trying to be docile. Maybe dressing like a hellcat turns me into one.

Luke grins, but it's not a happy-type grin. He definitely likes my defiance. Probably because it will afford him more punishments. He turns on the car. In the short drive to school, he listens to some EDM, which seems way too perky this early in the morning, but I'm not about to reach over and play with his radio.

He parks near the other guys' cars and gets out. I follow because that's what a good pet does. I'm hoping to get through at least one day where I don't get punished. Since punishments usually include pushing a boundary.

I follow behind Luke as we make our way to where the other guys hang by the entrance. A group of girls turns and sees us coming. Throwing a few evil looks my way, they wander off. I just smile at them like all is right in the world.

Any of them would probably love to service all four horsemen. Idiots.

Luke stops and I almost run into his back. I freeze before making contact.

"Are you going to hide behind Luke all day, kitten?" Eli's voice is soft and easy, like always, but with that hint of command behind it that draws a shiver down my back.

I take a deep breath and step around Luke.

"Fuck me," Caden says. He greedily takes in my body.

"Sweet," Jack adds with a huge grin.

Eli comes over to me and flicks my dangling earrings. "Did you find her like this or dress her like this?"

Luke's cough almost sounds like a laugh. I whip my head to look at him, but he's just as straight-faced as ever. "Found her."

"Where have you been hiding, kitten?" Eli grabs my hips, and I prepare for the bite of pain that never comes. His thumbs brush the bare skin above my jeans and the shivers multiply.

"How the hell did you hide, little nympho?" Caden closes in behind me. Really? Little nympho? I'm not sure it's better than *untouched*.

"I don't like her hair," Luke points out helpfully.

I'm tempted to hiss at him, but I don't. Caden and Eli pressing in on me has me on high alert. An awareness of them washes over me.

Caden reaches up, grabs one of my curled tendrils, and tugs it gently. "You can't grab it to hold onto, but it gets it out of the way for other things."

He trails a finger down the nape of my neck, and I noticeably tremble beneath his touch. Eli smiles wickedly down at me. Somehow, being pressed between two guys is starting to feel normal to me. I don't hate the feeling.

"I like her hair. She looks like Sporty Spice." Jack comes up beside me and tugs me from between the other guys to drag me into his arms. Eli's fingers brush across my stomach, leaving sparks in their wake. Jack pulls me in tight against his solid chest. "Which happens to be my favorite Spice Girl."

"Why do you even have a favorite Spice Girl? They've got to be like fifty years old now." Caden's tone is dismissive.

"More Posh Spice to me." Eli leans against the brick wall along the sidewalk to the entrance. He gives me a wink that makes my insides flutter.

"At least bring it into this decade. I believe Miley Cyrus has done a similar hairstyle," Luke says.

Everyone turns to look at him. Jack releases me from his embrace and holds me at arm's length to look me over. He shrugs and winks at me. "I'm okay with both."

"Stop manhandling Harper." Luke flicks his gaze over me. "At least she upgraded from what she tried to wear yesterday."

"Shouldn't we go inside?" I ask finally. Not that I don't appreciate being part of the delinquent gang hanging outside until the last possible minute. I'm just used to being in class as soon as possible.

The parking lot and hallways are practically filled with potential landmines. Of course, the biggest landmines now own me, but I also want to stay on their good side and not end up punished. The less interaction, the better.

"Eager to show off, kitten?" Eli rakes his gaze over me again.

Unfortunately, that captures Luke's attention. He grabs my chin and tips my face up toward him. "Who are you showing off for?"

I try so hard not to roll my eyes, but these guys are so frustrating. "Other girls. I've spent the past three years living in a fashion debt to stay away from your attention. Now I can dress however I like because I already have your attention."

They all give me various looks.

"If you're into girls, tell us now," Caden says.

I laugh. Bet they didn't think of that before now. They all look a touch worried. I could play it off and maybe that would get them to back off, but somehow lying feels like cheating. At least, lying about that.

"Oh, for fuck's sake. I'm not into girls. How could you know nothing of girl world? There's a hierarchy. From the top to the lowest. And in girl world, looks matter a lot. Not just if you have the right face, but if you take care of yourself and look good for you."

"I like your assets." Jack smiles and starts forward with his hands outstretched.

I back away until I run into Luke. He glances down at me like I'm an irritating fly, but he doesn't move away. Well, I'm not going to act like he's on fire and I need to get away as quickly as possible. Even if that's the way he makes me feel.

His eyebrow rises when I don't move, so I mimic him.

"Come on, hot stuff. Stop flirting with Death." Caden wraps his hand around my hip and drags me toward the building. "I'll walk you to your locker."

"I don't use my locker." I turn to watch the other horsemen fall in behind us.

"Nonsense. Everyone uses their locker." Caden turns down the hall where the seniors' lockers are. "Which one?"

"I honestly don't remember." I glance along the rows of similar lockers. "All I remember from freshman year is it was way too close to all your lockers, so I figured it was a lost cause." I shrug. "I just keep everything on me."

Caden stops and pushes me back against the lockers. His green eyes bear down on me. "You don't use your locker because of us? That's ridiculous."

I roll my eyes.

"Let's see, since you 'noticed' me, I've been publicly spanked and publicly humiliated asking for a boyfriend to save me, so yeah, I wonder why I haven't used my locker in three years." I press my finger against my lips like I'm thinking it over.

Caden laughs. It's a sharp but free sound that startles me into a grin. "Come on. You can use my locker if you need to. Just don't keep girly shit like tampons in there."

He grabs my hand and tugs me along after him. Frankly I'm in shock. He laughed and offered to share his locker with me. Do I even know these guys at all?

In the history of things the horsemen do, being nice isn't exactly on top of the list. If it even makes the list. I honestly don't know what to do with this information. Of course, they haven't all four publicly claimed a girl before either. Or really dated any one girl that I know of.

Caden tells me his combination and takes half my books out of my backpack to put in his locker for after lunch. I'm so stunned by his actions that I can't do anything but stand there.

Luke comes over and takes me off Caden's hands.

Caden winks and says, "See you next period."

My backpack is significantly lighter. Luke holds my hand and leads me to our class.

When I settle into my desk, I realize this morning they've all touched me in some way or another and I didn't flinch once. I let them pull me around and trade me between one another after only two days of being in their presence.

I'm fucked.

"Looking good, Davidson," some guy, who apparently has a death wish, calls out from across the class. Where was this guy yesterday when I needed a fucking hero?

"Shut it, Brewster." Luke almost growls the words.

I don't know what to do so I just keep my gaze toward the front.

"Make a note." Luke's warm breath brushes the small strands of hair on the nape of my neck, sending sparks across my skin. "Tomorrow, wear your hair like you did Monday."

I don't turn to face him, but ask, "So you can pull me around?"

His fingers tease the back of my neck, and a shudder rushes through me. "Either that or I'm sure Eli would love to get his kitten a collar."

I exhale as he moves back. I feel branded by his words and his touch. Luke's idea of not touching me is to touch me. He wants something on me he can grab so he can direct me where he wants me. He doesn't want a woman, he wants a dog, but I don't dare tell him that.

The feminist inside me bristles, but I keep my cool.

Not today.

Today will be punishment free. I'm confident.

HARPER'S PHONE

KENZ:

Girl!

ME:

Thanks for helping me shop

KENZ:

Should have done this years ago

ME:

I don't think younger me could handle this kind of attention

KENZ:

You would have had attention from guys
who aren't the horsemen

ME:

Maybe

KENZ:

Trust me

Someone would have snatched you up

CHAPTER 13

The First Strike

HARPER

When Eli told me lunch would be on the bleachers at the football field, I was ecstatic. No cafeteria means no humiliation, right? I almost skip my way to the field until I realize the horsemen and I are the only ones out here.

Sure, there are students closer to the doors, and a teacher wanders around the building now and then, but the bleachers aren't really an authorized part of the lunch area.

"Come sit with me, kitten." Eli pats the spot next to him. Again, his eyes seem warm and caring, but fuck, I don't trust it. I almost trust the coldness in Luke's eyes more than that warmth in Eli's. But I do what is asked of me because no punishment is my motto for the day.

I dig my lunch out of my backpack and hand a sandwich to Caden. He smiles like I just handed him a Super Bowl ring. As he grabs it, Eli holds out an apple for me.

I'm still leery of the fruit, but I take it and set it next to my lunch box. While I eat my other sandwich, the guys talk about football and the away game on Friday night. I don't have a lot to contribute to the conversation. It's the first game of the season.

Supposedly I'm grounded and won't be able to go. Not that I would normally go to an away game anyway.

"Tell your mom you're dating one of us." Jack sits down on the bleacher above me. "Then she'll have to let you come."

"Only one of you?" I raise my eyebrow and Jack smirks. "How would I ever choose?"

"I could be your boyfriend. Take you to fancy dinners and dances." Jack leans over and snatches one of my chips. "Moms love me."

"Moms won't let their daughters out past eight with you. But me" —Eli leans in close to me—"Moms adore me. Who doesn't want their daughter to date the wide receiver?"

"Please, they want their daughters to catch the quarterback." Luke leans his elbows back on the bleacher behind him and gives me a look that could only be called a smolder. "Moms know the quarterback is always the winner."

I laugh and turn to Caden. "What about you?"

Caden shrugs, no expression on his face. "Parents hate me. If you want to stay grounded for the rest of your life, you could say I'm your boyfriend. But since I want you to be free to play, don't."

Fuck, who got in this guy's head and messed it up? I feel the ridiculous urge to hug him, which is stupid on so many levels. But instinctually, he's one of mine for the year—until I can figure a way out of this arrangement. I don't like seeing him so down on himself.

"I bet my mom would love you best, Caden."

He narrows his eyes like I'm poking fun.

"My mom hates a kiss ass. She'd rather a guy be upfront with her and not try to do naughty things to her daughter behind her back while being a nice guy to her face." I finish my apple and put away the rest of my stuff before realizing there's still silence.

I lift my eyes, and Caden is smiling at me.

"Speaking of naughty things..." Caden starts.

I tense, waiting for the guillotine to fall. Fuck, what did I do this time? I finally look at the other guys. They watch me with anticipation, but I can't tell if it's because I'm about to be punished again or something else I might not like.

"What did I do now?" I ask in resignation because seriously, it's been a good day so far.

"We figure we need to start off slow with you." Luke brushes his hands off and walks down the bleachers until he's on the field. "So we're going old school for your first lesson."

Jack holds up his half-full soda bottle from lunch and joins Luke like they planned this whole thing out. "What better way to get your first kiss than with a game of spin the bottle?"

Caden starts down as Eli stands and offers me his hand. I stare at it for a second. Of all my firsts, giving this one to the horsemen isn't a hardship. It would actually be a relief to not still be waiting for my first kiss. If this had been a normal school, I would have attended a party in middle school where I would have played spin the bottle. And my first kiss would have been a peck from some random guy who I might have liked.

Now my first kiss will be with one of these guys, and I don't think they're the kind to just give me a simple peck. None of my firsts will be simple with them. If I give them everything they want, that is.

Sighing, I slip my hand into Eli's, and he helps me down to the field.

Eli pulls me down next to him as we all settle into a circle.

"I've never played this before." My palms are actually a little clammy and I rub them against my jeans. Out of these guys, I don't think I could choose who I want to kiss first. Part of me is excited to kiss all of them. Heat builds in my chest.

Luke talks as Jack puts the bottle in the center. "Obviously when we were younger, the ratios were a little more mixed. For our purposes, you spin the bottle and you kiss whoever it lands on. After that, instead of spinning the bottle, you'll just go around the circle and kiss all of us."

My eyes feel like they want to pop out of my head. "You're going to pass me around instead of the bottle?"

Eli laughs softly. "In a manner of speaking. We all want to be your first, which is why fate gets to decide this time. We all want to taste you."

A spark lights low in my belly and bursts into flames. Not kiss me. Taste me. I don't think this is going to be a tame peck on the lips.

"Are there any other rules?" I try to swallow down my nervousness. That buzzing feeling isn't all nerves though. Anticipation is running right alongside.

"Kisses are timed and hand placement is limited this time."

Fuck. My brain sputters to a halt. I hadn't thought of touching. "Hand placement?"

"Just spin the bottle, sweetheart." Jack nudges it in my direction. It's on a small wooden box instead of the grass. These guys think of everything. "We'll show you what to do. Trust us."

I look at the eager guys, ready to show me how to kiss. Normally, I wouldn't trust these guys at all, but when my eyes lock with Luke's, I know he's done this for me. That he's controlled all the variables to make me feel comfortable.

"Nothing more than kissing?" I raise my eyebrow.

The corner of Luke's lips tip up. "Maybe a little grinding but nothing more."

Grinding? That wild, horny bitch is ready to play with the big boys. Me, I'm not so sure. But I know Luke will pull back anyone who tries to take it too far. In a way, I'm trusting *him* with this. With my first kiss.

I'm trusting Luke Foster. Death himself.

The world must be ending.

Exhaling, I crawl closer to the bottle, close my eyes, and spin it as hard as I can. When I open my eyes, it's slowing its spin. I lift my gaze to see the guys all watching the bottle slowly wobbling between them.

It hits me that I'm about to kiss all of them. My insides heat up. This bottle just determines who goes first and who goes last. Each of their lips will press on mine and taste me.

I bite my lip, looking back at the bottle as it slowly stops. On Caden.

My heart pounds as I lift my gaze to his. He smirks.

"Come here, little nympho."

I swallow and look at the other guys. What if I do it wrong? What if my breath stinks? What if their breath stinks? Why didn't I think to have a mint? What if something is stuck in my teeth?

Caden's gaze softens when I take his hand. He's sitting on the ground, and I move on my knees to him.

"Straddle him," Luke says.

I don't look at Luke, but I almost do for confirmation. Fuck, these guys are getting in my head. Caden grabs my hips and pulls me onto his lap. I gasp as my center presses against his very large, very hard erection. At least I'm not the only one turned on by the idea of this.

"Put your hands on my shoulders." Caden's voice deepens a little and his tone is almost soft. I do as he says. He's solid muscle beneath my hands. He grips my ass and pulls me in tight against him. Heat builds in between my legs at the feel of him there. I remember last night, how he and Jack both got off on seeing me naked.

"Stop biting your lip, kitten." Eli's voice is close. They're all so close. This is so weird. Maybe too weird. I should just run away now and take the punishment.

I release my lip and meet Caden's eyes. They're so green. I can see flecks of gold in them. His eyes have always been intriguing, but this close, I could spend an hour just studying them. I take a breath, focusing just on him and not the others watching us.

"Just relax," Caden says as he leans forward a little, bringing his lips almost to mine. I inhale sharply at him being so close. His cinnamon scent surrounds me. "Relax."

His lips press against mine. My whole body lights up like Friday night football. He parts his lips. I try to relax and just be in this moment. His hips shift beneath me, and the sensation of his cock rubbing against my pussy makes me gasp.

He takes advantage and deepens his kiss. He's not gentle. It feels like he's conquering me. Taking over every part of me until I belong fully to him. His tongue sweeps into my mouth, and I can't hold back the moan at the delicious sensations flowing through me.

I can't help but surrender under his assault.

I don't want this to end. I want more. Somewhere in the back of my mind, I know this is wrong. I shouldn't be giving in to this. I shouldn't be loving this, but I can't help it. Caden's lips against mine feel fucking fantastic.

"That's time," Jack says.

Caden growls against my lips but pulls back. His eyes are darker as they meet mine. "To be continued."

He squeezes my ass and presses me hard against his erection. He brings his mouth close to my ear and says, "You smell good enough to eat."

That should not turn me on. This whole scenario should be a hellscape of punishment for me, but his kiss felt too good to be wrong.

"Come on, kitten."

Caden lifts me a little, and Eli guides me onto his lap next. It definitely feels weird to have kissed one guy and now I'm on another guy's lap. But as Eli pulls me in place against his own impressive erection, I bite my lip in anticipation.

"No biting," Eli says softly. "That's my job."

The things these guys say make that horny bitch inside sit up and pay attention.

"Hands on his shoulders," Luke reminds me. She even likes when Luke gives me orders. She'd probably be his damn lapdog if he asked her to.

Eli's dark eyes burn into me as I move my hands to his shoulders and he cups my ass. Before I can take a breath, his lips are on mine. Consuming me, devouring me. He parts my lips and takes my mouth. I whimper slightly but not out of fear.

Definitely not fear. My insides whip into a whirlwind of desire.

My hands tighten on his shoulders and I rock forward, pressing against his cock. He growls in the back of his throat and bites lightly on my lip.

His fingers dig into my hips hard enough to leave a mark. I want him to mark me, and I want to mark him too. I dig my fingernails into his shoulders, and he moans into my mouth.

Fuck, that's hot. I want more. I want him to claim all of me.

"That's enough, unicorn."

Eli pulls away. His eyes are so dark they're almost black. He gives me a knowing smile that makes me even wetter.

Jack is gentle as he tugs me onto his lap. This game should give me hives, not turn me on. But the moment Caden's lips met mine, it unlocked something. Maybe that horny bitch finally decided to take over, or maybe I just want this more than I want to admit.

Jack's blue eyes capture me. They're a deep dark blue with lighter shades toward the center, like a kaleidoscope. They all blend into a mesmerizing color I could spend hours looking at, memorizing.

As his hard cock settles in the cradle of my thighs, the memory of watching him last night, his hand stroking his cock as he visually devoured my naked body, sends heat pouring through me.

His thumb swipes over my lower lip and he frowns. "Try not to damage our girl, Eli."

Eli leans back on his hands and smirks at Jack. "She likes it a little rough. Don't you, kitten?"

I'm too turned on to answer him right now. Too hot to rise to the bait. This may have started as their game, but now it's my mission. I want to taste them all.

I press my finger against Jack's lips. What will his kiss be like? War conquers. Pestilence overwhelms. Famine...will he be greedy and keep taking? Jack chuckles and tugs my ass forward onto his lap, moving his hips to stroke his hard cock back and forth against my pussy.

I suck in a breath at the friction and the waves of molten heat that flood my body.

"Hands on my shoulders, sweetheart." Jack leans forward as I do just that. "Enjoy the ride."

His lips touch mine almost gently. I'm so shocked, my lips part. When he doesn't take my mouth like the others, I explore. I move my tongue against the seam of his lips, and he opens for me. I grow more daring as I do what felt good to me on Jack. He lets me explore and find out what I like.

When his tongue glides against mine, I moan and follow his movements. His hips roll under me, and I want to rock to feel it again, find that friction I've read so much about.

"That's time, kitten."

Jack pulls away and gives me a cocky smile. For a second, I forget I'm not supposed to give these guys anything. That I'm just a toy for them to pass around. I'm so keyed up I want to see what it's like to kiss Luke.

The kiss of Death.

The thought shouldn't thrill me, but it does.

Jack passes me to Luke. He steadies my hips against him. I already know how his cock feels against me, but I've never had him against my center.

"How do you feel, unicorn?" Luke pulls my hips against his and presses his large, hard cock against the throbbing between my legs. I gasp and automatically put my hands on his shoulders. "How does it feel to be touched by all of us?"

So fucking good, but I won't give him the satisfaction of that answer. They don't need to know I want this. That I want them. It's just hormones and evolution driving me. At least, that's what I try to convince myself.

He squeezes my ass and my eyes slide shut. His cock presses against my pussy and I want to cry out.

I need more.

"Please." The word coming out of my mouth makes something inside me flinch, but I can't remember why. All I know right now is Luke is about to kiss me, and I want it more than my next breath.

"Since you asked so nicely."

I can't even care about the gloating in Luke's voice. His lips crash down over mine, and I willingly open for him with no hesitation. It doesn't matter that I've just kissed three other guys. This kiss feels like my first.

His kiss is a claiming, marking me as his possession. Making sure I know I'm theirs and no one else's. In this moment, I would gladly give myself to them as Luke takes every piece of me he can get.

He explores my mouth like he's never kissed anyone before. He takes and he takes, and all I can do is give and try to follow his lead. I don't even try to hold back as I grind against the hardness pressed between my legs. Something is rising in me, building. A sensation I want to reach out for. I need to chase it.

Even I know this would feel better naked. My fingers curl into his shoulders as his hands tighten on my ass. My breasts flatten on his chest as I try to get as close as possible. He thrusts his tongue between my lips, the way I want him to thrust inside me. Later I will probably be horrified, but right now, I think this is the best thing ever.

"While this is hot as fuck, that's time." Eli's voice is like a bucket of cold water.

I pull away from Luke and see the smug look on his face. What the fuck just happened? I can feel the heat in my cheeks as I shuffle back away from Luke and my hip bumps against the box on the field.

I stare at the guys with wide eyes. What the actual fuck just happened?

"Come on, little nympho." Caden stands and holds his hand down to me. "Time to get your books for class."

They can't get me alone again. I know I want them. I knew that last night, but I didn't know how powerful that desire is. If they pressed me to have sex with them, right this minute, I don't think I would say no.

And that glint in Luke's eyes tells me he knows. He's fully aware of how little it might take to push me over the edge into not caring that three guys waited their turns while watching me make out with someone else.

I went willingly into their arms. Almost desperately.

Icy cold chills run down my back as I'm horrified at how little it will take for them to make me want more. How even now, my gaze drops to Luke's lips and I want them back on mine. My heart aches it pounds so hard.

I have to find a way out of this or I'll lose more than just my virginity.

HARPER'S PHONE

ME:

I'm in so much trouble

KENZ:

What'd you do this time?

ME:

Do you think I could go to a convent?

KENZ:

Where's the fun in that?

ME:

I don't need fun

KENZ:

Sure you do

Live a little, H.

CHAPTER 14

The Lull

HARPER

Eli drives me home after school. I'm still a little numb from how easy it will be to make me want them, but also still a little turned on and frustrated. He pulls into the driveway before he says, "Turn on your laptop tonight."

I glance at him as I go to open the door. "Why? I'm not being punished, am I?"

I didn't do a damn thing to deserve a punishment today. I made sure of it. Even if the second half of the day flew by in a daze. My lips felt swollen. My ass bruised from their touch. My panties damp with desire. My pussy throbbed with need.

Going to class turned on seems like enough punishment for the day.

"No punishment, kitten." Eli reaches over and tugs one of my tendrils gently. "We like to see you and until you aren't grounded, this is the best way."

I open my mouth to protest and then shut it. This is a battle I don't want to win. I like seeing them at night. It's safe with them in their rooms and me in mine.

As far as I know, no other girl has had this from them. It's all mine. They're all mine.

"Fine. After your practice is over, I'll open the window on my laptop."

"Good." Eli waits until I get out of the car before saying, "We can kiss you whenever we want now, kitten. Starting tomorrow. Only kissing though."

I give him a thumbs-up when I really want to flip him the bird. Great. Kissing I feel all the way down to my toes. I might as well kiss my virginity goodbye.

He chuckles darkly as I close the door and watch him pull out of the driveway back toward school. I shudder to think my first time might be the same as today. Passed from one asshole to the next. Maybe even timed.

The horny bitch cheers. I don't even know what to do about her. She would be happy to take all of them at once. I pause and scrunch up my nose. How would that even work? All of them having sex with me at once?

I've seen some romance books with threesomes in them, but I haven't searched for anything more. Maybe I should do some research.

I shake my head. I'm not having sex with all of them at the same time. Not if I have anything to say about it. They still want me to *give* them my virginity, so that can be on my terms. I make my way into the house.

"You didn't drive today?" My mom looks up from her phone as she sits at the kitchen island.

My asshole owners insisted probably won't cut it. "My friend wants me to ride with him."

"Him?" Mom perks up. "There's a him?"

There are four hims, and I can't stop thinking about those kisses. Does that make me a whore because I want them all? Does that make me *their* whore? I don't even know what to think anymore. For years, I haven't done anything with any guy. No guy has even tempted me.

But these guys. Every single one of them makes me want them. Every single one of them tempts me to lower my guard and let them take anything they want. Fuck, maybe Kenz is right and I should just give in and have one hell of a senior year fucking four guys.

Mom clears her throat.

Heat rushes to my face. "Uh, yeah, there's a him."

And his three friends.

"Oh." Mom looks a little shocked, and then she registers my outfit and makeup.

Things I've never worn before in my life because of them. Not that I can tell her why the sudden change in clothing is only partially about boys or why I felt it necessary to hide before.

She gets this mom look in her eyes, and I know I'm in for a talk.

"You know to be safe, right?" Mom straightens on her stool and pins me in my place. "Birth control pills won't protect you from STIs. You can't trust a guy when he says he's clean or a virgin."

I press my lips together to hold back the bark of laughter at those guys claiming they're virgins. "I'm not having sex, Mom."

Yet. If they get their way...who am I kidding? If that horny little bitch inside me gets her way, we'll be banging the fuck out of those guys. That thought doesn't terrify me like it once did. I'm so fucked in the head.

But I still want to find a way out of it. I have to. It should be my choice who I fuck. Not some guys claiming me as the last virgin.

"You have to be prepared. You should start carrying condoms." She stands. "I can go buy you some, so you have them. You can't rely on the guy to always have one. I know too many girls who thought in the heat of the moment, one time wouldn't hurt and ended up pregnant at our office."

"I'm not going to get pregnant, Mom. I have a future. I need to get out of this town and go to college where no one will have heard of—"

Fuck, I almost said the horsemen.

Her eyes narrow on me.

"Me. No one knows me." Not my smoothest save, but good enough. "I can start fresh. Trust me, I'm not going to get a boyfriend my senior year and let him complicate my life. Next year I'm going away to college."

Besides, I can't get a boyfriend while the horsemen own me.

I probably won't be a virgin by the time I go to college, but hey, how many girls are actually virgins in college? I don't need to tell anyone about my first time with four guys. Yeah, that probably wouldn't go over well with a future boyfriend.

Besides, I might not give them my virginity. Maybe I'll just end up a technical virgin. I might get away without parting my legs, but I know at some point they'll have me down on my knees. Jack's cock pops into my mind, and the feel of all of them against me.

Not really hard to imagine doing things with these four. Not after making out with them.

"Protection." Mom grabs her keys. "You need protection."

"Mom, really—" My words fall on deaf ears as she shuts the door behind her. I shake my head, but she might not be wrong.

Those guys push all the right buttons. Fuck, I even liked it when Luke spanked me. How desperate must I be to want the very guys I avoided for years? I go into my room and get out my homework.

I let my hair down and change into a loose t-shirt and shorts. I set an alarm on my phone to let me know when the guys finish their practice and then turn on some music while I work on homework.

I almost start to feel normal when there's a knock on my door. Like this is any other year. Focused on homework, getting good grades. Mom checking up on me.

"Harper?" Mom's voice seems a little hesitant, and then I remember why. So much for normal.

I squeeze my eyes shut and say, "Come in."

She's carrying a Walgreen's bag. "Now I know you think you don't need these, but I'd rather you be safe than sorry. I got two sizes. It's important to use the proper size of condom."

She sets the bag on my bed, and I wonder how red my face can get before my head explodes.

"I know you don't want to talk about sex with your mother, but know that you can. There are websites that can give you information on sizing. I'll try to answer any questions as best I can. If you need an appointment with the doctor..." She trails off. Mom works with an OB-GYN.

"Really, Mom, I'm fine. I'll keep the condoms just in case, but I really don't plan on having sex anytime soon." As long as I behave, they won't have a reason to punish me. Luke even said they would take things slow for me.

Of course, that was before I rode him like a wanton hussy.

"Sex is a normal part of life. I don't want you to feel ashamed because you want to have sex. It's natural. I just want you to be safe when it happens." Mom twists her hands together.

"You're right. I'll get right on that then," I tease. "It looks like you got me enough for the entire football team. Twice. Goals, right?"

"Maybe just try one guy at first, okay?" She smiles and shakes her head. "Just be prepared. Our mind doesn't always account for what our body wants."

I can feel my cheeks heat again. Yeah, I'm quite familiar with my body and mind not being on the same page when it comes to the guys. My mind shut down when they kissed me, but maybe that was because they were my first kisses.

I'm sure I'll get used to them kissing me.

"I'll be careful."

Mom nods and moves toward the door. "Honey?"

I lift my eyes to hers. We have the same coloring. Same dark eyes, same brown hair.

"Just be careful." She blows a strand of hair out of her face and gives me a considering look before she ducks out of my room. "I'll leave you to your studying. Gotta get those good grades for college. Dinner in thirty."

She closes the door. Careful, I wish I could be more careful. My alarm goes off and I open the program I never installed on my laptop. I don't think Luke installed it either. He doesn't seem like the tech type, but one of my horsemen did.

The window opens with four streams. I recognize each of their rooms, but they aren't in them yet. For all I know, they're going to go hang out at Caden's for a few hours and no one will be in their rooms.

I sigh. This will be my life, waiting for them to decide what they want to do with me until they get bored with me. That makes my heart ache a little, but I know it's coming. I'm just an average girl. Not enough to hold onto four guys who are the top of the social totem pole.

They may want me now, but it can't last.

HARPER'S PHONE

KENZ:

Do you think Mr. Wick will accept a drawing
of Shakespeare for our first report?

ME:

Maybe if you used the words of your essay
as the lines?

KENZ:

Boo! That means I still have to write it

And do a drawing

ME:

Something tells me English Lit means written
word

KENZ:

But a picture can tell a thousand stories

ME:

eyeroll emoji

CHAPTER 15

The Package

ELI

Not going to lie, I can't wait to get my hands back on Harper tomorrow. Instead of going to hang out at Caden's tonight, we all went home after practice. Catching me at home, Mom insisted on me eating dinner with her and Dad like we're some sort of Norman Rockwell painting instead of the dysfunctional shitshow we are.

I escape to my room as soon as I finish eating. The light on my laptop's camera is lit. I sit at my desk to see who's on. Harper's room is empty. I can hear movement in one of the windows and see Luke pass by his camera in only a towel.

Bet my kitten will be sad to have missed that. I see a flash of pink in the corner of Harper's camera.

"Are you there, kitten?"

She comes into frame. Her long brown hair falls in waves around her shoulders. The large shirt she wears hides her shape and does nothing for her. If this is an example of what she wore for the past few years, it's no wonder we missed her.

"Hey." She sits at her desk. "Just finished dinner. Where is everyone else?"

I shrug. "I just got here. Luke passed by in a towel, but I'm not sure if he was coming out of the shower or heading in."

Her gaze shifts to his room on her screen and she shrugs. "Any new torture for tonight?"

"Not that I know of." I lean back in my chair. "Unless you consider having kissed you only once torture."

A smile tugs at her lips before she wipes it away. "Are you saying kissing me was torture?"

"Not even for a second, kitten." I look toward my door. Dinner with my parents was torture though. It would be easier if they just divorced and found new partners who make them happy. Instead, they play this game of marriage chicken. Neither of them happy but wanting the other to decide to be the failure.

"Are you okay?" She frowns slightly at me.

"Worried about me?" I raise an eyebrow. I saw the way she looked at Caden today. Our girl is a natural nurturer. None of us has anyone to take care of us. Yeah, some of us have mothers, but ours aren't the nurturing kind. With the exception of Jack's dad, who stepped up to take care of Jack's little sister when she was born.

We all have each other's backs, but it isn't quite the same as having someone care for you.

She stiffens a little. "Wouldn't want you to take out your aggression on me."

I lean in and lower my voice. "Do you want me to, kitten? Take out my aggression on you? Show you exactly how it feels to have me take you?"

She catches her lip in her teeth.

"Last warning, kitten. Don't bite your lip again. Or I'll see to your punishment personally." I have plenty of ideas for our girl. Not all I want to share with the guys. We haven't discussed alone time with Harper yet.

Luke probably worries about our ability to control ourselves around her. He should. Our girl is hot as fuck and now she's not afraid to show it. Today she showed off that tight little body of hers at school. If she'd shown up in that the day before, we might have had some guys willing to fight us for her.

She releases her lip and pouts. "I didn't even know I did that. You'd punish me for something I didn't realize I was doing?"

"You're lucky we don't punish you for being a tease."

That has her sputtering. "What? When? I never—"

"You enjoyed grinding against each of our cocks today. Didn't you, kitten? Did you think we couldn't smell how aroused you were?"

She flushes a pretty shade of pink and glances over her shoulder at her door.

"If you don't want your mother to hear, put on some headphones, but if you mute us, you'll be punished."

Her eyes flash in anger, but she says, "Fine."

"First." I draw her attention back to me. "Take off that shirt. It does nothing for you."

Her eyes narrow and her cheeks flush red. I don't think it's embarrassment this time.

"That's an order, kitten. It's not like I didn't get a good look last night." I smirk at her, knowing it will piss her off a little more. I like our girl angry and spitting.

She stands and backs away from the camera so she's in view. She flips me off and then pulls her shirt off over her head. I should punish her for flipping me off, but then she might not let me see her angry.

Fuck me. The bra she wears is sheer lace. I can see her rosy nipples trying to poke through it.

"Happy?" She holds her arms out.

I raise my eyebrow at her sass. She definitely could use another spanking.

"Definitely happier." Jack's voice comes over the speaker. "Damn, sweetheart, were you wearing that all day?"

Her cheeks flush from embarrassment this time and she turns her back to go to her dresser. The shorts she wears are practically booty shorts. I'm tempted to tell her to pull them down and let me see the bruises I know I left on her hips, but she hasn't earned a punishment. Yet.

She shrugs a cami on over her bra and then comes back to sit in front of the screen.

"I still have homework to do." She tucks her hair behind her ear.

Jack leans closer to the screen and wiggles his eyebrows. "I can come over and help you with that."

"Jack," I chastise.

"What, you get her partially naked when no one else is around, but I can't go over to her house? You all can watch me help her with her homework." He wiggles his eyebrows at the word *homework* as if it's code for fucking her.

"If she needs help, I'll go." Luke sits at his desk with his blond hair sticking up from drying it. He's not wearing a shirt, and I watch Harper's tongue dart out to lick her lips as she checks him out.

"Why do you always get to have all the fun?" Jack tips back in his chair like someone took away his favorite toy.

"I have control."

Ah, yes, Luke's legendary control. I think that's the only reason the kissing didn't devolve into an orgy at lunch. Harper's usual vanilla fragrance had a deeper, muskier scent beneath it. Her knees clenched around my hips and the heat of her pussy cradled my dick as I feasted on her lips. I had to dig my fingers into her ass to stop from moving my hands to all the places Luke had deemed inappropriate for her first kiss. Fucker.

I think I missed some arguing because Jack looks belligerent while Luke seems smug. Harper's eyebrow is raised as she looks between the two of them.

"What'd I miss?" Caden flops down on his bed and crosses his ankles.

"Harper's lace bra," Jack chimes in.

Caden sits up and stares at the screen where Harper probably is. "Show me."

"Seriously?" Harper drops her pen. "I still want to graduate high school and get into college. If this affects my grades—"

"You'll what, kitten?" I lean in and her gaze locks on mine. "What exactly will you do?"

She glares at me, pulls the camisole off, and drops it to the ground. "Fine, have a look while I do my homework. It's not like you haven't seen them before."

She picks up her pen and focuses on something to the side of her laptop.

Caden smirks. "Much better bra than yesterday's."

She lifts her middle finger into the view but doesn't look at us. Luke's eyes narrow. Jack laughs out loud. Caden snorts. I shake my head. She was doing so well.

"The shorts too." Luke's tone brooks no disobedience.

Her lips press together. She stands and drops her shorts to the ground. She holds her hands out on either side of her and turns around in a circle.

When she sits back down, she picks up her pen again. Her cheeks are flushed pink, but that's anger for sure. Her jaw practically ticks, she's holding it so tight.

I want to know what she's thinking, but I know it will get her in trouble with Luke so I don't dare ask.

Instead, I focus on the bag on her bed. "What's in the bag, kitten?"

She sighs and looks back at the bed to see what I'm talking about. Her mouth opens into an *oh* and her cheeks brighten more. "Nothing."

"Well, now I want to know too." Jack puts his hands behind his head. "You wouldn't want to disobey now, would you, Harper?"

"It's private," she says through gritted teeth.

Luke leans in so his face fills the screen. "Nothing is private from us, unicorn. We own every part of you. Show us or I'll come find out myself."

A war plays out on Harper's face. I think she's actually contemplating Luke showing up in her room again. I know he says his control is good, but even I could see the cracks in it when he kissed her. If I hadn't stopped him, that orgy might have taken place. If we hadn't been at school, I would have let it play out.

"Show us or tomorrow you'll be publicly spanked again." I stroke my chin. "Maybe in the guys' locker room before practice this time."

She stands up in her bra and matching underwear and grabs the bag. "I mentioned a guy drove me to school and Mom, being a nurse, figured I needed supplies."

"Show us." Luke smiles coldly.

She pulls out two boxes of condoms, and Jack laughs.

"I think I like your mom, little nympho," Caden says with a wink.

She slides them back into the bag and sets them on the floor next to her desk. "It's not an invitation to use them."

"We won't need those, kitten." I decide to tell her the good news.

Her eyebrows scrunch together and she looks really fucking confused.

"We already decided we're going to fuck you bare." I raise my eyebrow and wait for the explosion.

Her mouth drops open. She grabs her cami top and tugs it back on. "No."

"What was that, kitten?" I smirk.

"No. You guys...nuh-uh. No way. Nope. No." Her hand reaches forward like she's going to close the screen.

"Don't close the laptop, Harper," Luke's voice bites out.

Her fingers dangle in the air for a moment, like she's debating disobeying again, but she puts her hand down into her lap.

"That would be stupid and reckless and...I'm not going to get a disease because..." She squints her eyes at us. "You guys get around and god only knows what is going on in your pants." Her nose wrinkles. "I'm not getting an STI because you guys don't want to wear a condom. Why? Because it doesn't feel good? Well, suck it up, buttercup, because I don't want whatever you're looking to transmit. This isn't even my idea. I was happy to go off to college a virgin, but no, you guys couldn't let one go, could you? Ugh."

Her arms are crossed over her heaving chest.

I'm not the only one smiling at her outburst, but Luke isn't having it. "Done yet, princess?"

"Oh, I'm princess now. What happened to unicorn? Am I more believable now that I don't want to have unprotected sex with four guys? Guys who I know have had sex before with who knows how many girls."

"Twenty-four and a half," I say, "if just blow jobs only count as halves. I always wear a condom and will gladly get you a report saying I'm disease free. The last time I had sex was two weeks ago."

Her mouth drops open as she stares at me.

"Thirty-two," Jack pipes up next. "Always wear a condom. It's been a week and a half since Caden and I tag-teamed Parker Ford." He arches his eyebrow. "I'll get you a report."

"Twenty-eight. Parker Ford was the last," Caden says. "Yeah, I'll get you whatever you need. I was against bare. I always use a condom, but for you, I'll make an exception."

Her eyes turn to Luke. He doesn't want to give her this, but if he wants her to trust us, he needs to. "Twelve. Not including blow jobs." Luke leans back in his chair. "Condoms were a necessity until you. And if you want test results, I can get you them. The last time I fucked a girl was two months ago."

Harper flinches when he says *fucked*. Her voice is soft as she asks, "Why do you want to fuck me bare then? If it has always been a necessity?"

"Because you're ours." Luke's voice is calm. "Because we've agreed to only be yours for a year. Because I want to *feel* your wet cunt wrapped around my dick when I thrust inside you."

Her eyes widen as she stares at all of us. We have a wide range of numbers of girls we've been with. Luke is the most particular when it comes to actually fucking a girl. His blow job count is probably at least three times as much.

"Have any of you had a girlfriend?" She twists her hands together.

"None of us," I say.

She straightens and puts her hands in her lap before looking each of us in the eye as much as you can with video chats. "Am I just your whore?"

"No." Luke rakes a hand through his hair. "You belong to us. That doesn't make you a whore."

"But we want to fuck you, and often, kitten."

When her eyes bounce back to me, her mouth opens and closes.

"Not tonight though." Luke effectively cuts off the conversation. "Do your homework, princess."

CHAPTER 16

The Tactical Advance

HARPER

I don't know what possesses me in the morning. I wake up to Caden's snoring and Jack's *Kilby Girl* alarm song. It's still weird seeing them in the morning. I glance over the sleeping guys before heading into shower. I don't close the laptop. When I come back into my room, I don't even think as I drop my towel and pull on my panties and a bra.

Standing in front of my closet, I hear a low whistle. I turn to find Jack watching me, his hand on his cock as he sits up in bed. My face heats, but I try to ignore the sounds he makes as I pull out a skirt and crop top for the day.

This is my life now. Beautiful boys who own me and want to fuck me. For now, they're on the other side of the computer. So I'm safe to do things I wouldn't do if they were in the room with me.

Instead of putting on my clothes, I sit on the edge of my bed and cross my legs while watching Jack stroke his cock. His blue eyes darken as he stares openly at my breasts, cupped in the bra and hoisted up. I study the way his hand works his cock, his thumb sliding over the tip and his fist coming down over it.

My insides heat more, but I try to ignore it.

I brush my hair and then bend over to work on getting it into the high ponytail Luke requested.

121

"Fuck, Harper." Jack's voice strains, and I look up to see him coming over his hand.

This is my life now.

I give him a small smirk as I notice motion in one of the other cameras. Luke is watching too. His boxers are on, but his massive cock is visibly hard. I tighten my ponytail and stand up to stretch, still only in my white bra and panties.

"Show me what you want to wear." Luke's voice is gravelly and deep. A shiver flows down my spine, filling me with liquid heat.

I pick up my shirt and, instead of putting it on, model it in front of my body. Setting it to the side, I show off the skirt next. I lift my eyebrow, daring him to comment.

He nods thoughtfully. "Behave today or I'll take those panties."

Fuck. If anything, his words make me wetter.

He gives me a knowing smile and his focus drops to between my legs. I'm not experienced enough to play this game yet. I put on my skirt and top and sit to put on my red Converse.

Retreating to the bathroom, I put on some light makeup. Some eyeliner and mascara, a touch of blush, and a swipe of lip gloss. Cherry flavored.

I return to my bedroom and pick up my backpack.

"Don't bend over like that in school, kitten."

I glance over my shoulder at Eli, who's putting on his shoes.

He smirks. "Wouldn't want everyone to see your panties."

My lips tighten, remembering the last time I wore a skirt.

"Unless you guys are the ones flashing them?" I raise my eyebrow and he laughs, dark and wicked.

His eyes linger on my high ponytail. I can almost feel the tug on it. I'm sure Luke won't be the only one grabbing it today.

Slipping my lip gloss into my backpack, I ask Eli, "Who's on pick-up duty?"

"I am."

I spin and find Caden in my room. "What are you guys? Ninjas?"

"Nah, but we won't be telling you our secret. Come on, little nympho, you've played with the boys enough this morning." He turns and heads out into the hallway.

I adjust my bag and follow him to the kitchen. He sits at the island and picks up one of the fake lemons Mom has out for decoration. I drop my bag on a chair and move to the other side of the island to make my two sandwiches for lunch.

"We could just buy lunch today," Caden offers as he watches me pull everything out of my fridge.

I shake my head. "I haven't eaten cafeteria food for years. Right around the time you guys started to make a reputation for yourselves."

"We're not that bad." Caden rubs his jaw and stands.

Ignoring him, I make the two sandwiches for us. As much as I can ignore the giant guy in my kitchen. He knows the horsemen are that bad. And I know he's behind me. But it isn't until I feel his warmth surrounding me that I try to move. His hands come to rest on the counter on either side of me.

"Is it your shampoo or perfume or body wash?" He leans down next to my neck and inhales. Heat floods my body.

I resist the urge to press into his warmth. "What?"

"The vanilla. It's like an ice cream cone I just want to lick all day." Caden sniffs my neck again, and I feel his lips against my pulse, which thrums harder.

My breath catches in my throat and I remain still, wondering what will happen next. The realization I'm alone with Caden in my house doesn't do me any favors. My pulse ratchets higher, and tingles scatter through me from his touch.

"Harper?" His mouth whispers against my skin.

"Mmhmm?" My chest is rising and falling fast, and there is no one here to stop him besides me. And I'm not that reliable.

"Turn around."

Fuck me. I don't want to turn around and I want to at the same time.

"Now." His voice is little more than a growl that shoots right between my legs.

I set the wrapped sandwiches to the side and turn in the cage of his arms. I lift my chin to look at him. His green eyes are darker than usual.

His lips are on mine before I can even blink. He grabs my ass and hoists me onto the counter, bringing our heads closer to the same height. My hands automatically go to his shoulders. My lips part beneath his, and he pushes my knees apart to step between them. His denim-covered cock presses against my panty-covered pussy.

"Oh my god," I say against his lips. Fuck, that feels divine.

"Not quite, little nympho." He chuckles before he devours my lips and rocks his hard cock against me. "If it were just you and me, I'd drive my cock inside you right this minute, but I'm not even allowed to touch that precious pussy yet."

He thrusts against me, eliciting a moan. I want him to touch me there, but I won't tell him that. I can't tell him that. My brain is fuzzy.

"You want it. Don't you, little nympho?" He leans back and grabs my chin. I open my eyes. "Fuck, you're hot. I swear you get hotter every fucking day."

I wish I had something to say to that, but my insides are on fire. Every time he rocks against me, sparks ignite and burn through me. Winding me up.

"Shit. You're going to get me in so much trouble." Caden claims my lips again.

His tongue parries mine for dominance as he holds my chin. He withdraws and I whimper, needing more.

"I'm not going to touch, but I want to smell you."

Say what?

Caden drops to one knee between my parted legs, leans forward, and inhales obscenely. He blows his hot breath over my damp panties, and I clutch onto the edge of the counter. Holy fuck, that should not feel that good.

He stands back up and hoists me down to stand before him. My legs shake a little but surprisingly hold me upright.

"You smell so fucking good. I can't wait to taste you."

My knees give a little, but I catch the counter behind me to hold me steady.

"You and me are going to have fun. Very soon." Caden kisses me as if we've been apart for years and then steps back. "Hurry up. We don't want to be late."

I feel like I just went through a hurricane. My legs are unsteady. As I pack the sandwiches and some chips into my lunch box, my hands tremble. My mind can't focus.

"Put some extra chips in there for me."

I risk a glance up at him. He gives me a huge, shit-eating grin. I take a breath and release the tension in my belly from being turned on with no relief. I'll deal with that later. For now, I'll focus on getting to know these guys when I can.

Finding the chinks in their armor will help me find a way out of this deal.

"Aren't you rich? Like really rich?" I grab another bag of chips.

"My parents are. Yes."

"Shouldn't you have a cook making you lunch or something?" I put our lunch into my backpack and turn to look at him.

"He doesn't give two shits about me. I'd rather eat something you made me." He smirks.

"I don't give two shits about you either." I try to keep my tone firm and unaffected, but his poor little rich boy story gets to me. I pick up my bag and head out the door.

Caden is right behind me. I feel his breath on the back of my neck and my knees try to give way again.

"Keep telling yourself that, little nympho. Maybe you'll actually start to believe it."

I STEP OUT OF CADEN'S CAR AND FALL IN LINE BEHIND HIM like I did with Luke yesterday. Except Caden stops and turns back to look at me. He grins and throws his arm around my shoulders to drag me into his side. Then he leads me to the others.

Jack comes up and lifts me off my feet before planting his mouth over mine. This isn't the let-me-lead type of kiss of yesterday, but a feel-it-deep-in-my-bones type of kiss. I put my hands on his shoulders to steady myself.

He pulls his lips from mine and leans forward to whisper in my ear. "I love cherry, sweetheart. I can't wait to taste yours. Thanks for getting me off this morning."

He deposits me on the ground and backs away with a smug look. I barely have time to think before Eli tugs my ponytail back playfully and takes his turn with my mouth. Each of them kisses slightly differently and each wants something different from me.

Eli wants to dominate me but doesn't want me to give in to him. I try to keep up, but fuck, it's only my second day kissing and I'm being passed around between four guys. Give a girl a chance to catch her breath.

Squeezing my ass, Eli sends me Luke's way. I stumble to a stop in front of him. He looks down on me and holds out his hand. I take it, not sure what's going to happen next, but he just leads me into the school. Holding my hand like we're in fourth grade.

Somehow that makes all this a little easier to handle and gives me some time to catch my breath.

He leads me to their lockers, and Caden puts my stuff in his again. Each of them kisses me before they leave for their classes except Luke. He stands beside me and when it's just him and me, he takes my hand and we walk to first period.

The hallways are almost clear and the bell is about to ring when Luke shoves me against the wall beside the door. He tangles his fingers in my ponytail and tips my head back. His light blue eyes are practically glowing as he drops his head beside mine.

He touches his lips against my ear as he says for my ears only, "Do you like being a little tease, princess? Do you like them pawing all over you? Wanting between your legs?"

When he tugs my ponytail, I whimper at the pain, even as sparks light up the fire within me.

"I'm only what you make me," I find the balls to get out.

He lifts his head, and his cold blue eyes pierce into my soul. "Then I should reap the benefits of my invention."

I don't have time to react before his lips claim mine. His kiss is all-consuming. He takes what he wants from me, and yet I still have more to give him. He presses his erection into my stomach, and I remember how good it felt between my thighs, rubbing against me. I'm almost ashamed to want it there again.

"Mr. Foster." Mr. Wick's voice is weary, like he's seen everything before and nothing fazes him. "Please release Ms. Davidson so you can both get to class."

Luke lifts his mouth from mine and stares into my eyes for a heartbeat before he wraps an arm around my shoulder. "Sure thing, Mr. Wick."

My face has to be the color of a ripe tomato. Luke's kiss has me spinning. I've barely started kissing these guys and already a teacher has caught me making out in the hallway.

Giving me no choice but to move with him, Luke drags me into first period and stops to help me sit in my chair before taking the one behind me. Mr. Wick drops his things on his desk and starts the lesson for the day.

Luke leans forward and tugs my head back by my ponytail. Kenz glances over with a concerned look before her gaze flits back to the front. "Remember, behave today or I'll carry those panties in my pocket."

Yeah, he's going to find any excuse to make me give up my panties. Today will be another day in hell.

CHAPTER 17

The Allies Or Foes

HARPER

I spend all of first period thinking about that kiss from Luke. My grades are definitely going to suffer from their attention, but it's only the first week of school. Not much happens in the first week. I'll be used to this soon. When the bell rings, I stand, determined to get away.

Luke steps into my path and grabs my ponytail. I will never wear my hair like this for him again. He closes the distance between us, and I draw in half a breath before his lips crash down on mine.

He grabs my ass and draws me into him, making me gasp. Taking advantage, his tongue explores my mouth like we have all the time in the world. He tastes like mint with a hint of bitter coffee. Heat rushes over me. As he crushes me against his hard body, wetness gathers between my thighs.

Losing myself to his kiss would be so easy.

Someone lets out a whoop, and I withdraw.

"Don't flash anyone those panties, princess." Luke's cold eyes dance with a dark light. He squeezes my ass.

"Only you then?" I lift my eyebrows as I gaze innocently up at him.

"Get to your next class," he growls and releases my hair.

I still beat the others to AP Statistics and have a moment to myself to take a few deep breaths to slow the racing of my heart. Besides being grounded, I don't have any way to fight against what they want to do to me.

Maybe I should give in less, resist more. What might happen? More punishments? Luke's eyes flash in my mind. Yeah, he'd like to give me punishments all day long. It's why he likes my defiance.

"Deep thoughts, sweetheart?" Jack slides into the desk behind me.

"Making plans to take down the patriarchy," I say over my shoulder.

"That skirt is heading in the right direction." Jack grunts in approval. "I know I'd go down for it."

I just shake my head. Caden and Eli slide into their seats. There are still a few minutes before class starts. Fuck it.

"What's on the agenda for lunch?" I ask.

Caden smirks, and I remember making lunch this morning. His hot breath against my damp panties. I cross my legs. Caden's gaze drops to them and he grins wickedly.

Eli turns sideways in his seat and his dark eyes drink me in. "Cafeteria, unless you want to find a quiet spot to be alone."

I lift an eyebrow and lean forward a little. "Is that allowed? I mean, Luke said you guys aren't trustworthy with me alone. I'd hate to get you all punished."

Eli's grin is positively evil. "You should worry about your own punishment, kitten. I mean, denying us a weekend because you're grounded ought to be worth...hmm, what kind of punishment do you think that's worth, guys?"

"Twenty lashes." Caden grins.

"You are not whipping me." Fuck that. I cross my arms over my chest. I'll tell my mom everything before I let that happen. Fuck the consequences.

"With my tongue on your sweet pussy." Caden's eyes dip down to between my legs, and I squeeze them tighter around the ache his words cause.

"Or her breasts." Jack leans in and trails his fingers down my neck. "I guess that would be more like twenty sucks or tugs."

Shivers course down my spine and I can feel my nipples tighten.

"You never got to play seven minutes in heaven." Eli's finger tips my chin up so my gaze locks on his dark eyes. "I'm sure we can find a dark closet all together—"

The door opens and the teacher walks in. I'm barely breathing. The images these boys filled my brain with are way too enticing. Being stuck with all of them in a closet, surrounding me with their heat, touching me wherever they want.

They all turn to face forward, and I inhale. I need to figure out a way out, and fast.

Kisses from three horsemen usher me into third period. I collapse in my seat next to Kenz.

"You look worked over." Kenz brushes a stray hair from my forehead.

"And they're only kissing me so far." I fan myself with my art book.

"Hi, Harper." Some platinum blonde in wedge sandals and a short skirt waves at me as she stops beside my chair expectantly.

Shit, do I know her? "Hey, you."

"What do you want, Penny?" Kenz says, emphasizing Penny.

Penny Wright.

Oh yeah, she's been in art with me since freshman year but hasn't said a word to me in all that time until today.

"You're so funny, MacKenzie. I'm just checking in with Harper to see if she needs a ride to the away game tomorrow."

I must look at Penny like she's an alien because her smile droops a little.

"I mean, we have room in our car. Me, Izzy, Nat, and Vicky always go to the away games and figured since you've never gone to one, it would be nice to have someone to sit with." Penny clutches her books to her chest and swivels on her heels like she's a little girl asking me over for a playdate.

"I'm not going to the game," I say slowly.

Her face falls. "But the guys—"

"I'm grounded. So the guys will have to make other plans." I give her a smile as an idea pops into my head. "You know, maybe you should keep them company this weekend. They'll be all alone at parties and probably need some relief after a hard week of school."

Her brown eyes narrow on me. "You won't be at the parties either?"

Maybe this girl likes me and not the guys. Weird. "No. Grounding means I can't go anywhere this weekend."

"How long are you grounded for?"

"Two weeks from Tuesday." I frown like I'm devastated and not dancing in my chair because I figured out a way to stay out of the horsemen's evil clutches. For a little while, at least.

She pouts. "That sucks. Can't you get your parents to reconsider?"

Not that I would want her to, but... "No, Mom's a stickler."

"I was hoping we'd get to know each other better." She smiles. "You should give me your phone number so we can keep you posted on what the guys do. We can be your eyes at the party."

"Oh, uh, sure?" What the hell is happening right now? I glance at Kenz, who shrugs. I rip out a piece of paper and scribble my number on it. When I hand it to Penny, she grins like I've handed her gold and not a scrap of paper.

No one has ever asked for my number before.

"I'll text you right away with my name, so you'll have mine." She starts to turn before she says, "Do you mind if I give it to Izzy, Nat, and Vicky?"

"Why not? Go crazy." I smile like I honestly give a shit. No one but Kenz, the guys, and my mom text me. Oh, and I get coupons from this pizza place I've ordered from occasionally.

Penny grins and hustles back to her seat.

"What the fuck was that about?" I whisper to Kenz. I glance back at Penny, who's sitting next to Natalie Edwards. They both wave at me as if we're best friends now.

"That clique always had boyfriends during high school. They lost their virginities the old-fashioned way to said boyfriends. My guess is they've heard of the horsemen's..."—she clears her throat—"sizeable assets and wanted to get a taste this year, but you've got them locked down."

"So the only access point to them is through me?" Fuck my life. "Not only do I have to put up with seduction and punishment from four dicks, but now every girl will want to be my friend to get on said dicks? Even though the guys aren't allowed to touch another girl?"

Kenz grins. "Something like that. Oh, don't forget the other guys. There will be the ones who want to earn favor with the horsemen. The ones who might want to pull a fast one on the guys and try to seduce you themselves to get back at them. And then the ones who will run when they see you for fear looking will earn them a beatdown from Caden."

"You know, senior year was supposed to be easy. The most stressful thing was going to be getting into college." I shake my head. Pulling out my pencil, I open my sketch pad.

"All because you still have a hymen." Kenz bumps her shoulder into mine.

"Lucky me," I grumble.

Ms. Sullivan begins class today by talking about our portfolios and what type of work should go into them for college. Something I'm not worried about, so I focus on the wire dragon sculpture in the corner. Ms. Sullivan keeps some of her students' art.

This one is from last year. Whoever worked on it was in a different class, but I saw it grow and develop over months. While the teacher goes on about portfolios, I start sketching the wire dragon. I've seen some of the other works by that artist, but whoever it is, they always sign it with a symbol and not their initials.

A sword through a crescent moon.

Not that I will get to know the artist, but I definitely admire their work. I can't wait to see what they make this year. Unless they were a senior last year. That thought makes me a little sad.

But they could be in this class.

"How long do you think the grounding will hold them off?" Kenz asks as Ms. Sullivan leaves us to do solo work for the rest of the class period.

I drag in a breath and exhale. "Hopefully the whole time. I might have to come up with another reason to get grounded that won't make them punish me. I think part of why they aren't pushing too hard yet is because of the webcams."

"Webcams?" Kenz's eyebrows almost meet her hairline. "They webcam you?"

"Shh." I look around to make sure no one is paying attention. Natalie waves at me, and I wave back before turning around. "They hacked my laptop and they have webcams in their rooms too."

"Have you seen their dicks? Because I heard Caden's is huge, like not even exaggerating." Kenz leans into me so we can talk low.

I sigh and blush. "I've seen Jack's."

"Hard or soft? How many inches? Is it thick?" Kenz pauses and purses her lips. "Brandon's isn't that long, but it's thick."

I open my mouth and close it. Having very little to compare Jack's dick to, I shake my head. "I'm not discussing dicks with you in class."

"When then?" She grins. "Oh, why don't I come over Friday night, and we can watch some movies and talk then? We can waste time until the guys get back from the game."

I smile. I could use some girl time. "Sounds good, but probably not a sleepover, just in case the guys pop on after the game."

Kenz's eyes sparkle. "We definitely have a lot to talk about."

Maybe together we can figure out how to get me out of this arrangement with the horsemen.

CHAPTER 18

The Weakness For My Enemy

HARPER

I'm still not crazy about the cafeteria, but this time Natalie and Penny follow me from art like we're going in together. Kenz knows the horsemen won't accept her following me around, and I don't want to put her in their crosshairs. I'm not sure what game these girls are playing but I'm sure the horsemen will set them straight.

I just hope they don't end up getting me in trouble. It's one of the reasons I keep Kenz away from them. They could punish me by punishing her.

I approach the table with the two girls right on my heels. Penny asks something about how I get my hair to look so silky. Hers is curly and perfect, so I'm not sure what she wants from me.

"Um, I wash and dry it," I say.

"Pick up a few strays, kitten?" Eli stands as we approach, and I shrug.

I didn't invite them to follow me. They just tagged along, but I really don't want to get on anyone's bad side. I already have four guys trying to ruin my life.

Penny laughs. "We were in art class together."

Yup, pretty sure that's not going to fly. I turn to the girls so the horsemen don't humiliate them too badly.

"It was nice talking with you." Hopefully I don't get punished because they were talking to me, and neither will they.

Penny looks at Natalie. Both of them are straining to keep their smiles on. "Did you want to sit with us for lunch, Harper?"

Caden's heat closes in behind me before he says, "Shoo, little pests. She's mine for lunch. Find your own virgin."

Fuck my life. I give them a what-are-you-going-to-do smile and a little shrug as their smiles fall.

"We'll talk later, Harper." Penny is as enthusiastic as ever as she and Natalie walk away fast.

I turn to face Caden.

"You need to be fierce with those kinds, little nympho." Caden takes my hand and drags me to his side of the table. He sits and pulls me onto his lap.

"What kinds are those?" I ask curiously and act as if this is completely normal for me to sit on Caden's lap for lunch. I pull out our food and divide it into a pile for him and a pile for me.

Eli holds an apple across the table. "The kind that will eat you up until you have nothing left to offer them."

"So I should be wary of you guys, then?" I take the apple and add it to my stack with a tight smile. I straighten my skirt a little because it rides up. There isn't much to it.

"We'll eat you up, but then you'll keep coming."

I wait for Eli to finish the sentence, but he bites into his apple and smirks.

It takes me a moment and then my face burns from the meaning. Yup, still can't hold my own with this lot. Don't know if I ever will.

Luke and Jack join us and Luke studies me as they both sit down.

"Embarrassed to be on Caden's lap?" Luke asks.

I glance over my shoulder at Caden and smile. "Nope."

I'm not going to elaborate on why my face is red if the others aren't, and neither Eli nor Caden seem to be forthcoming. So I eat my sandwich and check out the cafeteria a little more now that I'm not on display. Well, at least not humiliating myself in front of the whole lot of them.

Except for the tables near us, almost every table is full. The cheerleaders and the football players seem to be on one side of us, claiming a few tables. While a group of scantily clad girls—not that I can say much given what I'm wearing today—are at the same table as the other day, waiting for any acknowledgment from the horsemen.

I notice Penny and Natalie at that table with two other girls, who must be Isabella Baker and Victoria Martinez. Otherwise known as Izzy and Vicky. They sit on the far end, farthest away from the horsemen. I wonder if there's a hierarchy to that table.

Beyond that table is a group of guys trying to get those girls' attention. A few JV football players and good ol' Grant Perkins. When I accidentally meet Grant's eyes, he glares at me.

Yeah, no love lost here either, buddy.

"Harper." Luke's voice draws me back to the table.

I look at him and fight the urge to say *yes, your lordship*.

"Come here."

I glance back at Caden before I walk to stand beside Luke. I haven't done a thing for punishment unless talking to those girls counts. Fuck, that would suck.

But Luke doesn't know about that.

Luke leans back in his chair and meets my eyes with his cold ones. "Sit."

I glance at the chair next to him, but before I can make a move, he specifies, "On my lap. Facing me."

I run a nervous hand over my skirt and check to see if anyone is watching other than the four dicks at the table. Of course, a smattering of people at every table seem to be watching our little play.

"Hoping to see my panties again?" I raise an eyebrow.

"They are mine to look at. Now sit," he orders.

I take a deep breath and, holding the hem of my skirt, I straddle his lap. As I sit, it rides up, but at least that's under the table and mostly only visible to Luke and Caden. I place my hands on his shoulders. Grabbing my ass, Luke drags me into him until his hard cock rests against my pussy again.

Wetness gathers between my legs and I'm not sure my panties won't be soaking by the time he finishes with me. Will he punish me for getting his jeans wet? It would be his fault, after all.

He tips my chin up so we're face to face. "What are we going to do about this weekend?"

"Do?"

His fingers travel down my throat, sending sparks flying down to settle hot and throbbing where his cock rests. He wraps his hand around the back of my neck and holds me there.

"You're a smart girl, Harper."

"Been checking up on me?"

"Don't need to. I know you're smart." Luke must have eaten a mint, because I can smell the icy coolness on his breath and long to lean in and taste him again.

I'm broken. They've completely broken me if I want to lean in and kiss Luke Foster in the cafeteria. In front of everyone who's seen me spanked and desperate for a boyfriend.

His hand settles on my bare thigh, startling me. "What are you going to do about being grounded this weekend?"

"Um, stay at home?" I try to ignore the heat of his hand on my skin, but when it slides up my thigh, my breath catches.

"That doesn't sound like you're trying to be a team player, princess." He cocks his head to the side and his mouth is even closer to mine. I can feel his words on my lips. "You want to be a team player, don't you?"

"I didn't really sign up to be on the team in the first place, so..."

His hand slides up a little higher. My heart thumps faster. His fingertips slide along the hem of my skirt. I'm on fire sitting here. I'm surprised I haven't combusted into flames yet. My breath comes out in short bursts, and each inhale rubs my nipples against his chest.

He tsks me as his lips brush against mine.

Oh, fuck, that feels good. This would be so much easier if at least one of them didn't turn me on. I'll lose track of the conversation if he keeps this up. Which could be even more dangerous.

"Princess, we want you to play with us. You can't do that in your tower." Luke's voice turns cajoling, and fuck if I don't want to give in to him.

He toys with the hem of my skirt, which is already bunched at my hips, his fingers dangerously close to my panties. When he releases his breath against my lips, my pussy throbs. I'm worse than a bitch in heat when he's close to me.

"Luke." Eli's voice is a reprimand.

"What, Eli?" Luke's cold eyes meet mine and his fingers stop before they trail between my legs.

"Rules."

Luke slides his hand to my ass and draws me in tight against his cock. I can feel the fly of his jeans press against my clit. I suck in a breath. Without the added layer from my own jeans, it feels like there's nothing between his jeans and me.

His eyes darken and then his lips claim mine. As he nips and licks at my lips, I need to get closer. I slide my hands to the back of his neck and tangle my fingers in his silky hair. Fuck, that feels better.

I open for him, and he lays siege to my mouth while he grinds his hips against me. I can't breathe, I can't think, I can't do anything but feel this swelling inside me, thickening and twitching at his every touch. Fire burns through me, leaving me in torment. If I'm going down in flames, I'm dragging Luke with me.

The bell rings, and he pulls away. I follow his retreat and capture his mouth. His hands tighten on my hips, and I rub against him, taking the lead. My tongue slides against his. I tug on his hair as he groans into my mouth before Caden lifts me from Luke.

"You two can't play together anymore." Caden stands me up and straightens my skirt. He meets my eyes.

"You definitely need a time-out," Eli says as he rounds the table.

Luke stands behind me, his breath scorching my neck. Keeping the flames rising within me. I want to turn and find my way back to his lips and that feeling that had been rising within me. My body sways toward him.

"Nope, come on, little nympho. Time to go to our locker." Caden wraps his arm around my shoulders and drags me away. I glance over my shoulder to see Eli talking in Luke's ear.

Luke's gaze scorches me through before I look forward again.

I take a few deep breaths, and things inside me cool a little. Reason floods me. Fuck, what was that? My insides are still all weird feeling as

Caden opens his locker and switches out my books. The others don't follow us.

"Hey," Caden says softly. He brushes my cheek with his knuckle. "You okay?"

"Me? Yeah, sure, why wouldn't I be okay?" Just because I almost dry-humped Luke in the cafeteria. I'm fine. Peachy. One hundred percent golden.

Caden kisses me, and I return to the present. To the guy in front of me. To the softest kiss I've ever received.

Something inside me cracks open a little bit as I gaze up into his green eyes.

"Luke can be overwhelming when he wants something, little nympho." Caden hands me my backpack I hadn't even noticed he carried here. "It may be best for you to stay grounded this weekend and not try to sneak out like he wants you to. I can't believe I'm even saying this, but he'll cool down by Monday."

My brows furrow as I search Caden's eyes. "Why would you tell me this?"

"Because I want to play with you, Harper, and Luke might just get you into more trouble, which means longer before I can play with you." Caden kisses me again, but this time he pushes me back into the lockers and takes my mouth with his. My hands thread into his hair to hold him close. When he lifts his mouth from mine, I try to follow, lifting onto my tiptoes. He gives me a cocky smile. "I'll walk you to class."

Wrapping his arm around my shoulders, he leads me to my class before slapping me on the ass at the door. "See you later, little nympho."

I blow out a breath. These guys are going to be the death of me.

I take my seat and wait for Luke to appear. Right before the bell rings, he walks in. He gives me a heated look before he drops into his seat.

Yup, death of me.

CHAPTER 19

The Compromise

LUKE

Practice is short since we have a game tomorrow. Eli wants to talk before we turn on the webcams with Harper tonight. I know what he wants to talk about, but I have it under control. Fuck, mostly.

We all roll up to my house and go down to the rec room in the basement. Dad is out of town, so we have the house to ourselves. My rec room isn't as extravagant as Caden's, but I have a pool table.

I rack up a game as the guys get settled. Eli grabs a stick and chalks the end.

"Are we going to talk about this?" Eli asks, leaning against the wall as I grab my stick.

I line up to break. "No."

"You need to step away. We can deal with Harper for a few days." Eli's words are soft. He's not angry with me. We just know each other's limits. And for some reason, Harper is pushing mine.

"Worried I might break our toy before you get a chance to?" I break the balls, and two stripes go into the pockets. I straighten and chalk the pool stick's tip as I watch Eli. "She's just another virgin."

As if Harper could be more than that. She's the last. Yes, we own her, but that's all.

I pocket two more stripes before I miss, and Eli steps forward to work on the solids.

"She's not like the others," Caden pipes up after taking a long drag from his bottle of beer. He rests his head back on the couch and closes his eyes. "She's not as hardened."

"She hid from us for three years. She knows who we are and what we do. It's not like she's naive." I watch the solid go into the corner pocket.

Harper isn't like the rest of them, but she isn't soft or overly trusting. She's a firecracker bursting to be set free.

"She's like this untapped well of potential." Jack stands and leans against the wall to watch the game. "She wants more, but she's afraid to go after it."

Her wide brown eyes after kissing us in the field light up in my memory. Confusion and horror splashed all over her face. And desire. She wants us. She needs us to unlock the door and show her what she can become. How much pleasure she can take.

When I drew away today, she came after me. Her mouth hot on mine. Her hands digging into my hair until I wanted to spread her out on the table and take her in front of the entire student body. Show them how she's mine.

Eli misses his next shot. "She needs time. If we push her too fast, she'll balk. We'll hit a wall she won't be able to get past. For fuck's sake, the girl just had her first kiss yesterday."

She's also been starving for attention. She wants everything we can show her and fears it at the same time.

I blow across the chalked tip and line up my shot. He's right. I know he's right, but when she's in my arms I lose all sense of myself and only feel the need. The need to sink into her, claim her, mark her as mine. Prove to her she belongs to me. To us.

I squeeze my eyes shut and focus on the shot. When I open my eyes, I tap the cue ball. It clips the ball I want to go into the side pocket. It falls in easily.

"Fine. I won't push for this weekend, but I want this grounding gone soon. Especially if it's fictional." I line up my next shot. "She can come to terms with being owned by us."

"I don't think she'll ever come to terms with that," Jack says with a smirk. "I bet a hundred dollars she's hoping one of us fucks up this weekend and sleeps with someone else."

"How will you ever know?" Caden asks. "You a mind reader now? What am I thinking now, dickwad?"

"That you wish you were my type, so I'd suck your monster cock." Jack winks at Caden, who rolls his eyes.

"Actually I was hoping you and Eli would fall madly in love and leave Harper to me and Luke." Caden wiggles his eyebrows at him. "I swear I feel the tension between you two all the time. Eli's just afraid to give in to his darker side."

"Fuck off, Caden." Eli leans against the wall and turns to look at Jack. "Jack's and my love may be quiet, but we'll always have sophomore year."

"Not that shit again." I roll my eyes as I line up for the winning shot. "Eight ball in the far corner pocket."

"Just because you can't understand brotherly love doesn't mean it doesn't exist, Luke." Jack smirks.

"You tag-teamed two girls. It's not like he buried his dick in you." I take the shot and sink the eight ball. Putting my stick up on the rack, I grab a beer. "I have the Harper thing under control."

This desire to keep her all to myself will diminish. To take everything she has to offer. To feel every inch of her against me. To bury myself in her over and over again until my cum leaks out of her pussy, ass, and mouth. Until she is thoroughly, irrevocably mine.

Shit.

Yeah, maybe a weekend away from her will be a good thing. I'll find my control again. I'll get her taste out of my mouth and out of my head so when next week comes around, I'll be able to concentrate on breaking down her boundaries one by one.

"Eli, you pick up our girl tomorrow for school." I take a drink of my beer.

Eli nods. "Of course."

"Keep her in line tomorrow, Caden." I take another drink. "I'll focus on school. You all focus on her."

HARPER

Their rooms are empty. It's almost nine and they haven't even texted me. I suppose I should be thrilled and grateful they've left me alone. I finished my homework and watched some TV with Mom before coming upstairs to stare into their empty rooms.

No one told me to turn it on tonight. Jack dropped me off earlier with a kiss that stoked the fire inside me. I've got on long pajama pants and a camisole since a t-shirt simply won't do, and I don't want to change it.

I take out the historical romance I've been reading and get caught up in the story. It feels different to read the sex scenes now that I've been kissed. I keep thinking about that kiss with Luke in the cafeteria. I'm not sure why he melts my brain more so than the others. Not that the others don't make me melt, but I don't feel stupid for falling for their kisses.

A noise sounds on my computer. I look up to see Luke in his bedroom. No one else is in their rooms yet. He sits down at his desk and meets my eyes. My heart races and my stomach clenches.

"Have you had a good night?" His voice is low and there's a slight slur to his words.

I straighten on my bed and set my book down. "I did homework and watched some TV with Mom."

I want to ask what he did, but it's not my business what they do. As long as he didn't touch or fuck another girl that is. But I don't think he has.

"We drank and played pool," he offers.

I hesitate and then I ask, "Did you win?"

"Of course." He smirks. My pulse skips. "What were you reading?"

"Oh." I lift the book and set it down again. It feels weird without the others. It feels weird to talk to him like he's a human being and not just a guy trying to get into my pants. "It's a historical romance set in Regency England. Kind of like *Bridgerton*."

Eli walks into his room. "Good evening, kitten." His gaze goes to

Luke with his lips pressed together. I haven't forgotten how he and Caden stepped in at lunch. It's embarrassing that they needed to.

"Nobody has asked Harper to strip yet, right?" Caden says as he lies on his bed. "I could use something new for the spank bank."

"No one has asked her to take off anything," Luke assures him.

"That's a shame." Jack sits at his desk, and suddenly all the horsemen are here once again. Something settles inside me. It relaxes me to know they are all here with me.

Though I'm a little worried they'll want me to get naked again.

"I found something," Jack says as he clicks away on his keyboard.

I'm not going to ask. If I just sit here, they'll have no reason for me to strip. Well, besides the fact they're guys and like looking at naked women's bodies.

"What'd you find?" Eli rests against his headboard.

Jack smirks. "Our little virgin has a secret."

My brows furrow. What the hell is he talking about? I'm a really boring person unless he found some of the erotic romances I've read on my Kindle. Even then, it's not really a secret.

"Harper was on a competitive dance team until last year."

My cheeks flush with color. It was outside of school, and both Kenz and I were on the team. I needed something to pad my college applications since I'm not involved in much at school. "It's not really a secret."

Jack shares his screen, and he plays footage from our last competition. We did a jazz routine to "She's All I Wanna Be" by Tate McRae. Our outfits weren't uncommon for a dance competition, booty shorts and a tight crop top with long sleeves.

Instead of watching the video of myself, I study the guys.

Caden smirks while he watches me move to the music. Eli seems thoughtful, watching as if he's critiquing my performance. I can't see Jack, but I assume he's still grinning at what he's found. Luke watches without expression.

His gaze lifts to mine like he knows I'm watching him. A shiver races through me.

Jack changes the video to a bunch of us during dance class working on new choreography. The instructor put on Doja Cat's "Need to Know" and we were working on dancing in heels.

This time it's not me on stage with a dozen others, but me, Kenz, and Becca, a girl from the team. Becca is out front hamming it up, while Kenz and I do the routine behind her. I'm sure the guys focus on Becca. She's not from our school and older. She's hot and definitely has the moves down.

I take a deep breath as Jack ends the share. He grins at me. "Nice moves, sweetheart."

"Where did you find that last one?" I know it wasn't posted online. Hell, I don't even know if I have a copy of it anywhere. I think it was on Kenz's phone.

Jack winks. "A master never reveals his secrets."

"You gonna dance for us, little nympho?" Caden leans in toward his screen. His green eyes are hot on me.

I feel my cheeks heat. "I retired from dancing last year. It got to be too much with school, and I need all the time I can get to study this year with the AP classes I'm taking."

Please don't make me dance for you guys. I really don't want to do the whole peepshow thing, so I'm hoping I diverted their attention enough.

"But you definitely know how to move." Jack smirks. "I would dance first, but I'm afraid my skills aren't equal to yours."

"Maybe we can have a dance-off once I'm not grounded anymore." I give him a small smile and don't look at Luke. He's the one who would force the issue. He's the one who pushes a little harder than the others.

"It's a date, sweetheart." Jack winks again before he pulls up another class video where we're goofing off. By the end of class, most of us usually stripped down to shorts and sports bras because of the heat. In the video, we're working on a hip-hop routine and Kenz and I are messing around.

It feels more awkward and intimate than when they stripped me naked. At least then I knew they were watching. This is past me who hid from them and flew so far under the radar that I wouldn't be surprised if they didn't know my name.

I'm not sure where Jack found the videos or who he stole them from. I should ask Kenz what she has on her phone. It's probably too late if Jack already got it from her.

Caden is still watching, but Luke seems to be working on his homework. Eli alternates between watching and working on his own homework. I can't see Jack. I pick up my book and start reading again.

This is going to come back and bite me. Not now, but it will come up again.

HARPER'S PHONE

ME:

Do you have old dance videos on your computer or phone?

KENZ:

Yeah, why?

ME:

You might want to update your security

KENZ:

Shit

ME:

Yup

CHAPTER 20

The Tactical Retreat

LUKE

It's the middle of the night and I still can't sleep. I've gone and jerked off twice with visions of Harper's red lips and tight body in my mind. The way she moved in those videos makes me want her even more.

She's sleeping and so are the rest of them. I have her screen enlarged to watch her. Like some fucking creep. Of course, it would be worse if she wasn't aware of us watching.

She moans lightly in her sleep and turns her face toward me.

I'm obsessed.

I can't help it. She's in my dreams and constantly on my mind. It's what the guys worry about. That I'll push us too far too fast. That I'll end up hurting her because of it.

Broken toys aren't as fun.

Harper doesn't know I'm hanging by a thread. My whole life is about control. I can control this like every other aspect of my life. Like I've been taught to do.

She gasps lightly in her sleep, and I wonder what she's dreaming about. Her lips part. Fuck, I could spend days kissing those lips. Among other things.

"Luke," she moans. My name on her lips makes me hard again. Is she having a sex dream about me?

Her eyes are still closed and she shifts in the bed again. Needy little whimpers come from deep inside her. Whatever she's dreaming must be a pretty good dream. She inhales sharply and wakes up.

Her hand goes to her chest and she tries to slow her breathing.

"Bad dream, princess?" I whisper.

She gasps and her wide eyes find me in the dark.

"Luke?" Her voice is thick with sleep. For a second she seems confused, but then she shakes it off. She curls on her side to face me. "Why are you up?"

I shrug. "Couldn't sleep."

She nods, nibbling her lip while she thinks.

"What were you dreaming?" I ask. I want her to answer me. Tell me she's obsessed too.

"It's fuzzy now, but you were..." She bites her lip. "Or maybe because you said something? I don't know."

"Hmm. You should go back to sleep." I return my gaze to the ceiling.

"Can you tell me something good?" she asks. I look at her, and she gives me a self-deprecating smile. "When I used to wake in the night, Mom would tell me something good so I could go to sleep."

"There's not a lot of good in my life," I confess quietly.

"Mmm, probably more than you think. It doesn't have to be something huge. Like my something good would be I have a best friend, a good home. School is a little weird right now, but my classes are good." She yawns and snuggles down into her blankets. "You try. You have the guys."

"I have good friends who care about me. We're positioned to win the championship this year. I might get a scholarship to play ball at university." I swallow before I confess, "I have you."

Her eyes are already closed, and she's fallen back to sleep. I watch her as my eyes grow heavy. She's a good thing in my life right now.

I have her for as long as I can keep her, which means I can't break her.

HARPER

"Oh my god, I had a sex dream about Luke last night."

Kenz is sitting on my couch. Mom got called in to work tonight. It's just the two of us in the house. Kenz is leaving at ten to meet up with Brandon later. So tonight I'm on my own.

"What happened?" Kenz grabs a slice of cheese pizza and takes a huge bite. We already discussed Jack's dick size in as much detail as I could give Kenz while blushing furiously the entire time.

"Last night, Jack found a bunch of old videos of us dancing at competition and practice. He played them."

Kenz's eyebrows shoot up. "For the horsemen?"

I nod. "On webcam."

"Fuck, that's brilliant. I bet they were drooling by the end. We always looked good on stage." Kenz takes another huge bite of pizza. "What's that have to do with your sex dream?"

"I dreamt I was basically giving Luke a lap dance, and then he pressed me down into the bed while he kissed me. Then I woke up." I might have left out the part where his hard cock was grinding against my pussy, keying me up. I blush, remembering waking up aroused and being confused why he was there on the computer and not with me in my bed to finish what he started.

"Nice, but that's not a sex dream." Kenz takes a drink of soda and lets out a small belch.

"Okay, it was a sexy dream. If I hadn't woken up, I'm pretty sure it would have gone a lot further." I cave easily. She's right though. No actual penetration happened in the dream, but I wanted it. I wanted Luke.

Fuck, they're getting to me.

The movie plays in the background. We've both seen it dozens of times. I can't focus on it though. This whole day was kind of weird.

Luke seemed to be avoiding me for lack of a better term. He was there, and he even briefly kissed me in the morning, but the other guys definitely picked up his slack. Maybe seeing me dance wound them up because every class transition Jack, Eli, or Caden backed me up against a locker and kissed me thoroughly. Mind-numbingly breathless.

Maybe they were just making up for the years I went without.

My day was spent in anticipation of every break, every kiss.

I sat on Caden's lap during lunch, but I couldn't figure out what was going on with Luke. He ignored me. Maybe he was preparing for the game tonight. After all, he's the quarterback. I have no idea what his pregame ritual looks like.

The school we play is a half hour bus ride away, so they won't get home until late. The horsemen excused me from the webcam tonight. I'm sure I hid my disappointment well enough. Most likely they'll go to a party anyway, and I'd just see empty rooms. My punishment from the horsemen for being grounded is being grounded.

"Are you sure you don't want to stay the night?" I ask Kenz as I eat some pizza. I'm not crazy about staying by myself in the house when Mom works thirds.

She grimaces. "I would, but Brandon plans to sneak in later."

"Ah, yes, you have an actual boyfriend instead of four dicks who want to get in your pants." I laugh lightly, but I still don't know what to do to stop the guys from pushing me further. The kissing is...

I want to say nice, but the kisses are so far from nice. My whole being feels inflamed when one of them kisses me.

"Did you honestly tell Penny and her friends to go for it with the guys this weekend?"

It's my turn to grimace. "It seemed like a good idea at the time."

During art, Penny initiated a conversation again, and I assured her the guys were free to do what they wanted with who they wanted. I just hope she doesn't tell the guys I told her that because there will be spanking if she does. A little shiver goes through me.

Maybe I secretly want her to spill, so they have an excuse to punish me.

Yup, my brain is fucked up.

"If they touch or fuck another girl, it's my out clause." I shrug like the thought of them with another girl doesn't dig at something growing inside me. My stomach turns a little. "Then they don't own me and can't try to devirginize me."

"Well, they can still try, but you won't have to bow to their demands as easily as you do because they own you." Kenz collapses into the couch. "You know, I can barely keep up with Brandon. I can't even imagine having four horny guys after me."

"Here's hoping they decide to fuck someone else." I force a smile to my lips as a rock settles in my stomach. I mean, it would definitely be better for me if they found someone else to fuck, but I'll miss them. "It was kind of nice to be on the map for once though."

"Girl, you are squarely on the map. If those guys give up the chase, I'm pretty sure you'll find yourself under pursuit by at least four or five other dudes who want to claim you." Kenz smiles and shoves my shoulder. "You clean up good, and the boys have noticed."

"I would have preferred them to notice before the guys claimed me. Things would have been easier. Just one dick to hold off." I sink into the movie again, preferring an imaginary world over this one. This world is way too confusing.

I both want and don't want the guys in my life. Thinking of them breaking our deal makes me both happy and sad. Maybe I should ask Mom for a mental health check.

When the movie ends, Kenz gives me a hug. "Here's hoping your guys fuck around on you this weekend."

"Yeah," I say half-heartedly. Didn't Luke say it's been two months since he last fucked someone? That seems like a long time.

There are parties I won't be at. Not that I have ever attended a party, but maybe after this weekend, I can go. I'll have to find a boyfriend if the guys fuck up, because they won't quit until I do.

"Hey." Kenz pulls her shoes on and touches my arm. "Maybe they won't fuck around. They seem like guys of their word."

"I don't know what to think anymore." I shake my head and smile wearily at her. "Part of me wants to be free and part of me wants to keep kissing them and having their attention."

"They're hot as hell, and I can't say I blame you, to be honest. If it were me, I'm not sure I would last a week before spreading 'em." Laughing, Kenz opens the door. "I'll see you soon. Night."

"Night." I lock the doors and double check everything is off. I've never liked when Mom works the night shift, but I've been through it enough times to know I just need to go to sleep and tomorrow I'll wake up. Just like every other night.

I pull on a sleep shirt and shorts and crawl into bed. My laptop is closed, and I know they aren't home so there's no reason to open it. I roll over on my back and stare at the ceiling.

I refuse to open my laptop and be a creeper in their empty rooms. But deep inside, I know I miss seeing them before I go to sleep.

CHAPTER 21

The Ambush

HARPER

I'm still not tired though. Sitting up in bed, I grab my phone and pull up my messages from the girls in a group chat.

> PENNY:
>
> Wish you were here

> NAT:
>
> This is Nat. The guys are on fire tonight

> IZZY:
>
> Hey, this is Izzy. The other team is getting their asses handed to them

Penny is the only one who doesn't use her name every time she texts. I programmed all their names in earlier in the week, but I guess they just assume I didn't.

> VICKY:
>
> Vicky here. The other team has decided to play tackle the quarterback. Luke is getting hit a lot

PENNY:

> Everyone is holding their breath waiting for
> Luke to get up after a brutal tackle

My heart wrenches and I straighten. That's the last text. Why is that the last text? I glance at the time. The game should be over by now.

ME:

> What happened?

I lift the screen on my laptop and turn on the webcam app. Their rooms are empty. Just like I knew they'd be.

NAT:

> We won!

Oh, for fuck's sake. Yay, we won, but they don't say what happened to Luke. He must be okay, or they would have said something. Maybe he just had the wind knocked out of him. Maybe something is broken. Maybe he's at the hospital.

Didn't the guys say something about Luke's dad being out of town? What if he's all alone in the hospital?

VICKY:

> Party at Jason's tonight

I pull up the horsemen group chat. I don't have to ask about Luke specifically. I can just ask how the game went.

ME:

> How did the game go?

I stand and pace to the bathroom and back. I mean, obviously Luke's okay. They wouldn't be having a party at Jason's, whoever that is, if he wasn't. The guys probably won't be home until late tonight.

I glance at their empty rooms on the screen. Maybe Kenz knows something. I send her a quick text to ask if she knows what happened at the game.

KENZ:

Haven't heard anything. What does your
posse of wannabees have to say?

ME:

Penny texted saying Luke was down, but
then they said we won and there's a party
later

KENZ:

One less horseman for you *smiley face
emoji*

No. Well, yes, but no, I don't want that. I feel like I'm cut off from
everything and can't even ask if Luke's okay because I might show my
hand. That maybe I care a little about him. About all of them.

ME:

Do you know if the guys are on the way
back?

KENZ:

Brandon said he'd be here in thirty

You aren't really worried. Are you?

Luke is Death. No one takes down Death

ME:

Just curious

I drop my phone on my bed before I do something stupid like call
Luke. I can just imagine his gloating smile. Ugh!

A glass of water will help. I head down the stairs without turning on
the light. Midway down the stairs, loud knocks at the doors burst into
the silence. My feet stop moving. My heart clogs my throat. I freeze as
the escalating noise seems to surround me.

The knocks continue pounding like the hounds of hell want in.
Occasionally, a knob will rattle like someone is trying the locks. I back
slowly up the steps, one step at a time, to get to my phone and away
from the doors.

Then the noise stops abruptly. I hold my breath.

Clenching the handrail, I pause to listen over the pounding of my heart. Did they get in? With all the noise, would I have heard a door opening? The only sound now is the emptiness of night. I keep my eyes trained on the darkness of the lower level for any movement as I creep to the upstairs hallway.

I turn and bolt into my room. Lock the door and move anything I can in front of it. When it feels like I have enough blocking the door, I go to my bed and pick up my phone to call Mom. My hands shake.

Her phone rings and rings.

"Come on, come on," I whisper, my gaze fixed on the door. I search my room for a weapon, but the only thing that comes close is a piñata stick with ribbons on it from my tenth birthday party. I grab it and the weight of it in my hand feels good.

No sounds come from the other side of my door, but my pulse is chaotic and I can't stop shaking. The call goes to voicemail.

"Mom, call me when you get this."

I look at my phone and try to think. Maybe it was the horsemen playing a trick. Maybe it was some neighborhood kids, bored on a Friday night.

Okay, reason, come on, Harper, think. The guys just finished a game a half hour away. They aren't pounding on your doors. If they wanted in, they would come in.

The kids messing around scenario is more likely. My phone buzzes and I shriek a little.

I take a breath and answer my phone. "Mom?"

"Hey, what's happening?"

"Someone knocked on the doors for like five minutes straight. It's quiet now, but I'm up in my room." I don't tell her I'm scared shitless.

"I'll call the neighbor to check it out. Okay? Are you safe?"

I nod and realize she can't see me. I need to talk. "Yeah, that sounds good. Can you have them text when they finish?"

"Are you okay, sweetie?" Mom's voice is doing a lot to calm me.

"Yeah, just freaked out. Nothing like being all alone in the middle of a scene from a horror movie." I force a laugh that I know comes out sounding wrong. I'm trying to be mature, but I really want my mom here.

"I'd come home if I could." Mom covers the speaker and says something to someone else. "I'll be there in the morning. I'm going to call Francis and Bob right now."

"Love you, Mom." I know she has to work. It's completely unreasonable of me to want her here. I'm practically an adult, but I still want her to be here with me.

"Love you too, kid."

I grip my phone in one hand, and the other holds the piñata stick upright as I watch my door. The phone buzzes a second later.

> **KENZ:**
>
> Sorry to break it to you, but Luke just had the wind knocked out of him

> **ME:**
>
> Someone just pounded on my doors and I'm freaking out

> **KENZ:**
>
> *shock face emoji* Need me to come over?

> **ME:**
>
> No. Neighbors should be investigating

> **KENZ:**
>
> That's messed up. You sure you don't want me to come over?

I consider it for a hot minute. She's not asking just to be polite. She'd be over in a heartbeat if I asked, but I know she's expecting Brandon. Besides, I'm a big girl who will be fine after Bob and Francis make sure zombies aren't gathering around my property.

> **ME:**
>
> No. You keep that man of yours satisfied

> **KENZ:**
>
> You know it

No other texts have come in. Guess the guys don't check their phones, or I'm low priority since they know exactly where I am and what I'm up to. My phone buzzes.

UNKNOWN NUMBER:

All clear. –Bob & Fran. You can come down
and we'll check out the house.

I move the stuff from in front of my door and turn on the lights to head downstairs. With my piñata stick held high, I move slowly and check around every corner, turning on every light along the way. Finally, I make it to the back door where Bob and Fran wait.

There are still no noises of anyone in the house. That doesn't mean someone isn't hiding somewhere though. I open the back door. Bob has a bat in his hands while Fran holds her phone up.

"You okay, Harper?" Fran asks, stepping in, and she reaches out to grab my bare arm. I realize I'm still in my sleep shorts and sleep shirt without a bra. Bob moves past me into the house and starts going room by room.

Putting my piñata stick down, I grab a sweatshirt from the rack next to the door and shrug it on. Zipping it up, I say, "I'm okay. Just a little freaked out."

"We didn't find anything or anyone outside. Probably just bored teens." She shakes her head of curly red hair. It's tucked up in a handkerchief, almost in a Lucille Ball hairstyle. "Your mom wanted you to text her when we give the all clear."

I nod. "Thank you for coming over."

"Anytime. We were just heading to bed when your mom caught us. We know how she worries when she works." Fran pats my shoulder as I wrap my arms around my middle. "You're always welcome to use our guest bedroom."

I should be used to night shifts, but it's been a while since Mom has had to work them. It never gets easier. I've stayed at Bob and Fran's before. Their house has a weird smell and creepy dolls in the guest bedroom. "No, I'm good here."

As Bob walks upstairs, he calls out, "So far, so good."

"Did you want something to drink? I could make you a tea." Fran moves toward the kitchen island and looks at the cabinets.

"No. Thank you. I was heading to bed myself." Taking a deep breath, I say, "I'll be good."

I clutch my phone. My knuckles are white. I'm not sure if the guys will actually try to reach out tonight, given how late it is, but I didn't like the feeling of not being able to contact someone.

Bob comes down the stairs. "All clear. The doors are still locked and did their jobs. You just lock up after we leave and you'll be fine through the night. I'll keep an eye out for a while, but I doubt whoever it was will come back. I don't think we need to call the police."

"Thank you again for coming over." I smile at them as best I can.

"You need anything, you call us or just come over. Bob's a light sleeper, so he'll hear if you come knocking." Fran touches my arm one more time before Bob heads out the door.

He turns. "Make sure you lock it up tight."

I smile and nod. "I will."

"Sleep tight." Fran waves as they step off the porch.

I lock the door and double check the front door is locked too. I text my mom the all clear and pick up my piñata stick.

I honestly don't think I'm going to sleep tonight. With all the lights still on, I grab some chocolate ice cream from the fridge. In the living room, I settle on the couch and queue up a bunch of *Friends* episodes.

CHAPTER 22

The Calm Before The Storm

HARPER

Something wakes me. I sit up, confused. All the lights are on, and I'm on the couch. The TV is still working its way through season three of *Friends*. I pick up my phone from where it fell to the floor. Maybe that's what woke me.

I glance around, but nothing is out of place. I hold my phone above my face as I lie back down on the couch. More messages have come through. Pictures on the girls' group chat.

PENNY:

OMG you're missing the best party. Wish you were here

Nice way to treat a new friend who's grounded. Not that I'm really grounded, but she doesn't know that.

DEATH (LUKE):

Where r u?

I scrunch up my face at that. Home. Where does he think I am? I look at the time stamp and it's from around fifteen minutes ago. I'm tired and don't want to type anything that might get me punished, so I ignore his text, hoping he'll assume I'm asleep.

I shrug out of the sweatshirt and leave it with the blanket on the couch. Yawning, I turn off the TV. I grab my trusty piñata stick because I'm going to sleep with this bad boy all night, even if it is covered in purple and pink ribbons.

It's really stupid late now, and I'm pretty sure I can just crawl into bed and go back to sleep.

Leaving the kitchen light on, I turn out the others. No more knocks on the doors, and I'm sure Bob has long since gone to bed. The guys are probably out partying. Maybe Luke even texted because he's drunk and wondering why I'm not at his beck and call.

I snort laugh a little on the way up the stairs. My laptop is open in my room, and all the horsemen's rooms are still empty. Not surprising. I feel a pinch in my gut, as I can't help thinking about them getting laid tonight.

How would I even know unless someone else brags about it? I close my laptop, angry that they're probably partying hard somewhere and someone else is likely getting them off. I rub at the ache in my chest. Not that I want to get them off, but they made a promise.

I climb onto my bed and pull the covers over me. What dicks! They couldn't even keep it in their pants for less than a week. Maybe Kenz is right and I'll have a boyfriend by the end of next week. He'll protect and care for me.

The horsemen will have to find someone else to torment for the year. I sigh and close my eyes. At least my first kisses were really hot kisses.

I must have dozed off for a few minutes because suddenly the bed dips next to me. For a second, I think my cat is there and then I remember Mr. Snuggles died last year.

My heart thumps hard in my chest. My piñata stick falls, clattering on the floor next to me. The sound startles me into action. I jolt like I'm going to leap out of bed and run for the door when a hand closes over my mouth. I get out maybe half a scream.

"Harper, it's me." Luke's harsh whisper cuts through the panic. I grab at his hand covering my mouth. He removes it and I inhale.

"I lost a year off my life, asshole. What the fuck are you doing in my bedroom?" I spin on the bed to face him in the shadows of the dark. I shove at his shoulder, still more freaked out than worried.

He groans in pain, and everything in me chills out.

"Are you hurt?" I reach out to where I shoved, but his fingers wrap around mine to keep me from touching it again.

"The Tigers decided they didn't like me very much." Luke doesn't release my hand but holds it on the bed between us. "Where were you? Your camera was on, but you weren't here."

"I fell asleep downstairs after some kids messed around outside my house and freaked me out." I sit against the headboard of my bed. "The neighbors checked out the place, but I still couldn't calm down."

"Where's your mom?"

"She got called in." Somehow, in the darkness, it's okay to let Luke know we're here alone in my bedroom, completely unsupervised. My brain is slow to grasp things when I first wake up, but now I'm realizing all these things.

I'm in my sleep shorts and a sleep shirt, while Luke Foster sits next to me on the edge of my bed in jeans and a t-shirt. The room has a little light thanks to the streetlight that cuts through my curtains, but otherwise we're bathed in darkness.

Awareness slices through me. The air suddenly feels thicker, and his hand against mine is sending warmth and tingles up my arm. I should pull it away, but it's nice to have someone here. The creepiest thing about the noises was being all alone. No one here to help me.

"Where are the others?" I need to say something to unravel this tension welling inside me.

"Jason's party." Luke sighs. "I should probably go."

His hand starts to slip from mine, but I grab it. "No."

What the fuck am I doing? He stops moving and waits for me. I don't want him to leave. I drop my gaze to our hands.

"I—fuck it. I'm scared and don't want to be alone. I'm tired and want to sleep, but every little noise freaks me out. My mom won't be home for hours and I'm here alone." I keep my head down as I admit this to him, of all people.

I hate admitting any weakness. He could turn around and use it to torment me.

He doesn't say anything, but he doesn't move away either.

"Would you..." I take a deep breath. I can't believe I'm saying this. "Would you mind staying with me?"

He tips my chin until our faces are aligned, even if I can't make out his eyes in the dark. "I can stay."

My bed is a queen, so we won't even have to touch. I mean, he could sleep on the floor, but that seems pretty petty after I begged him to stay. "Thank you."

Luke nods and leans down to take off his shoes. I try to control my breathing as he stands and removes his shirt. His jeans come off next. In the darkness, I can just make out his form—not the details, but I've seen him this stripped down before.

Just never in the same room as me.

Scooting down in the bed, I move over to the side so he can slip in. I'm a ball of nervous energy as he lies down beside me. Both of us stare up at the ceiling. I realize I'm holding my breath and release it.

This is weird. Maybe it's too weird. Maybe I should suggest we go downstairs and watch a movie. We can just stay up all night and I'll sleep tomorrow.

"Stop worrying, princess. I won't maul you in your sleep." Luke's deep voice flows over me. "Boundaries."

I need to talk. I need to get all the energy out. "What were the guys doing at the party?"

"Fucking as many girls as possible." His voice carries no inflection.

Not believing him, I roll onto my side to face him. "Well, then this whole ownership thing is over."

He keeps his gaze on the ceiling. "That would mean fewer boundaries."

"Good for you. Bad for me." The light from the window gives me just a hint of his features. I swear I see a flicker of a smile on his lips, but I don't want to turn on the light. It would ruin the illusion that this is okay and safe. Being in bed with Luke Foster.

"Terrible for you." His hands go behind his head. His arms are sculpted muscles. My fingertips itch with the need to check to see how they feel. His warm skin, the solid strength beneath.

"Was it a good game?" I switch the topic before my mind wonders what kind of terrible things Luke would do to me. Like hold me down and kiss the hell out of me. Spank me for the hell of it. Pretty much anything with a little hell.

I bite my lip. My breath catches. No one is here to stop us from going too far. To pull us away if the passion takes over.

"They're normally an easy team, but they have some good defensive tackles this year." Luke seems to be ignoring the undercurrent of tension.

I inhale. "I heard you got hurt?"

His head swivels my way. "Worried about me, princess?"

"Who could hurt Death," I reply breathily.

"They definitely tried." Luke exhales and his minty breath teases my nose.

Something clicks in my brain.

"Wait. How did you get in if I have the place locked up tight?" Panic builds inside me. If Luke could get in, those people from earlier could too. They tried the handles. I start to sit up, but his hand holds my shoulder down.

"It's still a secret, but no one else can get in how we do." His hand is hot and heavy on my skin. I can feel the trickle of desire burning brighter from just that touch. Instead of easing me, it makes me more anxious.

"Somehow, that's not reassuring," I grumble.

"I thought you were tired." He shifts a little in the bed, but I try not to pay attention to the fact he's only wearing his boxers and is in bed with me. Alone. In my house. Alone. He shifts again, probably trying to get more comfortable.

"I was tired. I am tired. You startled the sleep out of me, I guess." I shrug. "Maybe we can go downstairs and watch a movie? I'm sure a nice zombie film or two will help me relax."

"Right, while we're at it, let's put on some good old-fashioned slasher flicks. That way, you'll never sleep again." Luke's voice is deep. "Maybe we can just find a show on serial killers to help lull you into dreamland."

"Maybe not." My voice has risen in pitch. "But maybe we could walk around the house to make sure everything is still locked up?"

"Whatever you need, princess." He throws the covers back and grabs his jeans to pull on. His hair flops over his eyes as he looks down at me. "You coming?"

Fuck. Yeah, maybe I'll be able to sleep after a stroll around the house. I push the covers off and stand. He holds his hand out to me and I take it.

Opening the door to the hallway, he turns on the light. Gripping his hand tight, I follow closely behind him as he opens doors and turns on lights. Logically, I know there isn't anyone else in the house, but earlier spooked me. Enough that I'm walking closer and closer to Luke.

He leads me downstairs. We open every door and walk through every room. After he checks the back door, he turns and grabs my hips, lifting me onto the island. He steps between my legs and tips my face up to his.

"All good, princess?" His hands trail up my bare thighs to rest on my ass and drag me in against him. "No more worrying about the boogeyman?"

My breath quickens as I search his light blue eyes. The hard press of his cock between my thighs stirs the desire these boys have worked relentlessly to awaken. I grip his bare shoulders, but I'm not sure if I intend to push him away or pull him closer.

This right here is dangerous. Luke is dangerous. Us being alone is dangerous.

Earlier, I feared something getting in, but this danger I've asked to stay with me. I've let him in willingly and now I have to pay the price. The cost might be worth it though.

My gaze drifts over his naked chest. A huge bruise is forming under one of my hands.

"Do you need some ice?" My fingers skate over it, feeling how it must ache. I swallow and lift my gaze to his again. "Does it hurt?"

"All the time, princess." His lips capture mine and he drags me into him.

This time last week, this kiss would have shocked me to my core. But now, after kissing four guys for most of a week, I just want more.

I tangle my hands in Luke's silky hair as he deepens the kiss, sliding his tongue alongside mine and building that winding tension inside me. He grinds his cock against my pussy, and I moan at the aching need.

He rests his forehead against mine. Our breathing is chaotic as his fingers clench into my ass almost painfully. When I tug on his hair, he meets my gaze.

"Why did you avoid me today?" The words slip out before I can think them through. My eyes widen. I just questioned a horseman. Yes, I've been wondering, but I had no intention of actually asking him that. And now I'm trapped, waiting for his answer.

Maybe I can backtrack a little.

"If it was because of the game, I totally understand, but the others didn't feel compelled to avoid me. Then again, they aren't the quarterback, and it must take a lot of concentration to do what you do out there on the field. And you're very good at what you do."

He touches his lips to mine, stopping my babbling. This isn't a normal kiss for us, but maybe it's normal for most people. He threads his hands into my hair. Instead of taking, his mouth glides against mine. He brushes his tongue along my lower lip, and I gasp, parting my lips for him as tingles of awareness race through me. This kiss is gentle and exploring and so damn dangerous. This is the type of kiss that could destroy me.

When I slide my fingers into his silky hair, he tips my head back and deepens the kiss. His lips are soft as he moves them over mine, continuing to taste me. My heart skips a beat as I lose myself in his kiss. It's not a battle right now. He kisses me like I mean something to him, like I'm not just another conquest.

He eases his lips away from mine and for a moment we share our breaths as we hold each other's heads close. My insides twist at the unfamiliar feeling growing inside me. They've made me feel desire and passion, but this longing, this need to hold Luke, to be close to him, is like nothing I've felt before. It's not a fire burning through me, but a low flame of something new. Something I'm not ready to look at too closely. After a moment, he steps back and holds his hands out to me. "Come on."

I search his eyes, trying to figure out what that kiss means.

Not getting anything from him, I take his hands, and he helps me down. Keeping hold of one of my hands, he leads me back through my house up to my room. My heartbeat eases as he only holds my hand. Once in my room, he shuts the door, locks it, and gestures to the bed as he turns off the light.

I climb in. Will he kiss me again? I want him to. I want to drown in the taste of him. He walks around the bed to the other side and takes his jeans off before he climbs in. His arms drag me to the middle, and his warm front nestles against my back.

"Go to sleep, princess."

He never answered my question, but now he's spooning me. When he doesn't move to do anything else but hold me, I breathe out the worry. He feels so safe and warm, like nothing bad can happen to me here in his arms. My eyes grow heavy and before I know it, I'm out.

CHAPTER 23

The Stand Down

HARPER

"Harper?" My mom's voice follows a knock on my door.

I startle awake, aware of Luke's heavy arm draped around my waist and my mom at my bedroom door. Which is thankfully locked.

"Sleeping," I call out in a scratchy voice. Luke's arm tightens around me, drawing me back into his warmth. Butterflies lift off in my stomach as he holds me against him.

"You okay after last night?" Mom's voice comes through the door.

It takes my mind a second to catch up. The prank, not Luke.

"Yeah, Bob and Fran went through the house, and I stayed up watching some TV before going to bed. Stayed up way too late," I call out. "Hoping to get more sleep now."

Luke's nose rubs the back of my neck, making tingles light beneath my skin. I want to tell him to stop, but I also want him to continue.

"Okay, I just wanted to check on you. I'm going to bed. If you need anything or want to talk, just wake me up. Love you."

"Love you too." I breathe a sigh of relief as her footsteps retreat from my door.

Luke pushes his hips against my ass, and I can feel his hardness. Heat flushes through my system, and I'm not sure all of it is from embarrassment.

I just slept with Luke Foster.

Luke's lips brush against the back of my neck as he says, "Need more sleep."

"Agreed." I snuggle into him and close my eyes again. I can deal with the fact Luke slept over later.

"If you keep rubbing your ass into my cock, we'll be doing a lot more than sleeping."

Ah, there's my cranky Death. I smile. "Boundaries. Unless someone has gone and fucked things up. Then I would have to kindly ask you to leave my room. But since we don't know if they fucked up, be quiet and get more sleep. It's only six in the morning."

"When are you going to let us fuck you, princess?" He tightens his arm around my waist. My panties dampen at his dark voice, his warm breath against my ear, and the hot press of his body.

"Probably never," I admit. "After all, it's my virginity. I should be able to give it to whoever I want."

"You want us." His tone is knowing. He's not wrong either. I do want them, but it's still this battle of wills and I don't want to be the one to cave.

"Maybe when you guys beg for it, I'll consider."

His chuckle is dark. "We'll see who begs first. Sleep now, princess."

If this turns into a game of sex chicken, I'm not only outmanned but also outgunned. These guys have much more experience than I do. I'm not sure if holding out will be good for me or end up horrible for me. They're being patient with me now, but how long will that last?

I must have dozed off. When I wake next, I'm face to face with a sleeping Luke. Sunlight pours in through my windows. Even though the guys leave their webcams on at night, there is nothing quite like having a living being in front of you completely asleep.

His features are relaxed and his lips part as he breathes slowly. I want to reach out and feel how soft they are, to brush the lock of hair that's fallen over his eye back. It's hard to believe he's here in my bed with me. That we only kissed last night, but he held me through the night.

Especially after those kisses on the football field and in the cafeteria. If we'd been alone then, things would have escalated quickly. Maybe one of us would have stopped, but maybe not. Last night he only briefly kissed me like that before pulling away.

I'm not going to think about that other kiss.

He's sleeping on his non-injured shoulder. The bruising is a lot more visible now than last night. Deep purple with a tinge of green. Fortunately it's his left shoulder and not his throwing arm.

Kenz has slept on my bed with me before, but we usually keep to our sides. Last night, Luke dragged me to the middle of the bed and that's where we stayed. Him holding me and keeping me safe.

My fingers itch with the urge to reach out and trace his features. To try to memorize the slope of his nose, the curve of his lips, the hard line of his brow, the fuzz of new growth on his chin.

I'm theirs. It's hard to come to terms with it, but deep inside I think I always knew it would come to this. I'm still not going to lie down and give up, but my will to fight is definitely shaken.

Luke could have taken advantage of me. He could have moved his so-called boundaries, but he didn't. Yes, he kissed me, but no more than he usually does. And that last kiss...I don't even know what to think of that kiss. Caden kissed me softly yesterday, but from Luke, it's a much bigger deal. He doesn't do nice and soft.

When he abruptly stretches and reaches for me, I can't help the butterflies that burst within me as he drags me into his chest. My ear rests against his beating heart. After a moment of awkwardness, I let my arm drape over his waist.

"Sleepovers should be part of the deal, princess."

I smile at his sleepy voice. "Not sure my mom would agree. Good thing someone thought to lock the door last night."

"You're welcome," he mumbles.

He rubs his scratchy chin against my head while keeping me against him. I try to pry myself away, but not very hard. Instead, I end up pressed tighter to him.

"Pretty sure that would have added a month to my grounding." And be for real this time. Sure, nothing happened between us, but Mom doesn't know that, and me swearing nothing happened probably would have fallen on deaf ears. Having a guy like Luke in my bedroom, in my bed, in his underwear at night alone is a huge no-no. She doesn't even need to tell me that.

"We can't have that happen." His arms hold me against him, but I feel them start to loosen a little. I'm cocooned in the bed with him. His heat engulfs me, warming me inside and out.

Is he falling back to sleep? I don't even know what time it is or how long we slept. I'm pretty sure it was after midnight when Luke came over. Maybe one or later.

Fuck it. It's Saturday. I snuggle into him and let his sultry cologne fill my nose. His skin is warm against my cheek and hands.

I imagine at some point they'll all want to sleep with me. Caden seems like a cuddler. Jack too. I wouldn't have pegged Luke for a cuddler and definitely don't think Eli is one, but who knows? Maybe I'll find out.

Luke's phone buzzes. He breathes out into my hair before letting out a soft, "Fuck."

For a second, it seems like he's going to ignore it, but then he rolls onto his back and reaches over to the nightstand. I squeak a little as he drags me with him, so my head is still on his chest but now my leg rests across his. His thigh between my legs. When I try to shift, he gives me a heated look that stills me.

He pulls up his texts.

"Anyone slip and fall into anyone's vagina last night?" I prop my chin on my hand on his chest to look up at him.

"You better hope not because if they did, then you're all mine, princess." His blue eyes scorch me when he glances my way. His blond hair is a mess, and it makes him seem more...human.

I force myself not to squirm from the possessiveness in his voice. It sends shivers down my spine. I remind him and myself, "Still own myself."

"Keep telling yourself that." Luke clicks on his phone for a few seconds. "Guys are going to grab breakfast before practice today. Is breakfast off limits for grounded people?"

He cocks an eyebrow.

"I do like breakfast." I bite my lip as I consider the consequences.

Sure, I can go with him to breakfast. Mom really won't care, but if I act like my grounding is lenient, what else will they want me to do?

"You do have to eat." His hand strokes up and down my back, sending tiny sparks through me.

"I did have a pretty tough night. Worst prank ever, followed by waking up to a creeper on my bed." I arch my eyebrow.

"A creeper you asked to stay the night." He clicks something on his phone and sets it aside. His fingers trail down the side of my face, and tingles spread through me. "What's it going to be, princess? Breakfast or not?"

<hr>

CADEN

When Luke shows up to breakfast in the same clothes as last night with Harper in tow, I'm not the only one who has questions. He disappeared from the party early. When I got home, I checked to see if Harper was on. Her camera wasn't active. We hadn't asked her to, so I didn't expect her to be there, but Luke wasn't in his room either.

Harper wears flared, low-slung jeans that cup her ass and a green cropped halter top that shows off her tits. Her long hair is loose around her shoulders and she doesn't have on any makeup that I can tell. She's fucking hot as hell.

I exchange a look with Jack and Eli. We may not get to the bottom of this until Harper leaves. Then we can interrogate Luke and figure out what happened last night.

"Good morning, cavemen. How was the party last night?" Harper asks as she sits and takes a menu.

"Thought you were grounded." Not that I don't want her here, but we have to establish what grounding is and isn't in her world. Especially if it's fake.

"Mom worked last night. She wasn't up to ask her if I could or couldn't. I figure breakfast out is a kind of gray area." Harper shrugs but the tips of her ears are tinged red. "That and I'm hungry."

She hides behind the menu. How long are we going to allow her to be grounded? Especially if Luke is chill again.

Eli sets his menu down. "If coming out to breakfast gets you more time, you will be punished."

"It won't." Harper glances at Eli over the menu. "Sooo...who got laid last night?"

"The party was good. You were missed." Eli doesn't look at her and doesn't see her pout since he didn't answer her question.

"If you say yourself, we'll need to talk." I straighten as I look at Harper before throwing a glare at Luke.

"I definitely did not get laid last night." Harper sets her menu down and purses her lips. "I got scared out of my wits, but definitely no penetration happened. Happy?"

"Did you scare Harper?" My eyes lock with Luke's. Cause that's not going to fly either.

He rolls his eyes before meeting mine. "No."

I narrow my eyes. He better not be lying.

"What scared you?" Jack asks.

"Some kids decided to beat on my doors last night for five minutes. The neighbors checked it out for me, but by then, whoever did it was long gone." She gives a shiver, and not one of the good kind.

"This ever happen before?" I ask. My brain spins at the possibilities, but I need a lot more information.

Her wide brown eyes meet mine. "No. I'm hoping it was a coincidence that Mom was working last night and not the reason for it. Mom rarely works night shifts though."

The waitress stops by and we all order. My mind keeps working around the "prank." If it even was a prank. It's never happened before, but she's never been claimed by the horsemen before either. That's the coincidence I can't get over.

If someone's targeting my girl, they better hope they're bigger or faster than me because they will regret it.

The server leaves us and I home in on Harper again.

Harper breathes out and says, "Luke stopped by last night, and I asked him to stay because I was freaking out, but nothing happened besides sleep. That's pretty much everything."

Huh. Luke promised us he'd maintain distance over the weekend after the lunch incident. All our eyes go to Luke.

"I left the party and went home. Harper's camera was on, but she wasn't in her room. I texted her and didn't hear back, so I went to check on her." Luke leans back and meets all our eyes. "When I realized she was safe, I tried to leave."

"Her webcam wasn't on when I got home." I can't help putting that out there.

Harper wads up a straw wrapper. "I closed it when I came upstairs after falling asleep downstairs. None of you were there by then, and it was a little depressing staring into your empty rooms, knowing you were out partying. So I shut it and tried to go to sleep. That's when Luke showed up."

Harper breathes out and looks each of us in the eye with determination.

"I'm not sure why this is important. We didn't fool around or have sex. We slept. I was scared and alone and he was there. End of story. No boundaries were moved and I'm just as you left me on Friday." She crosses her arms. "I hope I can say the same about all of you."

Her eyebrow cocks up, and she looks sexy as hell, staring us all down like we did something wrong.

"You honestly think we got laid last night?" Jack asks. "Not that it couldn't have happened. I mean, this Penny chick was all sorts of persistent, but we do have standards. Otherwise our numbers would be much higher, sweetheart."

Her cheeks flush red. "It's not like I don't have reasons to believe you would want sex this weekend."

"You can make us out to be man whores all you want, kitten." Eli leans forward with his elbows on the table. "But the reality is we don't spread ourselves around. We can wait for you to be ready."

Harper crosses her legs and swings her foot a little, apparently still not satisfied with that answer.

"If you'd left your webcam on, you would have seen us all come home alone around two a.m." I stretch back in my chair. "We had a tough game, trying to protect Luke's fragile ass. We celebrated with a few beers and a game of beer pong with the guys. Then we went to sleep."

"We're not letting you slip by on a technicality, kitten." Eli's gaze takes all of her in. "You won't get away from us that easily."

Her mouth opens and shuts, but she doesn't add anything.

"Does your mom work tonight?" I lean my elbows on the table.

"She shouldn't. She went in because someone called out last night." Harper pauses as the server stops with our food. It takes the poor woman two trips to load up our table.

"If she does, text us. We'll set up a schedule to watch outside, but we don't want to seem like stalkers if your mom is home." I cut up my pancakes.

"You don't have to do that. Mom should be home. Besides, you guys probably have stuff to do tonight." Harper keeps her eyes on her plate as she eats her eggs.

"Even if we have *stuff*, you take priority if someone is messing with you." I know I speak for all the horsemen when I say this. "We protect what's ours."

"It was just some kids playing around." She meets my eyes and gives me a small smile. "But thank you."

I'm not going to back off this, even though I give her a nod. The four of us haven't gotten to where we are without making a few enemies. While no one is willing to go after us, Harper is a prime target. We've never claimed a girl. Never shown public displays of affection with any girl. We've marked her as special to us.

And that can bring out the haters.

Jack tells Harper a play-by-play of last night's game. For her part, she acts interested as he goes on about how everyone was out for Luke's blood. Her eyes flick to Luke's shoulder. As for Luke, his control appears to be in place. Especially if he spent the night with Harper alone in bed and nothing happened. Who knows, maybe he just needed a cuddle. I snort and everyone turns to look at me.

"What?" I stuff my face with pancakes. Death needing a snuggle. That shit is funny.

"I should get home." Harper stands and gestures to the door. She takes a twenty out of her purse.

"Nah, little nympho, your money is no good here." I push her hand back.

"But I—"

"No. You want to thank me for breakfast? Give me a kiss on the cheek." I turn so my cheek faces her.

"You're so weird," she murmurs before kissing me lightly on the cheek.

"Webcam today and tonight. All night," I stress.

She waves me off as she backs away. "I'll text if anything happens."

She spins on her heels and leaves the restaurant. My gaze falls on Luke.

"It's just how she said it happened. We slept in the same bed, but that's all. We slept." Luke takes a drink of his coffee. "Don't we have a meeting with Coach today?"

"You go last next time," I say.

"I went last the first time," he points out as we all stand.

"No harm. No foul. Harper seems fine." Eli wipes his hands. "It was probably a good thing Luke went over there. We might not have gotten the story at all."

Eli's probably right. That doesn't sit well with me. How are we supposed to protect our girl if we don't even know what's happening to her? I can at least figure out who didn't travel to the game and make a short list of people holding a grudge against us.

If it was just some kids messing around, fine, but if someone's coming after what's ours, I won't pull my punches.

CHAPTER 24

The Strategic Confinement

ELI

Same shit, different day. Tonight the party is at the head cheerleader's house, Sidney Brown. We've fucked around with her group of girls for years. I'm confident they believe they're in a holding pattern. Waiting for us to take Harper's virginity and then everything will go back to normal.

Because I don't want them to traumatize our girl, I haven't disillusioned them. Yet. Besides, it's not like they don't have other guys they hook up with. None of us have been exclusive with anyone since we became sexually active.

We're sitting on the couches in the corner of Sidney's living room. Dance music pounds out of speakers on either side of the room. The furniture is along the walls, and the lights are low, with a few colored lights spinning from the ceiling like a fucking disco.

Luke, Caden, Jack, and I are putting in our appearance, making our presence known. Caden thinks someone who wants to get back at us is targeting our girl, but I don't know anyone with big enough balls for that.

To go against the four of us without fear of retribution?

I haven't met a guy like that in our school. A few get their panties in a twist when we humiliate them or Caden beats them up, but they fall in line. Like good little ducks.

Some senior girls are dancing together in front of us, rubbing up on each other like that's going to do it for us. A couple girls look like the hangers-on who followed Harper to our table the other day.

Ashley Kim, Emma Garcia, and Hannah Wilson work their way through the crowd to us. The only one missing is their boss bitch, Sidney. Ashley has black hair and dark eyes. She's Korean and tall. We've hit it quite a few times. She likes me being rough with her. Emma Garcia is a Latina with long brown hair and dark eyes. She's sweet on Jack, but I know that she's played with both Jack and Caden together. Hannah is possessive of Caden and his cock. If Emma were just with Caden, Hannah would probably rip her a new one. Both Hannah and Emma are tiny things but strong. Hannah is black with naturally tight curly hair and hazel eyes that stand out. I'd buy tickets to see a drag-out, end-of-the-world catfight between Emma and Hannah.

I lean back and cross my ankle over my knee so Ashley can't climb on my lap like she tends to do. Possessive little things. The other guys do the same.

"Can we help you, ladies?" Luke tips his beer back and takes a long drink.

"Where's your new pet?" Ashley looks around the room like Harper will magically appear. "Why isn't she here playing with you?"

"Did you already grow bored with your new toy?" Hannah asks with a fake-ass pout.

"Or can the virgin not come out to play?" Emma cocks an eyebrow at us.

"We gave her the weekend off for good behavior," I say with a smirk. These girls bore me. They keep trying to claim us, but we aren't down for that.

"Does that mean you all are free and clear to party?" Emma sticks her tits out and grins at Jack.

"Not tonight, ladies." Luke rises. "We've got a pressing issue to attend to."

"Like what?" Hannah crosses her arms and narrows her eyes.

"Nothing you'd like." Caden chucks her under her chin. "Find yourself your own virgin to toy with. I'm sure there are plenty of guys out there who would love a four-way with you all."

"We prefer our men experienced." Ashley grabs my arm as I stand to join Luke.

I look down at her hand. She just smiles at me like she doesn't know she's irritating me.

"Is that what you want, Eli?" Ashley presses in closer. "All three of us worshipping your body?"

I grab her chin hard. "I don't have the patience to deal with all your egos." I pry her hand off my arm and drop it. "We're leaving."

Caden and Jack follow me and Luke through the crowd. We stop and talk with some guys on the team. When a group of girls tries to stop us to chat, we skirt around them with apologetic smiles.

"Text her," Luke says as we walk out into the cool night air.

ME:

Status update, kitten

HARPER:

Another one? You guys are worse than my mother

ME:

Ticktock

HARPER:

All clear. Mom is home, and we're watching a movie. She wonders who I keep getting texts from

ME:

Tell her it's your boyfriend

HARPER:

Hahaha. No

ME:

Is she against or for you having a boyfriend?

HARPER:

For, but not four of them

ME:

Any incidents?

HARPER:

None

"She's fine," I tell the others as we pile into Caden's car. "But she's watching a movie with her mom."

"We can hang out at my house. I downloaded the game that released last week." Caden drives toward his house where we all parked earlier.

What I really want to do is play with Harper. I'm fairly certain the guys would agree with me.

"How long are we going to let this 'grounding' go on?" I ask.

"If it helps the girl adjust, I'm fine with it staying." Caden shrugs as he pulls into his driveway.

"Yeah, I don't see the harm," Jack adds. "Though it would be fun to play with her in real life, I think we might push her too far too fast if we had full access."

"Agreed. It sucks, but she seems to be getting more comfortable with us." Luke steps out of the car.

"Of course you would say that. You got to sleep with her last night." I can't keep the bitterness from my voice. "You took one of her firsts."

Luke laughs as we round the corner to the back of Caden's house. Luke opens the door and we head into the rec room. "I'm sure that's exactly the first you would have wanted."

"It doesn't matter if I wanted it. We agreed to take them all together. And that one we could have shared." I grab a controller and sit on the couch.

Caden stops at the fridge in the corner and grabs us all beers. "Wait. How does that even work? We all sleep together in one room or one bed? Because I don't want to wake up with someone cuddling me with raging morning wood."

"I wouldn't mind that." Jack winks at Caden, who just snorts a laugh. "I'm guessing Eli means your bed, as the rest of us have normal-sized beds."

"Exactly. No touching required, except Harper, of course." I bring up the game and start setting up my player.

Luke takes a swig of his beer. He doesn't seem very forthcoming about sleeping with Harper, but what can he say? It's done. Over with.

"No more alone time with our girl until she's no longer a virgin." I take a swig of beer as Caden sets up his character. "And all her virginity is gone. I think that would keep things fair."

"What about pickups and drop-offs?" Jack asks. He keeps flipping back and forth between choosing a male or female character. Mostly because of the chick's boobs and the guy's abs.

"It would be better if we stick with the current plan on rides," Luke states. "It's not like there's enough time to do anything with her besides get her to school or home. Her mom's schedule will change next week, so she might be home in the mornings."

"What about on camera?" Caden asks. His eyes meet each of ours. "I think our girl appreciated having Luke there when we stripped her bare."

"Give her a few more days, and then we'll decide whether she gets to keep her grounding through next weekend or if we're done waiting." Luke hits start on the game. "We can stick to kissing and grab ass until then."

HARPER

My phone buzzes again. Mom glances over at me as she pauses the movie *again*.

WAR (CADEN):

Status update

"Why don't you just go hang out with whoever is texting you?" Mom sets the popcorn bowl on the coffee table. "Not that I don't love having movie night with you, but someone obviously wants your attention more."

"It's nothing important. No one wants me to meet them anywhere." I lift my phone. Besides, with the way they've been at school, I'm thinking they'll push those boundaries Luke talked about last night. I don't know how comfortable I am with that.

Though I do like the kissing.

ME:

Same as previously

"What about that guy who dropped you off?" Mom sips her hot chocolate while eyeing me over the rim.

"You mean the one you bought me two boxes of condoms for?" I set my phone down and widen my eyes innocently. "You want me to hang out with him?"

More like with them, and they'd probably be more than happy if I said I could come out tonight. Though they've already said no condoms required. I cross my legs. Still not on board with that.

"Hmm, you make a very compelling argument." Mom turns back to the TV.

Penny, Vicky, Izzy, and Nat have all sent me pics from the party tonight at Sidney Brown's house. The guys all look good in their party duds, sitting on a couch, holding court. Penny even sent a pic of a group of girls talking to them. Of course, she got the back of the girls and it's dark, so I'm not sure who they are, but they might be some cheerleaders.

Eli texted me shortly after Penny sent her last update. So I'm pretty sure the guys are keeping it in their pants tonight. They assured me they could wait for me, which means I'm not getting out of this through that technicality.

The movie Mom and I have been meaning to watch is a zombie movie. But with the guys interrupting it, I'm losing some of the tension. Though I got into the movie over the past hour when no one texted to see if I was okay.

The guys are taking the prank from last night a little too seriously. It's kind of sweet, but a bit much at the same time. I'm home safe and sound with my mom. What else could they want? Besides me there with them to torment?

This time, my phone goes off a few times before settling down. I look down and see they're all from the group chat.

I lift my phone and don't bother reading what they sent.

ME:

15 fucking minutes left in my movie. 15

After that, I'm all yours

PESTILENCE (ELI):

Promises, promises

My insides squeeze at his text. I set my phone on the coffee table face down and clutch a couch pillow to my chest. "No more interruptions. Let's watch the end of this."

Mom chuckles as she clicks Play again. The movie wraps up nicely. At least, some characters survived. After, I help Mom clean up our dishes.

"Go chat with whoever kept pulling your attention away from the movie." Mom shoos me out of the kitchen.

"Fine, but I'm not using the condoms," I throw over my shoulder as I grab my phone and head upstairs to my room.

"That's not what they're used for. Do I need to demonstrate on a banana?" Mom calls after me.

"No, please don't ruin bananas for me."

Her wicked laugh makes me smile.

When I open my bedroom door, I hear their voices. They wanted me to leave the webcam on even though they were all away. I step in and close the door behind me. They can't see me yet, but they all pause talking at the click. I lean against the door and pull up their group chat from before.

FAMINE (JACK):

Come play with us, sweetheart

WAR (CADEN):

My new game sucks *frowny face emoji*

DEATH (LUKE):

We require entertainment

PESTILENCE (ELI):

Come dance for us

FAMINE (JACK):

I have the perfect song

WAR (CADEN):

Do it naked

Then my texts came through, and they didn't text me afterward. I grin as I reply to them now.

ME:

No on the naked dancing

I'm not something you only want to do when you're bored

I'm sorry your game sucks

It sounds like you guys are entertaining yourselves

"Are you going to show yourself, kitten?" Eli's deep voice wraps around me like smooth satin. A small shiver works through me and I take a breath.

CHAPTER 25

The Capitulation

I walk over to sit on the bed where they can all see me. They're at their own homes, still dressed up in what they wore to the party. They're all hot as fuck.

"Any more disturbances tonight?" Caden asks. He wears a black t-shirt with dark jeans as he sits on the edge of his massive bed. His black hair is slicked back, making his green eyes stand out more.

"Besides the incessant buzz of my phone? No." I lean back on my hands and wait for one of them to chastise me. They've been letting me get away with too much sass lately without punishment. I keep wanting to pick at them until one of them breaks.

Luke looks like he wants to, but he doesn't say anything. His eyes are particularly cold tonight. Maybe he got in trouble for sleeping with me?

Technically, it was a first. I'd never slept with a boy in my bed before. I definitely hadn't cuddled while I slept, but what they want from me is sexual. So I'm surprised they'd even care about that.

"What movie did you watch?" Jack runs a hand through his dark, artfully messed hair. He has on a light blue shirt that makes his blue eyes pop and skinny jeans that show off his leg muscles and perfect ass.

"*Train to Busan*." I'm not really here to entertain them, so I don't add more, but I'm hoping they'll keep me entertained.

"Isn't that a Korean zombie movie?" Eli asks, leaning forward. His black button-up makes his brown eyes appear almost golden. His thick brown hair is messed up like he's been frustrated with something.

"Yup." I have a day before I have to see them and likely will have done something bad enough to get punished, so might as well have some fun myself before then.

Caden's green eyes narrow at me and then he smiles slightly as he leans back. I swear if he had popcorn, he'd grab it and start popping pieces in his mouth. I give him a small conspiratorial smile.

"We should go back to the party." Luke stands. He's got on a dark purple shirt and dark wash jeans that fit him perfectly. I don't think the guy owns anything considered baggy. "Don't know about you guys, but I'm pretty sure the girls would give us lap dances. Don't worry, princess, we won't touch or fuck them."

"You have fun with that." I pick up my phone like I'm going to text someone else. I'm pretty sure he's bluffing, but the less time I spend with them, the less likely I'll end up punished. So either way it's good for me.

"Of course, we could just show up at your house." Luke rubs his finger against his chin. "I'm sure your mother would love to meet the guys you've been hanging out with, and we can explain to her why you were stuck after school that day."

Okay, that got my heart racing. First, my mom would not be cool with me hanging out with four guys. She might think I should get a boyfriend, but definitely not four of them at the same time. Especially when they aren't my boyfriends but my owners.

Second, I lied about the grounding and I don't know what kind of punishment that would earn me from the horsemen. Third, Mom would try to grill all of them and probably feed them ice cream while passing out condoms.

"What's the third option?" I drop my phone on the bed and lean forward to meet Luke's eyes.

"The third option, princess, is you entertain us until we're all tired enough to fall asleep." Luke reclaims his seat and reclines like the mythical figure of Death himself.

"And how do you propose I do that?" I raise an eyebrow at him.

"What would you do with your boyfriend if you had one, kitten?" Eli lounges in his chair.

"If I was actually dating and could go out, we would probably watch a movie or go to a party. Neither of which I can currently do." You'd think I'd be able to come up with one viable option, but it's not like I've had a boyfriend. "Staying in? Watch Netflix. Maybe play a board game."

"Games might be fun." Jack grabs his phone. "I have an app that will let you set up your own poker game."

"Poker?" I'm afraid of what he might say next about what the stakes will be. These guys like to get me naked.

"Yeah, strip poker." Jack winks at me. "Don't you want to see these guys without their pants?"

I can feel the heat in my cheeks and almost turn away to hide from them. Do I want to see? Yes. Would it be a hell of a lot easier if they're on their video screens and I'm on mine, rather than them being in front of me for the first time? Yes. Would I end up losing more than winning at poker? Also, yes.

"Not poker." I shake my head. I'm sure I would be naked long before any of them.

"How about strip never have I ever?" Eli's eyes glint. "You get to ask the questions."

"So I just wouldn't strip? Because my list of have-dones is relatively short." I try to catalog what I'm wearing: jeans, top, bra, panties, socks. At least the socks count as two.

"No need to be shy now, princess." Luke leans forward. "How about you can only ask us things you've never done? And we can only ask things we've done? So you don't strip on your own questions. Is that fair?"

I wish I could think several steps ahead like Luke seems to, but I can't see anything wrong with what they're saying. It just means I will probably strip every time a guy asks me questions.

"Wait." I hold up my hand. "How do the questions go? I ask one.

One of you guys asks one or all of you guys get to ask one." Because if it's the second, I'll be down to panties and bra after the first round.

Luke's smile is downright evil, but he nods and says, "Only one of us will ask a question for each one of your questions. To make it fair, of course."

That bastard totally would have done it the other way if I hadn't said anything. He wants me stripped naked. I reach over and grab my AirPods. Again, Mom might come by to say good night and doesn't need to hear multiple guys in my room.

"Fine, I'll start." I purse my lips as I think of something they've done that I haven't, but that I want to know. "Never have I ever sent someone a naked pic."

I stare at their screens as Jack stands and takes off his t-shirt. Eli pauses and then stands, but takes off a sock. Caden braces himself like he's going to stand, but just smirks at me and leans back in his chair. Luke doesn't move an inch.

Interesting.

"You aren't afraid someone will post them to the internet?" I ask Jack and Eli.

"They aren't of my face, kitten." Eli winks at me.

Jack laughs. "And we aren't ashamed of our bodies."

Okay, I get that. They keep in shape and aren't exactly hurting for female attention.

"Would you ever consider sending nude pics?" Eli asks as he reclaims his seat.

"Not right now. I'm still underage and really don't want someone to have revenge porn to use on me." I shrug. "But maybe in the future. I'm not ashamed of my body either, but I don't want to just show it to anyone."

Luke smirks. "We like seeing your body, princess."

Heat gathers in my chest. I just shake my head at him. "That wasn't voluntary."

"You dropped the towel, kitten. Luke didn't strip it off you."

I open my mouth to defend myself, but I can't.

I did.

I'm not sure what would have happened if I didn't. Or what kind of punishment he would have cooked up, but it would have been worse than standing naked against Luke. So I shrug.

"Again, not ashamed of my body."

"Good." Luke steeples his fingers before his lips. "Our turn. Jack."

"Never have I ever kissed four guys in one day."

My eyebrows rise as Jack takes off a sock. I blush as I lean down and take off a sock too.

"Okay, explain?" I look directly at Jack's blue eyes.

"I'm bi, sweetheart. And I've played spin the bottle where it's only been men." He shrugs like it's not that big a deal.

"Have you ever with..." I glance at the other horsemen, who all laugh.

"Kissed one of them, yes. Fucked any of them, no. They're all straight as arrows." Jack leans back. Now I'm curious who kissed Jack. "Your turn to ask."

"Never have I had a threesome." I bite my lip and watch them.

Everyone but Luke stands up and removes a sock.

"Never?" I raise my eyebrow at Luke. "Come on. Not even two girls and you? I'm not believing this."

Luke leans in, blue eyes flashing. "Never, princess. I rarely like sharing attention."

I cross my legs against the involuntary throb provoked by his words. I swallow and focus on the others.

"I know Caden and Jack tag-teamed Parker Ford, but have you with anyone else?" I don't know why I'm asking. It will only hurt more to know they've done all this before.

"A few." Caden brushes his fingers over his lips. "But mostly to get the technique down. It's not as easy as it looks in porn."

My eyebrows rise at that. I clear the lump from my throat. "And you, Eli?"

"Jack and I have done the same girl at the same time." He doesn't elaborate. Probably for the best. The heat in my chest doesn't feel like gentle desire, more like raging anger.

I wonder what girls in our school they've had a threesome with and if those girls are looking at me as if I'm going to join their ranks. Maybe there's a support group for girls who got fucked by multiple horsemen.

"My turn." Luke's gaze rakes over me. "Never have I ever watched porn."

All the guys stand up. Caden and Luke remove a sock. Eli removes his watch. Jack removes his jeans. They all look at me expectantly.

I sigh and reach down to yank off my other sock.

They all give me knowing looks.

"Look, even I'm curious. You don't have to have sex to watch sex." I arch an eyebrow at them.

"See anything you like?" Jack asks.

"Not particularly." I have no reason to lie about this. "Personally, I don't get watching porn. I mean, it was hard enough to find a guy that didn't look skeezy, and then it just looked very methodical. Like insert tab B into slot A, move to position two, and continue." I shrug and admit, "I prefer reading steamy romance or erotic romance."

"Any recommendations, sweetheart?" Jack winks.

"Ha, no. If you want to read romance, you can find your own books to read." I lean back and stare at the guys. What else do I want to know?

"Ticktock, kitten." Eli pulls my attention to him.

Pretty sure this one will have them all stripping.

"Never have I ever had a one-night stand." I wait for them all to take off something.

Caden and Eli take off their shirts, while Jack loses his boxer briefs. Of course his cock is hard. I think I'm becoming immune to seeing his cock. This is, what, the third time? He strokes it with his hand and my core throbs.

Okay, maybe not *immune* exactly. Desensitized, maybe.

I turn to Luke. "No?"

"I'm more particular about where I stick my cock." Luke's gaze wanders over me. "I prefer to use the same hole over and over again."

That should make me uncomfortable, but in a sick way, it turns me on. That horny bitch, who has happily stayed on the sidelines, raises her hand like he'll pick her. Too late. He's already picked me.

I clear my throat.

Both Caden and Eli have pants on, and Luke has only lost a sock.

Eli clears his throat and I meet his eyes. He raises an eyebrow, and I realize he caught me staring at his chest. He grins knowingly. "Never have I ever had a sex dream about someone in this room."

Oh, fuck. Like that's something I can control.

The guys all stand, and I wonder if it's me or someone in the group. That would be weird. Luke gives up his other sock. Eli and Caden lose their jeans. I've seen this show before though. Jack strokes his cock while he stands waiting for me.

I inhale and take off my shirt and toss it toward the hamper.

They all have cocky-ass smiles on their faces as they devour my boobs in a bra.

"Who have you dreamed about?" I ask.

"You, little nympho." Caden sits down and clasps his hands together between his knees. The corner of his mouth tips up. "Of course, you might have been being railed by the other guys too in my dream."

Shit. My already damp panties grow wetter at the image of all of them taking me.

"You, princess." I exhale before I look at Luke. "Want to discuss how many times and what positions?" Luke appears to be offering it with no ulterior motive. "It might be very educational."

I bark out a nervous laugh. "No, thank you."

Eli chuckles. "Same as both of them."

"I'm probably the outlier." Jack shrugs. "I've dreamed of everyone at different points, and my version of everyone together probably looks a little different from Caden's."

"That doesn't bother any of you?" I ask. It shouldn't, but I'm surprised it doesn't on some level.

"Why should it?" Luke shrugs. "We're attractive men and we're all friends. We can't control our dreams or fantasies, so Jack having a dream where he's pounding my ass while blowing Caden shouldn't affect our relationship."

My eyes widen and I blink a few times because now I'm worried I'll have that dream tonight. Fuck, that's a little hot.

"And you, kitten?" Eli brings me back to the conversation. "Who have you dreamed about?"

"Again, they're just dreams." I narrow my eyes at each of them. "I can't control who I dream about."

"Of course, princess." Luke's eyes twinkle.

Fuck. "All of you at different times over the years." I don't even pause to take a breath. "Mostly because one, you're hot. And two, I've spent hours trying to stay out of your way. Watching you so I wouldn't accidentally stumble into your sphere of notice and be picked apart or gobbled up. It makes sense that you would all creep into my teenage dreams as I explore my sexuality."

I can see the interest in their eyes, probably wanting to know about exploring my sexuality.

"And no, I'm not offering to go into details, so you can just stop and wait for me to figure out my next question." Because I really want to make Luke take something off.

It's easy to figure out what I haven't done because it's a lot. I could get all the guys naked except for Luke if I ask if they've masturbated. Yet, while I'm curious, I kind of don't want to be scared either and from all accounts, Caden is huge. Like bigger than porn dick.

"Come on, princess. What do you want to know?" Luke sits there, all cocky.

"Never have I ever watched someone else have sex while I was in the room." I lift an eyebrow.

Caden stands and drops his shorts. Yup, that's definitely big. I subconsciously cross my legs. Even as that horny bitch inside me nearly pants. Fuck, how will that fit anywhere in my body? I mean, logically I know it will, but damn, that's a lot.

Jack stands, his cock in his hand, and while Jack might be smaller than Caden, it's really not by much. I feel like I should get with someone smaller for my first time. Maybe find someone half that size just to stretch things out a bit.

Eli's laugh draws my attention as he stands and lowers his shorts. Yup, definitely not small either, and I've just doubled the number of real dicks I've seen in my life. I was right. It's not calming to know what they're packing, even if they felt fantastic pressed between my legs while they kissed the hell out of me.

At least then, those monsters were contained.

Luke stands and takes his shirt off. "Who turns down a live sex show?"

I raise my hand.

"Have you been offered one, kitten?" Eli sits on his bed and strokes his cock.

I swallow against the lump in my throat and hope the fire burning in my chest cremates that lump. "No invitation yet."

"Shame." Luke sits.

Caden clears his throat as he sits on the bed. His hard cock remains on screen as he lightly strokes it. His hand wraps around it, but I've seen Caden's hands. They're huge. I doubt my fingers would close around his cock.

"My eyes are up here, little nympho."

That fire licks my cheeks as I lift my gaze to his. "I know."

Caden chuckles dark and low. It tugs at something deep inside me and I feel more wetness gather between my thighs.

"Never have I ever..." Caden strokes his cock. "Watched a guy jerk off."

Fucker. They all know I've watched Jack get off twice. I stand and undo my jeans. I turn my back to them as I slip them down my legs and kick them off to the side. When I turn back around, Luke is standing and taking off his own jeans.

Only one last cock to get a look at.

"Yeah, that one is pretty obviously Jack. Unless you guys routinely watch each other masturbate?" I sit down in just my bra and panties.

"No, we don't sit around and jerk off together. Unless you're in the room, sweetheart." Jack's words make me pulse with want.

I kind of want to watch them all get off for me. To see the power I hold over them.

"Harper?" Mom's voice comes through the door with a knock. The knob turns. I quickly shut my laptop, consequences be damned, and lunge for a towel on the floor.

CHAPTER 26

The Price

HARPER

"Woah, Mom. I was just getting ready to take a shower," I say, wrapping a towel around myself as the door opens. Discreetly, I drop my AirPods on the bed.

"Sorry, sweetie. Just wanted to say good night and see if you have plans for tomorrow." Mom glances around my room, but obviously nothing is out of place because the guys were in their rooms and I'm in mine.

No cause for alarm. Luke didn't leave any evidence behind this morning either.

"Are you coming down with something?" Mom steps toward me with her hand raised like she's going to check my forehead. "You're pretty flushed."

I dodge her hand. "Probably because my mom almost walked in on me naked."

"I've seen you naked."

"Yes, when I was five. Things have changed since then." I straighten and tighten the towel around me.

"Sorry, so used to being a nurse and seeing all sorts of bodies that I didn't think anything of it." Mom laughs and shakes her head. "Maybe we can go out for dinner tomorrow night. That pizza place you like?"

"Sounds good." I kick at the floor with my bare foot. "So if that's it…"

"Yeah, yeah." She waves her hand as she backs out of my room. "Take your shower, get to bed."

"Good night, Mom."

"Night, Harper." She drags the door shut and I go to lock it. I press against it and take a few deep breaths.

Oh, shit. I shut the laptop on the guys. How pissed are they going to be at me? I kind of want to finish our game, but I also know I need to take that shower or Mom will have questions.

I walk over to my laptop and open it. I sign in and refresh the webcam.

They all stop talking and look at me.

"Mom came in the room. I have to take a shower because I told her I was about to. So I'm going to go do that." I gesture with my hand. Nervousness flows through me, making me babble.

"Princess." Luke's tone says he's not in the mood for arguments.

"Yes, Luke?" I give him my politest tone. After all, I basically slammed a door in their faces.

"As punishment, take your laptop in the bathroom with you and make sure the webcam faces the shower."

My eyes bug out and my heart pounds. "What?"

"Your body is ours, kitten." Eli sits forward. "Maybe we'll all get off while you wash yourself. Maybe we'll tell you exactly where to spend your energy in the shower. It doesn't matter. What matters is you take your punishment."

I swallow and nod. At least it's not in front of the entire school. I look at Jack. "No recording?"

I don't demand. I ask, but I really want to demand. That type of shit always gets out.

"No recording," he confirms.

"Fine." I carry my laptop into the bathroom and set it on the counter facing the glass-enclosed shower. It's not like they'll see much anyway with the steam. I disconnect my AirPods and turn up the volume.

I set the shower to warm and hang my towel beside it.

"We want to see you take off the bra and panties, princess." Luke's voice rings out in the bathroom.

Hoping my mom is downstairs, I lock the bathroom door and turn my laptop until the camera faces me. I give them the middle finger before I strip off my bra and drop my panties to the floor.

I give a little twirl before aiming them back at the shower. I glance at the screen and see the guys still have their cocks out. Well, except for Luke, who still has his boxers on. I wonder what they discussed when I closed the screen.

Shaking my head, I step into the shower and let the water course over me. I'm just going to ignore the men watching me. I stroke my fingers through my hair to help get it soaking wet.

Grabbing the shampoo, I glance toward them as I put some in my hand. Right now, they have a pretty clear view. Definitely not enough fog. I flick the water to hotter. It's a side angle. They can see the curves of my breasts and my stomach.

After I wash my hair and rinse the shampoo out, I reach for the conditioner when I hear a groan. I pause and look over my shoulder. My face flushes with heat. I immediately straighten up at the pretty graphic picture of myself that was on the camera.

No bending over. I'm pretty sure the guys didn't mind a flash of my pussy, but I'd rather not.

I wait for commentary, but nothing. So I put the conditioner in my hair, then wrap it in a bun and clip it to let the conditioner soak while I wash.

I reach for my pouf.

"Use your hands." Luke's voice startles me, and I turn to face them.

"What?" Maybe if I pretend I can't hear him.

"Wash yourself with your bare hands." Luke raises his eyebrow. "Or this won't count as your punishment."

Well, fuck. I squirt my soap into the palms of my hands and rub them together.

"Start with your neck." Luke's voice fills the room and my head as I reach up to wash my neck. Tingles work their way through me from my touch, knowing they're watching and probably want to be my hands right now.

I inhale, and the smell of vanilla wafts around me. I move my hands to my shoulders without Luke's word, but I can only wash my neck for so long.

"Arms next, princess."

"I know how to wash myself, dick," I murmur low enough he can't hear me over the shower.

I scrub my arms and reach for more soap.

"Your breasts." Luke's voice is a little deeper. Curious, I turn to watch them as I lather soap over my breasts. Eli, Jack, and Caden stroke their cocks while watching me, making my nipples harden and my breasts tighten. A pulse echoes between my thighs.

My arousal shouldn't surprise me at this point. It's all chemistry, after all. They're the best of the best of the males and they want to breed me. Not literally, thankfully, but our bodies don't understand that.

"Slower, princess. It's not a race. Trace your nipples with your fingers."

My eyes meet Luke's as I do what he asks. It feels like his hands are on me. My lips part on a gasp at the sensations flowing through my veins to settle between my thighs.

"Stroke underneath your breasts." He licks his lips as his eyes fall to my breasts, and I feel a gush of wetness.

"I think..." I clear my throat. This should not feel so good and wicked, but with four guys watching, wanting...fuck. "I think they're clean now."

Luke chuckles. "Fine, clean your stomach."

"Fuck," Jack shouts as he comes all over his hand. My pussy spasms in response. That shouldn't be as hot as it is to me.

"Get your sides. Smooth and slow."

I follow Luke's directions, but I watch Caden and Eli, trying to determine who is closer. Who should I keep an eye on? I want to hear and see them come.

"More soap, princess."

I get more in my hands and rub it together.

"Look at me." Luke's voice is practically hypnotic to me right now.

My gaze finds his light blue eyes. His mouth tilts into a slight smile.

"Wash your pussy, but don't look away from me."

Umm. He basically wants me to touch myself while watching him. Somehow even with a screen between us, it feels a lot more intimate than video chat. Last night, he held me as we slept. He kept me safe from the monsters outside.

I slide my hand between my legs and let out a small cry at how good it feels. Eli groans and his cock jets out cum. My pussy throbs against my fingers like a heartbeat.

"Eyes here, princess."

I glance at Caden, who is working his cock faster now. The throbbing doesn't stop, and I push my fingers between my lips to the wetness beneath.

"Harper." Luke's command draws me from Caden's cock. When I meet his eyes, the throbbing continues against my fingertip.

"Wash your pussy, but don't play." His eyes hold me captive as I do as he orders. I rub soap over myself and clean like I normally would, but every touch feels sharper and softer at the same time. I breathe out as his eyes darken.

"That's enough."

I stop and rinse my hands before washing the soap off the front of my body.

"Grab the scrubby thing," Luke orders.

Taking my pouf, I add soap and water to make it foam.

"Wash your back."

I stretch my arms to wash my back. My breasts thrust out and apparently, that's enough for Caden. He groans as he comes. My hands pause as I watch his cock strain in his hand. Fuck, that's going to be inside me. Soon.

I can't imagine them playing these games for long before they take it a step further. They can't get me alone. I'm not strong enough to resist the temptation they present. I want them, and all this does is prep me for them.

Make me want them more.

Caden gives me a grin. "It would be better with you here, little nympho."

My pussy throbs in agreement. I swallow and lift my eyes to Luke. He hasn't even stroked over the hard cock in his boxers.

Control.

Fuck, I want to break his control. To feel him surrender under my touch. To shake him to his foundation.

Luke smirks as if he can read my thoughts. "Scrub your ass good, princess. I want it so clean I could eat it."

Umm, say what? If my cheeks weren't already flushed from the hot shower, I would blush at the thought of what he might mean. Instead, I don't even try to imagine it as I use the pouf to wash my cheeks and then drag it through my ass crack.

"Firmer."

I follow orders and scrub. Tingles shoot through me like it's Luke's hand there.

"Good. Now wash your legs."

The other guys are all back at their cameras after cleaning up. They have their boxers back on, so I guess my show is done for the evening. I drag the pouf over my thighs before lifting my leg to prop on the corner ledge so I can bend and get my calf, forgetting about that particular angle until I hear a groan.

"Fuck, sweetheart. I'm going to fuck you in a shower with your ass just like that, where I can watch my cock glide in and out of your sweet pussy." Jack's words make me freeze. Well, at least outwardly. Inside, the heat reaches volcanic levels.

Curiosity makes me imagine what it would be like to have him behind me. His cock pressed against my entrance as he slowly eases inside. My insides are a riot of unfulfilled desire.

I straighten and wash the other leg, knowing they are all watching and wanting the same thing Jack does. To fill my pussy with their cocks. The shower hides the wetness of my arousal at least.

I wash my feet and then step under the hot water. Releasing my hair from the clip, I close my eyes as I rinse out the conditioner and the rest of the soap from my body.

"Aren't you going to shave your legs?" Luke's voice is pure temptation.

I'd have to assume that position again while they all watch me, staring at my pussy like it's theirs for the taking. Wanting to slide their cocks into me over and over again until we both come. Them hot inside me, filling me.

Fuck.

"No, I'm good."

Jack laughs.

Luke's eyes narrow on me, but I shut off the shower and grab my towel before he insists. I squeeze the excess water out of my hair and then dry my body. Wrapping the towel around my hair, I decide to just dry it, because no way am I walking around naked with the towel on my head.

I dry my hair and then wrap the towel around my body as I step out of the shower.

"Is tonight's peep show done?" I ask.

"Not until you're ready for bed, princess," Luke says.

"Fine." I move the computer to the back of the vanity and aim it better. Then I run through my nightly routine. I apply moisturizer to my face, brush my teeth—discreetly spitting—detangle my hair, and braid it. Then I moisturize my arms and legs.

I lift the computer with the thankfully quiet horsemen and bring them into the bedroom with me. Verifying the door is indeed locked. I drop the towel and go to my dresser to pick out panties, sleep shorts, and a camisole.

I step into the panties while bent toward the camera. Their eyes are glued to my breasts. I smirk at how easy it is to distract them with boobs. I pull on my camisole next and then my shorts.

Flicking my braid over my shoulder, I sit cross-legged on the bed.

"Do I get to watch you shower now?" I lift an eyebrow.

Luke smirks. "Maybe if you ever behave, it can be your reward."

CHAPTER 27

The Battle With War

CADEN

While I'm not happy about the constraints Luke puts on us, he does put on a good show. Fuck, my little nympho in the shower is my new favorite thing. Jack talking about fucking her. Shit, would watch.

Harper is pouting because Luke went to take a shower and left her on his desk. She unbraids her hair as she sits cross-legged on her bed. Eli's in bed with his book. Jack works on his computer. I know he has us on one screen and on the other, he's typing away.

Harper sighs as she runs her fingers through her wet hair. It's past midnight, but none of us seem ready to go to sleep.

When I tap my finger on my desk, she looks up at me expectantly. I give her a half smile and her face softens. I've never had a girl look at me like Harper does. Like I'm a big teddy bear and not a ferocious beast hell-bent on making everyone pay for their transgressions.

She makes me lunch and doesn't fuss when I manhandle her. In fact, I think she likes it when I manhandle her. Her big brown eyes look at the other screens where the other two are busy and mouths *what?*

I just wanted her attention. I don't know what to do with it now that I've got it. Holding up a finger, I lift my phone, texting her directly.

ME:

Bored. Wanna play a game?

Her eyebrow lifts at me as she reads my message.

HARPER:

What game?

ME:

Strip Rock, Paper, Scissors

She laughs, and Eli and Jack both look up at us for a second before returning to their work.

HARPER:

You can't make every game strip

ME:

Yes I can

HARPER:

Besides, I have like 3 items on and you have 1

ME:

Your point?

She smothers a laugh and shakes her head.

ME:

Fine, winner owes the other a kiss on Monday

Not a peck, but a no-holds-barred kiss

HARPER:

Best two out of three?

ME:

Sounds good. Prepare to go down, Davidson

HARPER:

Bring it, Ross

She sets her phone to the side and puts her hands into the classic rock, paper, scissors position: left hand flat with right hand fisted above it.

I put my hands in the position and nod to indicate we're starting. I tap my fist against my hand to the beat of rock, paper, scissors, shoot.

I throw rock and she throws paper. She holds her arms up in the air in victory. I'm not minding her victory as her breasts shift beneath her camisole and her midriff shows. I can't wait to get my hands on her bare skin.

Harper mouths *again.*

We tap our hands and both throw paper. I give her a smile and fist my hand. She follows, and we do it again. This time we both throw rock.

I lift my eyebrows. She narrows her eyes. But then we fist our hands and start again.

I chose scissors and she throws paper. I smirk at her.

She shakes her head and fists her hand. We do it again, and she throws rock and I throw paper.

Chuckling, I reach for my phone.

ME:

I win, little nympho

HARPER:

Technically, we win either way, right?

Glancing up, she winks at me.

ME:

Can't wait to move those boundaries. To
play with you more

Her eyes widen and she bites her lip as she reads my message. Is she wanting to play with me too? Fuck, I hope so, because I need that pussy in my life and Harper is a fucking bonus to it.

ME:

You ever sexted, little nympho?

She shakes her head.

ME:

Want to practice?

I raise my eyebrow. She glances around the screen again, but both Eli and Jack are still busy. Luke is probably jerking it in the shower after holding back while having Harper touch herself. He didn't let her play though.

Asshole.

She hasn't masturbated. He told us that, but damn, I could have watched that for hours. The only thing better than watching her get herself off would be me getting her off. Because I seriously want to get Harper off. With my fingers. With my tongue. With my cock.

HARPER:

I don't think we should

ME:

Why not? Scared?

HARPER:

No, but it seems like a first, and after the way you guys acted this morning with Luke and me sleeping together, I figure I should save my firsts for all of you

She gives me a sad face, and I give her a half smile.

ME:

Fine

But just so you know, I'd watch Jack slide his cock in and out of your wet pussy any day of the week

She blushes.

ME:

While watching, I'd prefer you to be sucking my cock, while he takes you from behind

Then we can switch and I can slip my hard cock into your tight wet pussy while Jack takes your sweet mouth

HARPER:

Caden!

ME:

What? You aren't participating

I glance up at her and wink.

ME:

Then, when you're soaking wet, I'll stand with you wrapped around me. My cock buried in your cunt

Jack will come up behind you and ease his cock into your tight asshole

We'll take turns driving in and out of you until you come so hard you drench both our cocks in your juices

She sets her phone face down on the bed. Her face is red as she glares at me. It's kind of ruined by her dilated eyes and her heaving breasts. I chuckle.

ME:

Want to watch me get off or should I go use the shower like Luke?

I jerk my head toward her phone. She shakes her head.

"Come on, little nympho. Aren't you curious?" My voice attracts the attention of Eli and Jack. Luke drops into view with his hair standing up and his chest bare.

Harper bites her lip. "No, I'm not."

"Yeah, you are. Maybe I should read aloud what I wrote to you." I lift my phone and scroll back. "That way, the guys can decide whether you should read what I last wrote."

She glares at me and lifts her phone. She reads my text. "Use the shower."

I smirk. "That doesn't sound like fun."

"Read his texts, princess."

Harper balks at Luke's voice.

"Out loud."

"Fuck," she whispers. "Fine." She glares at me one more time. "Caden. Bored. Wanna play a game?"

"Too far back, little nympho." I lean back on my elbows. My hard cock strains against my boxers. "Start with 'I'd watch Jack slide his cock in and out of your wet pussy any day of the week.'"

She presses her lips together and those angry eyes focus on me.

"Then I said, 'While watching, I'd prefer you to be sucking my cock, while he takes you from behind.' Do you want to continue from there? Or should I keep going?" I chuckle at the daggers her eyes throw at me. "'Then we can switch and I can slip my hard cock into your tight, wet pussy while Jack takes your sweet mouth.' At that point, you cried out my name—"

"I did not. I was trying to get you to stop."

"So I said, 'Then when you're soaking wet, I'll stand with you wrapped around me. My cock buried in your cunt. Jack will come up behind you and ease his cock into your tight asshole. We'll take turns driving in and out of you until you come so hard you drench both our cocks in your juices.'"

Her dark eyes flash murder at me, and I revel in it. I'm not a teddy bear. I'm fucking War.

"She almost didn't read my question of whether she wanted to watch me stroke it or if I should use the shower, but you answered, didn't you, little nympho?" I scratch beside my lips. "Though I'm guessing you actually would have liked to watch me again, but I'll take you at your word." I stand. "Oh, and don't forget about our kiss on Monday. I guarantee it will be downright filthy."

———

HARPER

I watch Caden the asshole walk offscreen. Fucker. I knew better than to put my trust in any of these assholes, but I got sucked in by his poor little rich boy act. That sweet kiss on Thursday meant nothing. It's a reminder that they're toying with me. The only reason they want me is because I'm the last and they'll do anything to push the boundaries until I have nothing left to give them.

His words coated me in heat and swamped me with desire. He left me here with the other horsemen still watching me.

"I'm game," Jack says, throwing me a wink. That's all I am to them. Holes to use.

Fucker.

Luke watches me carefully, like he's trying to dissect my every mood. Well, fuck him, I'm not a fucking science experiment. I'm more than a sex object too.

I get up and go into the bathroom. I need a break from them before I go off and get myself more punishment.

Taking my time, I braid my hair into side braids and use the facilities, which I wasn't about to do with the computer in the bathroom. I have some boundaries no matter what they claim. I'm not theirs.

I cross to my bed, pull down the covers, and climb underneath. Luke's scent wafts up, but I ignore that spark it lights within me. Without glancing at the screen once, I pick up my book and read.

I get a page in before Luke clears his throat. I almost chuck my book at the screen. Of course he can't leave it alone. Instead, I put it down on my lap and turn to meet Luke's eyes.

"Does talking about sex or the idea of sex embarrass you, princess?" Luke's eyes search mine.

I'm not sure what he'll find over video. Besides, there's not really a reason to lie. Though it may give them ammunition to use against me in the future.

I stop to think about it. "What he wrote about the act."

"Did it turn you on? Reading it? Hearing him say it out loud?"

Eli's gaze lifts from his book and meets mine. Why does this always feel like therapy sessions? Like they're trying to dissect me and get me over my perceived hang-ups. These boys go too fast for me to keep up with.

"Yes, it turned me on."

"Reading or—"

"Both. They both turned me on. Not that I can do anything about it," I add bitterly. Touching myself in the shower, I'm sure I could have gotten myself off.

"Of course you can, princess. Just say the word and we'll come over and make sure you come as often as you like."

My mouth opens and closes like a fish. Not exactly what I want, but I could imagine them willingly coming over to get me off. Unfortunately, I imagine they'll expect the same in return. Would they stop with just hands? Or would they keep pushing me until I give in?

And then what? What do they do once they get their prize? Do they become assholes again? Do they just keep taking from me?

"I'm good," I finally get out. No need for horsemen to infiltrate my room and get me off, however they plan to do it.

"Of course you are, kitten." Eli sets his book to the side. "You've never even had an orgasm, so you don't know what you're missing."

His dark eyes take in my hardened nipples beneath my camisole. A pull reaches inside me and grabs the strings of desire they've worked so hard to build up. Just a word or a look is enough to make me want more.

"I'd prefer to go slow," I bite out. I'd prefer to find a way off this crazy ride, but that doesn't seem like it's going to happen.

"Until you don't." Luke smirks.

"Meaning?"

"The first day we kissed, had we been anywhere but at school, we could be past this beginning part. We could be buried inside you as often as we want. And believe me, princess, we want and often."

I press my thighs together at the ache welling between them.

"We own you. And if we want to tell you, in detail, what we want to do to you, you'll listen. Have you thought about how it will be that first time, Harper?" Luke's voice spins around me like it always does, weaving his web until I'm helpless to resist him.

"All four of us touching your body. Playing with your breasts.

Sucking on your nipples. Our fingers between your thighs, parting you, entering you, stroking you. Our lips on yours, fucking your mouth with our tongues while our fingers and tongues fuck your pussy, until you are so dripping wet our cocks will slide into you over and over again, until you scream our names from coming so fucking hard."

Swallowing, I look down at my hands. I can imagine it. I've thought about it. It terrifies me how badly I want it. Want them. It shouldn't be this easy for them. They've stormed into my life and decided I'm theirs.

They own me.

With no consideration for what I want. Want to stay a virgin until college? Nah, we have a scorecard to check off and you're the last box we need to tick. And this will be no simple tick. Not just one guy. No, I have to take four because they say so.

Because they've decreed it without a single thought about who I am or what I want.

Can they make me want them? Yes. Who doesn't want the guys who rule the school to notice them and want them? But they don't give a shit that it's me, Harper Davidson.

I'm just holes to fill for them.

I turn away from the camera and turn off the light in my room. They can stare at the back of my head for all I care. They want to own me for the year and control my every movement.

But they only care about my body, and that might be enough for me to hold back that horny bitch inside me because even she has standards. They want a placid little doll they can fuck. I wanted to make it through senior year without them.

None of us are going to get what we want.

CHAPTER 28

Awol

HARPER

I spend Sunday sans horsemen. As soon as I wake up, I close the screen on my laptop and leave my room. Technically, they didn't say I needed to be on today. I get a few texts on the group chat, but I ignore them.

If they want to punish me on Monday, so be it. I'm just a sick form of entertainment for them. Fuck them.

I work on homework and get started on my paper for English class. When I work on my laptop, I flip the little cover over my camera and mute it. So if they are on, they can't see me. I doubt they'll be on. They have lives too.

I need a day away from them.

A day to clear my head and reaffirm my determination to get out of this devil's bargain I've made with them.

It shouldn't be that hard, but the problem is this isn't like contract negotiations where someone can easily renegotiate by adding something to sweeten the pot. This is hostage negotiations, where I'm the hostage.

I don't have a lot of bargaining power in my current position. I have one thing they want, but they've already decided I'll give it to them.

I need to remember the sheer evilness of the horsemen. The fact they want to embody War, Pestilence, Famine, and Death. These are not mere boys looking for a good time. They want utter and complete control and will do anything to keep it.

Not only am I hostage, but part of me doesn't want to escape them. That's the part I need to talk sense into. Their attention just makes me want more. It's not healthy.

In the evening, I call Kenz to see if she can come over to talk, but she's sick. Which doesn't bode well for school on Monday. We chat a little, but her throat hurts to talk. That's the problem with having only one best friend.

"You ready to go to Crusty's Pizzeria?" Mom stands in my doorway as I put the finishing touches on my statistics homework.

"In just one...minute." I press the final key to submit my homework. "Now I'm good."

I don't bother putting on makeup. I'm wearing dark skinny jeans that fit like a second skin and I pair them with a flowing peasant top. Not trying to be hot. Not trying to get attention. Just being me.

The me I could have been if it weren't for the horsemen. It feels good to own who I am. To not hide. I feel good after a day without the constant pull of the horsemen. Refreshed even.

My hair is a little wavy from the braids, but I leave it down. We make it to the pizzeria in record time.

After ordering at the counter, we take a seat at a four-top since the two-tops are all taken. I recognize some kids from school having dinner and some working in the kitchen. I really don't expect anyone to interact with me, since the guys have said I'm off-limits. Besides, they never interacted with me before.

So I'm relaxed and enjoying Mom time. Mom talks about work, and her schedule this week is the same as last week. Mornings. I talk about classes. I'm not worried about any of them yet, but we'll see how the semester goes...and how big of a distraction the horsemen will be.

Our pizza is delivered. We sometimes get the barbeque chicken pizza, but tonight we went with a classic pepperoni and sausage pizza.

"So we haven't discussed boys yet," Mom prods as she takes a bite.

"Not much to say. They exist. I exist. We all go to school together. Maybe some of them want to get in my pants. Maybe I want to get into some of their pants. But right now, I'm happy to just go along my own way and let them figure out my pants are on permanent lockdown."

"Ouch. Hopefully not permanent." Wincing, Mom drinks some of her soda.

"Permanently to high school boys," I clarify. "They aren't mature enough to deal with the consequences of their actions."

"If I didn't know better, I'd think you're bitter from unrequited love." Mom laughs.

"Yeah, not going to happen. No love lost here." Definitely not. I would never be stupid enough to give my heart to any of the horsemen. Could you imagine? They would chew it up and spit it back in my face.

I barely feel the electricity in the air, but I definitely feel something shift in the pizzeria. The hairs stand on the back of my neck and I raise my gaze to meet Caden's green eyes at the counter.

Fuck. My. Life.

Seriously, can't I get a break from the prick brigade for one day? Also, will he dare to come over to talk to me with my mom here? Oh, shit, Mom...

"Mom, if someone comes to our table, I'm grounded, okay?"

"What?" She looks around the restaurant, apparently not affected by the horsemen's gravitational pull. "What do you mean?"

"Just I can't go anywhere. I'm grounded. I'll explain later. Please, Mom." I hold her gaze with mine and hope she can read the desperation in my eyes.

"Fine, but I've never really had cause to ground you," she mutters as she takes a big bite of pizza. "Might be nice to have to parent you even at this late stage of the game."

Caden enters the dining area, and that's when I notice the rest of the assholes following behind him. He smirks at me as he sits in a booth a few feet away. Jack slides in next to him, while Eli and Luke sit on the other side. I can feel their glances at my back like lasers tearing at my flesh.

"I take it the table of jocks is the reason for your grounding?" Mom lifts her eyebrows at me as she glances over at the guys. Her eyes widen, but she keeps her glance quick enough that the guys won't know I've pointed them out to her. "Yeah, they would be a good reason to ground you."

"They've made it a point to *notice* me this year." That's about as much as I'm willing to say to my mom. That way, I won't get in trouble with the guys, and she won't accidentally cause any trouble.

"Are they bullying you, Harper Lynn? Because I don't care how big they are. If they're bullying you, I'll kick them in the balls myself."

"No, jeezus, Mom. Calm down. They aren't bullying me." Much. "They've just been interested in the permanently locked down pants of mine."

"Ah, nothing you can't handle, right?" She gives me a look that says say the word and their asses are hers. I can't help the grin that threatens to spill out at knowing my mom will always have my back.

"Definitely nothing I can't handle." I straighten in my seat. "Just boys being boys."

Even as those words come out of my mouth, I want to hand in my woman card. One small death to feminism, right here in Crusty's Pizzeria, courtesy of Harper Davidson.

Mom even gives me the side eye at that.

"Meaning I can handle their come-ons, and they'll take the rejection fine like they should." I nod to myself like I righted whatever cosmic wrong I just did. The thing is they won't take rejection fine. They'll bend me over and spank me in front of our entire school.

Maybe they'll even make it an assembly so everyone can show up this time.

Fuckers.

I'm really not looking forward to Monday as I've given them plenty to punish me over today, but damn, give a girl a break. They've been on me for six days. Even God gave it a rest on the seventh day.

For the rest of the meal, things stay relatively the same. I'm aware of the horsemen directly behind me while my mom talks about some of the odd cases of the week, including some interesting X-rays.

The server checks on us, and we ask for a box and the check.

He comes back a few minutes later with a box. "The guy at that table picked up your check for you. You have a nice evening."

Mom's eyes widen and she glances over at the guys with a hard look, probably trying to determine what game they're playing. I put my hand over Mom's to get her attention.

"They're all practically rich. I'm sure our thirty-dollar meal isn't even a speck of their weekly allowances." I don't know if I'll be able to talk her out of this confrontation, but I'm afraid a confrontation is exactly what they want.

Mom drops a generous tip on the table and stands. Please let her be ready to go and not about to—too late, she's heading straight for their booth with a smile on her face.

I grab the box from the table and try to cut her off, but I'm way too slow.

"Good evening, boys." Mom's got on her killer smile.

"Good evening, ma'am," Luke says. His eyes cut to me. "Harper."

"I wanted to thank you all for our meal. It was very kind of you." She's too sweet. Fuck, I can't control her any more than I can control the guys. Hopefully she doesn't blow me up too much.

"It was nothing. Seeing as how Harper was grounded and couldn't join us out, we figured we'd get your meal." Luke's emphasis on *grounded* tells me his game. I'm sure he'd love nothing better than for me to not be grounded so he can move his sadistic game forward. Finally get me alone with all four of them. Asshole.

"That's so sweet of you boys. Well, thank you." Mom smiles. Neither confirming nor denying my grounding. Man, is she smart.

I wish I could tell her everything. She'd know how to get out of this death spiral I'm in. But as an adult, she'd bring in other adults, and then things would get sticky.

"Yes, thank you," I add. I almost want to stick my tongue out at them. If I didn't think Mom would notice, I would give them a double bird salute on the way out the door. I already have to explain the creepers in my life to her once we leave.

"I'll pick you up for school tomorrow," Luke says. And my house of cards comes crashing down around me.

Mom's eyebrow rises. "You know Harper has her own car and can get to school just fine on her own."

Momma didn't raise no princess, fucker.

"I know, but I like to pamper her." Luke's gaze flicks to mine and I hope Mom misses the heat in them before they go back to cold.

"It's up to Harper whether she drives or rides, but she better be home on time." Mom's voice is stern enough to warrant nods from the horsemen. "Thank you again for the meal. Maybe we'll repay you sometime."

She walks away before they say anything more, and I hurry to stay with her because I'm not getting caught by one of them. Not here. Not today.

Tomorrow morning will be soon enough. Today is mine.

As I slide into the car, my phone lights up with a notification. Earlier, I put it on do not disturb for the day. I'm sure I won't appreciate what they have to say, so I ignore it.

Mom gets in. "Well, you go big when you go."

I shrug. Didn't really have an option. A few false promises to give me the sense I was making decisions, but not really. They determined they wanted me. They determined I wanted them. They always get what they want.

In the end, they wanted to own me, so they do.

"They're handsome young men. I assume this is the half of the football team you were talking about?" Mom puts the car into gear and drives us home.

"Not really half." I look out the window. I'm sure they want my webcam on tonight. I'm sure I'll do it and they'll have some sort of punishment to go with it.

Fuck it. If I'm already getting punished, I might as well go big like Mom said.

"I trust you, Harper. I don't trust any of them, but I trust you. So if you like any of them, I'll back you up, but if you want me to hate them, I can do that too."

Smiling, I glance over at her. "I'll let you know. I'm still not sure I like any of them. But they're persistent."

Mom makes a disgruntled noise. "Most men are when they want something. It's after they get it that they prove who they really are."

Yeah, that's what I'm afraid of.

HARPER'S PHONE

KENZ:

Why do I have to be sick?

ME:

Sorry

KENZ:

How's the dick parade?

ME:

Planning on getting punished

KENZ:

Fun

CHAPTER 29

Disobeying Orders

HARPER

I'm getting ready for school when my bedroom door opens. On a normal day, that would freak me out. But I know it's probably Luke, and he's most likely pissed off. I didn't look at their texts last night. Didn't even turn on my webcam. I also didn't sleep well, but fuck them anyway. I shouldn't need their faces to fall asleep to.

I'm done with their conditioning of me. Putting me between two of them. Kissing me like we're already fucking. Leaving bruises on my ass from gripping it so tight.

Finishing applying my lipstick, I glance in the mirror to see Luke on the end of my bed, hands behind him, holding him up. His blond hair falls over his cold eyes while his gaze rakes over me. He's wearing a dark green t-shirt and those jeans that must be custom-made for him.

Not that I'm dressing for them, but I'm sure he appreciates my skater skirt with knee-high skull socks and a black t-shirt with Venom on it. I put my hair into the two top knots again with framing pieces and go with a super dark red lipstick and dark eye makeup. No need to be dragged around by my hair today. My red Converse are the only spot of color in my outfit.

It suits my mood and tells the world to back the fuck off. Hopefully the horsemen get the message.

217

"Missed you last night and this morning." Luke's tone is deceptively easy.

It unnerves me as I slip my hoop earrings in. I expected anger and punishment.

"I took a me-day." I blot my lips. "Mom and I watched another movie, and I actually got to pay attention to it this time."

I turn. My skirt twirls around my legs. "Figured you all could use a break from babysitting me." I walk out of my bathroom and stand between Luke's legs. "Sorry you missed me."

His grin should have warned me. "Show me your panties."

I lift my skirt to show my black lace panties. "I need to make my lunch."

"I'll buy you lunch." He straightens and pulls me down to straddle his lap.

I put my hands on his shoulders like a good girl because punishment is back on the table and I don't want to end up pantyless in front of everyone. Maybe it would be a good idea to carry a spare set in my purse.

"What if I don't want cafeteria food?" This close, I can smell his cologne and his minty breath. My insides wind up. I might have missed this yesterday, just a little.

His hard cock, which I'm beginning to wonder if it's actually packaged meat he keeps in his pants, presses into me. After all, he's been reluctant to show it. "I'll take you out for lunch."

"Like a date?" I smirk at him. "Death is going to take me on a date?"

"Shut up, princess." He shakes his head and grabs the back of my neck to hold me steady. He captures my lips. I almost forgot how good it feels to be kissed by him. How desirable he makes me feel.

His tongue sweeps along my lower lip, and I want to deny him. I want to show him I'm stronger than that, but with a whimper, my lips part beneath his. My mouth is his. He's claimed it to be so, and I can't help but give in to the feel of his tongue brushing against mine.

He pulls back. Before I can lean in and recapture his lips, he sets me beside him on the bed like the kiss was nothing. What the fuck? I steady myself like I don't feel used. He rubs his thumb against his lips and dark red appears on his skin.

"No smearing lipstick, princess."

Anger flares through my system. I stand and glare down at him. "Don't kiss me then, Death."

Luke grabs my wrist before I can think to get away. I hear footsteps and look up to see Eli, Caden, and Jack walk into my room.

"Can't punish you without them." Luke tugs me between his legs. "Ignoring us, disrespecting us for a whole day. You've earned another spanking, princess."

"No, we don't have time. We have to go to school." I jerk on my arm, but before I know it, I'm down across Luke's lap. My skirt is over my hips. With my ass pointed to the others.

"Eli, will you lower Harper's panties?"

"What? No, you can't do this. Get the fuck off me." I struggle uselessly against the hand against my back. I have absolutely no leverage, and there's no way for me to overpower him.

Eli's hands brush against my hips as he slides my panties down just enough to expose my ass. I wish I could say that did nothing for me. I wish I could just ignore these guys and what they make me feel inside. Anger at my own body's betrayal flashes through me.

"This will go easier if you accept we own you, kitten." His hand brushes over my ass. Sparks light under his touch. "Every day, every hour, every minute. That when we text, you answer. When we tell you to do something, you do it."

"I'm not your fucking slave," I grit out, so furious I barely get out the words.

"How many?" Luke asks our audience.

"Fifteen," Jack speaks up.

Fuck Jack.

Fuck all of them.

They aren't getting any more pieces of me.

"You count, princess."

"Fuck you." I can't help it. I'm so done with their manhandling of me and their punishments.

He spanks me. "It's here or in the locker room with the football team present. Your choice, princess."

"It's never my choice, is it, Death? It's *your* choice. I don't have a fucking say in what happens to me." I'm so done with all this. They can all go fucking jump off a cliff.

"The punishment doesn't start until you count, Harper." He smacks my ass again.

I want to be belligerent and not say anything, but fifteen is a lot. I've only had two so far and my ass already hurts. Luke presses on the sting, and that not-unpleasant feeling erupts under my skin.

I hate them. I hate them so much.

"Ready?"

I almost say fuck off, but I hold my tongue.

He smacks my ass.

"One." Fucker.

He brings his hand down on the other cheek.

"Two." Fucker.

A hand that is most definitely not Luke's presses on my ass cheek. I jerk under his touch. Afraid of the *checking to see if I'm wet* test Luke mentioned last time. I can't even look to see whose hand it is. It stays on my ass cheeks. Those swelling feelings move within me as he rubs the ache away.

I will not get turned on by this.

I will not get turned on by this.

Fuck them and the horses they rode in on.

"Three. Four."

Definitely someone else's hand now, pressed against my sore ass cheeks. I clutch onto Luke's leg as I bite down on my lip. Not turned on.

"Five. Six."

And the last fucker's hands are on my ass. Larger hands than the others. These have to be Caden's.

I squirm under them, but I still have it under control. I'm not aroused by this. It's doing nothing for me except sending me into a rage.

"Seven. Eight."

Luke's hand rubs over my ass cheek again. Slower, more deliberate, working in circles closer and closer to my pussy. As he rubs, my pussy lips part and rub together. I was a little wet from his kiss already. That turned me on, but this won't turn me on. I refuse.

He removes his hands, and I brace myself.

"Nine. Ten."

Luke's hand and someone else's massage my sore ass cheeks, and they keep moving closer and closer to my entrance. I'm starting to question whether I can hold back any longer. The sparks gather beneath my skin, mocking my efforts.

"Eleven. Twelve."

The spanks aren't the hard part. The touching afterwards is. I want to part my legs and rejoice in the feeling swelling within me, but not with these guys. Never these guys.

Fuck, I can feel the wetness practically trickle out of me.

"Thirteen. Fourteen."

I can't fight it anymore. A moan escapes me as they touch my ass. It's sensitive, and the skin feels like it's on fire. I can't control my arousal. What these guys do to me. I wish I could tell them to all go back to hell, but I can't do any more punishment.

I have to go back to being the willing victim for now. But I don't have to show I like it.

"One more, princess."

I brace myself, but his hand doesn't come down on my ass cheek. He smacks me straight on my pussy. I cry out. A burst of pleasure sweeps through me. Not what I think an orgasm would feel like, but something not so nice and nice at the same time.

"What the fuck?" I screech out.

"Count or you'll get another."

"Fifteen."

I wait to see if he's going to rub away the hurt. Almost afraid he will. Instead, they all press a hand to the warmth of my ass while I hang like a broken doll over Luke's lap.

They step back and my panties are drawn up. My skirt is righted and Caden lifts me to stand.

My ass and my pussy are now sore. Wonderful way to start Monday morning.

Luke stands and hovers over me until I look up. He takes his palm and licks his fingertips. "I knew you'd taste good, princess. Go wash your mouth and pick something that won't smear or go without."

"And if I don't?" I don't say it defiantly, even though every bone in my body wants me to. I'm not sure I'm controlling the daggers in my eyes though.

"Then you'll go without panties for the day. As always, *your* choice, princess." The words are mockery and I feel them in my core.

I want to rail and cry and kick them all in the balls. Instead, I shrug off Caden's hold and go into the bathroom and close the door. I let out a ragged breath and take a quick moment to breathe.

After cleaning myself up and straightening my clothes, I choose a dark red lip stain. It's not as dark, but it won't smear all over Luke either. Not that I want to kiss any of them right now. The dark red still suits my mood.

I wish I knew how much I could get away with. Maybe they like the fight and me giving in to them. If I stop responding to their little games, will they grow bored with me? It's something to try at least. Better than willingly playing along and hoping at some point they'll decide to stop.

Be meek, hiding Harper. I meet my eyes in the mirror and they burn. I don't think I can hide anymore. For years, I did it without a second thought, but I was never as pissed off as I am now.

I shrug it off and leave the safety of my bathroom. The guys are downstairs. I can hear them talking in hushed tones. Fuck them.

I wish there was a way I could do to them what they do to me. Humiliate them. Make them squirm. Without giving any more of myself to them.

With my backpack on my shoulder, I march downstairs past the guys and outside to stand next to Luke's car. I wait there patiently while they file out of my house and head to their cars.

I swear if any of them try to kiss me, I'll bite their fucking lip and I'm sure it shows on my face.

Luke unlocks his doors. I slide into the seat and pull on the seatbelt.

He gets in and his super peppy EDM plays. I keep my gaze out the window, not wanting to engage.

By the time he pulls into the school lot, I've calmed down a little. I'm still going with the plan to stop reacting to them. It will be hard to not respond to their kisses, but at least I'm more used to kissing now.

Getting out of the car, I head for the school without waiting for

Luke. I don't stop for the rest of the guys outside either. I walk straight to Caden's locker and wait. No expression on my face.

They want a docile pet. Well, here you fucking go.

The guys join me after five minutes.

I hand Caden my books and lean against the locker. The guys exchange looks, but no one tries to engage with me.

Luke finally says, "Come on. Let's get to class."

I follow him down the hall and into the classroom. When we're seated, Luke leans forward on his desk.

"I don't like this new game, princess," he whispers before he leans back in his chair.

Good.

CHAPTER 30
The Concession

HARPER

By the time I get to art class, I sag into my seat.

ME:

Hope you feel better. Miss you

KENZ:

Binging shows and bored

Did you get your punishment?

ME:

Yes

But I'm trying a new tactic

KENZ:

I can't wait to hear all about it

Good luck

Keeping up the ice-cold bitch routine is harder than I thought. I'm not a hard person, but *fuck them* is my motto right now. I'm sure Kenz would approve.

They all seem confused and a little concerned about my change in attitude, so mission accomplished. Shouldn't have fucking spanked me first thing in the morning. Dicks.

I relax into my seat, even as my ass hurts, and pull out my sketch pad. I've been working on a sketch of a face for a while now. Death's face, soft in sleep, is etched in my mind. I need to get it out of there because that guy is a fucking lie.

The way he held me and cuddled me, protected me.

All lies.

Lies to get me to drop my guard to trust them. To want them. Fuckers.

The act of sketching helps center and calm me.

"Hey, you're Harper Davidson, right?" The guy standing in front of my desk looks familiar, like I've seen him around, but I honestly couldn't tell you his name. Kenz is much better with that.

"Yes?" I hesitate to engage. Kenz warned me about users. Which kind is he going to be?

Tall and well-built, he has blond hair and bright blue eyes. An easy smile hits his lips. He's like a nicer Luke, less ominous. Not quite as hot though.

"I'm Tanner Lewis." He pulls out Kenz's chair. "Mind if I sit here today? I tore my contact this morning, so it's hard to see the board from the back."

"Sure, but Kenz will probably be back tomorrow," I warn him.

"Thankfully, I'm getting new ones after school." He settles into the seat, and Ms. Sullivan begins the lesson.

I keep working on my sketch while she talks. I notice Tanner glancing over at me from time to time, but I ignore him. After half the period, Ms. Sullivan releases us to work on our projects.

"You've got a great eye," he says softly.

"Thanks." I'm still not in the mood to talk. My ass hurts more the longer I sit. Plus, next period is lunch. I have none with me. Luke promised to take me out, but I'll believe it when I actually see it. Not that I really want to go anywhere alone with him. Or his posse of fuckheads.

"I think I was in the sculpting class while you were in drawing, because I've never seen you in art class before this year." Apparently he wants to talk.

I put my pencil down and look at Tanner. Really look at him. He wants something. I just don't know what it is yet. "Sure, that happens."

He smiles now that I'm engaging. "You've been claimed by the horsemen this year. How's that going?"

I smile, but it probably looks like a grimace. "It's not like I had a choice in the matter."

"I missed last week helping my sister settle into her new school. It surprised me when someone told me they picked you."

I'm not sure what that's supposed to mean since I don't really know this guy.

"We were in history last year together, and I always thought you were cute." He gives me a crooked smile. "When they said no one would claim you in the cafeteria that day, I didn't understand why not. I mean, excuse me if I'm being forward, but you're hot."

"No one was willing to stand up against the horsemen. I don't blame them."

If what I'm suffering is when they like someone, I'd hate to see what they do to someone they actively dislike.

I ignore his compliments because I don't trust his motives. Is it to get closer to the horsemen or pull one over on them?

"Bunch of cowards in this school." He shakes his head. "I tried to stand up against them after what they did to my sister." He shrugs and looks down at his drawing.

"What happened to your sister?" I'm curious.

"They targeted her until she finally caved. It was last year. She hasn't been the same since. She transferred schools this year to get away from them." His eyes get a far-off look to them. "We're twins, so I tried to stand up to them. After all, I thought the guys were my friends until they got me kicked off the football team."

I hadn't heard about his sister, but I've basically been living with my head in a hole. It's not surprising I'm not privy to the inner workings of this school.

"That doesn't seem fair if you were just trying to help your sister."

The guys are jerks and I know this is a pattern with them. The only difference this year is I've got their full attention.

"Yeah, well, that's the horsemen for you." Tanner shrugs. "I wanted to let you know you aren't alone. If you need someone to help you, I can't sit by and watch them do to another girl what they did to her."

I'm still wary of him, but then he settles in to sketch quietly beside me. It's not like people are lining up to help me. Even my bestie can only do so much. I'll have to ask Kenz what she knows of Tanner's story.

When class ends, Tanner stands and nods to me. "I don't want to get you in trouble or I'd walk you to wherever you need to go."

"Yeah, I'd rather not face their wrath anymore today." My ass couldn't handle it.

"Here." He hands me a scrap of paper. "It's my number if you want to talk or need help. I hope you consider me an ally if not a friend in your war. Good luck."

Tanner backs out the door and heads off down the hall. I slip his number into my notebook before anyone sees it.

"You know." Penny moves up beside me. "I wouldn't let him sit next to you anymore. I don't think the horsemen like Tanner much."

"Yeah?" I'm curious what she knows. "Why not?"

She nods. "I just know he used to be a big deal on the football team until last year. I don't think he even gets invited to parties anymore. Poor guy. He's stupid hot though."

I nod thoughtfully. That only substantiates his story.

Penny smiles. "You're coming to the game on Friday, right? It's a home game and we'll all be there. We can sit together and then head to whatever party afterwards. It'll be loads of fun."

"I'm still grounded this weekend, so probably not. I wish I could though." Not really. I need to find a way to stay out of the horsemen's clutches. Mom might be amenable to "grounding" me more, but I'm not sure that won't get me in trouble with them.

She smiles easily. "Then the next one, for sure."

I nod and walk out of the classroom and toward the cafeteria. My feet are heavy like I'm walking to my doom. I don't even have lunch to eat today. And I trust Luke as far as I can throw him.

I have to reassemble the ice princess persona I've been using all morning, but it seems like too much work now. I just want to go home and forget the horsemen even exist. I'd go to the nurse's office and get sent home if I didn't need to save those days for when things really get to be too much.

The only good thing about today is I might have found an ally. Who knows, maybe more people feel the way Tanner does. Maybe I'm not alone in this battle.

Jack

I'm pretty sure we broke Harper. She's been skittish and defiant and even sometimes submissive, but today she was a hellcat until we broke her. Now she's nothing.

I walk up behind her as she drags her feet to the cafeteria. I wrap my arms around her waist and lift her off her feet. Not even a shriek of surprise.

"You're going to get us in trouble." Her words are flat. Not a bite or a hint of amusement. Nothing.

Fucking Luke and his plans. Great way to start the fucking week. Spank our girl. All together. And she'll fall in line after ignoring us all Sunday. Though I enjoyed pressing my hand against her warm ass cheek, feeling the muscles twitch beneath my palm.

"You're going the wrong way, sweetheart."

"The cafeteria is this way." Simple statement of fact.

"We aren't going to the cafeteria today." I set her on her feet and turn her around. "Luke promised to take you out."

I hold out my hand to her, and she sticks her hand in mine. It's loose like a limp noodle.

Fuck. I don't like this.

At least she's moving in the right direction now. I lead her out the doors to Luke's car. Everyone else is already in, waiting for us.

I open the back door and she climbs in. No muss. No fuss. No arguing. Nothing.

I inhale and figure today is going to suck ass, and not in a good way.

The guys all talk as if Harper isn't being a sullen little thing on the way to the wing shop. I study her to see if there's any spark left in there. I don't know about the others, but I'm almost afraid to kiss her when she's like this.

If she kisses like she just held my hand, no thank you.

Luke parks and we all get out. I turn back and look in at Harper sitting perfectly still in the center seat. My eyes meet Caden's over the roof of the car.

He nods. We both lean in. I unbuckle her seatbelt before Caden drags her out and throws her over his shoulder. She dangles there.

His hand covers her ass to keep her skirt down, and she lets out a small whimper. Her ass is probably sore. My eyes meet Caden's again. Yeah, this definitely takes the fun out of having a pet.

I like her better when she's feisty.

Eli and Luke have already gone into the restaurant to order. I hold the door open for Caden, and he strides through the tables until he reaches a booth toward the back. He sets Harper on her feet.

"Slide in," he commands her.

She does, and he slides in next to her while I sit across from her. She clasps her hands on the table in front of her and stares at the napkin holder like it's a show she needs to watch.

I pull out a napkin and hand it to her. She looks at me for a second and then takes the napkin and sets it on her lap. Then she returns to staring at the napkin holder again.

I do the same thing. Grab one and hand it to her. She glances at me before setting it before her. We go through the motions two more times before she sighs and looks at me as she puts the napkin in front of her.

I give her a smile. Luke and Eli arrive with drinks and pass them out. Harper focuses on her drink instead.

"Nothing?" Eli asks.

I shake my head. I notice Caden's arm move, pretty sure he just put his hand on Harper's thigh. No reaction.

Caden grunts and then glares at Luke, who sits next to me.

Luke leans back and studies Harper like he's trying to dissect her. She takes a drink of her soda and stares off into the distance.

We could just talk around her, but this all feels odd. Even when she ignored us before, she was engaged. Now she's like a lump we're carting around.

No one wants to fuck a lump.

"Did you order Harper the hottest wings they have?" I ask Luke.

"Figured she'd want them plain like her current behavior." Luke narrows his eyes at her. "Embarrassed the spanking turned you on, princess?"

She lifts her face and stares at Luke blankly. "No."

"Probably should have done it in the locker room. Apparently she likes an audience." Eli smirks as we all watch her for any fucking reaction at all.

She shrugs and starts folding her straw wrapper.

"I guess we could start every day like this." Luke rubs the corner of his mouth. "There are more pleasant ways to start a day, but if she's going to be sullen, then maybe spankings are the way to go."

Again she lifts her face but doesn't say anything.

Luke shakes his head like he doesn't know what to do with her. We still have a few minutes before they bring out the wings, but no one talks.

"You owe me a kiss, little nympho." Caden looks at Harper. "You ready to pay up?"

She nods.

Caden lifts her and puts her on the table in front of him, rattling the glasses. She puts her hands on his shoulders as she looks down at him with those empty eyes.

He leans in and presses his lips to hers. She doesn't do anything, just sits there. Yup, glad I didn't do that.

"I can do this the whole lunch until you respond, little nympho." Caden pulls her onto his lap. "The bet was for a no-holds-barred kiss. Do I need to punish you for not complying?"

HARPER

I want to glare at Caden for pulling this crap, but I manage to keep my face as placid as a lake. "You do what you have to do."

They've all been seriously quiet. Normally, they talk around me, but it's like I'm sucking all the energy out of the group. Good. Fuck them.

Caden draws me in against him, but he's not hard. That surprises me. I figured that was just a standard for being a horseman. Or maybe I'm being effective and he doesn't want a limp little doll he can easily control.

Maybe this will go better than I thought. Maybe a few days of this and they'll be done with me as a lost cause. I can go back to my normal life without the horsemen in it.

A twinge strikes my heart, but I ignore it.

Caden leans in, but instead of going for my mouth like I thought he would, his lips go to my ear.

"Technically, since Luke slapped your pussy, I think that should count as touching it." Caden's voice is dark and dangerous in my ear.

He wouldn't. Not here. I resist the urge to tighten my legs, but it would be useless anyway since Caden is between them.

"I could slide my hand under your skirt and against your pussy and have you soaking by the time the food gets here." His lips and breath move against my ear, lighting sparks. He hardens beneath me. I'm not the only one affected by his words. "A few more minutes of kissing and stroking and I could have you coming all over my lap. Would you like that, little nympho, for your first orgasm to be at a restaurant in front of all these people? Would that get you off more? Maybe you need a crowd to turn you on? If I slide my hand into your panties right now, will I find you hot and wet and ready for me?"

Fucking Caden. His hand slides up my thigh as he leans back to meet my eyes. I'm not going to win this game of chicken because this asshole will follow through. He'll slide his hand into my panties and find that his words make me wet. Feeling him swell beneath me, for me, makes me wet. His body pressed against mine is making me wet.

And I hate him and myself for it.

Fine, a kiss, and then I'll go back to zone-out Harper. I lean in and claim his lips while I clamp my hand down on his to stop his progress. I put all my rage and hurt into this kiss.

His other hand cradles the back of my neck as he deepens it, sliding his tongue into my mouth. A moan builds in my throat, but I hold it back. I may have to give in a little, but I'm not giving him everything.

He reclaims his territory, sliding his tongue against mine and biting lightly on my lips. Taking his time to show me exactly how much he can make me feel.

The kiss goes on until I forget everything I'm supposed to be holding back as he rocks his cock against me. The fucker. I squeeze my thighs around his hips to get him to stop, but he chuckles into my mouth.

"Food's here," Eli says.

Jack laughs.

Caden pulls back and glares into my eyes. "Stop being broken."

Fuck you. The words linger on my tongue, wanting to escape as I squint at him. Instead, I slide to the side and take my seat again. I take one of the many napkins Jack gave me and put it on my lap. Jack passes me some sauceless, boneless wings and some fries.

"Just how we like you. Naked." Jack cocks an eyebrow at me, hoping for a response.

I lift a wing and bite into it. Actually I prefer a mild buffalo sauce, but I'm not giving these assholes an inch more today. Caden got all the play I'm willing to put forth.

Jack presses his lips together and glares at Luke. Good. Get mad at the conductor of our orchestra and not me. He's caused this with every stupid thing he does. I can't believe I actually let him spoon me.

It will be a cold day in hell before I let that happen again.

CHAPTER 31

The Counterattack

LUKE

I let Harper have her little tantrum. It won't stop us from wanting her. We already know what lies beneath the surface. An animal waiting to get out. She has to learn to accept what she can't control.

And she can't control me.

As we head back to class after lunch, I shove her against the lockers like I've done countless times. She sinks back against it and stares vacantly over my shoulder.

"Caden was wrong, you know." I put my hand up around her throat to hold her head still as I lean in. I don't need a teacher overhearing me. Not that they could do anything about it, but my princess doesn't need some knight to charge in to save her.

She prefers dragons over knights. Even if she doesn't know it yet.

"If he wanted to slap your pussy, then he could have done that. But we haven't crossed into the realm of playing with your pussy." I kiss her neck behind her ear. "Yet."

No shiver. No struggle. No defiant look. Just calm acceptance.

Fuck it. I press into her and take her mouth with mine. No response. It's like kissing a corpse, and I'm definitely not into that.

"Though maybe Caden had the right idea." I stare into her brown

233

eyes. "Maybe we need to push a little harder. Escalate to keep you on your toes."

Her eyes focus on me, and I can see the hate in them. But when she speaks, it's with that same bored tone. "We're going to be late for class."

I take hold of her arm to pull her into the classroom. At her seat, I release her and continue to my own.

She had to know we'd punish her this morning. She ignored every text on Sunday. There are consequences to her actions. She knows that.

The class flies by as I consider what to do next. I could let her continue this game of hers or I could escalate to get a reaction. But if I do that, things will be more tense with the others if it fails.

When class ends, Harper heads out without me. Without even a glance in my direction. I wanted to keep our punishment private, but if she keeps this up, maybe it's time to actually do what we threaten.

I text the guys.

ME:

Situation not resolving. Thoughts?

ELI:

Let her have her wallow. She'll come back around

JACK:

This fucking sucks

CADEN:

Apply pressure. She's mad under all that

Of course she is. But she can be mad. This act is frustrating as hell. The problem is we don't know how long she can keep this up.

ME:

I've thought of two things. Escalate punishment or escalate interaction

JACK:

You want to break her permanently?

I'm not down with that

ELI:

Jack, you want to cave to her little tantrum?

ME:

We have to decide

CADEN:

Let her be today. We'll talk tonight after
practice. My house

Easy for him to say. He made her respond to his kiss. The rest of the day passes and instead of worrying about Harper, I focus on my classes.

Jack took her home after school and got no interaction.

After practice, we head to Caden's basement.

"Text her to put her camera on at nine tonight." I gesture toward Eli. He sends the message to the group chat with a note to respond.

She replies with a thumbs-up emoji.

"What do we do?" Jack runs his fingers through his hair. "I mean, this is all an act, right?"

Caden lounges in the corner of the couch. "Of course it's an act. Below that is the spitfire she always is. She's just punishing us."

And there's the rub. She's punishing us, and it's working.

"How long do you think she can keep this up?" I knead the back of my neck. She's already got us spinning, and it's only been a day.

"No idea. She hid from us for years before this." Eli shrugs. "It's possible she can bury herself under layers again."

"I don't think she's hiding." Caden grabs the remote and turns on the TV. "But we'll know for sure by what she wears tomorrow to school."

"I think she's trying to make us not interested in her." Jack picks up a football, tosses it in the air, and catches it. "It's actually pretty effective. I still want Harper, but I don't want her like this."

I lean forward with my hands clasped between my knees. "Give her tonight. No punishment. No interaction. Let her think she's winning. Maybe she'll drop her guard."

"And if that doesn't work?" Jack says.

I smile. "Then maybe she needs to remember what it's like when we aren't in her life."

———

HARPER

At nine o'clock, I turn on my webcam and then go in and take a shower. They didn't say I had to stay on the webcam, and I didn't give them a chance to tell me anything. I take my time in the bathroom and then head out into my room, already dressed for bed.

I chose a shapeless nightgown with *I heart coffee* on it that falls to my knees. Sitting at my desk, I work on my homework without even glancing at the guys' webcams.

No one says anything. I almost forget they're even there. I stretch up after a little while and finally glance at the screen.

Huh?

They're working on homework or off-screen. I'm surprised because usually they interact with me a little. Oh, well, less work for me.

There's still that small part of me that revels in the horsemen's attention. What if they start ignoring me again? Fuck, but that's what I want. I want them to leave me alone. Right?

Shaking my head, I go downstairs to refill my bottle of water.

"Hey, how are things going?" Mom looks up from the book she's reading at the island.

"Same old, same old." I stop and lean against the counter. "What're you reading?"

She holds up the book, flashing the cover of a man's chest draped in plaid. "The good stuff. How's the boy trouble going?"

I take a breath. "Well, I'm trying a new tactic. Ignoring them."

"How's that working for you?" Mom raises her eyebrows.

"So far, so good. I think if I continue to ignore them, they might decide I'm not worth the effort." I give her a smile. At least I hope it looks like a convincing smile. My stomach feels funny—not sick, just off.

She nods thoughtfully. "And that's what you want?"

"Of course," I say automatically. "You saw them. They're good-looking guys, but those kinds of guys are only after one thing, and while they may be genetically attractive, I need more than a pretty face to tempt me."

"I could see that." Mom turns her book back over. "But don't just judge them by their pretty faces. They're still people, and they have to be somewhat smart if they're interested in you."

"They just want me because I'm…unavailable." I gesture as I stumble over the last word.

"Maybe, but guys rarely stick around if they don't receive some sort of encouragement." Mom arches her eyebrows at me over her cover.

I shake my head. "Not these guys. No encouragement required. I think they just like the chase."

"Ah, but once they catch you, they'll find out you're a keeper."

I burst out laughing. "These guys aren't the kind to keep anyone. Not one of them has had a girlfriend."

"You've never had a boyfriend," Mom points out.

"Yes, but I don't go out with boys and don't have a boyfriend. They go out with girls. They just don't ask them to be their girlfriend."

"Are you interested in any of them? Seriously." Mom sets her book down. "I mean, not that you couldn't date multiple guys, but I would think that would get confusing and end with some hurt feelings. Is there one of them you like more than the others?"

Not that I have a choice to only like one of them, but Mom doesn't know that. I try to think if there is anything I actually like about the guys besides the attraction between us.

Eli, who is legendary for being rough with girls, is delicate with me. The way Caden looked at me the first time I brought him a sandwich, like no one has cared for him before hit me right in my feels. Jack needs to make me happy and he's always quick with a smile. Luke holding me through the night to help me feel safe.

I refocus on Mom. "I thought I might, but they have expectations that are way too high."

"Maybe you already exceed all those expectations." Mom blows out a breath. "Don't sell yourself short, Harper. You're a good package and if any of those guys don't see that, they don't deserve you."

"Thanks, Mom. I've got a little more homework to do. Night."

One of them would be easier to deal with than all of them. But that's not an option, and I'm not sure I would want to have to pick only one of them. As embarrassing as it is, I like all their attention focused on me. I like that these four guys shared my first kiss.

"Night." Mom waves me off and opens her book again.

I keep circling back to the thought of only one of the guys as I walk back to my room. Would it be any easier if I had to pick one of them to be my first? I mean, dick-wise, I'm pretty sure Jack would be the easiest to take, though he's not all that much smaller than the others.

If the real question is all or none, would I be stupid to pick none?

Setting my bottle on my desk, I sit in my chair. When I glance at the screen, they're all focused on homework or whatever they're working on. I study them while they aren't watching me.

They're all assholes, but I've had my moments with all of them. Physically, I'm attracted to them, but they don't really know me. Luke's seen me afraid and a little desperate for someone to stay with me. When I told them about the prank, Caden was ready to sit outside all night to watch over me.

But overall, my moments with them have all been sexually driven.

Then again, what more do I want for my first time? Someone to love me? Do I need love to have sex? Apparently that answer is no.

I breathe out a sigh and work on finishing my homework. No one speaks as I finish up and get ready for bed. As I lift my laptop to bring it to the bed, the other webcams all shut off.

What? Oh, fuck.

My heart ratchets up a beat. I check my network connection but it's still live. I guess they don't want to keep them on tonight. My chest feels hollow as I set my laptop on my desk and leave it open, just in case it's a trap to punish me more.

I'm just about asleep when a text comes in.

> **DEATH (LUKE):**
>
> On your own tomorrow morning to get to school, we have a meeting early

> **ME:**
>
> *thumbs-up emoji*

I roll over and stare at the screen. Weird. Maybe they don't want a submissive doll. Maybe my plan is working, or maybe they really have a meeting, but I'll take the freedom. Even if the victory feels a little hollow.

HARPER'S PHONE

ME:

Mission Ice Out seems to be going too well

KENZ:

Yeah?

ME:

Guess they don't want a passive doll

KENZ:

I can't wait to hear more

ME:

Get better. I need my ride or die

KENZ:

Wouldn't miss it

CHAPTER 32

Victory?

I dress for myself in the morning. Jeans and a t-shirt. My red Converse. I leave my hair down. When I get downstairs, I make my lunch, but don't make extra for Caden. Grabbing my keys, I head out to my car.

My car. I didn't realize how much I missed driving it until this moment. The freedom it gives me is almost euphoric.

I park in the far back of the lot away from *their* cars like I used to. Then I go in the side entrance so I don't have to pass them. I skip the lockers and head to my first class. Getting there early, I sit and just take a moment.

Kenz slides into the seat next to me and looks around before smiling.

"How is this happening? I haven't seen you without a dick attached to you since the first day of school." She grins.

I glance around before leaning in close to her and whisper, "I decided to give them what they wanted, a docile pet, for the day yesterday."

Kenz's hand is on her heart. "Oh, fuck, I thought you were going to tell me you gave in and had sex with them."

I chuckle. "No, still trying to get out of the deal."

"What are you going to do about your birthday tomorrow? Are we going to grab pizza and a piece of cake or not?" Kenz glances over her shoulder at the door, but Luke hasn't come in yet.

"I think we can manage it." I sit back in my chair and turn to face the front. "We can talk in art."

She nods and smiles. This feels right. Talking to Kenz. Not worrying about the horsemen.

When I take out my sketchpad, Tanner's number falls out. I almost forgot about it. I program it into my phone before crumpling up the paper and sliding it into my pocket to throw away later.

Imagine the punishment I'd be in for if the horsemen found another guy's number on my phone.

Luke strides into the room, and I feel a jolt go through me. Seeing him will get easier with time. He crosses to his desk and sits down without talking or touching me. I stay facing the front, but he still does nothing.

Finally, I bend over my sketch of the dragon sculpture and start adding some shading. By the time Mr. Wick comes in, I've almost forgotten Luke is behind me.

Class passes, and nothing happens. When it ends, Luke gets up and leaves. Okay? I'm still worried this is a trap, but this is okay. This is what I wanted. Them to not pay attention to me.

I take a breath and head to statistics. The guys come in late and again say nothing to me. They talk a little to each other around me as if I'm not even there.

Jack even turns around to flirt with the girl sitting behind him.

I don't know what to feel right now. My chest feels numb and empty, but there's this anxious little pitter-patter still pacing away in there. I mean, this is what I wanted. Their focus off me.

As I walk into art, I feel weird, like I don't exist. Like somehow I've become a ghost to the guys.

"You okay?" Tanner stops and takes my elbow.

I blink up at him. "Yeah, I'm good."

"What did they do?" he asks. His lips press into a thin line.

I shake my head. "Nothing. They've done nothing."

His brow furrows, but he releases my arm. "Do you need to talk?"

I force a smile to my lips and shake my head. "No, thanks."

My feet carry me to my desk, and I sit down. I can feel an ache welling inside me that I don't think I can contain. It feels stupid and big and weird.

"Ms. Sullivan?"

"Yes, Harper."

I stand and go to her desk. "Can I have the pass? I need to use the restroom."

"Are you feeling okay?" She eyes me with concern.

"Maybe." I don't know what's happening. She hands me the pass and I rush to the bathroom. I sit in the stall and look at my phone. The last text I have from any of them was from last night about getting myself to school.

It worked. One fucking day. A warm tear hits the back of my hand. One fucking day and they decided I wasn't worth the effort. Good thing I didn't give them my virginity.

I swipe at the tears on my cheeks, feeling stupid for letting them fall.

Good. I was done playing their game anyway. Now I'm free to do whatever I want without having to worry about punishment. Which means I'm not stepping foot in that cafeteria today.

That makes me a little happy even if my heart feels heavy.

I wash up in the sink and reapply some makeup to cover the red splotches. A minute of crying was enough for what they were to me. Just a passing fancy apparently. Fun while it lasted, but now I can move on with getting out of this town.

I return to art and sit next to Kenz. She squeezes my hand and gives me a smile, which I return. When lunch rolls around, I head to the tree on the side of the building. I could use a little sunshine and privacy.

I've just finished my sandwich when I notice Tanner approaching me.

"Hey, I see you've found my perfect spot," Tanner says.

I glance around. It's been a while since I sat here on the south lawn. Probably since the incident with Caden and Jack last year. "It's always been one of my favorites."

"Mind if I join you?" He gestures to the ground beside me.

"Go ahead." I breathe in the fresh air and feel the shackles of the horsemen fall off me. This is nice. Not worrying about the cafeteria and everyone getting a show.

My phone dings and dread builds in my heart. Are they looking for me? But when I check my messages, it's a picture from Penny. The guys have a few girls at their table for lunch.

Yup, that seems about right. I text her back a shrugging emoji and set my phone down. Back to normal behavior for the horsemen. Well, probably. I honestly don't know what the cafeteria in high school was like until this year.

From here I can see the football field. That day was only last week. All their attention focused on giving me my first kiss. At least I have a good story to tell. I take a drink from my water bottle.

"Did they ditch you?" Tanner asks, startling me. I almost forgot he was here.

"Apparently." Shrugging, I smile bitterly. "I'm not surprised I couldn't hold their attention."

"They do like to strike fast and then bail." He shakes his head and then looks up at me from under his blond hair. "Did they get what they wanted from you?"

I laugh at that. "No, not at all." Somehow, this victory feels bittersweet. They got some of my firsts but not the most important one, and there are a lot still left. "How's your sister? You said she transferred?" I eat a chip, needing my mind off the horsemen before I do something stupid and cry again.

"Mia. She loves her new school. So much less drama." He quirks a smile.

"Why didn't you transfer with her? You could have maybe been on their football team?" I forgot to ask Kenz about Tanner, but today has been such a shitshow. I'll try to remember to ask her later.

"It's a special high school. They don't really do sports." He shrugs as he eats his sandwich. "I wasn't going to play in college anyway, so it's not a big deal. I figure I can at least stay here as a reminder of what they did to her."

My phone vibrates, and I lift it. Kenz sent me a pic of the guys with those girls. The girls are all sitting at the table, but the horsemen aren't touching the girls.

ME:

Take a pic if any of the guys touch the girls

KENZ:

Okay

"Getting the scoop on the horsemen from friends?" Tanner leans in and sees the picture. "Didn't take them long to move on."

"No, it didn't." But something settles in me at seeing them not actually touching the girls. How often did I actually sit in a seat at that table?

An idea pops into my head. What if they're just punishing me the way I punished them?

What assholes.

"What about you?" Tanner asks. "What are you going to do now that you're free again?"

I grin as I look up at the endless blue sky. "I'm not going to go back to hiding, that's for sure."

He gives me a flirty smile. "You know, if you still need a boyfriend..."

"Oh." I blush. "I think I'll need more than a day to figure out what I want."

He nods. "The offer stands. If you want to take me up on it, just let me know. I'm all about getting under the horsemen's skin."

That rubs me the wrong way. Even though yesterday he said I'm hot, it feels like I might just be a game to him. A way to get back at the horsemen. And while I understand wanting to get revenge, I don't know if I would go so far as to be with a guy just to hurt them.

One, I don't think I have the ability to hurt them. Two, their pride might get a little bruised, but they have more than enough to keep them going. So in the end, it would still only be myself I was hurting.

"Thanks. I'll see how the week goes. You never know, I might need a hero tomorrow."

He chuckles and nods to my phone. "You have my number, right?"

I swallow. "Yes, I do."

"Text me so I have yours." He smiles like we're going to be great friends.

Fuck it. I pick up my phone and text him my name.

His easy smile is almost a relief after working hard to get one from the horsemen. "If you ever need me, you call and I'll come save you."

CHAPTER 33

Third-Party Aggression

HARPER

The afternoon is more of the same. By the time I'm walking out to my car after school, I feel almost calm. The guys have appeared to back off entirely, but I haven't quite gotten my hopes up yet.

When I get to my car, my tire is flat. I stare at it for a moment and then heave a sigh. This happens sometimes. One of my tires has a slow leak. I never remember which one it is.

I text Mom to let her know why I'm going to be late and throw my backpack in the car. Popping the trunk, I get out everything I need to change the tire.

Mom made me change my tire five times before she would let me get my license. She didn't want me to have to rely on the kindness of strangers to get myself out of a jam.

When the tire is off, I notice a slash mark in the sidewall. Either I clipped a curb or...

I stand and look around the mostly empty lot. No one is around. But suddenly it feels like eyes are on me.

I didn't clip a curb this morning. A smattering of cars are around the parking lot. Of course the horsemen's cars are still here. I don't know if they would do this to me. I don't know what it would give them besides me being irritated.

That bound up feeling I had when the knocking happened fills my chest. Trapped and not knowing who is out to get me.

Ugh. Fuck that. I have to finish this and get home. One step at a time. I put the spare tire on and get busy. When I lower my car, I hear a stampede of footsteps running toward me.

I stand and turn to see the football team running through the other end of the parking lot. Oh, joy. I roll my damaged tire to my trunk and lift it to throw it in before returning for the tools.

Someone stops running and stares over at me. I resist the urge to hold up my middle finger at Caden. He glances at where the others have gone but then cuts across the parking lot toward me.

I don't have any energy left to deal with these fuckers right now. I replace all the tools in their spots and close my trunk.

"What happened?" Caden glances at the spare tire before his eyes dart to my face and then my dirty hands.

"Flat." I grab a couple of napkins from my car door and scrub my hands with them. Not that they do much for the grease.

"This happen a lot?" Caden glances over his shoulder, but the rest of the team has moved on.

"Sometimes. I have a tire with a slow leak, but this tire—" I stop. Why am I telling him any of this? We're done. Finished. They've made it perfectly clear they want nothing more to do with me.

"This tire what?" Caden's eyes meet mine. "Harper, what aren't you telling me?"

He closes in on me, and I swear even his sweat smells delicious.

Fuck it. He'll leave faster if I just tell him.

"There was a puncture to the sidewall. I don't think I hit any potholes on the way to school this morning, so..." I shrug and back up against my car to get away from him. "You should get back to practice, and I need to get home."

His face goes hard, and his eyes narrow on me. "So someone slashed your tire?"

I shrug again. "I don't know."

"Show me."

"Caden—" I start.

"Harper, show me the tire." He closes in a little more and gives me a fierce look.

Sighing, I head to my trunk. He follows closely. When I open it, he pulls out the tire as if it weighs nothing and squats down to study it. The hole is pretty obvious, so it doesn't take him long.

He stands and searches the surrounding area like whoever's responsible will just be standing there with a sign saying *I did it*. Then he lifts the tire into my trunk and closes it, taking my keys and pocketing them.

"Come on." He grabs my arm and starts pulling me toward the school.

I plant my feet. "What? No. My tire is fixed. I'm going home. Mom is expecting me."

He stops and crowds me, but I hold my ground. "And I'm not letting you drive home in a car someone already fucked with. Call your mom and let her know the tire was more damaged than you thought and you're getting a ride from a friend."

"I could just call her to come pick me up," I throw back at him.

"Fine, but I'm not leaving you out here alone while you do and I need to get back to practice. Are you walking or am I carrying you?" He lifts his eyebrow. He'd do it too.

I glance around the empty lot.

"Fine." Being out here alone already spooked me.

I text Mom as Caden pulls me to the football field. Mom tells me she's still at the hospital and to grab a ride with a friend.

I sigh.

"What?" Caden stops. We're just outside the football stadium, and I can see a group of three guys looking our way. No need to guess who they are.

"Mom's at work." I glance up at him. Even though it's probably useless, I have to try again. "My tire is fixed. Give me back my keys and I can get home on the spare."

"No, you won't." Caden grabs my chin and lifts my face so that I have no choice but to meet his glare. "You'll sit on the bench like a docile little pet, or I'll spank you worse than anything Luke will ever do to you."

I open my mouth and then shut it. Arguing with him is pointless.

Besides, the horsemen may have backed off today, but that doesn't mean I'm not still fair game. If Caden decides to punish me, there's not much I can do to stop him.

He takes my silence as compliance and drags me over to the bench on the side of the field. "Sit. Stay."

I'm tempted to bark at him, but I roll my eyes and sit on the bench.

He tips my chin up, and his eyes narrow on mine. "If you leave, I will be in your bedroom tonight."

I bite my tongue to keep from saying *promises, promises.*

He leaves me to join the others. They talk for a minute and glance over at me a few times, but I try my best to ignore them.

The coach blows his whistle, and the guys get back into practice. My bag is locked in my car, so I don't have my homework to work on. I have my phone, but Mom is at work. Kenz is planning on meeting Brandon tonight. I'm not about to text the user girls. I could text Tanner to give me a ride home. He did promise to be my hero, but I don't really need saving tonight. Not any more than Caden has already done. Not that I needed anyone to save me. I fixed my tire and was ready to head home.

Am I creeped out because someone probably did it on purpose? Of course. And I would have discussed it with my mom when I got home.

Now I have *their* attention again. Just when I believed I was free and clear.

I pull up Candy Crush and play through my lives. That's the problem with the higher levels. It takes a while to get through some, and I fail on all five of my lives. I try to ignore the sounds of pads colliding and grunting men on the field.

At least Caden put me at the end they aren't currently doing drills on. I look around, curious if whoever is out for me is still watching. None of this started until the horsemen claimed me, but it doesn't make sense.

I mean, they could still be two separate incidents. The prank and the car tire. Someone punishing me for having the horsemen's focus on me. Because that's my fault. I scoff. Or maybe someone punishing me to get the horsemen's attention.

Some of the guys run sprints while Luke throws to Eli and another guy. The other guy doesn't seem that good. He almost drops the ball twice and fumbles it another two times.

When Luke catches me watching, I decide staring up at the sky is a much better way to pass the time. I lie down on the bench and stare at the endless blue sky. A cloud would make this so much better.

"Wake up." A hand nudges my hip. I go to roll away from the offending hand and meet with only air. My heart flips. My eyes pop open to see the ground rushing my way, but then I realize I'm floating there and an arm is banded around my waist. "Didn't know you were so accident-prone."

Jack. I lower my feet to the ground and stabilize myself before he releases me.

"I fell asleep." Wow, way to state the obvious. I shake my head, vaguely remembering staring at the empty blue sky.

"Apparently." Jack sits on the bench and looks up at me. He pats the space next to him. He's still in his practice gear, covered in grass stains. His black hair is plastered against his head.

Not fully alert, I drop onto the bench and realize no one else is out here with us. "Practice over?"

"Yes. Caden didn't want to leave you alone, but Coach wouldn't let him bring you into the locker room, even with you asleep." Jack smiles warily.

I nod. That makes sense. "I'm fine. You can go get changed."

"Not happening." He shakes his head. "I know about the tire."

"It's probably nothing. Just a horsemen groupie who wants me to leave her men alone." Ha, joke's on her. They already left me alone. My gaze focuses on the parking lot. Even though the sun is still trying to shine, the parking lot lights have turned on, creating more shadows.

"We don't like that you've been targeted twice now." Jack's voice is stilted.

"Me neither, but they probably aren't related. Friday night at eleven o'clock equals bored kids wandering around trying to not be bored. The tire? Maybe I didn't notice the damage and a week of not driving on it made it worse."

I don't know if I even believe my story, but it sounds good.

I sigh. "Caden wouldn't let me just go home, so I'm here. He has my keys. I'll wait until you guys are done if you want to go in."

His hand covers mine on the bench. Warmth spreads through me from his touch.

"I'm not leaving you alone, Harper."

I blow out a breath. I want to rail at him about how they left me alone all day today, so obviously I'm not a priority, but now that I'm a damsel in distress they want to swoop in and fix everything?

And they aren't using their nicknames for me. It's Harper this and Harper that. So obviously they've decided they've had enough of me. I don't bother looking at him as I let the disappointment settle in my chest.

After five minutes of silence, Jack says, "I like this time of day. That space between night and day when you can see both the sun and the moon in the sky. It's too bright for stars, but the lights come on because it's almost dark. It's this time in between where things aren't quite ready to end and not quite ready to begin."

"Twilight," I murmur and notice he's still holding my hand. I try to pull it away, but he tightens his hold on me. I turn to him to ask him to let go.

"I figure that's where you are." Jack squeezes my hand. He stares at the sky in the distance. "Stuck in the twilight. Not quite what you used to be and not quite who you could be. I guess that's most of us in high school. You don't have to be afraid of the change."

He turns his face toward mine, and I focus on his dark blue eyes, so close to the color of the sky at twilight.

"You don't have to stay the way you were, but I understand if you don't want to be what we want you to be." Jack shrugs and looks up at the sky.

"What do you want me to be?" My words are quiet. I'm almost afraid to break this peace between us.

"Free." His eyes meet mine and I can feel this swelling in my chest.

"Go get changed." Luke's voice shatters whatever moment Jack and I were having.

Jack squeezes my hand before releasing it and stands. For a moment, he and Luke just look at each other, as if they're communicating without words. Finally Jack walks off to the locker room, leaving me with Luke.

I fold my hands in my lap as he sits beside me. His hair is wet and standing all over the place. He's back in the jeans and t-shirt he wore to school today.

Something sparks inside me just being near him. I take a deep breath and blow it out because I'm not talking to this asshole.

He watches me, but he doesn't say anything or move. Just sits.

It's unnerving. I'm almost willing to take my chance with whoever fucked with my car over Luke Foster.

He licks his thumb and rubs it against my cheek.

"What the hell?" I try to move away, but he grips my arm with his other hand.

"You have grease on your cheek." He moves his thumb back to wipe at it.

"You're using your spit to clean my face?" I give him an incredulous look. That's something moms do to toddlers.

He smirks and whips off his shirt with one hand before using the inside to wipe at my cheek. He cocks an eyebrow at me. "Better?"

Swallowing, I try to keep my eyes from dipping down to his shredded body. His seductive scent is basically pressed to my face and unavoidable. My insides soften before I can lock that shit down.

I push his shirt away from me. "I'm good. Thanks."

"So touchy." He chuckles low and dark, tugging at that part of me that really wants whatever Luke is selling. At least he puts his shirt back on.

Yup, I'm done. I stand and walk toward the parking lot.

"It's getting dark over there, princess," he calls out.

I stop at the nickname. My heart beats a little harder. I turn around, but the world darkens around us, leaving him in shadow. I can't see his eyes or face to make out what he's thinking. Not that I ever know what Luke thinks.

"Let's get you home."

I lift my head at Caden's voice. I'm so confused right now.

CHAPTER 34

The Protection Pact

CADEN

Harper fights me every step of the way.

"Just get in the car."

She presses her lips together. "I'll drive my car home so I'm not leaving it for someone to take out the other tires. You can follow me."

"I promise to come pick you up tomorrow. And I'll call a tow truck for your car." I pull out my phone and look up a towing company.

Her hand blocks my view of my phone. "My car is fine. This isn't like some Mafia film where they've set my car to blow up when I start it."

I eye her car, wondering if I could tell if someone did that.

"Caden, seriously, the worst they could do is put sugar in my gas tank, and if you follow me, you can give me a lift if my car stalls out." Her hands are on her hips and her dark eyes flash with fire. She thrusts out her hand for her keys.

This is the girl I've been missing. The one who makes me hard, and it makes me want to do whatever she wants to keep her like this.

I lean down and get in her face. "Fine, but if it explodes, I'm riding into hell to spank your ass."

Her eyes soften, and her lips try to curl into a smile. "Deal."

Fuck, I want to kiss her, but we've made a plan. This isn't part of the plan, but I'm not about to leave our girl with a flat tire and a potential stalker-type person after her.

When I drop the keys into her hand, she spins on her heels and goes to her car. She meets my eyes when she turns the engine. Her car roars to life.

Damn. I really wanted to spank her, but at least she's alive.

I get into my car, and Jack looks at me.

"Is this smart?" Jack glances over at Eli and Luke, who are watching us.

"Just because it screws up Luke's plan to ignore her until she begs for it." I scoff. "He wouldn't have lasted that long, and we all know it. That girl gets under his skin."

"He's not the only one."

I grunt in agreement as we follow Harper's car to her house. I pull in behind her, and Jack jumps out as she heads to her door. After getting out, I cross over to her.

"Your mom isn't home yet."

Ms. Davidson's car isn't in the driveway. Luke and Eli park behind my car in a line so Harper's mom can park without blocking us in.

"Newsflash, Mom's rarely home. What's your point?" Harper crosses her arms and glares as Luke and Eli join us.

"Give me your key. We'll make sure no one's in there." I hold out my hand.

"You guys are overreacting." She holds out the keys and drops them in my hand.

"Thank you." I brush past her. Jack stays next to her as Eli and Luke follow me to the door.

Their home is decent-sized. Three bedrooms, three baths. We split up and check the whole house, including closets and under the beds.

"Call for some pizza delivery," I tell Eli. He lifts his phone and taps on the screen. I turn my gaze to Luke. "I'm not leaving until her mom is here. You can leave if you want."

His cold eyes narrow, but he shakes his head. "I'm staying."

"Fine." I go to the back door and hold it open for Harper and Jack.

"Seriously, you've checked the house. I know how to dial 9-1-1. You guys can head out and do whatever or whoever you planned to do tonight."

I grin at her back. That sounded a little jealous. "Why would we do anyone else?"

She shrugs as she opens the refrigerator. "You looked pretty cozy at lunch."

I close in on her back and hear her small gasp. "You weren't in the cafeteria today."

"I got pics from my friends."

Just like we figured she would. I reach around her and grab a Coke.

She sighs as she looks over her shoulder at me. "Anyone else want a drink?"

Harper passes out sodas and then sits in a chair in front of the TV and turns on Netflix. She scrolls through to a series she's halfway through and clicks Play.

It's a zombie show I've been meaning to try. So I settle into the couch to watch. Halfway through the episode, the doorbell rings.

Eli goes to get the pizzas and sets them on the island.

I snatch the remote from Harper's hand and hit Pause. "Time to eat."

She glares but follows me to the kitchen and pulls out some plates and napkins. We all take multiple slices while Harper only takes a couple.

"We don't eat in the living room." She nods to the table with four chairs and the bar stools at the island. She takes the bar stool at the end, and I grab the one next to her.

She rolls her eyes at me, but I just grin. I take up too much room, so the others are forced to eat at the table. Losers.

She bumps her elbow into me three times before she looks at me. "You're too big."

"That's what they all say." I wink.

She blushes. Damn, I've missed her blushes.

"You guys really don't need to stay," she grumbles.

"Yes, we do." I eat my pizza and drink my soda while she focuses on her own food.

When she finishes, I grab her plate and the guys' and take them to the dishwasher. She watches me like I might do something wrong. Who knows, maybe I will, but it seems like a pretty simple thing to load a dishwasher.

I grab her hand, drag her back to the living room, and wait for her to get settled before hitting Play on the show. Honestly, I'm a little lost since this is like episode six, but who doesn't appreciate zombie killing?

She glances at her phone as the show ends. Her brow furrows and she types something. Then she sighs and glances at me.

"What?" I ask as I turn off the TV.

"Mom's stuck at work." She curls into her chair and looks at all of us. "Seriously, I'm good. You guys can leave. It's not like it isn't safe in my house. I've been doing this since I was a kid."

"You might have had to be alone when you were a kid, but you don't have to now." Eli leans back and rests his head on the back of the couch. "We can relax here just as well as at Luke's or Caden's house."

"I don't know when she'll get home," she warns.

"Worried we'll be out after curfew?" Luke smirks. "Maybe we'll all get grounded."

She glares at him.

"Don't sweat it." I get her attention. "My parents and Luke's father aren't in town. Jack's mom is a doctor, and Eli's parents are too busy ignoring each other to notice he's not home."

Her brow furrows as she glances at Eli. Our little nympho has a soft heart.

"What would you do if we weren't here?"

<hr>

Harper

Hiding in my room probably won't reassure them that I'm fine on my own.

"Homework."

Caden nods. "Don't let us stop you."

Fuck it. It's something to do. I go over and wipe off the kitchen table before settling in with my books. My attention is split though between my work and the guys sitting around my living room.

Jack goes outside, comes back in with his backpack, and sits across from me with a grin. He pulls out his school computer and sets it up.

"Wifi?" He lifts a dark eyebrow at me.

I smile. "David's house. Password is *my favorite Henry Cavill is a dirty Witcher*. Capital letters, no spaces."

"Yours or your mom's?" He grins.

"Both." I shrug.

"Me too." He wiggles his eyebrows.

I shake my head and refocus on my homework. After a while, Caden joins us at the table to work on his AP statistics. He asks about a problem, and then Eli comes and joins us as we all discuss the homework.

"Why are there so many cars in the driveway?" Mom stops when we all look up at her from the table. "Uh, what's up?"

Her eyes find mine and she widens them.

"I drove to school today, and it looks like someone intentionally flattened my tire. The guys were at football practice, and Caden saw me changing it and worried something else might have been wrong with the car. So they followed me home and then worried someone might be trying to find me alone and..." I spread my arms out to indicate the guys at the table and the one in the living room. "We were just discussing our AP statistics homework."

"O-kay." Mom hangs her purse on the rack near the door. Her eyes linger on the empty pizza boxes in the trash. "I assume you've all eaten by now."

"There's some leftovers in the fridge," Caden points out.

"I appreciate you boys looking out for Harper." Pretty sure that's not all she wants to say, but I'll probably hear about it later. "I'm sure your parents are probably wondering where you are."

"They know where we are," Luke says, "but it's late and we should head out. We just didn't feel comfortable leaving Harper alone."

Mom nods, still looking fairly shell-shocked to find four guys in her house. It's hard to imagine her thinking of them as boys when they all tower over us. The guys pack up their books.

"Thank you." I don't know what else to say to them.

"Walk us out?" Caden meets my eyes and I nod. "Thank you for letting us crash your house, Ms. Davidson."

She pulls out the leftover pizza box. "Thank you for feeding us once again. I'm going to owe you guys a dinner one of these nights. I'm making Harper's favorite mac 'n' cheese for her birthday tomorrow night. It always makes too much. And we could use help eating the cake. You should come over."

When her eyes meet my shocked ones, she realizes her mistake. She mouths *sorry*.

"We didn't know it was Harper's birthday," Luke says as he stands next to me. "We'll definitely have to celebrate it."

Mom smiles. "We always have leftovers for days afterwards, so you'll be saving us from ourselves."

I gesture to the door before she invites them to a sleepover or something worse. "All right. Don't let us keep you."

The horsemen all say goodbye and assure her they'll be here tomorrow. Fantastic, insert eyeroll here.

I follow them out the door and as soon as it closes behind me, I cross my arms over my chest and stop on the bottom step. They pause to look at me. I should be snarky and taciturn about how I really don't need babysitters, but I decide to take one from my mom's playbook.

"Thank you." They didn't have to be this nice to me. So I can be nice in return.

"About today..." Jack starts.

I shrug and look down at my feet. "I get it. No worries. I'll let Mom know you guys won't be coming tomorrow. I'll park closer to the school so the cameras can see my car. You guys can go on with your lives."

After all, that's what I want too. I blow out my breath and raise my gaze to them when they don't leave. They all look a little pissed.

"What?" I can't stand the silence anymore.

"You really think we'd give up that quickly?" Luke smirks and shakes his head. "We just wanted to give you a taste of your own medicine."

I narrow my eyes at him. "Great. If that's how you want to punish me, feel free."

Caden chuckles, and before I can move, he wraps his arms around me and lifts me.

"Put me down," I say quietly, not wanting to grab Mom's attention.

"Nah, little nympho." He carries me off to a corner of the house where there are no windows and the light from the porch doesn't reach. He sets me down and the others crowd in around me.

My heart is already pounding, but at least they probably won't spank me. Not here where Mom might come out at any moment.

"We definitely don't want to miss your birthday." Luke steps forward, backing me into the side of the house. His hand comes up and toys with a strand of my hair. The backs of his fingers skate along my cheek. A fire lights inside me.

One day and I missed this feeling.

Even though I want to cave and let them do whatever they want—within reason—to me, I also don't want to make it easy on them to reclaim me.

"You seemed pretty cozy at lunch today. If you touched any of them, our deal—"

"Is still on, princess. You didn't think any of us would willingly let you slip through our fingers, did you?" Luke raises his eyebrow like I should seriously question my sanity.

"Still not going to be your sex toy, Death."

"We don't want a toy, princess." He leans in, and my breath catches at the rush of sparks through my veins. "We want you."

I want to shove him away and pull him closer at the same time. Instead, we stay there locked in a battle of wills. His pale eyes locked on mine. I want his lips on mine, but I won't be the one to cave.

"New rules, kitten." Eli's voice penetrates the fog trying to invade my mind. I don't release Luke's gaze to find Eli in the dark.

"What if I don't want any new rules?" I arch an eyebrow at Luke, daring him.

He smiles and slides a hand around the back of my neck.

"From now on," Luke says, "if you go radio silent on us, we will find you. No matter where you are or what you're doing."

"I suppose you'll spank me?" I press my lips together. It seems to be their go-to punishment.

"Not even close, princess." Luke closes the distance between us and kisses my jawline.

My lips part and heat rushes through me. "Then what?"

"We get to take something we want." His eyes lift to mine again.

My brow furrows. They want me to give them my virginity, so they definitely can't mean that. "Take something?"

"A first." Luke's gaze drops to my lips, and I feel a tug of desire inside. "Of our choosing. So many choices still. We've barely started to touch you or taste you."

Keeping his hand on the back of my neck, he wraps an arm around my hip and grabs my ass.

"If you try to ice us out, same deal." Luke tips my head back as his eyes lock on mine once more. "Do you understand, princess, or would you like a demonstration?"

Fuck. "I understand."

"Good. Now be a good girl and kiss your owners good night." Luke's eyes sparkle in the darkness. "Then go turn on your webcam and be ready for us."

I'm afraid of what that means, but part of me doesn't hate having their attention back. My gaze drops to Luke's mouth. Kiss my owners good night. Why that doesn't make me want to smack him, I'll never understand.

Instead, I press my lips briefly against Luke's. That's a good night kiss.

The others chuckle darkly, making my pulse race, and Luke shakes his head while clicking his tongue.

"Have you already forgotten how to kiss, princess?" Luke draws me in closer and lowers his head so his mouth hovers over mine. "You can do better than that. We could just take—"

I cut off his sentence with my lips against his. My hand goes into his hair and I tug on it as I open my mouth beneath his and kiss him like I've been dying to. I'm up on my toes. I didn't know how addictive their kisses had become until I went without.

I like kissing. I'm pretty sure I'll like whatever else they want to do with me, and that frightens me more than any threat they have about *taking* my firsts. Kissing is fine. I don't want them to move so fast that I can't keep up. And there's the whole condom discussion that hasn't come back up.

As I slide my tongue against Luke's, I can't contain the moan that slips from me into his mouth. I *really* like kissing. I'm not sure how long I kiss him, but I realize I'm going to have to go in or Mom will get worried, especially when their cars haven't left.

I break off the kiss, and Luke's eyes are hot pools. He smirks down at me.

"Much better, princess. See you soon." He squeezes my ass as he steps back.

Eli steps into his spot. I don't hesitate this time. I grab the back of his neck and push up on my toes as I bring his mouth crashing down on mine. He holds my ass as I take his mouth the way he always takes mine. Hot and ravenous.

The fire within me is raging hotter as Eli works my mouth the way he wants, dominating me until I can barely breathe. When I pull away, he tucks a strand of hair behind my ear.

"Night, kitten."

My heart settles as Jack steps into the space Eli vacated. I still feel bad for yesterday when he tried so hard to make me smile. I give him a smile now as I lean up with my hands on his chest to kiss him.

He lifts me by the waist so that it's easier for me to explore his mouth. Tingles shoot through me as we kiss each other, taking our time rediscovering. I could spend hours kissing each of them.

I meet his dark blue eyes. I won't apologize for the way I acted, but I am sorry I hurt him, even if he is a horseman.

"Night, sweetheart." He gives me a soft kiss before setting me down.

Luke and Eli are already at their car, and Jack walks over to stand near Caden's. I lift my gaze to Caden.

"Thank you for caring for me tonight." I can at least give him that much. He didn't have to do any of what he did, but he did it because he worried about me. I can't ignore how that makes my insides glow.

"Any time, little nympho."

I grin at his ridiculous pet name for me. "That's the one you're sticking with."

He shrugs with a mischievous grin. "It fits."

I shake my head and hug his neck to draw him down so I can kiss him. He meets me halfway. Our lips collide and open to each other. He lifts me by the thighs while pushing me back against the house.

Leaning into me, he grinds his hard cock between my legs, and I moan at the contact. Fuck, I missed this. I missed them. I'm so fucked right now.

Caden kisses me like he has to have me now, and I'm on fire from it. I wish I didn't feel this physical attraction with the guys. It would make it so much easier to deny them everything.

He lifts his mouth and rests his forehead on mine. "No more being broken, little nympho."

I nod and look up into his green eyes. I'm done playing broken, especially if it means they can just randomly do shit to me wherever I might be. That doesn't sound like fun.

"Stay safe. Lock your doors and let me watch you tonight." He captures my lips for another deep kiss before he lowers me back to the ground.

My knees feel weak and unsteady, but they hold me.

I walk back into the porch light and watch them load up in their cars to leave. I don't know how to feel right now. They never released me from the pact. And now, I'm not sure I want to get away.

Fortunately, I don't have to worry about that until tomorrow.

CHAPTER 35

The Fortifications

HARPER

Mom surprisingly has little to say about the guys when I come back into the house, but it's late and she's worked a long day. After a few minutes of catching up and discussing getting me a new tire this weekend, we say good night. I gather up my homework and move upstairs.

Even knowing they aren't home yet, I turn on my webcam and decide to text Kenz.

ME:

Horsemen are back on

KENZ:

sad face emoji What happened?

ME:

Had a flat. Guys saw me and made sure I got home okay

Mom invited them to my B-day dinner tomorrow

KENZ:

surprise face emoji What?

KENZ:

Yup. Pizza and cake for lunch, right?

ME:

I know. You're still coming, right?

KENZ:

Yup. Pizza and cake for lunch, right?

ME:

I'll check with the guys

KENZ:

Boo

ME:

New punishment

KENZ:

No more spankings? *winky face emoji*

ME:

Probably but they can also punish me by taking a first

KENZ:

shock face emoji

What does that mean?

ME:

shrugging emoji They get to decide what to take, but touching me or kissing me somewhere they haven't yet

KENZ:

fire emoji

ME:

I don't know what to do. Maybe I can't get out of this, so I should enjoy the ride?

KENZ:

What a ride it will be *grinning face emoji*

I stare at the screen with no windows of empty bedrooms on it. They shut them down last night and left me alone. I still don't know how I feel about what they did, but they wanted me to feel what I made them feel, I guess.

Confused, angry, hurt, a little relieved, but not as relieved as I thought I would feel.

I tie my hair into a messy bun to keep it out of my face and pull out my English homework to get started. I still need to graduate so I can leave all this behind me for college.

That gives me a moment of pause. What will the guys be doing for college? I never really imagined the horsemen outside of high school. I picture Ivy League schools and top ranked fraternities in their future.

A stream pops up on my screen, and Jack appears, sitting at his desk.

"Oh, I have you all alone. Lucky me." Jack leans back in his chair. "You should let down your hair, sweetheart."

I shrug. "It keeps it out of my face while I work."

He nods thoughtfully and leans in while looking over his shoulders suspiciously. He raises an eyebrow. "So how do I get you naked?"

I laugh and shake my head. "I'm sure if you wait long enough, someone will demand it. Or you could."

"Would you do it if I asked?" Jack gives me a smile and a wink.

This is a different tactic than the others use. They demand I take things off or change. Jack simply asks if I would if he asked. It's bound to happen tonight. It's rare they let an opportunity to strip me pass them by. I shrug.

"Probably. You've already seen everything anyway." My cheeks burn as I remember the shower and how they saw ever-y-thing.

"Lock your door." He gestures with his head.

"Already done." I raise an eyebrow at him, wondering what he wants to do.

"Take off your shirt." He leans back in his chair. "Please."

I grab the hem of my t-shirt and pull it over my head. I put on a black lace bra this morning. Jack whistles low.

"Fuck, sweetheart. I like you in lace." He licks his lips and a wave of heat flows through my system. He strips off his shirt. "Pants next."

I lift my eyebrow at him.

"Please." He smirks. Of all of them, Jack has always been an equal opportunity type guy. The first one to strip naked to help put me at ease.

I stand and push my jeans over my hips and down to the floor to step out of. Now he can see my matching panties. I don't turn around, because it's a thong, but I'm sure he can tell from the string-thin sides.

He stands and takes off his pants. No one else has logged in yet.

When he sits at his desk, he gives me a look that scorches through me. "Wanna get naked together, sweetheart?"

"Are you going to touch yourself, Jack?" I lean forward. Maybe I can get a little control of this entire situation. When they aren't in the room with me physically, my brain doesn't go on meltdown quite as quickly.

"You want me to?" He rubs his lower lip as he takes in my body.

I bite my lip and nod.

"Fuck, yeah." He slips off his boxers while I undo my bra and take off my panties. "Headphones and sit on the edge of your bed."

I put my AirPods in my ears and sit on the bed. Without the others around, maybe Jack will let me get off.

"Spread your legs and let me look at your pussy." Jack's words make my heart speed up. The graphic reminder of the shower floods my mind. He wants me to voluntarily show him every inch of my pussy. Fuck it, he's seen it already.

I do as he says and lean back on my hands, arching so my breasts thrust out. His hand strokes his cock as his eyes wander over my body from my tight nipples to my wet pussy. My core pulses and throbs with each of his strokes.

"Fuck, Harper. You don't know what I want to do to you." His voice is strained.

"Then tell me." I don't know where those words come from but I want him to. I want to know all the dirty things he wants to do to me.

"I want to taste every inch of you. Suck your nipples until they're sore and sensitive. Then work my way down to your sweet pussy and suck on your clit until you explode with pleasure, but I wouldn't stop there. Fuck, no. I'd keep pushing you over the edge until you couldn't take it anymore."

My breathing quickens, and I can almost feel his mouth on me. "Then what?"

His hand speeds up on his cock. What would it feel like to stroke him? To feel his hard cock in my hand?

"I'd lift over you and slam my cock into your pussy. Take you hard and fast until we can't breathe. I'd wait until your pussy shatters around me before filling you with my cum."

I bite my lip as he erupts all over his hand. Another feed logs in, and I watch Eli's gaze roam over me.

"I only got her shirt off, Jack." He raises his eyebrows. Jack stands to go to the bathroom.

"Not my fault I'm more charming than you. Be right back, sweetheart." Jack disappears.

I almost close my legs, but Eli says, "I like you like this, kitten."

I inhale and release a slow breath to cool myself down. Maybe letting them get a good look will stop any thoughts of punishment.

"Imagine all the fun we could have with you spread out before me." Eli's finger drags over his lower lip.

A wave of heat flows through me. I'm still turned on from Jack. The desire in Eli's eyes only makes me hotter.

"Take your hair down, kitten."

I sit up and bring my legs together.

"Stay spread open. I want to see your wet pussy." Eli's words in my ears make my insides molten.

I open my legs for him as I release my hair. Dropping my hair tie on the bedspread beside me, I work my fingers through my hair.

"Fuck," Caden says as his feed comes in. "What the hell did I miss?"

Eli chuckles. "Jack's been playing with the kitten on his own."

Luke's feed comes on, and I meet his gaze. He licks his lips, but otherwise doesn't make a move.

Jack returns to his chair, boxers on and all smiles.

"I do have homework," I mention as I lean back on my hands again. My hair falls between my arms.

"Definitely better with the hair down." Eli unzips his pants and pulls out his cock. He strokes it slowly. "Don't worry, we'll let you get back to your homework, kitten."

My heart races as his hand works his thick cock.

Luke runs a hand through his hair impatiently. "Touch your lips, princess."

I raise an eyebrow, but lift my hand. My lips are soft against my fingertips. Now this is a test. They want to see if I'll do what they say. As long as they're on that side of the computer and I'm here, I feel comfortable with what they want.

No one else is touching me, even though my body is on display. Their undivided attention is on me. Not some random girl sitting with them at lunch. Just me, and they get off on it.

"Suck on your finger," Luke says. I meet his eyes before sliding my index finger into my mouth and sucking on it.

I hear a rustle from someone else and turn to see Caden pulling his hard cock out of his pants. He smirks at me as my thighs twitch at the sight of his cock. Still big.

"Put another finger in your mouth and stroke them in and out while you suck them." Luke's voice is a little harsher. His hand moves on his lap, but he doesn't pull his cock out like the others.

Doing as he asks, I slowly pump my fingers in and out of my lips. I flick my tongue against them and my pussy throbs. Eli strokes his cock, and I can't help but wonder what it would feel like to have his cock in my mouth instead of my fingers.

Would his skin be soft or rough?

I move in sync with his hand, speeding up and slowing down with him. Eli groans and comes all over his hand. My eyes meet his and he smirks.

He may be feeling cocky, but fuck if I'm not feeling powerful getting these guys off. It's my body they're watching, wanting, and my mouth they long to be in.

I switch my gaze to Caden.

He wraps his hand tight around his cock and fists it as he moves. His green eyes focus on mine before slipping down to my fingers in my mouth. I ache with a need I can't quite understand.

"Add another finger, princess. Feel the stretch of your mouth around them," Luke's deep voice whispers in my ear, and I get even wetter. I'm wound tight and no one is even touching me.

Whimpering, I add the third finger and keep moving them in and out of my mouth while watching Caden's fist move over his hard, thick cock. I want to close my thighs and press them together to ease the ache between them.

Caden's words echo in my thoughts, how he'd fill my mouth while Jack took me from behind. I want to touch myself. I want to get off, but it's not allowed.

Oh, I can, if I ask one of them to come do it for me. They would probably take turns doing it, and I'd want to return the favor.

I'd want to wrap my hand around their cocks and stroke until they spilled all over my hand. Or feel them slide along my tongue between my lips as I sucked on them. I don't think they'll give me a choice to stop, and I wouldn't want them to. I want them to come down my throat so I can swallow them. Take their pleasure and make it my own.

Caden's face tightens as he groans. Cum covers his hand.

"Show's over, princess." Luke leans back in his chair.

I take my fingers out of my mouth, feeling empty. Picking up my panties, I grab a camisole and sleep shorts before going into the bathroom. My phone dings when I set it on the counter.

DEATH (LUKE):

I can still taste you

A rush flows through me, making me want to slide my fingers into my pussy and ease this ache. Even though I've never touched myself like that before, I'm sure I could manage. His words weren't on the group chat. Luke sent that to me where the others can't see.

Shivers flow down my back, but I ignore it while I get dressed and return to my desk. I meet Luke's eyes before focusing on my homework. I don't know if he wants me to respond to that text or not.

I don't know what to say. Is he talking about the kiss we shared earlier or when he tasted his fingers after smacking my pussy yesterday? I tuck my hair behind my ears.

When I slip into bed later, they're all getting settled for the night. They've upped the stakes of punishment. They want to speed things up. Move things to that next level. I'm not sure I'm strong enough to hold them off. I'm not sure I *want* to hold them off.

Their lights turn off, and I meet Luke's eyes in the dark. He watches me quietly, intensely. My eyes grow heavy as I try to keep this connection between the two of us.

I can still taste you. The words linger in my head. I'm sure I lose whatever battle we had going as I slip into sleep.

CHAPTER 36

Breaching The Walls

HARPER

"Happy birthday!" Mom's voice wakes me at six a.m. I glance at my nightstand where the guys are all still sleeping and gently close the screen so Mom doesn't see.

She walks farther into the room. "I wanted to be the first to wish you a happy birthday, and since I'm leaving for work, that's now."

I struggle to sit up and rub at my eyes. "Thanks, Mom."

Sitting on the edge of my bed, she pulls me into a hug. I snuggle into her warmth and fresh scent.

"I love you and wish you the happiest day ever." Mom pulls away. "I'll give you your present tonight after everyone leaves. Donuts are on the counter for you."

"Thanks." I rub at the sleep in my eyes some more.

She ruffles my hair and bear hugs me again. "Have a great day, sweetie."

"I will." As soon as she releases me, I slide back down into bed. "After I sleep more."

"See you tonight." Mom blows me a kiss from the door, and I stick my hand up to catch it. I snatch it out of the air and draw it under the covers with me. She chuckles as she shuts my door.

I open my laptop screen and fall back asleep. The bed shifts and my eyes open. "I don't need another hug, Mom."

A familiar masculine chuckle answers me. Wait a minute.

My eyes pop open to Luke sitting on the edge of my bed. "What's going on?"

"Happy birthday, princess." Luke hands me a small box.

Someone lies down behind me, and my eyes widen. I look over my shoulder at Caden. He has his ankles crossed and his hands behind his head as he winks.

"Morning, little nympho. You get two escorts from now on." Caden pulls me closer to him, even though he's on top of the covers I'm under.

Luke kicks off his shoes and lies on my other side. Heat creeps up my neck.

"Aren't you guys a little early?" I want to run into the bathroom and brush everything. I'm so not a morning person.

"Your mom woke us." Luke reaches over and straightens my camisole strap. Shivers ripple through me. "Since we were already awake, figured we'd make the most of it."

I turn the box over in my hands. "Do I open this now or later?"

"Now," Caden says.

"Okay, but first I need to use the bathroom." I look between the guys, needing one to move to let me out. They shrug, and Luke slips off the side.

I brush my teeth and use the bathroom and do the best I can do with my hair before returning to my bedroom.

Caden pats the bed beside him. I swallow as I return to my spot. This isn't other-side-of-the-camera safe. Luke closes in on me, trapping me between them again. They're both dressed for the day already, and I feel self-conscious in my pajamas.

Luke hands me the box again. This is really weird, but I take it, curiosity flooding me. Why would they get me a birthday present? Have they done this before? With other girls?

I take off the bow and gently unwrap the gift. What would the horsemen give a girl they've claimed for her birthday? Expecting some sort of item to show I'm their property, I open the jewelry box to find a beautiful silver Celtic knot band with a black inlay.

"This is lovely." I take it out of the box and slide it onto my right ring finger. It fits perfectly. "Thank you."

I lean over and kiss Luke on the cheek before moving to give Caden the same kiss. Caden turns his head at the last second so that our lips meet. Heat pours through my veins as he draws me in closer until I'm pressed along his side.

He releases my lips and presses my head down against his chest. "Go back to sleep, little nympho. You don't need to be up for another hour."

Luke rolls onto his side behind me and spoons me like he did before. I should protest, but they're both warm, and the weight of their gift feels nice on my finger. I close my eyes as I sink into them.

A hand stroking my thigh wakes me. My pillow is hard and a steady heartbeat echoes in it. I'm tangled up. I open my eyes and see my hand on Caden's chest.

His chest rumbles under my ear and I peek up at him. He looks like he's asleep, but then a hand strokes my thigh again. I look down and my thigh is pulled over his, and his hand is lazily stroking up and down.

I become aware of the other beast behind me. His body curls around mine, his erection against my ass and his thigh between mine, pressing against the ache forming. His lips move along the nape of my neck, and I inhale the heady combination of cinnamon and sultry spices. Decadent and tempting.

Caden's fingertips meet the edge of my shorts. Luke's arm is around my waist and his hand rests on my stomach. His mouth sucks on the back of my neck, and I release a moan.

His fingers clench into my stomach as Caden's grip tightens on my thigh. I'm suddenly awake and aroused being wrapped up in two of them. Them pressed against me. Fuck, I'm in trouble, because I don't want to leave this bed right now.

But I really should. This is dangerous. Playing with fire guaranteed to burst me into flames.

Luke drags a hand across my stomach and over my hip, then slaps my ass. I let out a startled cry. He chuckles. "Get up and ready for school before you make us all late, princess."

"I don't mind being late." Caden shifts and drags me more on top of him so I can feel how much he wants me. "Want to get off first thing on your birthday, little nympho?"

He thrusts his hips up against me. That's enough to make me scramble to my feet. I throw my hair back as I stand. My strap is down my arm and I fix that.

"Want me to help you shower?" Caden leans up on his elbows and his hot eyes trail over me. "I can help get those hard-to-reach spots."

Oof, my insides turn to goo. I don't have the processing speed to deal with two horsemen first thing in the morning. My mouth opens and closes as Caden's grin widens.

I shake my head. Slowly, I back away and shut myself in the bathroom. As I turn on the shower, I hear dark laughter from my bedroom. Taking a breath, I flick the lock.

In the mirror, my skin is flushed and my pajamas are all wrinkled. I look like I've been ravished, but I haven't...yet. I shake it off and focus on showering quickly and getting ready for school.

Unfortunately, I didn't exactly grab anything to put on after my shower. I wrap a towel around myself and walk into my bedroom. Caden and Luke sit on my bed. Their eyes track my every movement.

Walking to my dresser, I hold my towel tight while I grab some panties.

"Lose the towel, little nympho."

I swallow. If I don't obey, what will happen? Will he decide to cop a feel of my breast and slide his fingers inside me? A shiver races through me at how much I don't mind either of those things. Dangerous.

Instead, I drop the towel.

No punishment today. Especially if I'm going to like it and crave it.

Caden sucks in his breath. "Fuck, the live show is so much better."

"Right?" Luke agrees.

Pretending I'm alone, I pull on my panties and grab the matching bra. When I go to fasten my bra, hands grab the back before I can latch it. I didn't even hear Luke move. His heat just suddenly engulfs me.

"Allow me." His breath caresses my shoulder as he hooks my bra together. I try to hold back the shudder that ripples through me.

He drops His hands to my waist and he walks with me to my closet. His hands are hot against my bare skin. "What are we wearing today?"

"Uh..." My brain is on meltdown as Luke's fully clothed body presses into me from behind. My body craves to lean back into him. Feel his warm hands all over me.

He reaches for a red sundress, pressing into me. "This would be nice."

I nod. My brain is still barely awake, and having him close to me is making my blood flood the wrong part of my body. "Wrong bra."

"We can fix that." Before I can stop him, Luke unhooks my bra and drags it off me.

I resist the temptation to cover my breasts as I stand there in only my panties with two guys in my room. A shiver ripples through me again. I'm completely helpless to stop them from doing whatever they want.

Luke walks to my dresser and pulls out a strapless bra. He holds it up. "This one?"

I nod. Fuck my life. I have to trust they won't do anything I'm not willing to do. At least, as long as I'm not being punished. My gaze meets Luke's light blue eyes.

He wraps his arms around me, and I bite my lip to keep the gasp in from his heat surrounding me. He puts on my bra, and I hold it in the front while he hooks it behind my back.

"Much better." He drops a kiss to my shoulder. Sparks cascade downward, settling between my legs. He reaches around me and grabs the red dress. His body presses flush against my back, and I inhale sharply, filling me with his sultry cologne. He unzips the dress in front of me and then lifts it over my head.

No one has dressed me since I was little. This feels really weird, intimate, and a little erotic. I find the arm straps and let the dress fall onto me. He zips it up with the back of his fingers running up my spine.

I bite my lip to stop the moan that wants to slip out. Forcing myself, I step out of Luke's arms and turn around.

"Very nice." Luke gives me a partial smile. His eyes are hot when he lifts his gaze to mine.

"I agree," Caden says. "What do you think, little nympho? Would you like the live show too?"

What does that mean? My brow furrows as I glance over at Caden.

He strokes his hand over the front of his jeans, where his hard cock is definitely straining. My eyes widen. Oh, fuck.

"Of course she does." Luke turns my desk chair around to face the bed and grabs my hips. He sits down and pulls me to sit on his lap. Heat floods my face at the press of Luke's erection against my ass.

"I still need to dry my hair and do my makeup." I try to get up, but Luke wraps an arm around my waist.

"You'll have time if you help Caden out," Luke says against my ear.

Help him out? What the fuck does that mean? I flush with heat as Caden lowers his pants and sits in front of me with his erect cock in his fist. It's even bigger in real life, I swear.

I swallow as my gaze locks on him. He's long and thick. His fist overlaps a little on his cock. Would my fingers wrap around him, or would I need to use both hands? My panties dampen. I press my thighs together against the ache forming.

"Stand, princess." Luke parts his legs and I stand between them. "Lift your skirt."

I take a deep breath as my eyes are helplessly drawn to Caden's hand lightly stroking over his cock. What punishment would I get if I disobeyed? If I said no thank you? They can't take anything if they all aren't here. So the boundaries will hold for now...but later...

They can't move any boundaries or take anything if I obey. I lift my skirt so they both can see my panties.

"More?" Luke asks.

I look over my shoulder at Luke to see what he's talking about, but his eyes are on Caden's.

"More." Caden's green eyes focus on me.

Luke's hands go to the sides of my panties. He pulls them down, and I try not to move as they slip to my feet. I bite my lip at Luke's touch. Caden grunts his approval as his fist continues to move on his cock.

"More?"

I swallow. What next?

Caden's eyes meet mine when he smiles. "More."

"Sit, princess." Luke's hands guide me to sit on his lap. "Keep your skirt up."

Fuck. I do as he says and sit with my knees on either side of Luke's legs.

Caden's eyes go to my pussy, and wetness gathers between my legs. The sound of his fist on his cock makes my insides soften and need curls in my stomach.

"More?"

What more is there? Caden's fist moves faster on his cock, and an answering pulse throbs deep inside me.

"More."

Holding my waist, Luke spreads his legs so I'm forced to spread mine. He opens them obscenely wide. Wider than I did last night on the video call. Heat engulfs my face as Caden's gaze focuses between my legs.

My breath rushes in and out of me as Caden jerks off to my exposed pussy. The sound of his fist moving over his swollen cock is obscenely loud in my bedroom. The air is cool against my wet, aching pussy.

"Do you want his cock, princess?" Luke's voice is soft against my ear. A whimper escapes me as I lean back into Luke. His fingers tighten into my waist. "Do you want to suck on it? Feel the silky skin between your fingers as you pump it with your fist? Feel it against your wet pussy as he pushes inside you, stretching you, thrusting over and over again until you come all over him? Or would you want him to slide his thick cock between your ass cheeks, find your other hole, and press into it until you feel like you're going to die if he doesn't bury his whole cock in your ass?"

Caden groans as he comes on his hand. My pussy squeezes around nothing.

"That could have been inside you, princess. Hot cum filling you. I would have sunk into your soaking wet pussy and fucked you until you came again."

I whimper at Luke's words. My heart thunders in my chest and I need so much more. But I'm terrified to ask for it. Terrified to want it.

Caden stands and brings his hand to my lips. I meet his darkened eyes.

"Taste it, little nympho."

I flick my tongue over the warm, salty cum on his hand, bringing it into my mouth.

Luke groans behind me. Caden smiles.

"Maybe Luke will let you help him get off." Caden walks into my bathroom to clean up, leaving me with Luke.

I'm so turned on right now. Still spread wide open with my legs wrapped around the outside of Luke's. My pussy throbs. I have the taste of Caden in my mouth and Luke's hands around my waist.

"Slide your finger between your pussy lips, princess."

I do as Luke commands and feel how slippery I am. I gasp at the touch, needing so much more.

"Show me." His voice is low and dark in my ear, sending shivers down my spine.

I lift my wet finger in front of our faces. His hand captures mine and he draws my finger into his mouth and sucks on it. I moan at how good it feels and close my eyes.

Luke closes our legs and releases my finger. He lifts me to stand and helps me back into my panties. My breathing is chaotic and all I can think about is this aching need inside me. When he finishes, he turns me in his arms and nudges my face up with his knuckle.

"Want a taste?" His gaze is locked on my lips.

I nod helplessly. He lowers his mouth to mine and takes it. I can taste myself on his tongue and I'm sure he tastes Caden on mine. Our bodies press together as our tongues dance with each other. I whimper as he draws away.

"Finish getting ready for school, princess." His eyes are darker, his lips swollen from our kiss. I want to lean in and capture them again. To draw him against me, have his weight cover me. "Now."

I blink at his command and head to the bathroom. I run into Caden, who lifts me up and presses me against the door before slamming his mouth down on mine. Sweet mercy. My legs wrap around him as I cling to him. He takes my mouth with his tongue, stroking inside and making my pussy pulse. When he lifts his mouth, we're both breathless.

Leaning my head against the door, I stare into his eyes as I try to regain my breath.

"Thank you, little nympho." He lowers me to my feet and smacks my ass as he pushes me in the direction of the bathroom. "Hurry, we don't want to be late."

Shaking my head and trying to reset my brain, I get ready for school in a daze. After a few minutes, the routine of drying my hair settles me. I put my hair up in a high ponytail and dab on some light eye makeup. Red lip stain that matches my dress is the last touch. I glance at the ring on my finger.

It's simple and actually quite nice, but it's an odd choice for the horsemen to give a girl they claimed only a week and a half ago. Have they ever bought a girl a birthday present before?

I slip on some sandals and grab my backpack and a light sweater to wear over my dress before heading downstairs.

Luke and Caden are waiting for me at the island. One of them made a new pot of coffee, so I grab a cup before pulling the box of donuts over to me. I'm surprised the guys didn't eat them all. I pick my favorite, chocolate iced, and pass the box to the guys. They each grab one.

"So Kenz and I have this thing where we go out for lunch on our birthdays." I pick at my donut while I talk. "Is that going to be okay with you guys?"

I lift my eyes to meet theirs, worried they'll say no.

"Sounds like a plan. Where are we going?" Luke arches his eyebrows.

"Would you consider letting me go with her alone?" I take a sip of my coffee. This is the part I hate: having to ask them permission for things I've always just done. But right now, things are a little fragile between us, so I'm doing what I can to avoid more punishment.

Luke and Caden look at each other and then shake their heads.

I sigh. "Fine. I'll let Kenz know she can bring Brandon then."

CHAPTER 37

The Peace Talks

ELI

Jack and I wait at the school for the others to bring Harper. Jack sits on the sign while I lean against it. At least Caden was nice enough to position the camera for the little show he and Luke put on this morning. I get hard just thinking about Harper's flushed face as her pink tongue darted out to taste Caden's cum.

It's all good that our girl helps us get off, but I can't wait to fuck her. I'm all for us all fucking her, but I want her to myself sometimes too. We won't have that until she gives in to us.

Soon. Hopefully.

The red sundress looks spectacular on Harper and her ponytail swings behind her as she walks between Luke and Caden on her way to us. Jack jumps off the sign, walks up to her, and lifts her off her feet.

He kisses the shit out of her red lips. "Happy birthday, sweetheart!"

I walk up behind them as he swings her around and drops her in front of me.

"Happy birthday, kitten." I take the back of her neck in my hand as I lean in and kiss her. She opens beneath me and kisses me back. Maybe our little stunt of ignoring her paid off.

When I pull back, she smiles up at me. She touches the ring on her finger. "Thank you both for the present."

"You're welcome." Putting my arm around her shoulders, I walk her into the school. She steps over to Caden's locker when he opens it.

"We have lunch plans." Luke grabs his books from his locker.

I lift an eyebrow.

"Pizza and cake with Kenz." Harper bounces on her toes a little as she says it.

Today won't be a very healthy eating day, but I smile at her enthusiasm. "I look forward to it."

Luke wanders off to class with our girl while Caden and Jack hang back with me.

"Do we know anything more?" I ask as we head to our first period.

"The parking lot camera is a joke." Jack shakes his head. "The footage is blurry and too many people go that direction to fuck off during school. I couldn't even tell which one was Harper on the footage."

"I've got a short list of people who weren't at the game on Friday and could have targeted Harper." Caden scratches his head as we enter the classroom and sit in the back. "Unfortunately, we've pissed off a good amount of people, and Harper pointed out that it could be someone actually mad at her for being with us, which could mean a chick."

"We've been able to take down some wannabe queen bees before." I don't see the problem with taking down someone who is causing harm even if it's a chick. We just don't beat them up like some guys.

"We need more info." Jack shakes his head. "At least she's wearing the ring."

The ring has a built-in GPS that we can monitor. Luke wanted to put one in her like a real pet, but Caden found out about this tech ring. Pretty sure a microchip would have been a no-go for our girl. We've had it for a few days and her birthday was a convenient excuse to give it to her.

We each installed the software on our phones. Not that I think our girl will try to hide from us, but just in case whoever is messing with her escalates. We'd rather be safe than sorry.

HARPER

"So it's back on?"

"Apparently it was never off." I sketch on the drawing of Luke today. My ring flashes in the overhead lights. Still a weird gift, but I guess it says something to others.

"And your mom knows and is okay with four guys pursuing you?" Kenz shifts in her chair. "Because my mom would freak the fuck out. She almost caught Brandon in my bedroom a few nights ago and he's been my boyfriend for two years. She would have cut his balls off. My mom does *not* mess around."

I smile at the thought of Kenz's five-foot-tall, one-hundred-pound mom taking after Brandon with a carving knife.

"I'm not dating them." I shrug. "She knows they're interested and I might be interested in them, but nothing is going to happen."

Though she bought me two big boxes of condoms just in case. I shake my head.

"Yeah, but she invited them all to dinner?"

"She's suspicious and wants to get to know them." I shrug again. "She asked before I could even interject to stop her. Besides, they got me a birthday gift."

Kenz grabs my hand again. She studied it hard when I first showed her. "Brandon sucks at gifts. I don't think he'd ever get me a ring unless he was asking me to marry him and that's not for a really long time."

I pry my hand loose and get back to my sketch. "They're acting all sweet again, but I won't be fooled. They're assholes of the first order and they might be talented actors, but I'm not falling for it again."

They turned into raging assholes after one day of no communication. Yeah, I'm going to keep my guard up around them. But I also really enjoy what they do to me, and knowing they want me gives me a measure of control and power over them.

Tanner stops next to me and squats. He puts one hand on my desk to steady himself. "Hey, everything okay today?"

Kenz gives him the stink eye.

"Yes, fine." I gesture. "Kenz, Tanner. Tanner, Kenz."

"I know Tanner Lewis. How do you know Tanner?" Kenz turns the stink eye on me.

"Monday when you were sick." I close my notebook. "Tanner had to sit close to the board and since you weren't here, he sat in your seat."

"Your sister is Mia, right?" Kenz asks Tanner.

"Yeah, twins." He smiles.

Kenz presses her lips together. "You can go now."

"Wait, Tanner. What's wrong, Kenz?"

She's watching him distrustfully. "We'll talk when he leaves."

"It's okay, Harper." Tanner straightens. "I wanted to make sure you were okay after how they treated you."

"Umm, yeah, things are back to normal." I give him a small smile. Kenz shouldn't worry so much. Tanner wants revenge on the horsemen, and maybe I can use that to my advantage. "Nothing to worry about."

"Good. See you at lunch?"

I shake my head. "Kenz is taking me out."

Tanner nods and heads back to his desk.

"What the hell, H?" Kenz hisses at me under her breath. "Why is Tanner Lewis asking you about lunch?"

I sigh and whisper back, "Yesterday I ate outside, and he apparently likes to eat at the same tree I usually do."

"That can't be a coincidence." She turns and glares at Tanner.

"Seriously, he's just looking out for me because the horsemen scared his sister off and he didn't want me to feel like I was alone against them." I put my sketchpad away.

"Do you even know who Tanner is?" Kenz puts her hand over mine. "Has he ever talked to you before this year? Because that's sus."

"No, but I didn't really know Rebecca Forester either and I think she would understand what I'm dealing with. Or more, who I'm dealing with." I check my phone to make sure the horsemen haven't texted. I'm not getting punished on my birthday.

"Do you know what he did?" she whispers.

"No, but I know if his sister went through only a little of what I'm going through, then maybe he was justified in whatever he did. After all, they were on the team together. He thought they were friends."

"Harper, we need to talk about this because you only got part of the story, and if the guys know he's sniffing around you, they won't be happy." Kenz straightens in her seat. "We'll talk before the guys get there tonight."

I glance at Tanner, who gives me a crooked smile. Penny also warned me about him. I don't get a bad vibe from him. Maybe he's a little eager to get back at the horsemen, but he's just been friendly so far.

"Fine."

The bell rings, and everyone leaves for lunch. Kenz and I head toward the parking lot. Brandon finds us first and wraps his arm around Kenz's shoulders, drawing her in for a kiss.

"Happy birthday, Harper," Brandon says as we make it outside.

The horsemen stand from the sign they were sitting on as we approach.

"Where to?" Luke asks Kenz.

"Crusty's." She turns to me. "Are you riding with us?"

Eli wraps his arm around my shoulders, surrounding me in his warmth. "We've got Harper. Meet you there."

I smile at Kenz and shrug. Eli directs me to Luke's car and opens the back door for me. I slide in and Jack sits on the other side. Caden settles in shotgun and Luke drives.

"Good day so far, princess?" Luke meets my eyes as he backs up.

"Yes." It has been. Other than whatever was up Kenz's butt about Tanner, the day has been pleasant.

Jack turns my face to his and kisses me. Not a one-and-done type kiss, but an I've-got-time-to-fuck-your-mouth-right-now type kiss. My insides stir to life. We make out for a few minutes before Jack backs off.

Turning me his way, Eli kisses the shit out of me too. The good thing is I'm getting this kissing stuff down. The bad thing is that means they'll want to move on sooner rather than later. The way he works my mouth makes my panties dampen. Maybe I can get a month out of kissing and peep shows. Or maybe I only have days, depending on their moods.

We pull into the pizzeria and Luke parks the car.

Eli lifts his lips from mine. He traces my lower lip with his thumb. "I've been wanting to do that all day."

I smile at him. I really enjoy kissing these boys and that's going to get me into all kinds of trouble.

When we stroll into Crusty's, Kenz has already found us a table.

"I ordered when we got here." Kenz pats the seat next to her. She eyes the guys as they follow me. "Enough for the football team."

When I sit, Caden steals the seat next to me with a triumphant grin.

I just shake my head at him.

He grabs my face and plants a kiss on my mouth. "You look beautiful today."

Heat works its way up my neck at the compliment.

"Thank you." I turn to look at Kenz, who is looking at me with wide eyes. I shrug. What can I do? I can't control them. I can't stop them. If I'm too defiant, they'll help themselves to whatever they want. So I'm doing the best I can. Besides, I like the kissing.

"Okay, so this is weird with you guys here." Kenz puts her napkin on her lap.

"Kenz." Brandon gives her a warning.

"What? They better not try anything with me. She's my bestie, and I've been supportive of her and them. So sorry if I don't bow to their greatness." Kenz gives Brandon a look that makes him almost shrink in his chair.

Apparently Kenz inherited her mother's gift.

"Now, usually we talk about our lives, but since you guys are monopolizing my girl's life right now, there isn't much to talk about." Kenz gives them each a look.

Caden laughs. "I like this one."

Jack chuckles.

Luke eyes Kenz like he wants to crush her somehow, but won't because it's my birthday, and Eli watches me. When I meet his eyes, a smile tugs at his lips. I'm not sure what he's thinking but it must be dirty.

"Anyway," I say and put my hands on the table, "thank you for joining me for my birthday lunch."

The guys all nod and Kenz just shakes her head.

"I know you didn't invite them along, H." Kenz leans in. "Do you want me to call the manager and get them thrown out? He's my uncle's boyfriend and will do anything for him."

"No, Kenz. The guys are fine." I shoot her a look to say stop before she gets one of us in trouble. I'm afraid I'm going to be the one on the receiving end of the punishment if she doesn't shut it.

"Okay, okay. Peace." She smiles. "So how are the new outfits working out for you?"

"The ones we bought before school started," I add since I'm supposed to be grounded. "They seem to work just fine in attracting the right attention."

Jack shakes his head. "It's definitely a step up from what we found her in that first morning at her house. Sweatshirt and jeans."

"I was used to hiding, and it worked since you guys didn't even notice me until this year," I point out.

Caden slides his hand up my thigh under my skirt, and I almost jump out of my skin. He gives me a crooked smile when I give him a chastising look.

"I like Harper's clothes." He squeezes my thigh. "I prefer them off more though."

My face feels like it's burning along with my insides. The server clears his throat. *Jeezus.*

"Three pies?"

The guys direct the distribution, and I take a couple pieces of my favorite BBQ chicken. At least Caden's hand and mouth are now occupied. I definitely don't need him telling Kenz about this morning.

The talk moves on to Friday night's game, which I'm grounded from still.

"You're going to miss the first home game?" Jack asks. "Surely your mother will understand the importance of you being there."

"Which is?" I ask doubtfully.

"To cheer us on to victory." Jack winks.

"I'm sure you'll have plenty of girls screaming your names on Friday night and don't need one more." I take a bite of pizza and lift my eyes to lock with Luke's.

He's got that devious thinking look he gets sometimes. That's not usually good for me. I swallow my bite of pizza and drink some of my soda. He's making me nervous, but what's new?

He's Luke Foster. He makes everyone nervous. But he's working something out, and I probably won't like it. I'm sure he'll tell me soon enough.

CHAPTER 38

The Ceasefire

CADEN

We get done with practice and hurry to get cleaned up to go to Harper's for dinner and cake.

"Are you sure we don't have a girlfriend?" I ask Jack. "We're not getting laid and we're having dinner with her parent."

Jack slaps me on the back. "Dude, you're not wrong."

"I'm working on that." Luke sits on the bench to tie his shoes.

"Which part?" I ask.

"The laid part." He makes sure his laces are tight. "But not tonight. It's her birthday, so tomorrow."

That sounds ominous. I smile. "I like it when you fight dirty."

"She's at least back to normal again. Let's not push too hard." Eli shuts his locker and picks up his backpack.

Jack shudders. "I didn't like the Harper we got when we pushed too hard."

"It was just an act to get us to back down." Luke stands. "She found out she doesn't like the results of that. Harper likes having our attention. All of our attention. So let's give it to her."

I chuckle. "I've been trying to give her all my attention, but you won't let me go past kissing."

Luke meets my eyes. "I have a plan. We'll be respectable, nice boys so her mom doesn't see a need to ground Harper anymore."

"Still not convinced she's really grounded," I point out. Ms. Davidson didn't confirm or deny it, but who grounds a senior for coming home late after school?

Luke slaps me on the shoulder. "Come on."

We leave the locker room and head to Harper's house, parking on the street this time. I stop to check Harper's other tires on her car and there's no sign of a flat or anything.

When we knock on the door, Harper answers.

"Hey, come on in." She smiles as if she's actually happy to see us for once.

We all pile into her house. My immediate want is to corner Harper and kiss the hell out of her, but we have to be respectful young men tonight and not the hell-raisers we actually are.

Her cheeks are pink as her mom clears her throat. Ms. Davidson looks like an older version of Harper with a few differences. She's still hot for an older woman.

"So," Harper says, "this is Luke, Jack, Eli, and Caden."

Wiping her hands on a towel, Ms. Davidson nods at us. She's still got a suspicious glint in her eyes, but that tracks. After all, we're a lot for most parents who knew us growing up. Plus, our interest in her daughter isn't just friendly.

"It's nice to put names to the faces since you seem to be everywhere now."

"Mom." Harper forces a quick smile. "Why don't we go wait in the living room for dinner to be finished."

"Can I help you with anything?" Jack steps away from us, farther into the kitchen. "You work with my mom, Dr. Cathy Hill."

"Of course." She smiles and gestures to the lettuce and vegetables. "You could start the salad. Your mother is a very talented doctor."

Harper seems unsure what to do with the rest of us, so she leads us into the living room and sits in the chair, leaving us the couch. I give her the stink eye and for half a second consider lifting her and putting her on my lap, but I figure that will get everyone mad at me. Instead, I sit next to Eli on the couch.

"How was practice?" Harper asks. She fidgets with her fingers and glances toward her mom and Jack every few seconds. They talk quietly in the kitchen.

"Good." Eli smiles and leans back on the couch. "Did you figure out the problem in physics?"

Eli keeps the conversation flowing with class questions. Honestly, I don't know if Harper has any hobbies or what the girl does for fun. It feels like she just sparked into existence this year, but that's not the case.

We don't know much about her except the obvious. She watches zombie movies and shows. Takes art class. And the dance thing Jack found.

Normally I don't like to get to know girls, but it seems like if we're keeping Harper for a year, we should probably know more about her.

I glance around the room and my gaze stops on a photo collage of Harper through the years. Pictures from when she was a baby with a big grin and no hair. Pictures of a toddler with pigtails and that same impish grin. A little older Harper with a group of friends at a park.

Before I can get up to see if I recognize anyone, Harper's mom comes out of the kitchen and clears her throat. "Everything's ready."

We all stand. "What should we call you, Ms. Davidson?" The words pop out of my mouth.

"Oh." Harper's mom's face flushes. "You can call me Jennifer."

The back door opens, and Kenz stumbles in holding a half-dozen balloons and a large present. "Sorry I'm late. Do you know how hard it is to drive with balloons in the back of your car?"

Harper grins and steps forward to take the balloons. "Thanks, Kenz."

Kenz puts the gift on the entry table and faces all of us. "You guys again. Jeez, H, you sure you don't have boyfriends?"

Harper laughs awkwardly and grabs Kenz's arm. "That's so not funny."

"It totally is. Maybe not to you, but if this shit were happening to me, you'd be laughing your ass off," Kenz says, low enough I can hear but I doubt Jennifer can.

"Boyfriend or not, these guys helped Harper out and we're feeding them." Jennifer gestures to the table and the island. "Sorry, we don't normally have a lot of people over for dinners."

"No worries." Jack takes one of the bar stools. Eli and I take the others.

Glaring at me, Luke sits at the table with the girls. Serves the fucker right. He acts like Harper is his. He can pretend to be the boyfriend tonight.

<hr>

HARPER

When I sit next to Mom, Kenz sits opposite me instead of beside me. I shoot her an annoyed look as Luke takes the chair next to me. It's not like I can be sassy or catty to the guys in front of my mother. She already has enough questions about what's happening in my life.

Giving Luke a pleasant smile, I turn my attention to the guys at the island. This is so weird. I wasn't even going to tell them it's my birthday. Now we're all gathered in my kitchen like we're besties.

"We're not formal here. Go ahead and dig in." Mom pushes the mac and cheese my way.

After scooping some onto my plate, I pass it to Luke. His hand brushes mine, but he doesn't do or say anything inappropriate as he takes the dish. With little talking, everyone fills their plates.

As I put a bite of mac and cheese in my mouth, Mom asks, "So how was everyone's day?"

Her gaze goes right to Luke. He takes a drink of soda and sets it down. His gaze meets mine before he smiles at my mom. "A regular school day followed by practice. Fall is busy with football and games."

"What's your position on the team?" Mom pops a bite into her mouth but manages to look super interested in whatever Luke has to say.

"Quarterback." Luke leans back in his chair. "We've made it to State the last three years. We want to make it four before heading off to college."

"Are you going to play college football?"

"That's the dream, isn't it?" Luke smirks as he takes a bite.

I honestly don't know what the guys dream about. That isn't part of our odd dynamic. They try to get into my pants, and I try to avoid them. The future seems like forever away. I've made plans for mine, and I assume they have plans for theirs.

"What about the rest of you?" Mom turns to look at the guys sitting at the island. "Is football the long-term goal?"

"I don't think any of us have aspirations to play professionally, ma'am." Jack smiles at my mom. "This is really good mac and cheese. My mom only does the kind you microwave."

"Trust me, most days it's freezer mac and cheese, but Harper's birthday is special." Mom smiles at me and tucks a stray strand of hair behind my ear. "We don't always get to spend it together, but we always celebrate it."

I give her a smile back. Some years she's worked or I had dance. Usually, it's me and her for dinner, squeezed in whenever we can. Kenz and I do lunch. But now and then our schedules align.

"Thank you for my birthday dinner, Mom."

The guys all say thank you along with Kenz.

Mom asks me about my day, and I tell her about classes. Kenz adds in about lunch. The guys don't say much, but they eat a lot.

After the most awkward dinner ever in the history of dinners, Mom lights the candles on the cake.

Kenz and Mom lead the guys in the most surreal version of "Happy Birthday" in my life. Luke stands close to me as I lean in to blow out the candles. I don't know what to wish because I don't even know what's going on in my life right now. Do I wish the guys out of my life or do I wish for a pony? I mean, neither wish will get me far. Maybe I should just wish to get into college.

Luke brushes his fingers across the back of my hand as I blow out the candles, and my mind goes blank. My heart skips a beat, and the candles are blown out with no wish in sight.

Mom takes the cake back to the island and cuts it. Kenz hands me her present. I unwrap the box and open it to find Kenz's prom dress from last year.

"I'm not going to wear it again and I know you loved it. I figured you could wear it to homecoming since you probably have at least one date to take you." Kenz glances around at the guys. What she really means is I don't have to hide at home and miss out on the dances this year.

"What a fantastic idea." My mom lifts the dress out of the box. It's a shimmery silver dress with a pretty sheer overlay. We both tried it on last year and both loved it. Since I wasn't going to prom and she was, she bought it.

"Thank you, Kenz." I avoid looking at any of the guys. We haven't really discussed social activities outside of the ones where they get me naked, but I'm sure it will come up. I haven't even been to a party before. Everything was off limits because of potentially falling prey to one of the horsemen's notice.

Mom doesn't say anything as she returns the dress to the box. Taking a breath, I hold out my hand to my mom. "The guys got me this ring. They gave it to me earlier today."

Her eyes widen as she looks at the ring. Yeah, a ring is a lot for someone you aren't even dating, but they do want a lot from me.

"That's gorgeous. Well done, guys." Mom's eyes squint a little as she tries to figure out why the four of them would get me one ring, and an expensive looking one.

"Let's eat cake." I try to distract her from the fact that if four guys are trying to woo me, why would they all chip in on one gift. Complicate that with Kenz practically calling them my boyfriends, and I'm pretty sure I could give my mother a coronary by saying I have four guys, not just one.

Or maybe she'll just assume I'm playing the field and dating around instead of settling on one guy. Seems like a reasonable assumption. I'm young and don't have to have a boyfriend when I could date four guys who are all cool with the situation. Right?

She doesn't have to know that they want to do other things to me together, and that I want that too.

My brain blows a fuse at that last bit. Shit, is that what I really want? I want all of them?

Luke's cool gaze meets mine like he knows what I'm thinking. My cheeks heat and I look at the cake. I can sort through my feelings later in private.

We pass out slices, and everyone gets a piece. Kenz talks about our art class and how this year's project is going to be hella hard. Caden helps my mom with the dishes, and we spend more awkward moments talking about school before it's time for everyone to go home.

Kenz never got a chance to tell me about Tanner, but I also forgot to ask her about it. I walk the guys out to their cars, and Mom waves and says goodbye to everyone. When we get to their cars, Kenz waves as she drives off.

"Happy birthday." Jack hugs me. It feels nice and safe and appropriate after tonight's dinner.

The others murmur happy birthdays as they each give me a hug good night. Luke is the last, and his hug feels like he's never hugged another person in his life.

"We're going to have to work on your hug," I say softly in his ear as he releases me.

"Trying to fix me, princess?" Luke yanks gently on my ponytail.

I shrug. "Who knows, maybe you're human after all."

"I wouldn't go that far." He releases my hair and gives me a nudge toward my house. "Go inside. We'll make sure you get in before we leave."

"I think I can make it across the lawn without getting kidnapped." I shake my head but walk to the house anyway, waving at the door before going inside to face my mom.

CHAPTER 39

The Taunt

HARPER

"They seem nice." Mom sits at the island covering the last bit of cake with plastic wrap.

I snort-chuckle at anyone thinking the horsemen are nice. "I suppose they can be."

"They gave you a ring? Like all of them? Together?"

I hold up the ring, admiring the glint of silver against the black. My insides tumble over each other. "It's a nice ring."

I wonder if it's just another way to mark me as theirs. I'm just glad they don't insist I put it on my left hand. That would be too weird.

"It's a very expensive looking ring." Mom shakes her head. "Maybe I don't understand dating these days."

"We're not really dating. They didn't even know it was my birthday until you told them. So they had to scramble to get a gift."

"Well, for scrambling they did a really great job." She shakes her head and then raises her eyebrows. "Do you want to explain what's going on?"

"What do you mean?" I hedge, glancing down at the ring to avoid her knowing eyes.

"Four guys bought you a ring for your birthday. They've made it clear they want to insert themselves into your life. Is this a dating thing?

Does everyone date in groups these days? I would expect a more equal ratio of guys to gals, but I'm not even sure what that means anymore."

I sigh and sink onto the stool next to her at the island. "I don't know either, Mom. This is all as new to me as it is to you."

She puts her arms on the island and turns her face to look at me. "Are you dating them?"

I chuckle. I can't help it. Dating them? They own me, but I can't tell my mom that. "Dating might be too strong of a word. How about hanging out?"

Smiling, she shakes her head. "So is this a hang-out-one-on-one situation or all together?"

My cheeks heat like they're on fire. "Mom!"

"What I mean—" Mom cuts herself off, flustered. "Will they be taking you out on actual dates or will you just be 'hanging out' in a group?"

She does the air quotes, and I hope she means doing things together and not *doing* things together.

"The guys are really close, and we've mostly just spent time at school. So currently, we all just hang out together." I'm not sure my face can get any hotter.

She pushes out a breath. "Okay, that's all the parenting I can handle right now."

I chuckle. She glances around the kitchen.

"There aren't many leftovers, so that's a bonus to hanging out with four football players." She nudges my shoulder playfully. "They also helped clean up, so there's nothing left for us to do. Except for me to give you your presents."

I smile and wait at the island while she heads into the other room. She comes back with an envelope and a small box.

"Okay, before you get excited, it isn't much, but I've been working a lot to get it to where it is." She hands me the envelope.

"Okay." I open it and it's the statement to a college savings plan. While it isn't enough for all four years, it's a substantial amount and will make a good dent. "This is amazing, Mom. This will definitely help."

She smiles. "I know it isn't enough, but you should get some scholarships and financial aid to make up the difference. If you go in-state, you might get a full ride."

I haven't talked to her about college much. While in-state is a good deal, I don't want to stay close, where the horsemen have so much power. I want to get away from them, but moving away from my mom will be hard.

Tentatively she pushes the box toward me but holds onto it. "Before you open this..." She sighs and looks at the gift. "We don't talk about your father. I know you don't remember much about him, but I loved him once upon a time. He gave me you, and I'm grateful to him for that."

I nod. Dad is a nonfactor in my life. He ducked out on us when I was five. I have a vague memory of the smell of gasoline and oil, leather, and a scratchy beard.

"We weren't the only thing he left behind. I think it's appropriate for you to have this now." She shoves the box in front of me.

I don't know what she's talking about. As I unwrap the box and open it, a key falls out. I raise an eyebrow at her. This is all my dad left behind? "A key, wow, I'll treasure it."

Shaking her head, she takes my hand and pulls me outside and back to the garden shed. I haven't been in here since I was a kid. Mom hired a service, so the lawn mower and tools never get used.

"It's really not much, but I'm sure it could be if you wanted to fix it up." She pulls open the doors and grabs the edge of the drop cloth covering stuff in one corner. As it falls away, it reveals an old Harley-Davidson motorcycle amongst some boxes and gardening tools.

My mouth drops open. "What?"

It's gorgeous.

Mom smiles, but it's a little sad. "This was his pride and joy. I'm not sure why he didn't take it with him, but I always figured he'd want you to have it."

"This is amazing." It's black with chrome accents. It needs a wash, and I don't even know if it runs. "Thank you. I love you so much."

I turn and hug her.

"You're it for me, Harper. I love you to the moon and back."

THE NEXT MORNING, I'M STILL FEELING GOOD. LAST NIGHT, the guys and I did our homework and went to bed. No one asked me to strip, which was nice. I woke up to the guys' alarms and not two guys in my room. So bonus.

When I come out of my shower, I don't even bother with the towel. At my dresser, I pull on panties and a bra. Someone clears their throat. I turn to the computer screen to see Jack sitting there with a huge smile on his face.

"Can I help you?" I turn back to my closet and reach for a mini skater skirt.

"You'll get lines with those panties." Jack's voice is loud, and I notice Luke dressing in the background.

"So should I go without or...?" I cock my hip.

"Probably a thong would work, but if you want to go commando, I'll be hard every time I see you today." Jack reaches into his boxers and strokes his cock. He chuckles. "Let's be honest, I'll be hard either way."

I think I'm getting too used to seeing Jack's cock. Maybe that's part of their strategy. I slip my panties off and reach into the drawer to pull out a white thong. I bend to pull it on.

"Fuck, Harper. You sure you're grounded, because I'm ready to kiss something besides your mouth."

My pussy throbs at the implication. Shaking my head, I pull on my skirt and look for the crop top I want. It's the one that falls off one shoulder. I snatch it off the hanger and put it on.

Since they were nice about the ponytail yesterday, I figure it might be safe to put my hair up today, especially since it's supposed to be hot outside.

Luke sits at his desk as he puts on his shoes. I grab a pair of sandals and slip them on. Luke's gaze rakes over me, and I feel the heat through the screen.

His blond hair falls over his icy blue eyes. He's wearing a black t-shirt and jeans today. Jack's wearing a navy t-shirt and jeans. His dark hair is brushed back out of his face, and his dark blue eyes focus on me with a smirk.

I lean over the chair so my face fills the screen. "Am I driving myself today?"

"We've got you, kitten. Don't bend over in school." I glance over my shoulder at Eli staring at my ass and Caden closing in on it.

"Worried someone else will see my panties today?" I don't bother straightening as Caden grabs my ass. His fingers are warm as they massage my cheeks. Sparks sizzle through me.

"Princess," Luke says, drawing my attention back to him on the screen, "behave or the only one who will have those panties is me."

"I'm not sure they'll fit you." I give him a wide-eyed look before grinning. He narrows his eyes.

"Get to school." Luke stands and leaves his room.

I close my laptop and straighten into Caden's chest. I lean my head back and look up at him. Tingles course through my system as his heat surrounds me. "You just going to hold my ass all day?"

Caden chuckles. His fingers flex and my insides melt. "I might."

"Let her go, Caden. We need to get to school." Eli shakes his head as Caden backs off. When I get close to Eli, he leans into me. "If I see your ass again at school, I'll spank it."

I give him a fake pout before heading downstairs to the kitchen. At the island, I make two sandwiches. Caden comes up behind me and squeezes my ass again. It feels good, but I might be getting a little desensitized to them grabbing my ass all the time. I didn't even jump.

Of course, that's their plan, to push me along to what they ultimately want.

"If I could touch your pussy right now..." He lets that statement hang in the air. Caden's fingers slide beneath my skirt over my ass, teasing the line of my thong. My breath catches as heat rages through me. They've all touched my bare ass after the spanking, but not like this.

He draws my hips back against his hard cock and grinds against me. Shivers race through me and I'm not sure I'm breathing. Definitely not desensitized. Leaning down, he says directly into my ear in his deep voice, "We should just fuck and get it over with."

That should not feel so good. My brain is on meltdown and I can't get out the rebuke to his statement.

"Behave, Caden." Eli grabs an orange from the bowl and peels it. "We have time to wait until Harper is ready."

"Don't worry, little nympho. Next time I'll bring Jack, and he'll play with us." Caden kisses the back of my neck, and I can't stop the shiver that races down my spine. Part of me wants him to play with me now. The other part is terrified to want him.

And I need to remember this is all a game to them. *I'm* a game to them. That helps cool me down.

"Yeah, that sounds like a bad plan." I pack up the sandwiches, and Eli hands me a wedge of orange. I smile at him as I take it and pop it into my mouth. The citrus bursts against my tastebuds.

Turning in Caden's arms, I press my hands against his chest. "Time to go, big guy."

He smirks down at me and then lifts me up to set me on the counter. He claims my mouth, thrusting his tongue inside in rhythm with his hips against mine. My legs wrap around his waist like they have a mind of their own. The tension winds within me as I take whatever he wants to give me.

He groans. "Let's just skip to the fucking, little nympho. You're going to love it."

Dropping my legs, I dodge his mouth and push on his chest. He steps back even though I couldn't really move him if I tried. He lifts me down to my feet.

"Let's get to school." I take in a deep breath filled with cinnamon and orange.

I enjoy playing with the boys, but on my terms.

I walk around the island and bend down to retrieve my backpack right in front of Eli. He smacks my ass, and I grin at him.

"Dangerous games, kitten." He yanks me against him. "Very dangerous."

He captures my lips, drinking me in like a fine wine. I feel drunk on these boys. When he releases me, I'm warm all over. "School now."

CHAPTER 40

The Trap

Slow isn't working for me. Not when every day our girl chooses to torment us with flashes of skin and color on her already gorgeous lips. It makes me want to escalate things and soon, but I know I shouldn't.

It's a matter of control and I'm supposed to have it, but Harper shreds it. Every time we kiss, I need more from her. Yesterday in her room, when I had her spread on my lap, I could have eased my cock into her and she wouldn't have complained.

I'm not sure how well that would have gone over with the guys, given our plans, but at least one more boundary would be gone. The biggest one, her virginity.

I glance up at the clock. It's almost the end of third period. Almost time for lunch, and I don't have a plan. Our girl is frying my brain. And I'm not the only one feeling the effects.

The other guys feel it too. We need a plan for this weekend. We need to make her ours fully. She's had enough time to adjust to us. She's amped up for us too.

I need to punish her and make her walk around in that short skirt without her panties on. Or I can give her another choice. A more pleasurable option, or take something away.

The bell rings. I grab Eli on the way to the cafeteria. "We need to punish her."

"Fuck, man. She hasn't done anything wrong." Eli shakes his head, but he gives me a sly smile. "I'm all for punishing her, but she has to disobey us."

"Then let's find something she'll refuse to do." I rub my hands together.

"Cafeteria?" Eli nods down the hall.

Harper hates the cafeteria. She hasn't been in it all week. She's always spooked as hell to even enter it. It'll be perfect to catch her disobeying.

"What's the plan?" Eli asks as we head for our table.

Those who sat near our table scatter. By the time we're all seated, more people will be in the cafeteria knowing that the horsemen and their girl will be in attendance. They haven't had a show all week. But today...

Caden and Jack follow our girl in, their eyes focused on her ass in that small skirt. She's gone from invisible to a fucking tease.

"I don't have a plan yet." I watch her, waiting for her to meet my eyes. Those brown eyes lift to mine. I can't resist smiling at her, and she hesitates with her next step. Her eyes widen. Not so cocky now. Caden doesn't stop. He wraps his arm around her to bring her to our table.

She's been so obedient. So careful not to get punished, especially after Monday.

Caden sits beside me and tugs Harper down on his lap. She starts to move to the side, but he holds her hips.

"Stay."

She glances over her shoulder at him and that defiance flashes in her eyes for a hot second before she shrugs. She takes out two sandwiches and two bags of chips and scoots one set toward Caden.

"Thanks, little nympho."

Eli offers Harper an apple. She takes it and glances at me. Her eyebrow goes up, as if she's trying to figure out what I'm searching for. Can she tell how much I want and need to punish her?

Jack sits back and watches all of us like we're a play put on for his amusement. I glance around the cafeteria. Most people are chatting quietly while everyone tries to keep an eye on our table without being too obvious.

I have to decide whether or not I want to put on a show. I'm all for punishing Harper, but it's also nice that she seems more comfortable with us. We just got that back. I don't want to break the trust that's building.

The guys and I talk about the game tomorrow. Eli glances over at me now and then, probably wondering what I plan to do. The problem is I don't want Harper uncomfortable because of all the people watching. I want to push her comfort levels with us and only us.

Which means Plan B: get rid of the grounding myth.

Lunchtime is almost over when I say to Jack, "Take Harper home after school."

Jack grins like he's won a prize.

"After practice, we're meeting at Caden's house."

Harper looks over at me, trying to seem uninterested.

"Sorry, princess, you'll have to sit this one out since you're grounded." I give her a smile and look at the table of girls near us who are all trying to get our attention. The few I allowed to sit with us on Tuesday keep looking over here longingly. "Though you could help us out."

Eli's brow raises as he follows my gaze.

"Since you're detained this weekend, you can choose a girl from that table to take your place." I steeple my fingers against my lips and gesture toward the table of willing females. "Any of them can do what we require of you. Since we won't be putting our cocks in their cunts."

Harper's eyes flare as she looks over at the girls. "And what exactly would you have me do?"

I lean my elbows on the table and stare into her eyes. "Things we can't do at school. Things you should get more comfortable with. Things any of those girls would willingly do for us."

I don't look at the guys. They don't know this is a bluff. Harper won't want another girl touching us. She likes having us to herself. I've seen the jealousy in her eyes when she mentioned the girls at our table.

But I want the lie of her grounding gone. I don't want to wait over a week to have her on her knees before me.

"Only me. That's what you swore." She leans in, giving up any pretense of the mild little virgin. "You won't touch or fuck another girl."

"But you took yourself off the field when you got grounded. So you can send in a substitute." I look over at the table of girls. "Don't worry, we'll just play a nice game of spin the bottle, but we won't be kissing each other's mouths."

Harper's lips purse and her cheeks redden, but I know it's that temper she keeps in check. That bit of defiance she tries so hard to fight. So afraid to get punished. Probably because she likes my hand on her ass.

She glances over at the table and, as if the girls know we're talking about them, they all turn to face us. They look like hungry she-wolves as they take us in.

"Fuck no. It's against the rules." Harper tries to stand, but Caden holds her hips down on his lap. "If you do this, I'm out. One hundred percent. You can pick one of them yourself to be your little fuck toy."

"Then show me your texts with your mother." I hold out my hand calmly.

Her fingers curl around her phone, pulling it toward her. Her gaze drops to it and she bites her lip.

"Kitten."

Her head jerks up and she meets Eli's eyes as he shakes his head. She stops biting her lip.

"Shit," she says under her breath.

"Either show me the texts from your mother about being grounded or be punished." I put my hand down and glance at Eli. That bastard looks smug. I'll have to ask him about that later. "Five, four—"

"Fine." She stands, and I figure she's going to hand over her phone. "Punish me. You want my panties so every other guy in this school can try to get a look at my naughty bits, go right ahead."

That was a little loud. Sure enough, guys are paying attention and checking out our girl. If she wore this type of outfit before this year, she never would have made it to senior year as a virgin. One of us would have claimed her, or some fucking lowlife would have snapped her up and had what's ours.

"Would you like me to take them off here in front of everyone or would you rather corner me in a bathroom stall?" She arches her eyebrow at me and there isn't an ounce of fear in her eyes.

A smile pulls at my lips slow and steady. She's just told me her grounding is a lie. Her willingness to be punished is all the evidence I need.

I stand and approach her. She holds her ground until I crowd her into the wall. When I press against her and smell her sweet vanilla scent with that undercurrent of her arousal, I feel victory course through my veins.

I dip my head down so only she can hear me. "I have all the information I need, princess."

Her fingers clench and she huffs out a breath. Her dark eyes snap up to mine. "I'm not picking out a whore for you to use."

"I never wanted you to." I put my hand around her neck and squeeze lightly. "You're the only toy I want to play with, and tonight you'll be joining us at Caden's."

HARPER

Fuck. My. Life.

Eli warned me not to bite my lip, and I've been diligent not to do it in front of him. And Luke's endgame was to get me to admit I wasn't grounded after all. Sure, I never said I wasn't, but the fact I was willing to take a punishment instead of showing him the texts was proof enough.

I'm fucked.

Jack is quiet on the way to my house. When we pull into the drive, he clears his throat.

"We wouldn't have."

My eyebrows furrow as I look at him. "What?"

"Fuck." Jack presses his hands against the steering wheel. "We made a pact with you. None of us will touch another girl. We meant that shit. I meant it. I mean it. Right now, I swear to you even if Luke takes this game too far, I'm not down for that."

Huh?

"He was bluffing the whole time anyway." I shake my head. "He just wanted me to admit to not being grounded."

"Don't underestimate Luke. If he's willing to bluff something, he will go through with it if push comes to shove." Jack reaches over and tucks a stray hair behind my ear. "We've known since that first night you lied."

"What? How?" Maybe Luke did install something on my phone.

"The shopping bags, sweetheart. Moms don't generally let you go shopping for new clothes when you're being punished." Jack smirks.

Luke was in my room that night. The receipts and all the bags were right there for him to see. Jack knew what clothes I had already.

"Why did you guys go along with it then?" I'm so fucking confused when it comes to these guys.

"You needed time." Jack slips his hand behind my neck and pulls me to him.

"Time to get used to the idea of you guys fucking me? I don't think a week and a half is long enough." I stare into his blue eyes as he focuses on my lips.

"Maybe." His lips take mine, and I open up beneath him. I can't seem to help myself. Kissing is still new and the way it makes me feel is indescribable.

Warmth buzzes along my veins, making me squirm in my seat.

He lifts his mouth from mine partially and smiles against my lips. "I have to go to practice. Be ready at six. Eli is picking you up."

Fuck.

"I suppose I'll be punished for not following orders." I slump back in my seat and grab my backpack.

"Maybe we'll just play more spin the bottle, or maybe some strip poker." He wiggles his eyebrows at me suggestively. I wish that idea didn't make my insides melt.

"Bye, Jack." I get out of his car and head inside.

Mom's car isn't in the driveway, so I check the schedule. She's not supposed to be at work right now, but sometimes she has to pull a double shift if someone can't make it into the hospital.

ME:

Home. Should I get my own dinner?

MOM:

Stuck at work. Be home when I can. Be safe.

I bet if I told her four guys want to fuck me without condoms, she'd ground me for real this time. But pulling her into this still isn't a good idea.

I set my phone down and drop my head to the cool granite of the kitchen island.

What the hell am I going to do?

I grab my phone and text Kenz.

ME:

You there?

KENZ:

What's up?

ME:

Mom's at work. Wanna come over for a few?

KENZ:

Be there in a jiff

Placing my phone to the side, I take in a breath. I need to do my homework and I need to eat. I'll worry about the horsemen when Kenz comes over.

I get about half of my homework done and eat a salad before Kenz shows up.

As soon as she's through the door, she throws her arms around me. "How are the assholes?"

"Still assholes by all accounts." I pull back, and we go into the living room to sit on the couch.

"Did I tell you yet you look hot today?" Kenz makes suggestive eyes at me.

I laugh. "Maybe a little too hot. I'm pretty sure Caden would have fucked me on the kitchen island this morning if I'd let him."

"Seriously? Holy shit. That would have been epic." Kenz pulls out a large bag of peanut M&M'S and takes a handful before passing the bag to me.

I take a handful and nod. "Now they know I'm not grounded and are coming to pick me up."

Kenz's blue eyes widen. "So what all have they done with you?"

"Kissing mostly." I don't want to go into all the naked sessions of them jacking off to me. Or Caden and Luke in my bed yesterday. And tasting Caden's cum. Fuck, I get hot just thinking about yesterday morning and Luke sucking my juices off my finger.

"Did you really tell them off in the cafeteria? And then Luke fucked you against the wall?" Kenz grins like a madwoman.

"Ew, rumors suck." I shake my head. "I told them off, but Luke didn't even kiss me in the cafeteria."

"You told them off? Good for you." Kenz pops an M&M in her mouth. "What happened?"

I explain what Luke wanted me to do and then about the phone.

"It was a fucking trap, and I walked right into it like a dumbass. I should have just picked out a chick and called their bluff." Leaning my head back against the couch, I stare up at the ceiling. "I'm worried they plan to do tonight exactly what he said he wanted to do."

It ran through my mind as I worked on my homework.

"Which was?"

"Spin the bottle, but you don't kiss mouths." I cringe. I can only guess where they want to kiss, but of course, my mind goes straight into the gutter. Especially how Luke primed me to suck cock the other night.

"Tits or pussy?" Kenz wonders out loud.

"Possibly dicks?" I add. "I mean I've seen all but Luke's."

Kenz's eyebrows shoot up. "Are they big? I've heard they're big."

"Not small. Not gonna lie, I'm going to be walking funny once they finally take my virginity."

Kenz laughs, and I can't help but join her. This whole situation is ridiculous. But the guys aren't normal guys. They exude power and they own their titles. And the way they kiss and touch and talk to me makes me want them more and more.

"I've missed talking to you." That's the worst part of this. The horsemen take up all my time.

"I miss talking to you too. I haven't even gotten to tell you how much Brandon and I have been having sex." Kenz leans forward. "Like a lot. It's like once you take the plastic off, you just want to keep playing with it."

"In the past week and a half?" I look at her skeptically.

"There's a few places at school that are awesome to fuck in." Kenz gets this glassy-eyed look and a grin that might as well be the cat that got the canary.

"I'm sure I'll be introduced to them as soon as they take me for a test drive." I lean back, toss the rest of the M&M'S in my mouth, and chew.

"It isn't all bad, is it?" Kenz asks softly. "They seemed a lot more tame than I would have expected at lunch and dinner yesterday."

"The humiliation hasn't been fun. But there have been moments." Having their attention isn't awful. Holding their attention will be next to impossible once they get what they want though. I twist their ring on my finger. "What if they really only want my virginity and once they get it, they're done with me?"

"Isn't that what you want?" Kenz gives me a confused and worried look.

"I—" Ugh. "Fuck, I don't know. They promised a year."

Their attention is absolute. Their touch is addictive. Their kisses all-consuming. I'm guessing fucking them will be epic.

"I wouldn't get too comfortable." Kenz pulls her legs up under her. "The cats are going to go into heat, and then the claws will come out."

I haven't been privy to the gossip mill since I now star in most of the stories. "How bad is it?"

"The girls are watching. They're waiting for an opening." Kenz shrugs. "Right now, they aren't fighting it because they think the same as you. Once the guys get what they want, they'll be back on the market again."

"So if that doesn't happen?" Not that I think I can keep four guys satisfied, but it's possible, right? Gah, why would I even think that? I should be glad if they decide to fuck off after getting me. It would definitely make my life easier.

"I wouldn't trust any girl if I was you." Kenz pulls a face. "You can trust me. I'm your bestie and have a guy. I've been learning to do this thing with my tongue—"

"Oversharing." I shake my head. "I'll let you know when I need tips."

Kenz laughs. "I'm sure you've got the best teachers already."

CHAPTER 41
The Captive

HARPER

ME:

Studying with a friend tonight

MOM:

Don't forget your condoms

ME:

thumbs-up emoji *eye roll emoji*

Pretty sure if the guys are going to take it there tonight, they won't be using condoms. I haven't even thought that far ahead. My foot taps restlessly on the floor. Unless their tests came back not clean, which I'm sure they would have said something by now.

I'm nervous enough about having sex with them, but add in not using condoms... It wasn't something I thought I'd have to worry about until college, and then if I was in a committed relationship, it might make sense. Though we're kind of in a committed relationship of sorts.

As soon as Eli pulls into the driveway, I'm out the door. He's promised punishment. Before he can put it into park, I slide into the passenger seat and fasten my seatbelt.

"I'm ready."

Eli smirks. His brown hair is in disarray from his shower after practice. He has on a t-shirt and gray sweatpants that leave little to the imagination. "Afraid to be alone with me, kitten?"

"Not at all." I blush lightly at the lie. "Just don't want to keep the guys waiting."

"Tomorrow, I'll bring your punishment when I pick you up for school." Eli puts the car into reverse and gives me a smile. "Besides, Luke's in a mood, so you'll get all the punishment you can take tonight."

I already figured that out and have a plan of my own. It will probably bite me in the ass, but at least I'll have gotten one over on Luke.

Anxiety pricks at my skin. Alone in person with all of them. This is going to go sideways quickly, and there's not a lot I can do to step out of the way of the oncoming train.

Eli shifts into gear, and we drive out of my cookie-cutter neighborhood until we reach the fancy neighborhood with old mansions lined up one by one.

I've never been to Caden's house. Even the times he invited the whole class to birthday parties when we were little. Mom usually had to work and couldn't get me there and pick me up, so I just didn't go. Later in middle school, that's where all the boy-girl parties were.

The closet everyone else knew from seven minutes in heaven is in Caden's house. In high school, it's become party central. How many teens have lost their virginities in this house? And not just to the horsemen. Am I about to add to the number?

I tug at the hem of my skirt, suddenly mad at myself for not changing into jeans and a sweatshirt. Maybe a chastity belt?

"Stop fidgeting, kitten. You're safe with us." He parks in the driveway and kills the lights.

"Am I?" I can't help my response, because come on. Other than a few times, I've been safe on the other end of a camera. Now I'm about to walk into whatever punishment Luke has planned for me. I wasn't exactly thrilled with the last spanking I received.

And of course, there's always his threat of spanking while checking how wet I am. A shiver works its way down my spine. I'm not sure that's a boundary I want to cross tonight.

"We want to fuck you, kitten, but we want you to want it. No one is going to force you. We'll give you sucky choices, but at least you'll be able to pick your poison." Eli reaches over and tugs gently on my ponytail. "If you want to leave at any point, I promise I'll take you home."

"Any time?" I want to believe him as I look into his deep brown eyes, but how can I trust him? How can I trust any of them? They all stir something inside me, and part of me is desperate to explore that. But trust? That's a tall order.

Especially since I'm not sure I can trust myself around them.

"Any time," he confirms.

They still terrify me. I feel like I'm a plaything to them, not a person.

"Hey." Eli touches my chin and nudges it up, so I look him in the eyes. "I swear to you. I will protect you, even from my brothers if it comes to that."

"Why?" I have to know. Is this just another game? Or will Eli actually help me?

"We all promised you, kitten. We don't take that shit lightly. When we offer our protection, it's absolute." Eli smooths his thumb over my lower lip. Awareness races through my system, crashing over the anxiety.

I swallow. "Have you ever done this with a girl before me?"

Eli smiles and leans forward to press his lips against mine briefly. "No. We weren't lying when we said you're special. You're ours, Harper. Just trust us to keep you safe."

I push away the burst of tingles from his kiss and nod. "Don't make me regret this."

"I don't want you to regret anything." He opens his car door and comes around to open mine. Holding out his hand like he always holds out an apple to me at lunch.

I brace myself before I slip my hand into his and let him lead me into the lion's den.

Caden's house is enormous, with intimidating columns surrounding a double door that has to be over seven feet tall, but Eli leads me around the back to a door on the lower level. As soon as we open it, we hear music playing and the guys' deep voices. Eli wraps his arm around my waist and draws me into a large room with a huge TV and an even bigger sectional couch.

Jack and Caden stand as soon as they see me. Luke glances at me through his lashes, giving me a smoldering look that makes my insides burn.

Before the other two can claim me, I walk over and stop in front of Luke. He leans back and gives me the smile that makes my toes curl, like he knows I want him. I wish he was wrong.

I'm going for brave cockiness here. "You want my panties?"

He raises an eyebrow.

I open my purse, take out the panties I wore all day, and hold them out to him. I give him a smug smile. "Here you go."

He straightens and stands. Right into my space. I don't back up a step, refusing to be intimidated. His body brushes against mine as he looks down at me. His hand closes over the panties in my hand. "Thanks, princess."

He brings them up to his nose and smells them. I'm partially mortified and partially turned on. I figure this part of the evening has concluded, so I move to step back.

His hand whips out and grabs my ponytail, tugging my head back. He shoves my panties in his pocket and pulls me into his chest. The heat of his body engulfs mine, and the fire inside me grows hotter.

"Who said we were finished, princess?" His smile is cold, but it doesn't make me want him any less.

"I think I preferred unicorn," I snark up at him like I've lost my damn mind.

His smile warms. "What are you wearing?"

"The same thing I wore to school," I grit out. His hold on my hair is a little painful, but tolerable. My heart thunders in my chest. I'm a stupid girl, walking into a lion's den and thinking I can go toe-to-toe with this lion. He'll eat me alive before he's done with me.

"So if I check under your skirt?" He lowers his hand as if he's going to do it.

I draw my lower half away from him as much as I can. "I'm wearing panties."

He releases my hair and sits back down, then waves his hand in the air like a fucking king. "Show me."

I don't dare take my eyes off Luke, but I can feel the other horsemen watching. This isn't like the webcam. I can't just shut the screen and wait for punishment tomorrow. Not that I have, but they couldn't touch me on the other end of the webcam.

I just got here, and I poked the lion because I thought I could get away with it. Maybe I *have* lost my mind.

"Anytime, princess."

My breathing is heavy as I force my hands to lift my skirt. This isn't the first time I've shown him my panties, but it's the first time in front of all of them. Luke's focus is on the black panties I put on instead. I might as well be waving a flag in front of a bull.

His blue eyes darken. "What type of punishment should we give Harper tonight?"

Fuck. I already knew I'd get punished. I begin to lower my skirt.

"Hold it up or you'll take the skirt off, princess." Luke's voice makes me raise it back up.

My face is hot as I swallow and look at the wall. While these guys have seen me naked, somehow it feels different with all four of them in the same room and no mother to interrupt us.

"I say she loses the panties and we play your alternative version of spin the bottle."

I jerk my gaze to Jack, who smirks before dropping his gaze to my exposed underwear. Heat pools in my belly.

"Definitely lose the panties, but seven minutes in heaven." Caden leans back against the couch and licks his lips. Want makes my knees weak, but I stay upright.

My gaze lands on Eli. If I say the word, he'll get me out of here. I think. But what if that was just to convince me to come in? I can't trust any of them. Not really.

Eli smirks. "Harper should choose between either spin the bottle with kissing not on the mouth or seven minutes in heaven. Lady's choice. No penetration."

Caden grumbles, and I remember this morning. I'd be trapped with one of them alone in a closet for seven minutes. Which is a long time. Without panties. Sex didn't have to take longer than seven minutes.

"What will it be, princess?" Luke's voice draws me back. The backs of his fingers brush my thigh and stroke gently back and forth. My lips part at how good his touch feels. "Seven minutes in heaven or—"

"The other thing. The kissing not on the mouth." I don't trust a single one of these guys on his own, but with the others, I know they'll pull someone back if it goes too far. Including me. Hopefully. "What are the rules?"

Luke stands. "If you want rules, it will cost you your panties."

I kick off my shoes and drop my skirt to hang again. I reach under and pull down my underwear, feeling the cool air on my already damp pussy. Instead of bending down, I put my hand on Luke's shoulder to steady myself as I lift my panties to my hands by bending my knee.

"Rules please." I push my panties to his chest.

He takes them and smiles. "Since you asked nicely."

Once again, he inhales the scent from my panties, but this time he tosses them to Eli. I watch each of the horsemen smell my panties and then pass them on. I don't want it to turn me on, but gah, does it.

Caden gets them last and smirks at me as he pockets them. I feel bare to all of them even though my skirt covers me. Luke takes my hand and leads me over to a rug where a bottle is already waiting. Low gaming chairs sit around the bottle. The kind that practically sit on the floor and rock. But there are only four of them.

This time it's a beer bottle with the cap still on. Luke lowers to one of the gaming chairs. He pats his lap and says, "Sit."

I lower myself onto his lap, careful to keep my skirt covering me. The others join us and sit in the other chairs in a circle around the bottle. Pressing my knees tight together, I swallow, feeling Luke's erection against my tailbone.

"The rules?" I ask hesitantly. I'm sure I won't like them, but better than being devirginized in a quickie in the closet.

"No hands. Only mouth and tongue. You spin the bottle, princess." Luke wraps a hand around my waist and leans us both forward to touch the bottle. His smooth athletic pants do very little to hide the feel of his erection sliding between my legs.

I catch my breath before I can release a moan.

"Whoever it lands on, the coin toss decides whether you give, heads, or receive, tails the kiss."

Another game of chance. The last one screwed me over royally. This one might really screw me period.

"You're only allowed to kiss a place on someone once. Same goes for us. The order is the same for everyone." Luke's voice in my ear and his cock against my pussy fuck with my brain. "Neck, then chest, then stomach, then thighs, and finally pussy or cock."

My core clenches at those last two. No matter what, I'm so going to lose this game.

"You'll sit with me the first round, and then the next round you'll sit with Eli, and so on. A round is four spins of the bottle."

I glance at Eli and feel the heat in his eyes down to my bones. What's the likelihood that I'll land a bottle on the same guy and get five heads or five tails? That at least seems in my favor. I might get away without anyone under my skirt. Besides the guy I'm sitting on, of course.

"No hands, princess. If something needs to be exposed, the person receiving will expose it." Luke sits back up and the pressure he'd put on my throbbing pussy goes away. Shit, I want it back. "Except you."

"What?" I look back over my shoulder. Fuck, he's pretty. His blond hair is tousled with no product to restrain it. His light blue eyes lock on mine, daring me to look away. I don't think I could if I wanted to.

"When you need something uncovered, the guy holding you will do it. You won't use your hands at all. And you aren't allowed to leave the lap you're on." His eyes seem warmer right now.

So they're going to strip me and keep me pressed between two of them at a time. I wish that didn't turn me on.

This game will be the end of me. "How much time?"

"Thirty seconds," Eli says.

Shit.

CHAPTER 42

The Invasion

HARPER

I stare at the bottle, fully aware to reach it I will flash my naked pussy at Luke as I lean over to spin it. Already I don't like this game. I could use my out, but once I do, what will happen? More public humiliation?

Spanking in the locker room with no panties? My pulse kicks up a notch. Spanking isn't all bad, but I really don't want other guys watching or looking under my skirt.

I glance around at the boys waiting for me to spin. These guys are getting to me. Making me feel so comfortable with them that I won't question having sex with four guys. Maybe I'll even want it, because part of me already does.

I'm definitely attracted to each of them, and having all their attention focused on me is heady.

I always knew at some point they would move on from only kissing me and grabbing my ass. This is going to happen. No penetration means no actual sex, but how many rounds of this are we going to play?

I just had my first-ever kiss a week ago, and they're definitely going to get to second base tonight. But I don't think I'm ready for third base. My core tightens.

"Spin the bottle, princess."

Fuck.

My.

Life.

I take a deep breath and lean forward to spin the bottle. Luke's hands grab my hips to steady me, and I feel the kiss of cool air against my warm pussy again. I spin it and sit quickly back down, making sure my skirt is between us.

Helplessly, I watch the bottle spin until it stops on Eli.

Jack flips a coin. I hold my breath as it falls.

"Tails."

They've all touched my neck before and yeah, it sends tingles, but it can't compare to them kissing my mouth.

Eli smiles. "I'll play nice, kitten."

Luke grabs my ponytail, tipping my head back with a tug.

Eli kneels before us, his hands behind his back, and kisses my neck gently at first. When he opens his mouth and licks along my artery, my pulse kicks up a notch and sparks ignite under my skin, scattering along my veins. He trails his mouth down to where my neck and shoulder meet, and then he sucks and scrapes his teeth along the tendon.

I bite back a moan, but can't control the wetness gathering between my thighs. I close my eyes and try not to be drawn in.

"Time." Jack's eyes burn with desire.

When Eli stops, I release a helpless whimper.

This is a dangerous game, but I don't want to stop playing. I'm here and this is happening. I can't help the curiosity this feeds. After all, it wasn't morality or pride keeping me from losing my virginity. It was lack of opportunity.

"Spin." Luke's voice is ragged in my ear.

I lean forward and spin the bottle again. Luke's fingers bite into my hips. He hisses as I lower myself down on him.

The bottle slows and stops on Jack. He flips the coin.

"Heads." Standing, he walks over to us, his crotch in my face.

My eyes narrow at his.

"Where do you want it, sweetheart?" With a cocky smirk, he lifts his eyebrow.

"Neck," Luke says with a tone to stop fucking around.

Jack kneels before me and puts his hands behind his back. Luke scoots forward with me, his arm around my waist to help stabilize me, so I can reach Jack's neck. Glancing up, I get lost in Jack's dark blue eyes.

He smiles. "Anytime, sweetheart. The timer doesn't start until your lips touch skin."

Luke leans his chin on my shoulder. His smooth, dark voice murmurs in my ear, "And trust me, princess, we can go all night."

Fuck. I'll do what Eli did, just a bit less. Jack's apple scent surrounds me as I kiss his neck. I could just stay like this. My lips are on his neck. Technically I'm kissing him.

Luke trails his nose along my nape and his hand tugs my ponytail. "C'mon, princess," he taunts. "You can do better than that."

Luke massages my hip, inching my skirt higher. I gasp against Jack's neck and as soon as I move my mouth, Luke stops lifting my skirt. I trail my tongue up Jack's salty skin to his jawline and suck a little.

"Fuck," Jack hisses out. His body is tense, but he keeps his hands to himself. Curious, I trail back down to the spot that lit me up when Eli sucked there. I nip Jack's skin and lave the spot before latching on with my mouth. Sucking on his hot skin sends heat down to my center.

"Time. Good girl." Luke pulls me back on his lap, and my eyes meet Jack's. His are heated and his pupils are blown. Do I look just as aroused?

My breathing is ragged. Luke pinches my hip, making me cry out, and I spin to look at him. Asshole. Jack slips back to his chair and adjusts his hard-on, while Luke gives me a smirk.

"Spin the bottle," he says.

If Luke's inhale is anything to go by, I'm a little more careless when I spin the bottle. The others won't let him take more. So if I make Luke a bit more uncomfortable, sucks to be him. I sit back in his lap and squirm to get comfortable.

"Princess, if you want to ride my cock, all you have to do is ask nicely." His voice in my ear sends shivers cascading through me and pooling into liquid heat between my thighs. His desire for me is intoxicating.

"Keep dreaming, Death," I whisper back.

The bottle stops, pointing at me. I lean back against Luke.

"Do I spin again?"

"Why, princess? It's pointing at me." Luke grabs my ponytail. "Turn around."

"Tails," Jack says. FML.

I swallow. Careful not to flash anyone my goodies, I stand and turn to face Luke. Though I don't know why I bother with my skirt. If this game continues, I'm going to end up flashing them all. But somehow the skirt makes me feel safe. It's an illusion, but fuck, I need it.

"Straddle me."

Oh, shit. I'm not even sure he's wearing boxers under those athletic pants. He gives me an impatient look.

Lowering down onto him, I bite back a moan as his cock presses against my pussy fully. With my legs spread around his hips, my pussy lips spread as well. His cock nestles against me in a way I've never felt before. I resist the urge to rub against him to see how it would feel.

The only thing keeping us from rubbing skin to skin are his silky athletic pants.

His eyes are definitely not as frigid as usual. The heat from them almost makes me combust.

Those eyes trail over me. I'm confident I'm leaving a wet spot on his pants. I can barely think with him pressed against me so intimately.

I release a breath, but then catch it as he leans into me and scrapes his teeth up my neck.

Holy fuck. A trail of fire burns in the wake of his touch.

He consumes my neck, kissing, sucking, biting, until I'm a hot mess on his lap. He's found a spot that links directly to my pussy, making me rub against his hard length for friction.

"Time, Luke." Eli's voice is firm.

Luke pulls away and stares into my eyes, victorious. "Turn around and spin the bottle, princess."

My breath is coming in pants, but I do as I'm told. Carefully, I stand and drop back down on his lap, feeling the wet spot on his cock from me.

"One more time, princess." Luke's voice sends a shiver down my spine.

When I spin and go to sit, he flips my skirt up in the back and drags my hips down, so my bare, wet pussy rests on his smooth, satin-covered dick. I'm beyond caring at this point. It feels good. Too good.

The bottle lands on Jack, and he holds out the coin. "Tails."

"Fuck." Caden tips his chair back, and I get a good look at the bulge in his pants. My breath catches as my thoughts stall on the image of him stroking his cock in my room. I lick my lips.

His gaze falls to my mouth and he gives me a knowing smile. Fuck. I'm not sexually savvy enough to play this game.

Jack slides in front of me and waits for Luke to tug my ponytail and head to the side. As soon as I'm in position, Jack trails his mouth along my jawline before slipping down to where my shoulder meets my neck. Once there, he sucks and bites my sensitive skin.

Luke angles my hips a little, and I feel him thrust against my throbbing pussy. My breath catches in my throat. I want to think I'm stronger, but these boys take no prisoners.

I didn't think I could get any wetter, but I was wrong.

This is why those other girls gave it up to these guys. I'm about ten seconds from saying fuck it myself, but there's enough fear keeping me in check. First off, they want to do me bare. Second off, I can't forget Luke's comment about them all being there. I assume they'll all partake as well. I'm not quite that horny yet.

And I'm not giving it up that easily. Fuck them.

"Time," Caden calls.

Jack moves back to his spot with a smug grin on his lips.

"Time to move, kitten." Eli holds a hand out to me and I stand. When Luke reaches up to support my hip under my skirt, I glare down at him.

Giving me a wink, he drags his hand down my thigh.

"Sit, kitten," Eli says. Apparently I don't have to trust these guys to want them. I know they're preparing me to have sex with them. Putting me between two of them, getting me accustomed to having two guys surround me as they work my body. They've been doing it since the beginning. Crowding in on me, two at a time.

I wish I hated it. I wish I didn't crave it.

I lower to his lap, careful to cover myself with my skirt.

"Don't be embarrassed, kitten," Eli says in my ear, tugging my hips back against his erection. "You want us. It's natural."

"Nothing about this is natural." I quickly spin the bottle.

"Four men in the prime of their lives. Some girls would kill to be where you are. Wanted. Desired. Needed." His words caress my ear and send a pulse through me. "We're all waiting on you, kitten. And we'll continue to wait."

The bottle stops on Caden.

"Finally." Caden comes forward and kneels before me. When Jack tosses the coin, Caden leans over to see. His eyes meet mine. "Heads, little nympho."

This is only the second time I've had to give, which means maybe I won't end the night with their dicks in my mouth.

Necks are far less intimidating in comparison. Besides, I kind of like the way they taste. Salty. And they smell so good.

Caden smirks. "This game goes too slow. We should skip some parts."

I narrow my eyes. That would not be good for me. "Why?"

"You're probably hoping we'll run out of time and not get to the grand finale." He's not wrong. Caden's green eyes are darker as they search mine.

"Were you hoping the bottle would pick you more, Caden? Do you want to be the first cock I put my mouth on?" I lick his neck, knowing the timer will start, but I keep talking against his skin as I nip and lick between words. "Or do you want to be the first to kiss my pussy? After all, you were the first to kiss me. Maybe you want all my firsts. Maybe you think you've earned it. Maybe you think I owe it to you for demanding monogamy."

His skin is hot beneath my lips, and his scent almost makes me think of those hot cinnamon candies. I suck at the spot just below his ear. Aware that I'm turning him on as much as it turns me on.

"Rules suck, don't they?" I whisper, knowing Eli hears me too.

"Time."

Caden sits back on his feet. The fire in his eyes damn near scorches me. "Feeling cocky, little nympho? Remember, you only have three more turns before you're on my lap."

He rises to stand before me, his cock at my eye level. Grinning evilly, he meets my eyes. "I've always liked to play with my food before I *eat* it."

My core clenches again.

Caden moves back to his spot and adjusts his erection. I should end this now.

I lean back against Eli. If I asked, would he take me home? Back to my cold, empty house. If I leave, will they turn on their webcams tonight or will they leave me alone? Or will they take a first of their choosing? Will Luke follow through on his bluff to have another girl here in my place, doing what I won't do?

My stomach burns and twists at the thought of another girl willingly kissing them and them kissing her. That's not happening. If they've claimed me, then I claim them too. Even if I'm not willing to fuck them anytime soon, they can wait until I'm ready. Even if that's never.

Determined, I spin the bottle. Eli's hands lift my skirt a little when I sit back down on him. Instead of skirt fabric, I feel sweatpants against my pussy and his hardness presses against me. I bite back a moan. Fuck, that feels good.

Maybe I am a little nympho. Maybe that's what they hope I'll become.

CHAPTER 43

The Escalation

HARPER

The spinning bottle stops on Jack. Grinning, he palms his cock before removing his hand from his pants. He walks around the bottle and drops to kneel before me. My mind goes numb waiting for the verdict. Hoping for heads. Flipping the coin in front of me, he catches it, revealing the coin.

"Tails," he says.

My stomach sinks.

Eli grabs the bottom of my shirt and lifts it over my head before I can react.

"Wait," I say and cross my arms over my bra. Nope, no way. I need to leave.

"Don't you want us to make you feel good, kitten?" Eli's voice drops in pitch and strokes over my ear. My traitorous body softens against him. He undoes the back of my bra, but I don't move my arms. "You weren't shy this morning. Why be shy now?"

The obvious answer is they weren't actually in the room with me. His fingertips slip under the straps of my bra and brush against my bare shoulders. Desire pours through my veins at his light touch.

If he removes this, I'll be in just a skirt. With four horny horsemen.

Who's to keep this from devolving into something I'm not ready for?

Jack cups my cheek, making me meet his eyes. "Relax, sweetheart. We aren't having sex tonight. Let us make you feel good."

"No touching, Jack," Luke reminds him.

My gaze finds Luke, and he gives me a satisfied smile.

"Rules of the game, princess. No one but the one you sit on can touch you with their hands, and only to remove clothing. Jack's right. No sex. There's still some time." Luke leans forward. "Tonight is about feeling good."

Fuck, he's right. Everything has felt really fucking good, which is why I'm worried things will go too far. They want everything from me, but I want to hold something back. Some piece of myself they can't claim.

"No penetration." Jack's words make my gaze return to him. "Let us find out what you like, sweetheart."

Fuck. My curiosity will be the death of me. I know they don't really want *me*. They want the last virgin, who happens to be me, but with all of their attention and desires focused on me, I can't help wanting it all.

Eli drags the straps down, and I let my hands fall to my sides. Without my bra, I feel so much more vulnerable. Jack sits back on his heels and just looks at my breasts. It isn't the first time they've seen them, but it's the first time in person for Eli and Jack.

Jack's gaze is intense. What if in real life, they aren't what he was hoping for? Just when I'm about to cover them back up, he speaks.

"So fucking gorgeous." He presses a kiss to my nipple.

"Oh." A shock wave courses through me to settle between my legs. He glances up at me with a mischievous grin.

When Jack takes my nipple into his warm mouth, I gasp as that shock wave rocks through me again. When he sucks, my head tips back and my brain shuts down to focus on the pull and tug on my insides.

Eli holds my hands and shifts below me, making his sweats-covered erection rub my bare pussy. I can't breathe. It feels like I'm being wound so tight. So fucking tight that I'm going to burst.

Jack flicks my tip with his tongue. His soft hair teases my skin.

"Oh, fuck," I whisper.

"Time."

Why?

Jack sits back. My breathing is chaotic, and something is right there, just out of reach and fading with every second. Jack blows his hot breath over my wet breast, making it tighten and ache. I lean back against Eli. My chest still heaving.

As Jack backs away to his chair, he strokes his cock slowly. "Tastes like ice cream."

My gaze darts to Caden. Remembering his words from the morning he smelled me. His hand rubs his erection and he stares at my chest, making heat climb inside me.

"Can't wait to get a taste." Caden's words make me drenched.

"My shirt?" I manage to get out, trying to control the reckless spiral of my desire.

"You don't need it, kitten." Eli shifts me on his lap.

The friction makes me moan. I'm restless and on the edge of something, but I can't quite get there.

"Spin the bottle, princess."

My arousal drips down my thighs as I lean forward to spin the bottle.

"Fuck," Eli hisses.

I glance over my shoulder and sit on his lap. "What's wrong?"

"Nothing's wrong, kitten. Just a huge case of blue balls." He gives me a self-deprecating grin.

I haven't looked at Luke, but when the bottle slows down, it stops on him. Everything inside me clenches at the heat in his eyes. I'm caught in his gaze as he stands and walks over to me.

"Heads, sweetheart."

Luke kneels before me.

"What are you waiting for, princess?"

I swallow and try to think what I've done before. "You're the last neck."

"Are you sure, kitten?" Eli's voice wraps around me. "I haven't had the pleasure yet."

I glance over my shoulder at him. Eli scoots us closer to Luke. He tightens his arm around my waist above my skirt to hold me in place. His arm rests on my bare skin, making sparks ignite.

Luke leans in, and when I press my lips to his neck, my bare chest rubs against his t-shirt, making my nipples ache. He smells like sin and tastes like heaven. I explore his neck with my lips, tongue, and teeth. Sucking and biting, leaving marks that will remain until tomorrow.

Good, those girls at the other table can see I've claimed what's mine.

Under me, Eli shifts and rubs his cock against my pussy. I want their hands on me. I want Luke's shirt gone. Suddenly I'm the one eager to move things along. After all, when I get to *chest*, they lose their shirts.

"Time," Caden calls out.

Eli drags me onto his lap. Luke stares at me with so much heat I want to throw myself into his arms. His eyes flash even hotter before he returns to his chair.

I spin the bottle in a haze of lust. The bottle stops on me and Eli.

"Tails."

I swallow as he helps me stand and I turn to look down at him.

Holding out his hands, he says gently, "Come here, kitten."

His eyes are soft, and I want to trust him, but I know better. I take both his hands and he guides me down onto his lap again, this time straddling him. His cock twitches under my bare pussy. Fuck. I don't know how much more of this I can take before I explode.

Or worse beg for more. Beg them for release.

His eyes are dark pools as he says, "Lie back, kitten."

When I relax against his thighs, he takes my nipple into his mouth. He doesn't tease like Jack did, but suckles me as his cock presses against me intimately. Those shock waves ripple through me, keying me up, making me arch up into him. Making me need. Making me want. Something more.

His hands hold mine to keep me from grabbing. From digging them into his hair to hold him closer.

He kisses across my chest to the other nipple. Everything sharpens down to his lips as they close over my breast. I gasp and squirm against his erection. Just when I can't take it anymore, Luke calls out, "Time, princess."

I whimper with frustrated need.

Eli pulls me to sit, his mouth so close to mine his breath brushes against my lips. The fog of desire has me in its grip. I want to fall into his dark eyes and lose myself. I start to lean in.

Hands under my arms pull me away from Eli, making me stand. I almost protest as his heat is taken away. The coolness against my bare breasts pulls me a little out of the fog. Enough to remember where I am and who I'm with.

"You're mine now, little nympho." Caden sits in his chair and draws me down. He slouches. When I sit, his hard, thick cock is right under my pussy. He wears silky shorts that aren't as thick as Eli's sweats.

Heat sizzles over my bare skin and I'm so much more aware of every sensation. The coolness of the room hardens my bare nipples. The ridge of Caden's shorts presses against me intimately. Luke's sultry gaze on my body sets my temperature to boiling.

I can't seem to settle down. I'm anxious, knowing something is lurking right out of my reach. That I might not get there with their insistence to stick to thirty seconds each time they touch me. But somewhere, even in the fog, I know the limit is a good thing.

"Spin the bottle, sweetheart." Jack's voice draws my attention as I sink into Caden's warm, solid chest. His heat comes through his shirt, drawing me closer. Like a mouse mesmerized by a snake, I'm helpless against wanting these boys.

I blink a few times, trying to regain control. Shit, what the hell is happening to me? My control keeps slipping away. No longer caring what happens as long as they keep touching me. Almost scared they'll stop.

I do what I know I need to and lean forward to spin the bottle.

"Fuck me," Caden curses under his breath before I sit back down in his lap. The bottle spins and spins. It stops on Luke.

I couldn't stop this game if my life depended on it. I want more. I want to taste them. Feel their lips on my breasts and where I ache the most, between my legs.

"Heads."

Luke's eyebrow goes up. Crossing over to me, he takes his t-shirt off and tosses it behind him. Fuck, he's gorgeous. Magnificent. Cut from marble. A warrior frozen in time. Is he as cold as he looks? I reach out with my hands.

"Not so fast, grabby." Caden catches my hands and holds them behind my back. "Mouths only."

I wet my lips and lift my gaze to Luke's. He looks amused. While I'm afraid of keying them up, I can't resist pushing and trying to make them feel as shredded as I am. Especially Luke.

There's something about tempting Death that thrills me. I want to break his control. I want him to beg me for more so I can withhold it and torture him the way he tortures me.

I smirk up at him before I flick his nipple with my tongue.

His skin is so hot.

Pressing my lips against his pecs, I open my mouth and suck his nipple. When I get a moan from him, heat spirals through me, and I bite down gently and tug slightly on his tip.

"Fuck, princess." His hand grabs my ponytail and he tugs my head away. His eyes burn me. "You're playing with fire."

"Luke." Eli's tone is a warning. A warning neither of us cares about right now.

I arch my eyebrow at Luke. "Isn't that the point?"

"She still has time, Luke." Eli's hand strokes his cock inside his pants.

"Fuck." Luke releases my ponytail and resumes his position with his hands behind his back. "Just remember when the next spin lands on me—"

"*If* it lands on you." I move to his other nipple and do the same exact thing. Suck, bite, tug.

"Time."

I sink back against Caden and give Luke a knowing look. Innocent as my body is, my brain has plenty of experience. Years of reading. Imagining a day when I'd be free to experience everything.

I'm safe from sex tonight, but that doesn't mean I couldn't come from what they do to me. And fuck it, I want to come. I should get something out of this experience besides a lack of virginity and a slutty reputation.

Luke sits back in his chair, and feeling a little cocky, I spread my legs open a little. He leans forward. His gaze on my eyes.

"Spin the bottle." His gaze drops between my legs, and I feel a crazy pulse and throb of energy there. He raises his gaze to my breasts. My nipples are already hard, but I can feel them tighten and my breasts grow heavy under his heated gaze.

I could end this night as a technical virgin and part of me doesn't care.

CHAPTER 44

The Escape Plan

HARPER

The bottle points directly at me. Fuck. My gaze tracks Jack as he tosses the coin.

"Tails."

Swallowing hard, I stand and turn. Caden's green eyes are so dark as they meet mine. His hands grab my hips and pull me down on him tight. A moan escapes me at the contact. I long to rub against him, feel that friction build, but he's holding on by a thread. That particular button is one I'm not willing to push. Yet.

"I haven't gotten to taste you at all." His gaze moves over my neck down to my breasts and it feels like a physical caress. The urge to squirm is almost overwhelming. He lifts his gaze to mine and he smirks. "I call for a rule change."

My eyes widen. What the fuck is that supposed to mean?

"What would you like, Caden?" Luke asks almost nonchalantly.

I can't take my eyes from Caden's.

"This is going too slow." Caden's eyes glow with mischief. "I propose since little nympho here is shirtless, that we all move up to the chest portion of the evening."

My throat feels dry as I try not to squirm against him at the thought of his mouth on my breasts.

"You want to skip neck?" Luke asks.

"And stomach too." Caden licks his lips. "You can handle more, can't you, little nympho?"

That would be fewer turns until dicks.

"Wait a minute," Jack says. Maybe he's willing to stand by the rules.

"She hasn't even done anything to me." Eli leans forward. He takes in all of me. If I weren't already on edge, his gaze would push me to it and make me want to fall off it for him.

Luke holds up his hand. "Please turn around, Harper, so we can include you in this conversation."

Caden groans, but helps me stand and sit down on him, this time facing Luke. I reach for my shirt, but Caden grabs my hand.

"No, little nympho."

I lean back against him and cross my arms, barely covering anything. Luke sits across from me, shirtless too. My hopeless gaze drags over his abs and the solid evidence of his arousal in his athletic pants.

Luke steeples his fingers before his lips. "I'm fine with moving to breasts and skipping stomach."

His normally cold eyes drop to my breasts. I almost bite my lip in anticipation, but my gaze flicks to Eli watching my mouth with a smirk. His words about punishing me make me stop from making that mistake again.

"Princess."

I turn back to Luke, conscious of how naked we'll all be if they strip off their shirts.

"Do you want to bump all the guys up to chest?"

I don't know how much longer we'll be playing, but it would definitely speed up getting to their dicks and them to my pussy. And that I'm not okay with. Shouldn't it be too soon? Shouldn't it be my decision instead of being left to fate?

Eli tugs his shirt off with one hand. "I'm okay with skipping parts."

His chest is as cut as Luke's, just a little tanner. Jack takes his shirt off next. These guys are ripped. My mouth waters. Sure, I've seen them over webcam, but the live show is so much better. Caden leans me forward as he removes his shirt and then tugs me back against him.

I hiss as my bare back touches his hot, naked chest. Unlike the fabric of his t-shirt, friction holds us together.

Gorgeous male flesh surrounds me. All of their cocks strain against their pants. This is a dangerous situation with no outs. I can't just leave. They drove me here.

Maybe we should end this game. They swear it won't lead to sex tonight, but how easy would it be to change the rules again? Maybe the whole waiting for test results will hold them back. Maybe.

I'm sure they have condoms on hand if it really comes to that. Would I even stop them?

My gaze lifts to Luke's. He grins that evil grin of his that sends butterflies exploding in my stomach. His eyes lift to Caden's. "Care to share?"

What? Share? That's not part of the game. Caden pushes me to stand. I press my thighs together against the aching need clawing inside. My curiosity is definitely driving the show here.

"I can do the honors." Taking my hand, Jack brings me down on his lap. I don't have time to fix my skirt, so my bare pussy presses against his sweatpants instead of the back of my skirt. His chest is hot against my skin as he reclines and draws me against him. I press my legs together.

Fear tickles my spine even as anticipation climbs with it.

Caden and Luke move to my sides and kneel. My breath catches. I should protest, but fuck if I don't want to feel this.

"The timer's ready." Eli's eyes hold mine. "Whenever you two are ready."

Oh, shit.

It's my last thought before Caden and Luke lean in and latch onto my breasts. I draw in a sharp breath. Caden flicks my nipple with his tongue as he sucks on my breast, taking as much into his mouth as he can. Luke's eyes meet mine as he flicks my nipple with his tongue before gently biting down and tugging.

I let out a little cry. My pussy is drenched, pulsing. I close my eyes, overwhelmed by the sensations coursing through my body. Desire, lust, need, longing.

Jack holds my hands as Luke and Caden feast on my breasts. Sliding his hips beneath mine, Jack rubs his cock against my pussy. Instinctively, my legs part, wanting more.

When I open my eyes, Eli stares between my legs. I widen them more, letting him be part of this too. Needing him to be part of this.

They kept winding me up with every touch, and then I float down a little less each time they withdraw. I don't want to float down anymore. I want to soar.

"Time," Eli calls out.

At the same time, "Shoop" by Salt-N-Pepa blares into the room over our heavy breathing. I freeze. Luke and Caden sit back on their heels. Irritation crosses Luke's face as he turns to look at my purse.

The realization of the ringtone penetrates through the fog of desire.

"Shit." Standing, I grab my top and pull it on. I rush to my purse and pull out my phone. "Mom?"

"Where are you?" Her voice is concerned. "Your car is here and—"

"I'm fine." Inhaling, I look at the guys. Luke raises an eyebrow like I'm putting him out. I resist the urge to give him the finger. "I'm just…" Fuck. What the hell am I doing? Letting the guys accomplish their goal. I close my eyes. "…studying with friends."

"Do you know what time it is, Harper Lynn? And a school night. You need to come home. Now." Mom's voice is sterner than I've ever heard it.

"I—"

"Now, Harper." Mom cuts the call.

Closing my eyes, I take a deep breath. I'm not used to my mom needing to reel me back in. I haven't taken advantage over the years. Really, I've been the model kid, but she knows four guys are very interested in me.

Movement makes me open my eyes. The guys tug their shirts on. Eli grabs my bra from beside his chair and heads to me.

Part of me is relieved Mom called when she did and part of me is frustrated beyond anything I've ever felt. That buzzed feeling still floats through my blood. I was so close. Eli hands me my bra.

"Thanks." I shove it in my purse instead of taking my top off to put it back on. I don't want to be naked in front of the guys again so soon. My gaze lifts to Eli's. "I have to go."

He promised to take me home if I asked.

"We heard." Luke steps beside Eli. "I'll take you home."

I can't meet Luke's eyes. Will they punish me for this? Sure, it isn't really my fault, but most of what I get punished for isn't my fault.

Eli draws me into his arms and hugs me. I tense up, wondering what's next. As I realize he's just offering me comfort, the tension eases from my body and I return the hug.

When I step back, I glance at Jack and Caden. A wry smile graces Jack's face, while Caden has a sour look. Their disappointment is apparent, but when Mom calls, that's the end of the evening. Parent trumps horsemen.

Luke takes hold of my elbow, and I hiss at the contact. I'm still keyed up and sparks flow from the simple touch. My gaze darts to his, and his light blue eyes capture me with the heat still lingering in them.

My body throbs with want.

"Come on, princess, before you turn into a pumpkin." Luke leads me out of the basement and into the cool night air. At the sudden loss of warmth, I shiver. Luke wraps his arm around my shoulders and pulls me in close against him.

It stirs something odd in me. As aggressive as he always is with me, this feels comforting, like something just for me. It reminds me of the night he slept at my house. Like he's protective of me. My heart pounds a little heavily and I swallow down the weird feeling stirring in my chest.

"I'm not going to get punished for this." I'm not. My mom wanting me home on a school night isn't my fault, and he can't say that it is.

Besides, the ache between my thighs is punishment enough. I doubt I'll fall asleep, even with what I assume will be my nightly show of Jack and whoever else getting off. While I'm not allowed to do a damned thing about this ache unless I want all of them to do whatever to get me there.

"Is that a question or a statement, princess?" Luke's tone is cool as we reach his car.

"My mom is right. It's a school night, and I should be at home doing homework or getting into bed." Not stripping and making out with four guys. My life has changed. I'm not sure for the better.

He steps away as he opens the door for me. I shiver at the sudden cool breeze sweeping over me.

I wish I had something more to wear than my skirt and top, especially without my underwear, but I know not to ask for it back. After I slide into the seat, Luke closes the door and walks around.

Without a word, he starts the car and puts it into gear. The silence is a little daunting. I straighten my skirt over my thighs and wish I'd taken the time to put on my bra. At least then, I'd feel a little less vulnerable.

I can't stop thinking about possible punishments. Eli has something to punish me with tomorrow, but he doesn't worry me. He wants to have me alone when he punishes me, and I'm beginning to trust him a little. At least, more than I trust Luke.

"If you're going to punish me, can we just do it now before I get home? I don't want to worry at school about you dragging me in front of everyone and—"

Luke hits the brakes, effectively cutting off my speech. Fuck, that worked.

Oh shit, that worked. I can't believe I pushed him to punish me when we're alone. My pulse flutters and I straighten my shirt and skirt as he pulls off on the side of the road.

We haven't really left Caden's neighborhood, so the houses are spread out and no streetlights keep the darkness at bay.

I didn't really think this through. My words ran away with themselves. I don't know what to say to make Luke forget it and not end up with even more punishment.

The dashboard lights illuminate Luke's face. Closing his eyes, he takes a breath and turns the car off. Darkness and silence fall over both of us. I don't know what to expect, but I do know that being alone with a horseman I've recently teased is probably not a good thing.

Especially Death himself.

CHAPTER 45

The Parley

LUKE

Patience and control have been my mistresses for a long time. I've needed to hold myself in check. My father requires it of me, and I'm not allowed to fail him.

But Harper tests both. She needs a steady hand, and right now mine are shaking.

Her breath hitches in the darkness. The scent of her arousal still lingers in the air around me. The feel of her lips and tongue against my skin plays over and over in my mind. The guys and I hoped we could move the boundaries to get some relief from the massive hard-ons Harper leaves us with every day, and show her what we have to offer her.

The girl has never experienced an orgasm. Tonight she got so fucking close. And then her mom called and ended all the fun.

Harper wants her punishment. Or rather doesn't want to be punished, but wants it now when I'm so fucking keyed up, I'm about to explode if I can't sink into her warm, tight pussy.

Honestly, I wouldn't have punished her for this, but then Harper had to get mouthy about it. She can't seem to help pushing me. Making me need to punish her.

Like she can dictate when and where she gets a punishment. She's mine to control now, but she pushes at the edges of her cage just a little every time. Seeing if I'll allow her to run free. Now that she's mine though, she'll never get away. She just hasn't figured that out yet.

"Luke, I didn't mean—" Her voice is softer, and I can hear just a hint of fear, trying to get out of what she's asked for. That hint of defiance she can't seem to resist.

"Stop, princess." Taking a breath, I have myself under control enough to do what I have to. Though I haven't completely decided how to punish her.

"I—"

"Come here." I push my seat all the way back and hold out my hand to her. Tonight we would have broken her down until she came with us around her, watching her fall apart for all of us. It wouldn't have mattered whose tongue was in her pussy. It would have been all of us.

She shrinks away from my hand. "You can punish me tomorrow. I swear."

I snap my fingers and hold my hand out. Impatience tugs at me, but I can't let it win.

She sighs, resigning herself to my will. When her hand slips into mine, something settles within me. I reel her in. She raises up on her knees, a shadow in the darkness, but she hesitates.

"Straddle my lap, princess." I keep emotion out of my voice. I can control the lust flooding my body. Even if I have the worst case of blue balls ever.

She still hesitates.

I release a breath.

"This will go faster if you just submit. You wanted punishment," I remind her. "Come and get it."

Her hand tightens on mine as she slips over the center console and straddles my lap, sitting on my thighs instead of against me where she belongs.

Tsking her, I grab her hips to bring her against me. I'm still hard. I swear I always am around her. If I thought the others would be cool with it, I would take care of her virginity right now and get it out of the way.

But we agreed. And I have control. Even with her bare pussy pressed against my pants, I can control my lust. I don't move my hands from her hips.

"Take off my shirt," I order.

This close, even in the dark, I can make out her features. She's unsure where this is going. Unfortunately it can't go very far because our game got interrupted.

"Hurry, Harper. We need to get you home so you don't get grounded." I slip some boredom and arrogance into my tone.

She reaches for the hem of my shirt and pulls it over my head, dropping it onto her seat. I return my hands to her hips.

"Now take off yours."

"I don't—"

"Fine, tomorrow after school, we'll have our own personal pep rally for the game in the locker room. Fifteen spankings in front of the football team should remind you who owns you."

Her shirt joins mine on the passenger seat. My shoulders relax, but she's tense, trying to hold herself away from me. Her breasts are magnificent. Just the right size without being too large and so fucking responsive. I'm surprised she didn't come when Caden and I sucked on her nipples. She had to be close.

Her hands rest on my shoulders, probably to keep herself away from me.

"Did you enjoy tonight?" I ask her. The darkness surrounds us, closing us in.

"Did I enjoy being forced to be practically naked with a bunch of guys in the same room?" Her tone is a little judgmental, but I know she loved every minute of it.

I catch her ponytail in my hand, bringing our bare chests together, and tip her head back. She gasps, and I can feel her tremble against me. I bring my mouth close to her ear.

"Not everything we do has to be a punishment, princess."

"You mean I should just lie down and get it over with?" Her voice wavers, as if she's afraid to say what she's saying.

"Maybe." I shift so that her clit presses against my cock. "We don't even have to move to the backseat. I could just slide right into you. Right here, right now. Fuck you until you see stars."

Her breath catches. I capture her earlobe between my teeth, and her fingernails dig into my shoulders. I suck on it to soothe the pain.

"I don't want to have sex with you." Her voice is small and unsure. The dampness of my pants where she presses against me tells me she lies. She may not be ready to accept that she wants us. But she does.

"Princess, you won't lose your virginity in the quarterback's car."

Some of the tension eases out of her body.

"At least not tonight." So many plans to make. "You won't lose anything without us all there."

She had a taste tonight of what it's like to have three of us on her at once, while Eli watched. We just have to keep pushing those boundaries until she's begging for it. Craving that sweet release with all of us.

Using her ponytail, I tilt her head back again. So that we're eye to eye. Her breath rushes out over my lips and her brown eyes widen as she looks into mine.

"How should I punish you?" I whisper against her lips, but I don't kiss her. I ease my hand under her skirt and grab a handful of her ass.

She jerks forward to get away from my hand, rubbing her sweet pussy against my throbbing dick. She whispers against my lips, "Luke, I need to get home."

"Do you need to be punished, princess?" I release my grip, but stroke along her ass cheek with my fingers. "Do you want me to spank you?"

She shakes her head slightly.

"This is your opportunity. You pick how I'll punish you."

HARPER

This feels so fucking different from Caden's basement. I was in this position tonight already, but then we had three other guys to pull him and me back if we lost control. I'm alone with Luke in his car, practically naked, on his lap.

I wish I could taunt him and push him away. If I truly didn't want him, I don't think he would force the issue. Somewhere there is a line that not even Luke will cross. The problem is, I'm still keyed up from all the stimulation in the basement and I'm not immune to any of these men. Especially not Luke.

He's beautiful and so put together that I fight the urge to ruffle his hair. Pretty sure that wouldn't go over well for me.

With every breath, my breasts rub against his warm chest. My nipples are hard peaks. I can taste his breath on my lips, the hint of mint.

He wants me to think and make a decision while his erection presses against my pussy, and every inch of his hot flesh against mine sends sparks sizzling through my body to settle between my thighs.

His lips hover over mine, and I can't help thinking of how good it felt to kiss him on the football field and again in the cafeteria. How close I got to coming from his lips on mine and his cock rubbing against me intimately.

"What will it be, Harper?" Luke's lips whisper against mine.

My breathing comes out in pants as I try to search his eyes in the darkness. Who will draw him back this time? Do I want someone to stop him? Do I *need* someone to stop us?

I throb against the feel of him between my legs.

My brain has officially left the building, and I must have no self-preservation because I lean in and claim his lips. He yanks my ponytail, but not to disengage. He angles my head to the side as he deepens the kiss. His tongue strokes against mine, sending heat flooding through my veins and pooling low in my stomach.

Wrapping my arms around his neck, I press my body into him. Hot skin against hot skin. I can't seem to get close enough to him. The fingers on my ass are likely to leave bruises with how tight he's holding onto it.

A mass of sensations, I whimper into his mouth. When I rock my hips against him, he moans, making my insides burst into flames. His lips leave mine and trail down over my jaw. Using his grip on my hair, he tips my head as his lips and tongue and teeth follow my jugular, teasing, torturing.

I roll my hips against his, knowing I'm making a mess on his pants again but not caring. Needing the friction. Needing him not to stop after thirty fucking seconds and leave me hanging on by a thread. So close to the release my body craves so badly.

He meets the motion of my hips with thrusts against me. Teasing and tantalizing my neck with nips and kisses and licks. I wouldn't be surprised to find so many hickeys no amount of makeup will be able to hide them. Marks claiming their territory. When Luke's mouth settles on that spot where my neck meets my shoulder, he bites down.

I moan as everything inside me winds tighter. His fingers flex on my ass cheek like he's trying to make sure they don't leave that spot, but I need so much more. My empty core pulses. I want to tip over the edge into whatever is waiting for me on the other side. And I know he can get me there.

"Luke?" I need to know I'm not alone in this. That this attraction tears him up as much as it does me.

"Fuck, Harper." His mouth finds mine again. He releases my hair and his other hand finds its way under my skirt, gripping my bare skin to help guide my hips against his. He slides his length against my clit, winding me tighter and tighter.

I break from his lips for a moment to search his eyes.

That fire and darkness from earlier blazes in them, even without light. I want to let him consume me until nothing is left but ashes. A glint enters his eyes, and it should scare me, but I need him to release me from this tension and pressure.

He shifts me. His hips still lead mine, but he presses me back against the steering wheel and then dips his head to take my nipple in his mouth. My lips part and my fingers thread through his soft hair as sensations course through me. He tortures me the way I tortured him, but this time no one will call time on us.

The pressure keeps building with no relief, until I feel like I might burst from it. His mouth finds mine again. His covered cock rubs against my throbbing clit as he devours me, taking everything I have to give.

"Let go, Harper," he whispers against my lips.

Suddenly as if waiting for his command, my body unravels. Time freezes as euphoria floods me. My lips part and I cry out against his mouth, clinging to him as wave after wave crashes over me. It's too much. Sparks release like fireworks through my blood, lighting up my whole body. I gasp against his mouth.

All those times I'd been so close to this and never tipped over. Fuck.

His hips don't let up, keeping me in the moment, drawing out my orgasm. Until he groans, his cock jerking against me as he comes. The tension releases from him as he sinks back into his seat, drawing me against him.

He kisses me with that softness again before he holds me. I don't have the strength left to resist as I collapse against him. I sink into his warmth, unable to gather my scattered thoughts.

I rest my cheek against his shoulder as his hand strokes my back. Tiny flutters surge through my pussy, clenching around nothing.

Fuck, that was just... fuck. I should have masturbated. If I'd known this was the end result.

"Feel good, princess?"

I nod and rub my cheek against his shoulder, inhaling his sultry cologne and breathing out. I want to rub on him like a cat until I get off again.

"We need to get you home."

I can't look him in the eye as he helps me return to my seat. I give him his shirt and pull my bra out of my purse, putting it and my shirt on. He starts the car. When the dash lights the interior, I catch the dampness on the front of his pants and blush.

He takes my panties out of his pocket, and I think he's going to hand them to me. Instead, he lifts the waist of his pants and wipes at his cum. Blushing, I look out the window at the darkness surrounding us.

He slips my panties back in his pocket and puts the car into gear.

I'm not sure what to say. I didn't intend for any of that to happen. Public humiliation stormed my mind, and then desire and lust clouded it over until all I could think about was the slide of his hot body against mine.

"You'll come to the game tomorrow, and the after-party." Luke's tone doesn't leave any room for me to decline, so I don't say anything.

At least my body no longer feels like it's on fire. The rest of the drive is in silence. When he pulls up to my house, the light is on in the kitchen and the curtain flutters in the window.

Luke parks the car. "Don't get grounded, princess."

"Don't keep me out late on a school night, Death," I shoot back, unable to resist.

His cool eyes meet mine. I'm still not sure what to make of what happened in this car, so I drop my gaze to my hands in my lap.

"I don't think my mom knows what grounding is," I admit softly as I undo my seatbelt and start to open the door.

Luke grabs my ponytail, not as rough as usual, but I still feel a slight bite of pain. He turns me to face him and takes my lips. I wish I could stop responding to him, but my will isn't that strong.

When he breaks the kiss, he smirks. "Tomorrow night you party with the gods."

CHAPTER 46

Infiltration

HARPER

"Were you out with those guys?" Mom asks as soon as I close the door. She has her arms crossed as she leans against the island.

"Yes." I can just imagine all the marks on my neck tell her exactly what I was doing tonight.

"Is this going to be an every night thing? Do I need to worry about you?" Mom's gaze travels over my clothes.

Even knowing she can't tell I'm not wearing panties, I blush and worry my whole appearance might be a bit rumpled from all the heavy petting. What can I say? One of them is my boyfriend? Not really. They make me do things? Yeah, that'd be bad. They own me? Parental red flag. They just want to fuck me all year? Even bigger red flag.

"We're...just hanging out. Taking things slowly." I stumble over the words. If having felt four different cocks between my legs while they took turns kissing my body is slow. Not to mention dry humping one of them in his car until we both came on the way home.

Yup, real fucking slow.

Mom's eyes narrow, but she sighs and her arms drop. "Just be careful, Harper."

"I will." I tug at the hem of my skirt. My gaze lifts to my mom's tired face. As much as I want to run to my bedroom and shower, I pause and say, "Are you okay, Mom?"

She gives me a weary smile. "Just a long day at work. I'm sure things will calm down soon."

"Do you want me to fix you something to eat?" I move toward the fridge, intending to pull out some lettuce and veggies for a salad.

"I'm fine, Harper. You should head to bed. You have school in the morning." Mom turns and picks up a plate to carry over to the sink.

I want to talk to her about the guys. I want her read on this situation. Maybe she can figure out a way to help me out of this. But as she turns away, her shoulders slump with exhaustion, and I know I can't put any more burdens on her. Besides, she might decide to get other adults involved, and even though she would think she's helping me, that would only be bad for me.

"Good night."

"Good night, sweetie."

I make my way to my room and sit at my desk. No one told me to turn on my webcam tonight, but I can't help opening my laptop and starting mine, curious to see if they're there too.

Caden is in his room on his bed, looking over a notebook. Jack is working on something, maybe homework, at his desk. Eli is reading a book in bed. They glance my way when my video starts.

"You okay, kitten?" Eli asks.

"I didn't get in trouble if that's what you're asking." I slump back in my chair. Who knows what kind of punishment they might give me for *actually* getting grounded.

Jack quirks an eyebrow. "No, sweetheart, we want to make sure you're okay."

I glance at Caden, and his eyes are trained on me. The guys seem to actually care about me a little. Maybe they worry about pushing their plaything too far. The memory of what Luke and I did in his car floods my mind. My cheeks heat as I drop my eyes from theirs.

Do I actually feel guilty? Like I cheated somehow? Fuck that.

"I need to take a shower and get to bed, but I'm fine." I can't help but wonder if Luke will tell them what happened.

He's not in his room yet. I don't expect him to get there for a while.

The guys return to their work, and I go into my bathroom, shedding my clothes. When I step under the hot water, I remember every minute of tonight. Lips on my neck and breasts. The pressure of their erections against my pussy. The heat in their eyes as they watched me with the other guys.

By the time I get out of the shower, I feel wound up again. I slip on panties, sleep shorts, and a camisole before towel-drying my hair and weaving it into a quick braid.

When I return to my room, the guys are on their beds in their boxers. Luke walks into his room and his eyes meet mine. I suck in a breath as my pussy throbs like a Pavlovian response.

Needing to do something, I move my laptop to my nightstand and get under the covers.

My phone buzzes with a message notification. I glance at the screen. It's from the group chat.

FAMINE (JACK):

Since our playtime got cut short, want to help us out tonight, sweetheart?

I glance at the screen with my eyebrows knotted. What new torture is this?

ME:

Help you out?

FAMINE (JACK):

We'll show you ours if you show us yours

I meet Jack's gaze, and he winks.

PESTILENCE (ELI):

She's already seen ours

WAR (CADEN):

Only if she lets me see all of her. When she bent over to spin the bottle, I only got a glimpse, but I want a longer look

Will Luke tell them about the car? He lifts an eyebrow, as if daring me to mention it. What will they think of Luke and I getting off, just the two of us? They were upset when we slept together. Will he get punished and if so, can I dole it out?

ME:

What do you want me to do?

PESTILENCE (ELI):

Put your headphones on, kitten

I connect my AirPods to my laptop. Luke joins the others as he settles on his bed in just his boxers.

"Is your door locked, kitten?" Eli gestures with his head toward my closed door. "No more interruptions."

I get up and open the door to see if Mom is still up or if she's headed to bed. The TV isn't on and the lights are all off. I shut my door and turn the lock. Taking a deep breath, I return, but before I can sit on the bed Caden clears his throat.

"Move your computer to the desk again." Caden nods his head. "It'll be a better angle for us."

I open my mouth to protest, but before I can get a word out, Jack says, "No talking. We don't need mommy dearest wondering who you're talking to."

Anticipation trickles down my spine as I move the laptop to the desk.

I sit on the edge of the bed and wait for them to tell me what to do.

"Take off your top." Jack moves closer to the monitor and smiles.

I take off my camisole. The cool air in the room caresses my already tightened nipples. I lean back on my hands and thrust my chest out.

If they want a show, I'll give them a fucking show. Since none of them can do anything about it, I feel a lot braver than I did sitting with them around that bottle, their mouths on me. A shiver runs through me.

"I was really looking forward to eating your pussy tonight, little nympho." Caden's voice flows over me like a caress, making my pussy pulse in response.

I cross my legs against the ache. They want me naked, but I'm not going to just remove my clothes for them without getting something in return.

I grab my phone.

ME:

It's only fair when I take something off, one of you should take off something too

I only have two items of clothing left, but fuck it, they each only have their boxers. They all got to see me, but I still haven't seen Luke naked.

Jack stands and flings his boxers across the room. Holding his hands out to the side, he slowly turns in a circle. His cock is hard, red, and straining against his stomach. His ass is tight, and everywhere I look are toned muscles.

I start to bite my lip but stop and glance at Eli. He quirks a smile and lifts an eyebrow but doesn't say anything.

"Your turn, princess." Luke waves his hand.

I shimmy out of my shorts. The red panties I'm wearing are mostly just bits of lace.

Caden groans. He holds up my black panties he pocketed earlier. "I'll trade you these panties for those."

Smiling slightly, I shake my head as I resume my position, leaning back, legs crossed. I wait to see who will do the honors.

Caden peels off his black boxer briefs. The guy has a legit monster between his legs. Long and thick with veins running along the engorged length.

I swallow the lump in my throat as he turns. He's all muscle. He's the offensive left tackle for a reason.

He sits on the bed and fists his cock. I feel an answering pulse between my legs. I'm not sure how I would have reacted if I'd had to kiss his cock tonight. I don't know if I would have known where to start. It's a lot.

"Kitten." Eli's voice pulls my gaze away from Caden's hand wrapped around his cock. I meet Eli's dark eyes. "Your turn."

I stand and turn my back to them. I slide my hands into the sides of my panties and lower them slowly to the ground before stepping out of them. Taking my time, I straighten back up. I smile at the chorus of groans and glance over my shoulder.

"Turn around," Luke demands.

I sit on the bed with my legs crossed. Still withholding that part of me.

Laughing, Eli drops his boxers.

Eli turns to show me everything. Tight ass, muscled back. He's built leaner than Jack and Caden, but it doesn't mean he's any less built. I don't have any complaints about their bodies.

They're gorgeous and they know it. Which is why they're all arrogant, entitled assholes.

Eli leans against his headboard. His eyes darken as he wraps his hand around his cock and strokes it slowly. Heat bursts through my body.

"Spread your legs, Harper." Luke's voice pulls my gaze away from watching Eli stroke himself.

I raise my eyebrow and nod to him. He has to go first before I give them what they want. My skin feels tight and I'm soaking wet again.

When Luke stands, I involuntarily lean in. He doesn't tease me the way I teased them. He takes his boxers off, revealing his thick cock. Honestly he's the closest in size to Caden. My legs tighten.

Even now, my body prepares for them. My breasts are heavy, my nipples are tight, and my pussy is so drenched lubrication won't be an issue. Need winds in my stomach as my core clenches, aching and empty.

Luke's body is built lean like Eli, and he's just as cut. Instinctually, my body wants these perfect male specimens. In a normal world, they'd fight over who could claim me. But nothing about the horsemen is normal.

They want to share me. That thought shouldn't make me wetter.

Luke leans against his headboard. He strokes his hard cock a few times, but he already got off once tonight. If I were in charge of punishment, I'd deny him his orgasm.

CHAPTER 47

The Negotiations

Harper

"Open your legs, kitten." Eli's voice coaxes me. It's heavy with lust.

They're far away from me, not in the room, which emboldens me. I scoot backward on my bed until my back is against my headboard.

I bend my knees. They want to see the most vulnerable part of my body. They've already seen all of me, so this shouldn't be as terrifying as it is. But something about this seems more intimate. My insides feel like they're on fire.

"Come on, sweetheart. We've shown you ours. Show us yours." Jack's voice is deeper and calming, without a hint of his usual amusement.

Holding my breath, I slide my legs open to the sides and clench at my bedspread.

"Are you wet, kitten?"

I can't decide where to look as the guys all fist their cocks. My gaze settles on Eli as he rubs his thumb over his tip and spreads his precum down his shaft.

Opening my mouth, I remember I'm not supposed to talk. I shut my mouth and glance at the closed door. I don't want to grab my phone and text them, so I nod.

It's no use lying. They know how wet they make me. They felt me dripping all over their dicks during the game. Just because my body is on board with what they have in mind doesn't mean I want to want them.

Maybe giving in tonight will end in pleasure like in the car with Luke. That orgasm was amazing.

Luke says, "Touch your neck the way we kissed it."

Okay, new game. I inhale and lift my shaking hand to my neck, tracing the line that Luke's mouth took in the car. Slowly dragging it down the side. Tingles chase my finger like the guys are the ones touching me.

"Did you like our mouths on your neck?" With my AirPods in, Luke's voice is like a dark consciousness in my head.

I nod as my eyelids grow heavy.

"Where, princess?"

I drag my finger to the spot where a hickey is already. It's tender. They all sucked and bit me there, marking me as theirs. I can almost still feel their teeth on me. My breath stutters in and out.

"What about your breasts?" Luke whispers.

I catch my lower lip between my teeth and nod.

"Show me. Use both hands. Show us what we do to you."

I drag my hand over my nipples, remembering their slick tongues and sharp teeth and hot mouths surrounding them, drawing them in. My eyes shut and my knees fall out to the side as I run my hands where their mouths were just a while ago.

"We didn't get to hold your breasts in our hands. Show us."

I've touched my breasts before. Showering, putting on a bra, tugging them into position, but nothing feels like touching them at Luke's command while Eli, Caden, and Jack watch. It's like they're on the bed with me. Their hands trailing over me lightly. My lips part. I arch my neck back, needing more. Needing Luke to drive me wilder.

"Do you want to see what you missed, princess? Do you want to feel what we would have done to you if you stayed?"

I open my eyes and meet Luke's darkened ones as I nod. My gaze darts to the other guys. Eli squeezes his cock at the base as he slowly pumps up and down. Caden is rougher with his strokes. Jack grins when he notices me watching his hand ease up and down his cock.

When my eyes settle on Luke, his fist moves rhythmically up and down, tugging at something low and needy in my gut.

"Listen to my voice and do what I say."

I nod helplessly, as much of a mess as I was in the basement with Jack's cock under me, pressing against my pussy, Caden and Luke sucking my breasts while Eli's dark gaze held mine. I want what Luke will hopefully give me again.

"Keep one hand on your breast. Run the other lightly down to your stomach. Run your finger over your waist. A lot of guys skip the stomach, but so much anticipation happens when you're between two needy spots like your breasts and your pussy.

"Both crave attention. Both want our mouths on them, and don't worry, princess, you'll have mouths on your breasts and pussy at the same time. One of us will eat you out while two of us will tease, lick, and suck your nipples. And someone will claim your lips until you come all over us."

Fuck. He's painting an image I can almost envision. No one has touched my pussy. Not them and barely me. But I've had their cocks rub against me there and know how potent that touch can be.

"Fuck, Luke. Make her touch her fucking pussy already." Caden's impatient voice makes my eyes pop open. He grins wolfishly. "You know you want to know, little nympho. Once we eat you out, you'll beg us for more and more until you have one of us between your legs twenty-four seven."

Shit. My pussy gushes at the image of his dark head between my legs. I dip my finger south but stop so that it stays on my stomach. My gaze finds Luke's in the camera.

"Do you want it, princess?" Luke cocks his head. "You want me to guide you to your first orgasm with all of us watching?"

I arch my eyebrow. My first orgasm was in his car with him grinding up into me and his lips devastating mine. If I rat him out, will he punish me? Fuck it. If he wants to play it this way, fine. I nod.

"Fuck," Jack hisses as he comes all over his hand.

Caden's laugh is dark and fills my ears.

"Close your eyes, princess." Luke's voice once again fills my head. I do as he asks. "Pluck your nipple like you did mine. Run both your hands down over your stomach and onto your thighs. The best part of kissing your thighs would have been the smell of your arousal surrounding us as we tortured the sensitive insides of your legs. Coming so close to the promise of kissing your pussy without actually kissing it. Our mouths watering wanting to taste you. Light touch, princess. Trace from your knee up. Stop there."

My breath is coming in pants as I let him lead me. Giving him this control over me.

"Open your eyes, kitten." Eli's voice pries my eyes open. "Watch us for this next bit. I want to see your eyes."

Luke chuckles darkly into my ears. "Imagine if you'd been able to kiss our cocks, princess." Luke's hand pauses its stroking and he lifts it away. "Where would you have put your mouth?"

They all stop touching themselves. Jack is already hard again. They wait for me.

I straighten and glance at the door. If I'm quiet enough, Mom won't hear. She was pretty tired.

"Tell us, little nympho."

I lick my lips and run my hands over my inner thighs like Luke told me to do. Heat courses through my veins as my pussy pulses, longing for more. I look at their cocks. Each one a little different. I try to imagine what I would do.

I clear my throat and whisper, "I'd kiss the tip."

As one, they all trace their thumbs over the tips of their erections. I crawl to the end of my bed to see better. Sitting on the edge, I spread my legs. The focus isn't really on me right now.

Power fills me at their groans. I imagine what I would have done once I got over my initial reluctance.

"I'd part my lips and suck lightly on the tip." Their hands follow my commands and fuck, is it a power trip. Channeling every romance book I've read, I continue. "I'd kiss along the underside down to your balls. I'd want to see what happens when I lick them."

Eli shivers as he drags his fingers down his balls. An answering pulse rocks my pussy.

"I'd suck your balls into my mouth to see what it feels like." They all cup their balls. "Then I'd run my tongue back up to the tip before taking your cock into my mouth. I'd wonder how much of you I could fit inside. Taste your skin with my tongue and then run the edge of my teeth gently along it."

"Fuck." Eli comes in jerky streams of cum over his hand.

I lick my lips, and Caden groans. His hand squeezes the base of his cock as his eyes meet mine.

"I'd wish I could use my hand too, so I could touch more of you instead of just the tip. I'd run my hand over your shaft while I sucked the tip like you sucked my nipple in your mouth."

Caden curses as he comes. Jack also comes again and sinks into his bed.

Luke is still holding out, but he's already come once tonight. He gives me a wicked smile.

"My turn, princess. Stay where you are. I enjoy seeing you this close. Spread your legs wide. Take your fingers and hold your pussy open for us. Let us see where we'll be spending all year with our mouths, our cocks, our fingers."

Shivers race through me as I do as he asks. Even though my body is flushed with both heat and embarrassment, I'm beyond caring about what's appropriate. I need what he's going to give me, even if I'm doing it to myself.

Eli and Caden have recovered, but Jack looks spent. He still watches with a grin on his face.

"Take your finger and press against where you feel the pulsing."

My eyes go to Luke as I do as he says. My soft pussy is wet and slippery, but as I press on my clit, I want to close my legs against the pressure.

"Don't close your legs." Luke's dark command hangs over me as I part my legs farther. "Good. I would press my tongue against there to savor your taste and feel your slick pussy under my tongue. Then I'd dip down to circle your opening. Trace it with the tip of my tongue until you can't help but buck against my face, waiting for more. Longing for more."

I do as he says, feeling the pressure building, ramping up.

"I'd slide my tongue into your pussy just a little."

I dip the tip of my finger inside me and let out a gasp at the feel.

"Is it wet?"

Fuck. I nod.

"Spread it around your clit. Use two fingers and rub in a circle. Imagine my tongue pressing against you. I'd close my mouth over your clit and suck. Then I'd slide back down to taste your cunt again, but this time I'd press in a little farther."

My heart pounds as I watch Luke leisurely stroke his cock while I follow his orders so he can watch. I figured I'd spend the entire year hiding again. Instead, I have the attention of the horsemen, and I've gone from never having been kissed to second base with four guys.

Part of me wishes we had gotten to this part of the game, so I could feel their tongues moving over my pussy, spearing inside me, sucking me. Part of me even wishes I could have done everything I'd said I would do to the guys.

But fear would have lingered around me. Worried one of them would take it further. With them on the camera, the fear disappears. I can end this if I want to.

"If we were using hands, I would slide a finger inside you while I sucked your clit."

I slide my finger deeper and use my other hand to tease my clit. Masturbation had never appealed to me before, but I've never felt a need like this. A craving. And to be honest, I didn't know what I was missing.

Sure, books describe it, but the feel of their mouths on my breasts is an experience I won't ever forget and couldn't replicate with my own hands no matter how hard I tried.

"Does it feel snug, princess?" Luke's voice is strained as I lift my gaze to his window. He looks close to the edge himself.

"So fucking tight," I whisper.

His eyes darken. "Add another finger. Keep rubbing your clit. Pump them in and out. Slowly. Show me how wet you are, Harper."

I give him a questioning look.

"Show me your fingers."

I slip them out and hold them up so he can see the wetness on my skin.

"Taste it."

I wrinkle my nose for a second, but fuck it. I bring my fingers to my lips and trace my tongue along the wetness. Slightly salty and musky.

Luke groans, and that feeling of power wells within me. "Slide them back inside you. Both of them. All the way in."

My breath rushes out of my lungs as wetness coats my fingers in my snug pussy.

"Look at us. Keep your eyes on us and don't you dare fucking close them." Luke's commands make my pussy clench around my fingers.

I groan.

"Harper."

My eyes pop open and I nod. Keep my eyes open. Got it.

"Do what feels good. Pump your fingers in and out of your pussy while you rub your clit. I want to come when you do. We all do. So when you get close, let us know."

My eyes widen. I look at the others. Eli leans in. His hand slips over his cock from tip to balls. Caden tugs on his cock. Even Jack has rallied and is once again hard. Fuck. My pussy squeezes my fingers.

Luke's movements are precise and controlled. His strokes almost perfectly measured, and I fall into a rhythm with him. Following him like it's his cock inside me. My fingers circle my clit, finding a spot that winds me tighter and tighter.

His strokes quicken, and I follow his pace. Their breathing is heavy in my ears. My gaze bounces between all of them as they all fall into the same pace. I imagine them each inside of me and it doesn't disturb me. No, it makes me want more. I wish I had more hands to touch me the way they could if they were here in this bedroom with me.

Caden would be sucking as much of my breast as he could get into his mouth as I stroked his cock the way he does. Hard and quick, a little tight. Eli would take my mouth with his cock, letting me tease the tip with licks and sucks until he thrust it deeper, making me take as much of him as possible.

Jack would take my other breast, running his fingers down to my pussy, playing with my clit like I am. Pinching it slightly and rubbing it just enough to wind me tight. And Luke...

Death himself would take my pussy. Thrusting inside me, pressing on all those nerves until I couldn't tell where I ended and he began. He would keep his pace steady. His eyes would burn with fire and darkness and destruction as he took me. As they all took me.

"Oh, fuck," I whisper. My eyes widen as it builds to be too much. "I—"

I cry out as my pussy convulses around my fingers. I keep my eyes open as they all come with me. Their hands milking the last bit out of them until they're spent. I take my hands off my body and lay back on the bed to stare up at the ceiling. Not caring that the guys can still see my pussy.

"Good, sweetheart?" Jack's tone is playful.

I nod and then realize they can't actually see my head at this angle, so I whisper, "Yes."

"Sleep naked tonight." Luke's dark voice curls in my ear and my pussy clenches in an aftershock.

CHAPTER 48

The Surprise Attack

HARPER

Morning comes way too quickly. Last night, I crawled under my sheets and fell asleep right away. When I wake up, the guys are mostly awake. I roll out of bed and take a quick shower before dressing.

It's a game day at Sherman High School, so that means wearing school colors, a shortened schedule, and a pep rally in the afternoon. This is all business as usual, but this year, I don't think the guys will let me get away with the extra-large school t-shirt I usually wear.

Our school colors are blue and silver, so I find a blue crop top and some low-slung jeans to wear. I part my hair down the middle and weave two braids with blue ties on the ends. I keep my makeup light and walk downstairs in plenty of time to make my lunch and eat a little breakfast. I start the coffee maker and get out what I need.

"Sleep well?" Mom's voice startles me as she steps into the kitchen. She's worked every morning this week, so I thought I was alone again. I glance at the schedule and see it's her day off.

Remembering all that happened last night makes my cheeks flush with heat. "Yeah."

I'm in the middle of making two sandwiches and already have two bags of chips in my lunchbox.

Mom lifts one of the bags and narrows her eyes. "Eating for two?"

"No, definitely not." I shrug. "Caden likes it when I bring him a sandwich, and it's not that hard to make an extra."

Mom grabs a coffee cup and pours some of the coffee I made into it. She sips while studying me with a puzzled expression.

I sigh and put the sandwiches in my lunchbox. Finally I can't take her silent judgment anymore. "What?"

"I'm just trying to figure out what's going on with you." She sits at the island and puts her cup in front of her. "First you say there aren't any boys you're interested in this year, and the next day someone is taking you and dropping you off at school. You need new clothes, which bravo for your new style. Loving it. Then I meet four guys who buy us dinner, make sure you're safe alone, and buy you a ring for your birthday. Then you stay out late on a school night. I'm just trying to decide whether or not I like these changes."

I take a drink of my coffee. Not all these changes are my choice, but I can at least address part of it without things blowing up in my face.

"I always worried about attracting the wrong attention in previous years, so I always dressed not to be seen." I shrug and take a sip. "This year, I wanted to start it out right and decided I don't need to worry about getting attention."

Because I already have the attention I was previously hiding from.

"I take it that drew some wanted attention from your four football players." Mom arches her eyebrow at me suggestively.

Wanted? Not really. Not at first, but the more they push, the more I can't help wanting them. I still worry once they get what they want from me, they'll decide they want someone else. But they seem to be stuck with me for a year unless I find a way to renegotiate the terms of my enslavement.

"Harper?"

I lift my gaze to her, realizing I was lost in my head and didn't answer her.

A knock sounds at the back door. Fuck. Eli.

I take a breath and open the door. "Good morning."

Eli reaches for me, but I back away and glance at my mom. His hand drops to his side and a perfect smile forms on his handsome face. His hands go into his pockets. He has his football jersey on.

"Good morning, Ms. Davi—Jennifer. I hope you slept well."

Mom's face goes from surprise to suspicious. "Are you the reason Harper was out late on a weeknight?"

He doesn't miss a beat. "Sorry about that. I was finishing up an assignment for our AP statistics class, and Harper mentioned she was home alone. Since she's awesome at stats, I asked her to come to my house and help me. We lost track of time."

Yeah, Mom's not buying that. She smiles like she does when someone wants something she doesn't want to give them. Right now, she's not an Eli fan, which may eventually work in my favor.

"You don't mind that Harper makes Caden lunch?" She takes a sip of her coffee as she eyes him over the rim.

"She makes him a sandwich. I give her an apple." Eli glances at me with a sweet smile. "We're all okay with Harper giving us whatever attention she wants."

"Hmm." Mom gives me a look before she nods at Eli. "Football player too. That doesn't leave a lot of time for a girlfriend, does it?"

"He's not my boyfriend." I stuff my lunchbox in my backpack and toss it on my shoulder.

"Not yet anyway. Harper's a hard nut to crack." Eli wraps his arm around my shoulder and pulls me into his side. His warmth seeps into me, and I resist the urge to melt into him.

"We really have to get going. I'll see you tonight, Mom?"

It's supposed to be her day off. She sets her coffee mug down and shrugs. "Hopefully. The hospital has been short-staffed lately. I'll text you if I have to go in."

"We were hoping to go to a party after the game tonight. What time should I have Harper home?"

Eli is still trying, but I can tell each time he puts on his charm offensive, Mom gets a little more defensive. I wasn't lying when I said she would like Caden best. He may be a brute of a man, but he's honest about who he is.

"Cameron and Nora Jacobs are your parents?" Mom narrows her eyes slightly on Eli.

"Yes." Eli smiles like my mom knowing his parents will help his case.

"Harper knows when she needs to be home." Mom gives me a look like *this guy?*

I shake my head with a small smile. Not just this guy.

"See you later." I push Eli toward the door.

"Nice to see you again." Eli tosses one more smile her way before he goes outside.

I don't bother to look at my mom's expression. She's not impressed and she'll definitely have something to say about him later. But what can I say? I don't really have an option? Yeah, that will go over so fucking well.

I'm just lucky two guys didn't show up in my bedroom again. That would have never flown this morning.

Eli holds open the car door for me and then goes around to the other side to let himself in. We're halfway to school when I realize Eli hasn't given me his punishment. Mom kind of surprised both of us.

Well, I'm definitely not going to mention it. I also don't want to bring up any of the firsts from last night. I still don't know why Luke didn't tell them about the car. Maybe he did later. The real question I don't want answered is this: did what happened in my bedroom move the boundaries? It was me touching and not them, but they were there. I swallow down my nervousness.

I glance at Eli, but he's not looking my way.

He parks in the school parking lot, and I reach for the door, eager to escape being alone with him.

"Don't think I've forgotten." His voice stops me from opening the door.

I look over my shoulder, giving him my best innocent look. "Forgot what?"

He shakes his head and crooks his finger at me to come closer. I turn and settle back in my seat.

He reaches out and pulls on the braid closest to him. "I always loved tugging on girls' pigtails."

"That doesn't surprise me."

His fingers linger on the bruise on my neck from them. A rush of heat pulses through me at the slight ache. "Were we too rough with you last night?"

"No," I say softly.

His hand goes to the back of my neck and he draws me close. My breath catches as he closes in. His lips capture mine, stirring those feelings throughout me. My eyes close as I sink into the kiss. Now they've conditioned me to want more.

I feel something cold against my neck and pull away. My fingers go to the leather strap he's fastened on me. My forehead scrunches and I tip the visor down to look in the mirror.

"A collar?" It looks like a choker, but it most definitely is a collar.

"You need a reminder that you're owned, kitten. You don't own your body anymore. It's ours." His finger slips into the ring attached to it and tugs my face back to his. "The only one allowed to bite your lip is me."

He takes my mouth in a brutal kiss. It's rougher than any kiss he's given me since that first kiss. He bites down on my lower lip and then licks over the stinging wound. My body must have its signals crossed because heat floods me at the pain.

"Remember who you belong to, kitten."

When he releases me, I sit back a little dazed and a lot turned on as I touch my swollen lip. Eli's eyes are dark when he gives me a smile that doesn't quite reach his eyes before he turns to open his door.

I drop my hand. Maybe this will be a good reminder that these boys are not the guys they're pretending to be to get into my pants faster. They have been kind and patient, coaxing me out of my shell, but when it comes down to it, these aren't nice boys.

Eli opens my door and holds his hand out to me. I take it warily, but Pestilence seems to have taken the backseat again. Eli wraps his arm around my waist, tucking his fingers into the front of my jeans over my hip bone and drawing me in tight against his side.

Where are the boundaries now? Last night, they only got to kissing my breasts. But in my bedroom, we all played out a fantasy, and while hot, it had been a lot safer over video than being alone with my horsemen.

I didn't consider the boundaries when we were getting off together.

As we approach the others, they're all in their jerseys. A few cheerleaders stand in front of the three of them. The girls are in their uniforms too. Short skirts and tight sleeveless shirts, blue with silver piping. Their hair is pulled up into ponytails with blue and silver ribbons.

When the cheerleaders turn, I notice they each have a number on their cheeks, and they correspond with Luke, Jack, and Caden's jersey numbers. A little pulse of jealousy ripples through me. Especially as they seem real comfortable touching the guys' arms.

Jack disengages and struts over to me. Squatting, he wraps his arms under my ass, lifting me off my feet. My hands latch onto his shoulders to hold myself steady. I don't have time to react before his mouth is on mine. My lip is sore from Eli's bite, but I can't help returning Jack's kiss.

He might be an incurable flirt but he's also very affectionate. His lips trail down my cheek to my neck. My insides soften.

"Good morning, beautiful," he whispers in my ear, sending a little thrill through my blood.

"Put me down, Jack." I tug on his dark hair. His laughing blue eyes meet mine.

"Nah, I like carrying you around. Caden is right. We should just carry you all day." His gaze drops to the collar on my neck and his eyes darken visibly. "Though it's clear Eli has marked you as our property."

My fingers touch the collar. It's not exactly something I would normally agree to, but I gave up that right apparently. As long as I go along, I don't get punished. It hasn't all been bad.

"Stop hogging Harper." Caden steps into me from behind, pressing his warm body against mine. Trapping me between him and Jack, Caden kisses the nape of my neck. My panties are already damp and it's not even the beginning of the school day.

The cheerleaders remain beside Luke, whose focus is on me. I can still hear his voice in my head, telling me how to touch myself and what he wants to do to me. Desire floods through me.

When the cheerleaders notice the attention has shifted from them, they finally stop preening and turn to glare at me. Before I can return their attitude, Jack claims my lips and Caden's lips trail over my neck. I can feel the evidence of their desire against my lower half. My eyes close as I let them feed the building lust.

"Slut." One girl coughs the word as they pass us on their way into the school. The girls all burst out laughing.

Caden chuckles against my neck. "If they only knew, little nympho."

The words are like a splash of ice-cold water in my face. I pull away from Jack and press against his shoulders. "Put me down."

"Come on, sweetheart." Jack's blue eyes dance with mischief. "They're just jealous."

"I don't need to be groped all the time." I sigh, knowing I won't be released until they're ready to put me down.

"I disagree." Caden draws my hips against his to grind his hard-on against my ass. "You need to be groped a hell of a lot more."

Frustrated and angry, I don't know what to do, but I know I need down, and now. I shouldn't want any of this. Even though somehow, when they get me alone, I lose all sense. They call to a part of me that is so fucking curious and touch starved that I can't help but want them.

"Put her down." Luke steps in.

Jack lets me slide down his front with a smirk on his lips. "We need to skip to the good bits next time we play spin the bottle."

"We need to play seven minutes in heaven," Caden says from behind me. His hand cups my ass cheek. "We'd be moving a hell of a lot faster."

I don't say anything. I never wanted any part of this. It's not my fault they want a virgin sacrifice and I'm all that's left. The reminder that I'm not someone they chose but who was left over makes my heart thump harder.

"You could always go after those cheerleaders." I glance over my shoulder at Caden. "I'm sure they wouldn't mind being with you guys. Problem solved. You leave me alone and go back to fucking whoever you want."

Caden's eyes narrow on me, but before he can do anything, Luke draws me out from between Jack and Caden.

"Is the collar not enough, princess?" Luke takes my hand and leads me into the school. "Do you need a reminder of who you belong to? Because I'm more than willing to put our little pregame spanking back on the table. Or maybe something more entertaining."

I want to bite my lip to keep from railing at them all, but my lip fucking hurts thanks to Eli. It seems like they all want to try my patience this morning.

Well, fuck them too. "Whatever you want to do. Why not just strip me naked and parade me around for the entire school to see your whore."

Luke turns to glare at me, but I don't give a shit.

"Why not? Prove that you own me. I'm sure you can find a leash to go with my shiny new collar." I flick it with my fingernail and glare into his eyes.

"I have the perfect punishment for you." His eyes have a malicious gleam in them, but I ignore it.

"Punish me. It's not like I have a choice in the matter." I glare at him, so fucking over this. Luke drags me along behind him as I stew in my own thoughts. Fuck him. Let him parade me around naked, what do I care. Everyone already thinks I'm a slut.

I'm so sick of being manhandled. Sure, I like it a little. And the kisses and touches are, well, mind-blowing. But it doesn't mean I want to fuck four guys and confirm the label of slut. I haven't even fucked anyone and the stigma is already attached. All I wanted was to get through my senior year with no incidents with the horsemen. Now, in less than two weeks, my life revolves around their wants and desires. Not mine.

Maybe I want to have sex. Maybe even with them. But it should still be my choice.

I barely register when Luke turns right instead of going to their lockers. Not that I need to go to their lockers. I still have everything in my backpack. Though it's nice not to lug the heavy thing around all day.

It's not like I can go anywhere on my own anymore anyway. They just want to control every aspect of my life. Behind me, the others follow us to who knows where.

What's going to happen after I give them my virginity? How long before they stray? I'm just a novelty to them. Something to use and then throw away. Or worse, something to keep so only they can play with it, but then they only bring me out when they need me or can't find anyone else to play with.

They have more than enough feminine attention. One female won't be enough for them. Fuck, they all came two times last night. Three for Jack. I don't even know if I have enough stamina to keep up with them.

Luke pulls open a door and tugs me into a dark space. I pull my head out of my ass and look up as the others crowd into the small closet and the door closes behind them, taking all the light except for a slice spilling through the bottom of the door.

Oh, fuck.

CHAPTER 49

Guerilla Warfare

HARPER

There's no light for my eyes to adjust to. It's just inky darkness and the heat of them, the horsemen.

They surround me, crowding me in the darkness. My heart stops as I realize I've let them draw me into a trap because I wasn't paying attention.

I'm not sure if asking what the fuck is happening is a wise thing to do at this point. They aren't talking. The only sounds are some lockers closing in the hall beyond the door and our breathing.

Luke still holds my hand, but otherwise they're barely touching me. And yet, they're so close I can feel the heat off their skin. My heart kicks up a notch. This isn't good. I dropped my fucking guard and now I'm alone in a situation where they control me once again.

I swallow the lump forming because Luke threatened me with punishment. What fresh hell is this?

"Shouldn't we get to class?" I ask, ashamed at the catch in my voice. I want to be strong, but I don't know what to expect. That little burn of anger still boils in my stomach, but being this close to all of them has my senses heightened and awareness washes over me.

"Nah, little nympho, we've got time for a round of seven minutes in heaven."

My heart lodges in my throat. "What? We're at school."

I back into a body. I'm not sure whose. Someone lifts my backpack off my shoulders and it disappears into the darkness. My vulnerability doesn't escape me. The only thing they want me to *give* is my virginity. All those boundaries we crossed last night don't leave much left.

"You need a reminder of what we can give you," Luke says.

My heart clatters in my chest.

Strong hands come up to grab my arms, and I'm held against a large chest. Caden?

Their heat surrounds me as they close in, making the sparks inside me riot. That part of me that begs for their touch warms up.

"Am I not supposed to have a say in what happens to me?" My voice is high as panic surges within me.

"You have to be quiet, princess." Luke presses in on me from the front. "We wouldn't want you to get in trouble."

He doesn't say *they* would get in trouble. And why would they? A hand passes over my bare midriff. A shiver ripples through me as my stomach trembles beneath the touch. I feel the others close in against my shoulders.

"Did you ever wish you could join the parties in middle school?" Luke's voice weaves around me in the dark, luring me into submission. "That we would have chosen you?"

I try for reason.

"Luke, we need to go to class. We don't have time for whatever this is." My voice trembles out of me.

Whatever they have planned, I'm powerless to stop it. I enjoyed last night, but I was safe, alone, touching myself. I even felt a little safe at Caden's house. I had Eli's word he would take me out of there if I needed him to, but I never put him to the test.

Because part of me knew Eli's word was an illusion, and I didn't want to know they had me trapped. They could have done anything to me, but they didn't.

But now? If I cry out, someone might find us, and then those safeguards they left in place last night might be taken away. I'm curious what they have in mind, but also terrified they might push me too far. That I'll give in too much.

"In eighth grade, we could have taken you into a closet and shown you how to kiss. How to touch. How to make us feel good, and made you feel good in return." Luke could lull me into compliance with just his voice.

Then I remember Eli this morning, and Jack and Caden. The possessiveness and the arrogance of what they can get from me.

I'm not sure what will happen in this closet, but I can't let them think they've won already. A hand sweeps up my side under my crop top. My skin tingles beneath the rough palm. My heart beats like a frightened rabbit's with starving wolves bearing down on it.

"We can't play this at school." I try to sound stern, but my voice shakes as I attempt to reason with them. "Someone could open the door, and you guys might not get in trouble, but do you think my mom won't really ground me if I'm found in a closet with four guys?"

"Good thing we have a lookout then." Jack's voice comes from my right.

I can't see anything in the darkness. Only the shadows of the guys' legs from the light creeping in under the door.

A phone lights up the space in front of me. Luke looks diabolical in the weak light as he smiles down at me. His blond hair and cold eyes make him seem untouchable. I swallow the fear rising in my throat.

"It's only seven minutes, Harper. What can happen in seven minutes?" Eli's words are smooth and not at all comforting. All those things I worried about last night with seven minutes rise to the surface. But I'm not pantyless in a short skirt now.

"I don't want to give you my virginity in a closet at school." I look up into Luke's eyes, knowing you can't negotiate with Death. His eyes are cool with an evil glint in them as his thumb moves on his screen. I look down and see seven minutes on the timer.

"Easy, Harper, we aren't taking anything you haven't already given us. You made your choice outside. You keep trying to push us onto other girls, but that's not how this game is played. We don't want any other girl. We want you. We'll show you just how much we crave you."

I open my mouth to try to reason with them, but the light goes out as he sets the timer. Luke captures my mouth in an all-consuming kiss. I'm powerless to stop my response to him. I crave his kisses. Hands are on me everywhere at once. I can't keep track of where the hands come from, but my shirt lifts and my bra slides off my arms.

Multiple hands tease my nipples from all angles. There's no escape from their touch and each stroke burns like fire on my skin, heating my insides and flowing to throb between my legs.

A pair of hands are on the button to my jeans. Wait. My hands clasp over the front of my jeans to keep them from opening them farther.

"Hands," Jack whispers.

Luke lifts his mouth from mine. "Let go, Harper."

Fuck those words. Luke takes my mouth again and his tongue tangles with mine. For a moment all I can focus on is how they glide against each other. Fingers tweak my nipples, making my pussy pulse in time with their touches. Distracting me.

It's effective, because someone slides their hands over mine, pulling my hands from my pants, and I let them. My arms are raised above my head and held together by one hand.

I try to get my mouth away from Luke's so I can think, but my head presses into Caden's chest, holding me in place. My jeans open and a hand slips down the front. I gasp as they stroke along my panty line.

My breasts feel heavy and tight as my nipples are continuously stimulated and tugged. Lips caress my shoulders and neck. I get wetter, wanting more, needing more. My system is overloaded with sensation.

Someone pushes my jeans down, and some sense flows back into me. We're at school. Fuck. I try to twist out of their hold even as sparks race under my skin at their touch. Hands run over my panty covered ass and hips. As hands slip under the edge of my panties, I tug at my captured hands. We shouldn't be doing this here, but Luke's mouth captures all my noises.

His kiss makes my brain fuzzy. Mouths kiss my shoulders and neck, making it hard for me to breathe.

My panties slip down my thighs, and a hand slides between them, touching the same skin I touched last night. I suck in my breath as one bold finger strokes over my clit while another finger finds my opening and presses against it. Oh, fuck, that feels amazing.

A bolt of desire spears through me, wanting to feel them inside.

Jeans scrape against my ass as I shift. It's too much. Someone's lips replaces their hand on my breast, pulling my hardened nipple into a warm mouth. My pussy gushes with need. Luke abandons my mouth but then Jack captures my lips.

Thrusting his tongue into my mouth to tease mine. I like kissing and they fucking know it.

Hands on my thighs spread my legs open. The tickle of hair against my inner thighs is the only warning I have before someone's tongue teases my clit. I gasp against Jack's mouth, frozen while my body registers the foreign touch. The finger circling my entrance eases inside.

All things I did to my body for them last night.

Heat floods my body as desire and lust flow through me. I can barely think as the tongue flicks over my clit and the fullness of his finger moves inside me. Just like I did last night, stroking in and out. My hips rock with the movement, craving more.

I moan and lean into their touch. Letting go, giving into the sensations bursting through me.

Caden's large hand holds one of my breasts. His thumb circles my hardened nipple. I'm pretty sure Eli is sucking my other breast as Jack keeps my mouth occupied with his. I think Caden's other hand is on my wrists, holding them tight above my head. Not that I'm trying to get away.

And Luke...his tongue and fingers are making my hips sway with need. Desire overwhelms me. Any rational thought leaves me as the desire dominates me. I'm building to something that will shatter me, but I'm helpless to fight against it.

I give in to the pleasure and allow myself to enjoy it, experience it fully.

They taste me everywhere, my nipple, my mouth, my clit. Caden's hand glides down the side of my body, leaving behind a trail of sparks. Another finger from behind me joins the one inside my pussy, both moving in tandem. They stretch me more than my fingers did last night.

The tension winds and builds within me until my knees weaken. As if sensing my submission, the hand holding my wrists slackens and I slip free of their hold. An arm wraps around my waist to hold me upright.

My fingers dig into Luke's hair as he sucks my clit into his mouth and Eli's hair as he flicks my nipple with his tongue.

Jack trails his mouth down my neck and keeps going until he latches onto my other breast. I tip my head back against Caden's shoulder. So fucking overwhelmed and ready to explode.

Caden nudges my face with his until his lips find mine. He thrusts his tongue into my mouth in time with the fingers in my pussy. All of us strain together as they wring pleasure from my body with their hands and mouths.

It's so much more than I imagined last night. So much better.

The darkness fades into a burst of white-hot heat as I come so fucking hard I can't breathe. My whole body tightens like a string on a bow, arching into their touch. They don't stop touching me. As I sag against Caden's chest, their hands ease me down from the high. Caden kisses me like he's never tasted anything so good.

Luke's alarm goes off, and all the touching stops. They don't take their heat from me though. I take several deep breaths as the guys slowly dress me. I can't move to help them. Taking stock, I feel overwhelmed and so fucking good at the same time.

Luke captures my mouth. I can taste myself on his lips and I want more.

He leans in close to my ear and whispers, "Just as sweet as I imagined."

CHAPTER 50

The Reconciliation

CADEN

Luke approached us this morning about the seven minutes in heaven punishment he devised, but we didn't think we'd implement it first thing. Fortunately for us, Harper was in a mood and popped off.

Her body sags against mine as we file out of the closet. No one is in the hallway, and we're definitely late for first period, but it was worth it.

I help her stand and wrap my arm around her waist as I carry her backpack and lead her to my locker. Her head rests against my shoulder and she doesn't pull away.

She's seriously dazed. I lean her against the locker next to mine while I take care of her books. I've paid attention to what she needs for her next few classes.

Her brown eyes are blown with desire. Her braids survived the manhandling well. I reach out and straighten the bottom of her shirt. Her eyes focus on mine and I give her a half smile. She blinks at me.

Luke confessed about his little tryst in his car with my little nympho. Bastard.

The plan is to share her firsts, not take her off somewhere alone and claim her first orgasm. We need to put a leash on that fucker. Obviously Luke can't be trusted alone with Harper.

Last night was fucking amazing watching her masturbate while

Luke guided her on screen. I could get off to that for hours. But feeling her shatter with my finger buried in her pulsing cunt, while capturing her cries in my mouth…fuck, I could do that shit until Harper cries for mercy and begs me to fuck her.

My already hard cock twitches, but that bastard will have to wait until my little nympho is ready.

I lean down to bring my face to her level. Her eyes focus on mine again. I touch her cheek with the backs of my fingers. "You okay?"

She nods warily. A bruise has formed on her bottom lip. I run my thumb over it, and she sucks in a breath. My gaze lifts to hers.

Fucking Eli is rough with his toys. Not that I'm gentle, but I take care of what's mine. And this girl is mine as much as she is theirs.

Her wanting us to go back to the cheerleaders riled us all up. Fuck that. She's ours and we've only just begun to get a taste.

"Let's go, little nympho."

Her eyes spark a little at the nickname, but she falls in line with us. With the pep rally today, we're on a shortened bell schedule, so it won't be long before she's in second period with me.

Luke steps up on Harper's other side. He meets my eyes over her head. I read the concern in his eyes. She seems more rattled than usual, but she's not pulling that shutdown shit again. Maybe we pushed a little too hard.

But she's ours and she needs to own that shit instead of trying to push us off on other girls all the fucking time.

I watch as she meekly follows Luke as he leads her to their class.

She's a fighter. She'll come back around. She has to.

The morning flies by, and soon I'm standing outside the art room waiting for Harper to come out for lunch. Normally I'd wait in the cafeteria, but she was still acting a little dazed during second period.

Not that I blame her. We stripped her bare in a closet at school and gave her a bone-melting orgasm. I can't wait to taste her. Now we just have to get her on her knees before us.

When Harper walks out of the classroom, she's smiling and relaxed as she listens to Kenz. The other girl notices me and touches Harper's arm.

"Ready for lunch?" I move away from the wall.

The smile fades from Harper's lips, and she swallows before she nods. Girl hasn't said a word since the closet. At least not to us. I know Luke thought we couldn't break her, but we're a lot, especially when we come at a girl more than one at a time. We've never come at a girl all four of us.

I look over at Kenz. Her blue eyes widen when I make eye contact.

"You can come sit with us for lunch," I say. Maybe she'll help our girl feel comfortable.

"Uh." She glances at Harper and then at me. She gestures over her shoulder. "I'm supposed to meet Brandon."

Harper gives her a smile as Kenz steps away from me.

"I'll pick you up for the game tonight." Kenz waves as she hurries away.

Harper falls in step with me, but I'm so done with this broken shit. Dropping behind her, I wrap my arms around her and lift her off her feet.

"What are you doing?" she squeaks out as her hands press against my arms.

"Carrying you since you're acting like a baby."

"I'm not acting like a baby. Caden, put me down."

No one is around in the hallway. I walk over to a dark classroom and pull open the door, taking Harper into it. After setting her on her feet, I lean back, blocking the only exit.

She watches me warily, hands out in front of her as if to ward me off. Like that would stop me. At least she's trying.

"Did we do anything you didn't want?" I ask, crossing my arms over my chest. "Because the only one who got off in that closet was you. Trust me, first period was uncomfortable with the hard-on I was sporting."

Her cheeks flush red, but she steps forward. There she is. That tense coil inside me unwinds. I fight the urge to smile at her and keep my expression stern.

"Because that's what *I* wanted?" She rolls her eyes. "I love having four men maul me into an orgasm first thing in the morning at school."

"Sounds like a good time to me." I rub the corner of my mouth to conceal the smile trying to form.

"Do you think I wanted to come at school? It's one thing at your house, but here? That's supposed to be private."

I scratch the back of my neck. "You consented to be owned by us. That's part of it. Wherever, whenever we want. Your body responds beautifully to ours. You're just too damned uptight."

"I'm uptight?" She stomps over and thrusts her finger into my chest. "You all are fucking whores who don't care where you stick your dicks. The only reason you're even remotely interested in me is because I'm a virgin and the last one in our class. Otherwise you never would have even bothered me."

"Is this because we didn't notice you before this year?" I step forward, letting her rile me, feeling that familiar burst of heat race through me.

"I've known you guys since grade school, and you've never noticed me before last Monday. Yeah, I hid from you guys, but we shared classes every fucking year. If you wanted to notice me, you would have."

"You mean like when you were beneath the tree when Jack and I were playing football last year. You pulled your legs out of the way so I wouldn't trip. When I landed, I saw you, Harper Davidson. Your flushed cheeks, your dark hair pulled back in a ponytail, your brown eyes wide with surprise. I smiled at you and the next second, you were gone like a fucking illusion."

She gasps, and I take her distraction to wrap my hand around the back of her slender neck.

"Why should I notice a girl who doesn't want me to notice her? Who slips so easily into the background she just becomes part of the scenery?" I close in until my mouth hovers above hers. That spark of awareness between us makes me want to do so much more than just taste her mouth, but we're on a time crunch, because at some point, someone will come looking for us.

Her dark eyes are wide and questioning, searching mine. Fuck.

"I saw you, Harper Davidson, but I knew you didn't want me to, so I fucking ignored you like you wanted. I can't ignore you anymore though." I catch her lips with mine. I'm gentle even though I want to conquer her, prove to her once and for all I'm in this thing. I'm into her.

Her bruised lip has to hurt, so I barely press my lips against hers. Soft and coaxing.

After a second, she kisses me back just as softly. Her hands come up to capture my wrists, holding onto me like I'm a fucking lifeline.

I can be that for her. I *want* to be that for her. The one she reaches for when she needs someone to center her. I lift my mouth from hers and press my forehead against hers to breathe in her sweet vanilla scent.

"Forgive me for wanting you so bad after ignoring you for so long. I've wanted you before. I just forgot." Rubbing my nose against hers, I draw her into my chest for a hug. "I need you to be okay, because I want all of you."

Her hands settle on my back. She inhales and lets out a shuddering exhale. She sags against me like she did after she came in the closet. This time, I hold her just as tight. No matter what, I'm not letting go.

HARPER

Caden takes my hand and leads me into the cafeteria and to the horsemen's table. I can't believe it.

He saw me.

He remembers me.

Fuck, that shouldn't make my heart leap into my throat.

Taking his seat next to Luke, Caden pulls me down on his lap. He's being really gentle with me, and I appreciate his care. I need a moment after the closet. Overwhelmed doesn't come close to describing it.

I won't lie to myself about what happened. It was hot, and I liked it more than I thought I would. I might not object to a repeat performance, but not at school.

I have to remind myself that their desire is usually fleeting. But they were angry about me trying to push them onto other girls.

I hand the sandwich I made for Caden to him. He smiles at me when our eyes meet. My cheeks grow warm and I drop my gaze to my sandwich.

The others don't pay attention to me as they talk about tonight's game. As I eat, I surreptitiously look at each of them. They aren't acting any differently toward me. Honestly it seems like, if anything, they're ignoring me.

Except for Caden.

A little flutter of anxiety works its way into my heart. I don't need constant attention, but after last night and this morning, you'd think they'd be a little more attentive. A little more affectionate.

Fuck, listen to me go on about wanting more attention. This is good. Let them ignore me and not put on a show for their willing subjects.

The cafeteria is busy as always. I've eaten about half my sandwich when I notice movement toward our table.

Sidney Brown, Emma Garcia, Hannah Wilson, and Ashley Kim approach our table as if they own the school and the horsemen. Their matching cheerleading uniforms show off their athletic bodies. As the most popular senior girls, they definitely own the school, but no one owns the horsemen.

Every girl wants to be these girls, and every guy wants to fuck them. They have the looks. They're cheerleaders. Their makeup and hair are perfect. Their bodies are curved and strong.

Sidney rakes her gaze over me with disdain. The cheer captain is a tall blonde with green eyes. All leg, which her cheerleading skirt shows off to perfection. Everyone is envious of her.

Caden's hand tightens on me, and I lean back against him as they approach. His warmth fills me. I've never been on the receiving end of the cheerleaders' hatred. I doubt they even know me outside of a few shared classes.

Color me curious what these girls want from my men.

Umm...the horsemen, not my men. It's dangerous to even think I have any ownership over them. No matter what they promised. What they'll continue to promise until they get what they want, and then who knows.

"Luke." Sidney stops in front of Luke, who gives her a once-over.

"Can we help you?" Luke looks like a king deigning to speak to one of his many subjects. He checks out the tall cheerleader with a sort of disinterest that should insult her.

Ashley puts her hand on Eli's shoulder and leans against his back. "We partying tonight, boys?"

Ashley Kim has attitude for days. Almost as tall as Sidney, she's slender and beautiful with huge brown eyes. Between her gorgeous Korean mother and her handsome father, Ashley got the perfect mix of features to make her unique and stunningly beautiful.

Emma is even bolder and sits on Jack's lap. She puts her hand in his hair and jerks his head back to look up at her. Emma is a petite Latina with a curvy body. Her dark eyes take in everything. Even when she's flirting, she always seems observant.

My insides boil. Not going to lie, I want to start the biggest catfight ever, but only because of our agreement. Not because I actually want these guys all to myself.

CHAPTER 51
The Declaration

HARPER

My gaze lifts to Hannah, who gives me the bitchiest look ever. Hannah is also a petite flyer. Her brown skin is dark and gorgeous. Her light hazel eyes are arresting as she glares at me.

I narrow my eyes at her. Caden kisses my shoulder, drawing my attention back to him. Something eases inside me as he gives me a look that says not to worry about her. Not with him at least.

Now the other guys. They might be another matter entirely.

Luke smirks at Sidney when he answers Ashley. "It *is* at Caden's house, like always."

"Nice dog collar, Harper." Hannah's tone is condescending. Putting her hand on her cocked hip, she thrusts her breasts out. They're bigger than mine, but the guys really haven't complained.

My fingers touch the collar. I almost forgot about Eli's collar with everything that happened this morning. It seems so insignificant after what happened in the closet.

"That's got to be the stupidest thing I've ever seen." Emma laughs on Jack's lap.

"You might need to take your bitch for a walk, Caden." Ashley's eyes land on me. She huffs like I'm not even worth her notice and looks away.

"I got it for her." While Eli doesn't remove Ashley's hand, he also doesn't seem to welcome her touch.

"Baby, you could have gotten me one." Ashley's tone is babyish when she speaks to him. Her hand threads into Eli's hair. I roll my eyes. "I love when you put your hands around my neck."

These girls make me want to gag. I put the rest of my sandwich away, no longer hungry.

"Why are you here, Sid?" Luke leans forward and gives her a frosty look.

Sidney's eyes turn calculating. "Next week is senior night at the football game."

"So?"

"Come on, Luke. The cheerleaders always wear the senior football players' jerseys during senior week. It makes sense for you to give us your jerseys. It's not like you have a girlfriend." She looks at me pointedly.

I don't even flinch. I'm not their girlfriend, nor do I claim to be.

Not getting a response from me, she returns her attention to Luke. "You know we're always party ready. We can come to some arrangement we'll all find mutually satisfying."

Did this chick just offer to have sex with the guys for their jerseys? What else could that mean? I try to lean forward a little, curious about how this all works, but Caden keeps me where he wants me. His hand stays on my bare stomach.

This is all fascinating. After all, I don't know what the hell happens with the popular kids. I've always stayed as far away as possible. Is it just blow jobs or full-contact sex?

Emma puts her hands on Jack's shoulders as she bats her long lashes at him. "Let us take care of you at the party. I can do that thing you like."

As Caden leans back, he draws me with him. He remains silent. His hand rests on my bare midriff. His thumb strokes just below my bra under my crop top. I wish I could say his touch doesn't affect me, but tingles skirt beneath his fingers.

None of the other guys bother to look at me. Are they considering this offer since I don't seem willing to give it up anytime soon? They did want me to pick someone to fill in last night. Pretty sure video peep shows won't cut it for much longer.

Especially after the closet. My cheeks warm and so does my pussy. Fuck.

Hannah still seems really put out that she can't gain Caden's attention.

"Come on, Caden, what can this little virgin do for you?" Hannah stands next to Sidney with disdain in her eyes as she dismisses me. There it is.

Because not putting out should be looked down upon. But then again, I'm also being called a slut. So which one is it? Virgin or whore?

Hannah's not wrong though. The only thing I can offer the guys is my virginity. There's no guarantee sex with me will be satisfactory. If I even get to the point where I'm willing to give it up.

I might literally be awful at sex, but I don't have any bad habits yet either. So there is that. They can teach me how they want me. I squirm a little on Caden's lap because that doesn't sound awful.

Caden's chin rests on my shoulder. His cheek rubs against mine, filling me with warmth. "Maybe I'm sick of sloppy seconds."

My eyes widen as Hannah's eyes narrow and her lips purse. Oh, she did not like that.

"Sure, unless it's Jack's. Everyone knows you two share. Even the virgins." If looks could kill, Hannah would have slayed me. Shit, if she knew that I have all their attentions, her brain might explode.

Emma tugs on Jack's hair, and her eyes go to Caden. "I love when you two play games with me."

Laughter wells inside me at these girls being possessive over the guys. Like the horsemen keep it in their pants for anyone, but I manage to keep the laughter in. Even I might have a second of jealousy, but honestly, why bother? They made a deal with me. My compliance for their monogamy.

Of course, this deal with the cheerleaders could be my out. If they touch one of these girls, then our agreement is null and void.

I would be free of them all.

Putting my hand over Caden's, I lean my cheek against his. He's not so bad when he's not being an asshole, but I thought that about Eli too. My lip still stings as a reminder to not trust them.

No matter their momentary kindnesses, there's always some other reason behind it. Eli wanted me inside, so he offered to take me home at any point. Last night they didn't want me to close my laptop, so they were kind and patient.

This morning, they had full control of the situation and took what they wanted. Whether or not I wanted it.

I squirm again on Caden's lap remembering the feel of them touching me everywhere. He lets out a low growl in my ear, and my panties dampen.

Sidney watches all our interactions with laser focus. I can almost see the gears spinning in her brain.

"May I?" She gestures to the chair across from Luke.

Luke waves two fingers and gives her a slight nod. If my appetite hadn't vanished when these girls stepped up, I would love to have some popcorn to watch this show. I can't wait to tell Kenz about this later.

Sidney sits in the chair. Hannah crosses her arms, a pout on her full lips, and drops into the chair next to her.

Ashley must feel bolder, as she sits in Eli's lap. Neither Jack nor Eli have touched the girls sitting on their laps, but they also don't remove them or ask them to get off. Maybe I should add that girls can't touch them either. Of course, renegotiations usually mean I lose something.

"We know you have some unfinished business," Sidney sneers in my direction, "but we've had a longstanding relationship with you guys. What would it look like if we didn't wear your jerseys during senior week?"

Luke leans forward with his hands together on the table. His blond hair falls over his eyes as he regards Sidney like a potential business partner. Not someone he's bumped uglies with.

Sure they're pretty, but they're both so frigid. What would that even look like? *Ew.* I do *not* need that image. I'm going to have to invest in some brain bleach if I have to continue to hang out with these guys. It's bad enough I know they've been with girls at our school, but to witness the girls trying to get with them, that's a new level of ick.

"Do you think we care what it looks like for you?" Luke gives her a smile that doesn't reach his eyes. "We're not available and neither are our jerseys."

Red creeps up Sidney's neck. Her lips flatten, but then she eases into a smile. If I could, I would ask her to give me lessons, because this girl just won't back down. She's tenacious.

"Look, Luke. Everyone understands you're toying with Harper for now, but it won't last. We all know how quickly you lose interest." She gives me a look that says I'm no exception. I don't react. I'm not stupid. Her gaze takes in Luke with a familiarity that shouldn't make my stomach pitch the way it does. "You'll want to pick up where we all left off. We understand you guys don't want to be tied down but need access. We provide that."

"We won't need that access." His nonchalant look is cold.

Sidney laughs without humor. "You think without our permission other girls will be available for you once you finish whatever this is?"

Luke's smile sends chills down my spine, and it's not even directed at me. "We've made arrangements for this year." His gaze flicks to me for a hot second. My Pavlovian response to his attention is getting annoying, but it's not my mouth that grows wet for him. He returns his cold eyes to her. "So if that's all you needed, you can leave."

Yeah, that doesn't thrill Sidney. They're denying these girls the status the jerseys of the horsemen would provide them. Sure, they're at the top of the girl social ladder, but the horsemen are the cream of the crop.

"Look, every girl on the squad needs a jersey, and there are only so many varsity football players." Sidney shifts tactics from being their uncomplicated sex—though I can't imagine anything with these girls is uncomplicated—to appealing to their reason.

I can't believe she's still trying. Luke just told her no in the nicest way I've ever seen a horseman say no. If she keeps pushing, what will happen? Will he punish her?

What would that involve? Would he spank her like he did me? Would that be my out clause because he touched another girl? Or maybe it's different if she pushes because of who she is. I'm not sure how the social hierarchy of the school works in actuality. I stayed as far away as possible. The little I know is from growing up with these people and what Kenz tells me.

"You don't want what we're offering. Fine." She gestures to the other girls. Emma and Ashley leave Jack and Eli's laps. Hannah joins the other two behind Sidney's chair. "We aren't exactly hurting for options, but your girl might not have the greatest year if you put a target on her back."

Caden's hold on me tightens. Hell, even I know this. The horsemen have never claimed a girl before. Not like they have with me. Kenz warned me the girls are waiting in the wings, waiting for the horsemen to get bored with me. I know the guys promised to only be with me for the year, but I don't really believe that will happen.

"Don't threaten what's ours." Luke's tone is bored but his eyes are deadly.

"Maybe if you want to protect your pet," Sidney spits the word *pet* out, "then consider how our two groups might be beneficial to each other. Putting your jerseys on us will keep the target off your bitch's back, but if you ignore us, you guarantee she has a fucked-up year. You can't be everywhere she goes during the day."

Luke chews on the words for a moment. Caden's thumb rubs against my thigh. She has a point though. I'm not exactly the scrappy girl who can take on the popular girls. Or any other girl who thinks I'm in her way. I'm someone more comfortable in the shadows. I don't think these girls are the kind to get dirt on their own hands, but they can definitely make my life uncomfortable.

"Harper." Luke commands me with his voice.

Caden stands me up. My stomach feels cold without his large hand on it. I move hesitantly to Luke, trying to seem like a non-threat to the cheerleaders.

My heart beats loudly in my ears. I don't know what Luke wants with me or what point he's about to make that has to do with me, but I miss the security of Caden's arm around me.

Luke holds out a hand, never taking his gaze off Sidney. Taking a breath, I slip my hand into his. He draws me closer to him. Like we do it all the time, he guides me to straddle him on the chair, keeping me to one side of his lap as he never takes his gaze from Sidney. My hands automatically go to his shoulders, and I watch the side of his face as he smiles at Sidney.

"Don't threaten Harper unless you want to see your social status fall faster than your panties do." Luke runs a hand over my back.

I wish I could say I remain unaffected, but his touch is a drug I'm slowly becoming addicted to. Tingles race along my spine and settle between my legs. A full-body tremble goes through me. Everything in me softens at being near Luke, and hearing his voice in my ear might as well be an aphrodisiac. He makes me so fucking wet.

"But we can be reasonable." Luke's other hand slides up my jean-covered thigh.

My breath catches as desire clouds my brain. A muscle tics in Luke's jaw, and I want to lean in and kiss it.

These boys are seriously fucking with my mind. Luke's hand stops on my ass.

"You can use three of our jerseys each day, but our girl will wear one each day next week. We'll swap out jerseys every evening." It's a short week since Monday is Labor Day. "You can decide amongst yourselves who will have to find someone else's jersey to wear."

"But," Eli stands on one side of the girls, towering over them, while Jack stands on the other, blocking them in, "if you do anything to Harper, we won't stand for it. She's ours and under our protection."

A tight, needy part of me beats a little harder at his words. I've never belonged anywhere in this school. Never belonged to anyone. Not since I was a kid.

"Not just for right now," Jack states.

They've claimed me before, but this time feels different. Maybe because these girls can offer them something I haven't been willing to give them yet.

"I don't care if you're chicks." Caden stands and moves behind Luke and me. I raise my gaze to his face as he glares at the cheerleaders. "If anyone hurts Harper, I won't pull my punches."

Sidney stands and nods. "Noted. We'll expect the three jerseys over the weekend. You can tell us the schedule to make exchanges. Pleasure doing business as usual."

I turn slightly to look at the cheerleaders. The girls don't look pleased with this arrangement. This isn't finished, but I'm the one who will have to deal with the ramifications.

Sidney meets my eyes, and my stomach bottoms out at the hatred there. Luke grabs my chin, and our eyes meet for a second before he takes possession of my mouth. He arranges me the way he likes me on his lap, and I whimper at the feel of his hard cock pressed between my thighs.

It's a power move. That's all. They've claimed me, and the girls tried to test that. My heart leaps into my throat at their protection. But I wouldn't need it if it weren't for them.

As Luke deepens the kiss, I lose all sense of everyone around us. The world could literally end and I wouldn't want to stop this kiss.

When Luke lifts his mouth from mine, he traces his thumb over the sore spot on my lip. His eyes follow his thumb before he looks over at Eli. "Careful with our girl. We don't want her to have an excuse not to put her mouth to use."

Eli nods. A whole different sinking feeling hits my stomach as Luke's eyes meet mine. "You painted such a detailed picture last night."

Shifting slightly beneath me, he rubs against a spot that sends sparks flooding my veins. His thumb pulls my bottom lip down slightly as he slips the tip of his thumb against my teeth. "We'll have to find time tonight to play our own games."

CHAPTER 52

The Unknown Ally

Harper

We won the game. Of course. Kenz and I sit in our normal spot toward the top of the stadium. I'm glad I have her here with me because the looks I get from most of the girls and the Cheermonsters aren't friendly at all.

Penny, Izzy, Vicky, and Nat wave to us from down front as they stand to leave. They wanted front-row seats and even saved us spots next to them, which I have to admit was impressive. Close seats go quick at the games, but Kenz and I always sit towards the top of the stadium. I give them a wave back, and Penny holds her phone up to indicate she'll text me. I nod.

The word must not have gotten around since lunch today about the standoff between the Cheermonsters and the horsemen. That I'm the only chick the horsemen are interested in this year. Or maybe Penny still hopes being friendly will grant access.

Kenz leans against the back of the stands, and I settle in next to her.

"I can't believe the Cheermonsters actually tried to bargain with sex." Kenz shakes her head as we wait for the rest of the stadium to clear out before we even think about heading down. I don't really want to get stuck in the crush of people. "I mean, is this an every year thing or special this year? So many unanswered questions."

"They tried to claim the horsemen, and the guys weren't having it."

"So the party tonight?" Kenz smiles and grabs my arm, shaking it hard. "I can't believe you're finally going to a party. Your first party."

"It's not like I have a choice in any of this." I look out over the field as the crowd moves down the cement bleachers and filters out of the stadium. The field is empty, but I can't help thinking of the horsemen's and my lunch out here. And the kisses.

Shivers roll down my spine as the memories of the closet drift through my mind. It wasn't all bad, but it was terrifying at the same time. They aren't slowing down. If anything, they're shredding boundaries right and left. They have full access to my body besides penetrative sex.

"If you're worried about tonight, just hang out with me and Brandon." Kenz pats me on the shoulder. Like it will be that easy.

I laugh. "That'll work until you two disappear to have sex."

She laughs and nods. "You're right."

Our laughter dies as we watch the people leaving.

"Are you scared?" Kenz glances at me. During the game, I told her about what happened in the closet and last night

I take a breath. "Of the horsemen? A little. Shit, Kenz, you should see Caden's dick, and the rest of them aren't exactly little."

Kenz leans in and whispers, "There's a reason they're legends."

"I'm sure the rumors don't come close to the truth." I shudder.

We meet each other's eyes and giggle. Fuck, I've missed this. Sure, we have third period together, but we never get to just hang out anymore. At least not as often as we did in the past. She always made time for me, but the horsemen own my time now.

"It was on webcam, so it's possible the camera added to the size." Kenz bites her lip.

I shake my head. "I got to see Caden's up close and personal on my birthday, and I'm sure I'll get to see it again in person tonight."

"Already?" She squeezes my hand.

"Not intercourse. At least I don't think." I stare at the field. Luke made it clear earlier that he wants me to put my mouth to use, meaning blow jobs. No idea what sort of game they'll have for this decision of what order they get to take my mouth and for how long. All I can think is how sore my jaw will be. "I just hope Caden doesn't go first anymore. I mean, he's enormous. You've seen his hands."

Kenz gets a distant look in her eyes. "I've seen his hands. Even his fingers would put a lot of guys to shame."

My cheeks flush with heat. In the dark, I couldn't be a hundred percent sure, but I'm positive Luke and Caden were the ones whose fingers were inside me. Theirs were definitely bigger than my two fingers. Even now, my panties get wet thinking about them all touching me, driving me to explode.

"That look is interesting." Kenz cocks an eyebrow.

"This whole thing is weird." I meet her eyes, and we dissolve into giggles again.

"I'm so glad we got to hang out tonight," I breathe out when I can. "At least for the game."

"It's a weird year," she says. "Who knew you should have gotten laid over the summer like everyone else?"

"I wish someone would have let me know it was a race." Grinning, I bump her shoulder. "I could have been a contender."

"If I'd known, I would have held out a little longer." Kenz blushes.

"No, you wouldn't have." I laugh. "Besides, it's not your fault deflowering horsemen rule our school."

"Oh my god. You should offer them your precious flower. Maybe they'll be so confused they'll let you go." Kenz laughs again, and I join her.

"I can almost see Luke's disgusted face at me calling it that." I take a deep breath to settle my insides. "They're lucky I'm not a prude, just someone who didn't want to get swept up in the drama."

"So you think it will happen soon?"

"That I'll give them my precious flower?" I can't even get the words out before I dissolve into giggles.

"Harper?" a male voice asks.

I'm still smiling when my gaze collides with brown eyes in a very familiar face. Surprise fills my voice when I realize who it is. "Nico?"

He climbs the stairs two at a time as I stand. His arms go around me and pull me into his hard chest. Last time I saw Nico Lee, we were in sixth grade. Shocked, I let him hug me close and draw in his scent, fresh, like rain.

When he left, we were the same height, but now he's as tall as Luke, and from the press of his body against mine, just as cut with muscle. I draw back and smile at my old friend.

His black hair and dark eyes are familiar, but his face is more angular with a square jaw. He definitely grew into his Korean father's looks. His hands remain on my arms as he looks me over.

Fortunately I remember where we are and who might come out at any moment.

"What are you doing here?" I step away from his hands and glance down at the field. The guys should still be inside, but I don't want to risk it. I don't want Nico to get hurt.

Nico was my best friend once upon a time, until his family moved for his father's work. The horsemen won't care about that though. All they care about is keeping me their property.

"Dad's company transferred him back here, so I'm back for our senior year." Nico runs a hand through his thick black hair and gives me a flirty smile. "You grew up well, Harper."

Heat courses through me at the look in his eyes. I'm way too familiar with that particular look. I'm just not used to it coming from someone who isn't a horseman.

"Hi, I'm MacKenzie."

I completely forgot Kenz is here. "This is my best friend, Kenz. Kenz, this is Nico. My best friend who left me to go to New York."

While Nico holds his hand out to Kenz, I try to rein back in my weird feelings. Nico is attractive and built like one of my horsemen, but I already have four guys trying to get in my pants.

If Nico had stayed, I might not have had to hide from the assholes. Tingles rush through me when he reaches out and touches my arm. If he'd stayed, I might have had a boyfriend. I did have a crush on him when he left.

"I was hoping to find you here." Nico's dark eyes fall on me again, and my heart kicks up a notch. "I don't start school until Tuesday. When I called your house, your mom said you'd be here."

He talked to my mom. What all did she tell him?

"So much has happened." Nico smiles, and it's a really good smile that makes my heart beat a little harder. I'm hopeless. "I was hoping we could hang out tonight and catch up, or sometime this weekend."

Before I can open my mouth, Kenz says, "There's a party. You should totally come with us. I was worried about leaving Harper alone, but if you come, then I can wander off with my boyfriend."

Nico turns to her. "That sounds great."

Meanwhile, I'm mouthing *what the fuck* to Kenz behind him. When he turns back to me, I smile. "Yeah, you should totally come with us."

"Great. Let me go tell my parents. I'll come back and find you." Nico grabs my arm and his hand trails down to squeeze mine. Sparks follow his touch. What the hell is wrong with me? I've already got four men. "I'm glad I ran into you. I've missed you."

My pulse kicks up another notch. "I've missed you too."

He heads down the stairs and off toward the section where the parents sit. Wearing jeans and a tight t-shirt that show off his fit body, my old best friend has grown into a man I don't even know anymore. One who could give any of the horsemen a run for their money.

"Holy shit, Harper. He's hot." Kenz shakes my arm.

"Fuck." My heart finally slows down and icy cold realization floods me. "What did you do, Kenz?"

"I invited the hot as fuck guy who hugged you to a party. You're welcome." Kenz waggles her eyebrows like this is a great idea. Does she want to see him beat into a bloody pulp?

"With my four asshole protectors. Who I don't think will allow me to retroactively claim a boyfriend, even if Nico were interested in me in that way—"

"He's most definitely interested. The way he looked at you. Fuck, I got hot and bothered. I might need to drag Brandon off as soon as we get to the party. You'll be occupied getting reacquainted with Nico." Kenz has officially lost her mind.

My phone buzzes in my pocket a few times. When I check it, I murmur, "Shit."

WAR (CADEN):

You got a ride, little nympho? *winky face emoji*

FAMINE (JACK):

I've got a ride for you, sweetheart

DEATH (LUKE):

You still riding with your friend?

They weren't happy when I told them I'd ride with Kenz to the party, but it makes more sense than waiting for them. They have to finish getting cleaned up, plus the bonus that it would give me more time away from them. They mess with my mind when they're near.

ME:

Kenz will drive me. See you soon.

Kenz bumps my shoulder, and I put my phone down as Nico climbs the bleachers back to us. His dark eyes hold mine and my breath catches. I'm so fucked.

CHAPTER 53

The Old Friend

HARPER

"Can I grab you a drink?" Nico asks me as we walk into Caden's downstairs. Kenz and Brandon are right behind us.

My stomach drops as I remember last night. It seems like so long ago that they had me practically naked, writhing on their laps, and I'm walking right back into their trap. No parents, no one to stop them. What fresh hell will tonight bring?

"Harper? Drink? Hey." When he gets my attention, Nico nods toward Brandon, who paused to kiss Kenz. He bends down, bringing his mouth close to my ear. "This going to happen all night?"

Tingles ricochet through me. Fuck, that shouldn't feel so good.

"With them? Yup." I draw in a breath as someone bumps into me, pushing me against Nico's hard muscles. My hand lands on his abs and I resist the urge to run my fingers over the ridges beneath them. Heat floods my body.

I'm so fucked. The horsemen will see it on my face when I look at Nico and know. I don't want them to humiliate him like they did Grant. Nico doesn't deserve that. What if he tries to stand up to them, and they do what they did to Tanner Lewis?

He's just starting school here again.

It's his senior year, and if they blackball him, maybe he won't stay. Fuck.

Maybe I should push him away now so he doesn't get hurt. Then I look up into his dark eyes and I'm sunk. Awareness courses through me.

Nico holds my arms and glares over my head at whoever ran into me. "You okay?"

"Mmhmm." Fuck, I can't talk right now because all I can focus on is how perfect Nico's lips are. Full and beautifully shaped. What would they feel like against mine? And the way he smells. His rain scent makes me want to breathe him in.

"Maybe you should come with me to get that drink." His eyes twinkle. "I'm afraid you'll get run over and I'll never find you. It was bad enough losing you once. I'm not about to do it again."

I don't miss the undertone in his sentiment. Maybe last week I would have confused his statement for friendship, but now I know what it sounds like when someone wants you.

I let my gaze flow over the crowd, looking for the horsemen as Kenz and Brandon move with us toward where the drinks are displayed. Caden has to be here already, right? It's his house.

How do I explain this to them? Hey, here's my best friend from elementary school. This means I'm off the hook, right? Because I'm pretty sure I can get busy with him even though I really enjoyed getting busy with you guys. My cheeks feel like they'll burst from the heat that floods them.

I don't know what other options are available. I don't even know if they'll let me hang out with Nico once they find out. Maybe I should take off with Nico right now and go somewhere to talk. Give him all the info about the horsemen. Let him know what he's stepping into.

Nico leads me with a hand on the small of my back. Tingles spread through me from the simple touch. Now and then, he'll reel me into his side to keep someone from running me over. I turn my hopeless gaze back to Kenz, but she just grins and gives me two thumbs up.

Pretty sure I'm getting publicly spanked again. The guys won't like this development. No guy at school stepped up to be my boyfriend. I don't think they'll accept an amendment for when new guys start school. Showing up with a smoking hot guy to their party won't go over well. Especially one who keeps touching me.

And who I wouldn't mind touching me even more. My stomach sinks and my heart twists. This is all *their* fault for making me want more. For opening my mind to more. Maybe my touch-starved body just craves it now.

"What do you want?" Nico looks over the open bottles and bends down to reach into one of the coolers. "Still love Cherry Coke?"

My heart damn near chokes me when I smile, remembering summers when we'd race into the kitchen to grab cans of Cherry Coke. We would giggle so loud Mom would yell at us to stay outside. "I haven't had a Cherry Coke in years."

"Then I have a mission." He winks as he digs in the cooler. Kenz grins and Brandon draws her into the crowd.

The hairs on the back of my neck stand on end and a warmth I've gotten too familiar with over the past weeks closes in on my back.

"Princess." Luke's deep voice in my ear does wicked things to my lower half. I melt into his heat, needing it.

Nico straightens at that moment. He's smiling down at the can in his hand. "All I can find is a regular Coke, but I swear we'll hit every store tomorrow to find you a Cherry Coke."

When he goes to hand it to me, his dark eyes focus on the blond god behind me, standing way too close. Possessively close. I'm resigned to being permanently red-faced at this point. Maybe I can still find a way to make Nico walk away, so they don't humiliate him before he even starts school.

"Hey." Nico hands me the Coke. I take it as his eyes spark with recognition. "Figured I'd run into you sooner than later. How you been?"

Wait, what?

Luke's hand slips over my hip as he draws me back against him. He rests his chin on my head, and I wish I could see his face. What the hell is going on?

"Nico, good to see you." His voice sounds like he's welcoming a friend. Luke holds out his other hand to Nico. They do this weird, complicated handshake thing that no one but them could possibly know. What the fuck is happening?

"You back for a visit?" Luke asks.

Okay, Nico was in football when we were in elementary, but he hadn't been friends with the guys. He'd been my friend.

"Nah, man." Nico's eyes dip down to Luke's possessive grip on my hip before he lifts his gaze back to Luke's, skipping my face. "Came back for my senior year. Dad just got the news, so it was all rush rush. Sucks to move, but since it was somewhere I know people, I thought why the fuck not. And of course, Harper is here."

Luke's fingers tighten into my hip as his thumb dips beneath the waistband of my jeans to tease the top of my panties. My breath hitches and I want to squirm under his touch, especially with Nico watching.

I'm used to the other horsemen watching, but Nico doesn't know what's happening. Even though the basement is stuffed to capacity, it feels like it's just me, Luke, and Nico.

I don't really know what to do in this situation. It's not like I'm not used to being between two men I find attractive.

That's pretty much my life now.

"I didn't know you knew Harper." Luke presses into me from behind.

"Used to be best friends. Right, sunshine?" His dark eyes dip down to capture mine.

The old nickname makes my face warm. I'm glad Luke can't see me.

"Yeah, we lived down the street from each other," I get out. Nico's eyes search mine, trying to figure out what Luke and I are to each other. I haven't moved away from his touch. But besides his possessive touch, Luke hasn't claimed me in any other way.

"You going to join the football team?" Luke asks. "We could use Apocalypse. Our other wide receiver has butterfingers."

"Of course. I'm going in and talking to Coach Tuesday before school. The rest of the guys here?" Nico glances over our shoulders. "You want to go sit and catch up?"

Apocalypse? What the fuck is that supposed to mean? I didn't even realize Nico knew the horsemen. Every word that comes out of Nico's mouth makes me wonder if I really knew my best friend at all.

Luke must give Nico the dude nod, because he leads the way with me in front of him. I don't know where Luke's taking us, but he doesn't take his hands off me, and I can't see Nico behind him. My nerves ratchet skyward with every step.

Is this a trap? Will they punish Nico for talking to me when he doesn't know the rules? Or punish me for not filling him in on the deal? Either way, this is going to suck for one or both of us, and I lost my opportunity to warn him.

High schoolers crowd the room, unlike last night when it was only the four horsemen and me. The lighting is low, and music fills the space. Luke's hand never leaves my bare skin, practically burning the imprint of his fingers on me. I'm sure he'd like to.

He turns me and the leather sectional is ahead of us, tucked away in the room's corner. Eli, Jack, and Caden turn as one to watch us approach. I haven't changed from the school day, so I'm still in my blue crop top and low-slung jeans.

They've all changed since the game. Jeans and tight t-shirts show off their muscles. Their hungry eyes roam over me like they haven't seen me in days, rather than a couple of hours.

I shiver against Luke. I've been processing what happened in the closet all day and dreading what they'll have me do tonight. Okay, dreading is a little strong. I'm curious and they make me want more, but there's that hint of fear inside me.

When they finally notice Nico following behind, Jack stands with a grin on his face.

"Dude." Jack's arms are wide as he closes in on Nico and lifts him off the ground.

Nico laughs and pounds his fist against Jack's back. "I can't believe you've let yourself go, Jack."

Jack sets Nico down and holds him at arm's length. "You get more disgusting the older you get."

Caden and Eli step up and they both do the same handshake Luke did with Nico.

"Visiting?" Caden steps back.

Luke leads me over to the couch and sits in the corner, pulling me down onto his lap. I almost roll my eyes at his territorial behavior, but I don't need to keep pressing for more punishment.

Nico's gaze flicks to me with a confused look before he smiles. "Moving back."

The guys all reclaim their seats, and Nico sits on the other side of Luke and me.

Jack reaches into a cooler and hands a beer to Nico before sitting on his other side. "You back for good?"

Nodding, Nico opens the beer and relaxes into the couch. "Figured it would be a good time to reconnect with my friends before college."

"We could use you on the team. Eli's great, but we need another wide receiver. The other guy is a sophomore who can barely hang with us."

They all talk about tonight's game and football this season. I take a drink of my Coke as I try to figure out what's happening. The guys all seem relaxed, even with Nico here. Of course, as long as Nico is here, I might not be forced to play any new game. So score for me.

As I check out the room, Grant Perkins, the guy who had to put his underwear in his mouth, glares at me from one side, but when I look again, he's gone. Shaking it off, I try to focus on what's going on around me.

While the rest of the basement is packed, there's almost a bubble around us no one dares to enter. Nico blends in with the horsemen. He seems at ease with the guys, but his gaze keeps coming to me.

I should have told him the deal, but who wants to tell your friend that four guys have decided to own you for the year? More like they demanded a virgin sacrifice and I'm the only one left.

In the car, Nico didn't ask if I'm seeing anyone, and I didn't offer any info because again…virgin sacrifice.

Caden takes my Coke out of my hand and drinks some before handing it back to me with a wink. Luke's fingers stroke the back of my neck beneath my hair, sending shivers down my spine.

I'm just glad I'm wearing jeans tonight. While I love wearing skirts, these guys like to take advantage of them. I'm not convinced they would keep their hands from slipping under it, even with everyone else watching us while trying to appear like they're not paying attention.

Not that jeans stopped them this morning in the closet. My pussy pulses and I release a sigh. I'm doomed. That part of me that's so fucking curious just wants more. More touches, more kisses.

My eyes meet Nico's dark ones. More guys?

Luke's fingers cradle my skull as he massages the back of my head. That feels really nice. I want to lean in and close my eyes, but I'm aware of Nico's presence. It holds me back more than anything else could have. I realize I've given in to these guys more than I've fought them off.

Even this morning, if I wasn't so deep in my feelings, I would have known they were taking me somewhere I might not want to go. Then again, if I had stopped them, they might have gone to Plan B: the locker room pep rally with me starring as the spankee.

Fighting them off would have been impossible, but when I gave in to them, it was explosive.

The problem now, as Luke's fingers work magic on my scalp, is I want to lose myself in the heat of him. My gaze rises to his. His pupils are blown, as I'm sure mine are too. Will he kiss me?

Suddenly Luke tenses beneath me and his hand goes to the back of my neck. Outwardly, he's just as laid back, but he's coiled and ready to pounce. I straighten and see the cause.

The Cheermonsters have decided to join our party. Sidney, Emma, Hannah, and Ashley stroll toward the couch like someone invited them forward, breaking the "barrier" surrounding us. They all have on barely-there tight crop tops and skirts that offer little coverage. While I have a slender body, these girls have sculpted muscles.

"How's the party, boys?" Sidney comes to a halt in front of Luke. She cocks her hip and tosses her long blond hair over her shoulder. The others fall into formation behind her just like they're doing a routine. Well, a routine where they're all bitchy.

"No complaints." Luke's other hand dips into the waist of my pants, and I try not to react. I know it's a power move, another possession like earlier in the cafeteria, but like that kiss from earlier, my body can't tell the difference. Heat pours through me, settling between my thighs.

"Did you need something?" Jack asks.

"Just figured you let anyone over here." Sidney nods toward Nico. "Since you have your little bitch and a guy none of us have seen before."

Nico cracks a smile. "You don't remember me, Sidney? Why am I not surprised?"

Nico really is gorgeous. I always thought he was cute when we were growing up. Both of us were on the outskirts of the popular kids. It never bothered us because we had each other. Then he had to move, but I found Kenz eventually.

"Should I?" Sidney turns to the other girls. Emma and Hannah shrug, but Ashley Kim steps forward.

"It can't be." Ashley's eyes narrow on Nico, probably taking in how good he looks. Because he's hot. Just as hot as any of the horsemen.

"Ashley." Sidney almost commands her with her name.

"Nico moved away when we were young. Our families were friends." Ashley almost sneers as she backs up. "He wasn't much to look at back then."

Nico's smile grows. Obviously he knows he's something to look at now. Never thought he'd grow up as cocky as the horsemen, but he's equal to them in desirability.

"Then the question is why are you letting another loser into your ranks?" Sidney's gaze flows over me as the first loser.

Luke's smile turns feral. "You ladies don't remember your place, do you?"

Luke passes me to Caden before he stands to get in Sidney's face. Caden tucks me in against him and puts his hand possessively on my bare midriff. I lean back against him, craving his heat. Nico's eyes widen at the sight, but then his face clears, as if he realizes now isn't the time.

Eli and Jack stand behind Luke. Nico hesitates for a second before he joins them. My jaw almost drops open. What the hell is going on?

"Does he look like a loser to you?" Jack asks.

The girls' eyes eat up Nico's cut body, then move up to his sharp jaw and his thick hair. From my side, I can see his perfect ass and sculpted back under his t-shirt. Nico Lee is definitely not a loser.

Though he never was to me.

Hannah steps forward with interest in her eyes as she focuses on Nico. "What's your deal?"

I almost want to growl at her, but I have no standing to keep him as mine. I already have four guys committed to being all mine this year, and I'm committed to them.

"Nico will join the football team," Luke says, his gaze not wavering from Sidney's. It's almost as if they're having a battle of wills. "He's one of us."

Sidney's calculated gaze goes to Nico. "You don't let just any football player hang out with you."

"Nico isn't just some football player." Eli steps forward. "He's a horseman."

Say what?

———————

The story continues in THEIR TWISTED RULES

Meet C.S. Berry

C.S. Berry is a combination of my love for writing and my love for reading. She began as an experiment and took off into something I absolutely adore. It's not often you can do what you love and it works as a career. As for me, I love reading and romance and heroines seriously getting railed. I assume since you've read my books, you do too.

If you want to discuss books or anything with me, come join my Facebook group, C.S. Berry's Spicy Executive Suite. And you can always catch me on Instagram @csberry.

Oh and me, I have a lovely family who aren't allowed to read my books. But are so proud, they keep leaking my pen name. My dog and cats don't care about my writing as long as I sit still long enough for them to snuggle.

XOXOXO,

C.S. Berry

Keep up with C.S. Berry
View the shop: csberrybooks.com
View the Patreon: patreon.com/csberry
Join her Newsletter on her website
Join the Facebook Group:
https://www.facebook.com/groups/csberryreaders
Checkout her Website: csberry.com